THE COMPLETE CASEBOOK OF HERLOCK SHOLMES

The Complete Casebook of Herlock Sholmes

CREATED BY
CHARLES HAMILTON
INTRODUCED BY
NORMAN WRIGHT
DESIGNED & COMPILED BY
MIKE HIGGS

THE COMPLETE CASEBOOK OF HERLOCK SHOLMES

ISBN 0 948248 91 2

PUBLISHED BY
HAWK BOOKS LIMITED
SUITE 309
CANALOT STUDIOS
222 KENSAL ROAD
LONDON W10 5BN
ENGLAND

DESIGN: MIKE HIGGS GRAPHICS

PRINTED IN FINLAND

Herlock Sholmes

by Norman Wright

When, in 1886, an impoverished young doctor named Arthur Conan Doyle penned the opening lines of a novel he intended calling "A Tangled Skein," he little realised the phenomenal consequences of his action. In his notebook he had roughed out two characters to be named Ormond Sacker and Sherringford Holmes, but by the time the novel was completed he had made a few small changes. The title had become "A Study in Scarlet' and the main characters, Dr John H. Watson and Mr Sherlock Holmes.

With that story a legend was born: a fictional character of such potency that now, a century later, there are still those who regard his creation as a living being. Sherlock Holmes has become the best known detective in the world. His adventures have been translated into practically every known language and his exploits have been encompassed by every medium of communication. He is the universal fictional character, his name is known from the icy wastes to the tropical jungles by boys and girls aged from nine to ninety.

Such eminence inevitably caught the eye of parodists and remarkably early on in his career Holmes became the host feeding a plethora of parasidic parodies: Chubblock, Sheerluck, Sheerflop, Herlock and the like. Such satires, while not always pleasing to Conan Doyle, served to stimulate and extend the legend. Sherlock Holmes was such a robust creation that, despite the slapstick stupidity of Homes, Soames, Combs and the rest of them, their existence was more a homage than a slander.

But back in 1886 publishers were tardy in taking up that first story and the manuscript began a tedious journey back and forth gathering a crop of rejection slips along the way. Eventually the firm of Ward Lock offered the author £25 for the copyright, provided he did not object to it being "held over till next year." Doyle objected to both the delay and the outright payment, preferring instead a royalty on the book. But the publishers prevailed, maintaining that, as the story was to appear in an annual containing work by other contributors, a royalty on sales would give rise to some confusion. Doyle acceded and Sherlock Holmes, the world's first consulting detective, eventually appeared before the public, together with "two original drawing room plays," between the colourful covers of "Beeton's Christmas Annual" for 1887.

The first meeting of the two characters was memorable—"Dr. Watson, Mr. Sherlock Holmes," said Stamford introducing us.

"How are you?" he said cordially gripping my hand with a strength for which I would hardly have given him credit. "You have been in Afghanistan, I perceive."

"How on earth did you know that?" I asked in astonishment."

Poor old Watson would continue to be astonished many times during their sixty recorded cases. The sitting room in their lodgings at Baker Street was usually the scene. Holmes would take some trifling object left behind by an unknown client and, basing his deductions on the object, flesh out such a full picture of the owner that Watson would be incredulous and declare it absolutely impossible to glean so much from so little. After Holmes had explained the reasoning behind his deductions Watson would chuckle and say how absurdly simple it had all been!

In a rare recording made in 1928, Doyle explained how he came to create Sherlock Holmes. "I was when I wrote it, a young doctor and had been educated in a very severe and critical medical school of thought, especially coming under the influence of Dr. Bell of Edinburgh, who had most remarkable powers of observation. He prided himself that when he looked at a patient he could tell not only their disease, but very often their occupation and place of residence. I thought I would try my hand at writing a story where the hero would treat crime as Dr. Bell treated disease, and where science would take the place of chance. The result was Sherlock Holmes."

"A Study in Scarlet" was successful enough to be reprinted the following year with illustrations by Charles Doyle, the author's father. The story was very well received in the United States of America, and resulted in a commission for Doyle to write a further Sherlock Holmes novel for the Philadelphian firm of J. B. Lippincott Co. to appear in the February, 1890, issue of "Lippincott's Magazine." The story was entitled "The Sign of Four" ("Sign of Four" in all U.K. editions). It is a memorable tale that introduced many of the touches that became enshrined in the Holmesian myth: the metropolis wreathed in dense fog, the gaslit streets, the chase in the hansom cab, of course, the distraught young client. It was an exciting story with far more pace than its predecessor. It twisted and turned through the foggy London streets leading Holmes and Watson on the trail of a murderer and a fabulous treasure. It was one hundred percent Holmes, with no secondary plot to slow down the action as there had been in "A Study in Scarlet."

The popularity of Holmes and Watson sprang from "A Study in Scarlet" and "The Sign of Four," but it was consolidated in the pages of "The Strand Magazine," a monthly periodical launched by George Newnes in January 1891. Doyle conceived the idea of writing a series of short stories featuring his detective. Unlike a serial, readers would be less put off if they missed an issue of the magazine. The first story, entitled "A Scandal in Bohemia," appeared in "The Strand Magazine" for July 1891. It was followed by eleven further short stories that were quickly collected and published by George Newnes in 1892 as "The Adventures of Sherlock Holmes," Doyle dedicated the volume "To my old teacher Joseph Bell, M.D."

A second series of twelve stories began appearing in "The Strand Magazine" in February 1893, and eleven of them were collected as "The Memoirs of Sherlock

'A REVERIE.' Compilation of Sydney Paget's illustrations from 'The Strand' magazine, March 1911.

Holmes," published by George Newnes early in 1894. Those two dozen adventures were unparalleled successes and firmly established the Sherlock Holmes myth. Part of their success was due to the distinctive illustrations of Sydney Paget, who deviated from Doyle's original description of the detective and made the character less hawklike. Paget depicted the cosy and comfortable Baker Street scene with all of its familiar paraphernalia: the deerstalker hat, the cane chair, the inverness cape, the chemical table and the worn dressing gown. The mental image of Holmes that we all have was created as much by the illustrator as by the author.

Many readers of "The Strand Magazine" for December, 1893, must have had their Christmas festivities ruined when they opened their favourite periodical and saw Paget's full page illustration entitled "The Death of Sherlock Holmes." For Doyle had grown weary of Holmes, almost jealous of his creation's popularity, and in that story (ominously entitled "The Adventure of the Final Problem") killed off the detective sending him hurtling over the Reichenbach Falls locked in a death grip with his greatest adversary, Professor James Moriarty, the Napoleon of crime.

Even before Holmes' apparent watery death the imitators had been at work. "The Idler" had a run a series of "Adventures of Sherlaw Kombs" in 1892, and "Punch," that perennial purveyor of humour, had 'Picklock Holes' plunging to his doom at about the same time as the genuine Holmes!

Readers may have been deprived of the genuine article but there was no shortage of parodies. They cropped up all over the place, often in the most unlikely of magazines. "A Few Adventures of Mrs. Herlock Shomes" by "KA" appeared in "The Student: a Journal for University Extension Students" in 1894. The hitherto unknown Mrs. S. endeavoured to continue from where her late husband had left off. While Mrs. Shomes was sorting out "The Identity of Miss Angelica Vespers" in "The Student," 'Chubblock Homes' was making his comic debut in "Comic Cuts," a halfpenny comic paper published by Harmsworth. A few months later Chubblock transferred his allegiance to another halfpenny comic, "The Funny Wonder," where he eventually achieved the distinction of becoming the comic's cover character.

The copyright laws in the 1890's were such that the performing arts could purloin Holmes with impunity. "Under the Clock," a one-act play featuring Holmes and Watson, opened at the Royal Court Theatre, London in November, 1893, and ran for almost one hundred performances. One of the first full length theatrical adaptations was "Sherlock Holmes," a five-act play first produced in Glasgow in 1894. The play ran for over a decade. Probably the best known theatrical appearance of Holmes and Watson was in the play "Sherlock Holmes" written by William Gillette and first produced in New York in November, 1899. While writing the play Gillette had written to Conan Doyle asking if he could marry off Holmes. Doyle had acidly replied, "You may marry or murder or do what you like with him." After a successful run in the U.S.A. Gillette brought the play to England. His timing could not have been better, for Doyle had reluctantly agreed to write another Holmes story and "Sherlock Holmes" the play opened at the Lyceum Theatre, London, on the 9th of September, 1901, just as the second instalment of "The Hound of the Baskervilles" appeared in the pages of "The Strand Magazine."

"The Hound of the Baskervilles" was a superbly-crafted tale. Even the over-use of its plot for films, radio and television plays, and comics has not taken the edge off its appeal. But if Doyle had imagined that one story would stifle the demand for more Holmes he was mistaken. Editors clamoured, cajoled and tempted and at last Doyle capitulated and resurrected Sherlock Holmes. His return was announced in the September, 1903, edition of "The Strand Magazine." "The news of his death was received with regret as at the loss of a personal friend. Fortunately, that news, though based on circumstantial evidence which at the time seemed conclusive, turns out to be erroneous. How he escaped from his struggle with Moriarty at the Reichenbach Falls, why he remained in hiding even from his friend Watson, how he made his re-appearance and the manner he signalized his return by one of the most remarkable of his exploits will be found narrated in the first story of the New Series, beginning in the October Number." The story was entitled "The Adventure of the Empty House." Twelve further stories followed in quick succession, and the thirteen short stories were collected in 1905 as "The Return of Sherlock Holmes."

Doyle was never able to shake off the detective, though fresh exploits never again appeared as frequently. Between September 1908 and April 1927, nineteen short Sherlock Holmes stories were published in "The Strand Magazine" and eventually collected in two volumes, "His Last Bow" in 1917, and "The Casebook of Sherlock Holmes" in 1927. The final full length Sherlock Holmes novel, "The Valley of Fear," was serialised in "The Strand Magazine" between September, 1914, and May 1915, and published in book form by Smith Elder and Co. in 1915.

The parodies and pastiches of the Sherlock Holmes stories had, for the most part, been short-lived affairs but in 1915 a series of parodies began, that continued for almost forty years and comprised almost one hundred stories. "The Adventures of Herlock Sholmes" began in "The Greyfriars Herald" on November 20th, 1915, with "The Adventure of the Diamond Pins." It was followed in the succeeding weeks by a further seventeen short stories of the detective. Many were skits on tales from the Holmes canon: "The Freckled Hand," "The Yellow Phiz," "The Bound of the Haskervilles." Others poked fun at the wartime shortages. All were deliciously satirical, and although the humour and the mood was irreverent, they were written with a feel for and a love of Doyle's original. They often began with Sholmes and Jotson in their Shaker Street apartment and, before Mrs. Spudson showed in the client, there would be delicious moments over the breakfast table as Sholmes, true to form, delighted and amazed Jotson with his powers of deduction.

"I see that you have not shaved this morning, Jotson."

"Shomes how could you possibly know——"

He laughed. "Is it not a fact?" he asked.

"It is a fact, certainly. But how you guessed——"

"It was not a guess, Jotson." Sholmes frowned a little.

"I never guess. I leave guesswork to the police. It was simple deduction, Jotson, simply explained."

The dialogue was a joy, the dry delivery often adding a biting edge to the humour. The stories were written under the byline of Peter Todd, a pen-name that concealed the identity of one of the century's most prolific writers,

'SHEERFLOP SOAMES ' One of a whole series of strips drawn by D.C. West.

Charles Harold St. John Hamilton, a man credited with writing over one hundred million words under at least twenty-six pen-names.

Charles Hamilton was born in the West London suburb of Ealing on 8th August, 1876. He was a great lover of books, devouring everything that came his way. He began writing early in life and had his first story accepted for publication when he was only seventeen years old. From that moment his pen was never idle. Much of his early work was for the boys' papers and comics published by Trapps-Holmes, and even in those early days his output was prodigious. In the 1890's he began contributing stories to the firm that was eventually to become the Amalgamated Press, a firm he was associated with for almost half a century.

Hamilton's great forte was the public school story, a genre extremely popular with young working class readers during the the first forty years of the century. Hamilton's work was always in demand, for his stories were humorous, well characterised and, above all, they were very well written. His first really successful series of stories began in a story paper entitled "The Gem Library," launched in 1907. At first his tales featuring the boys of 'St. Jim's School' alternated with adventure stories. But from issue number eleven, entitled "Tom Merry At St. Jim's," he became responsible for the paper's main weekly offering and, under the pen-name of Martin Clifford, turned out hundreds of tales of Tom Merry and his friends.

"The Gem Library" proved so popular with readers that a year later a companion paper entitled "The Magnet Library" was launched. Charles Hamilton was asked to devise a new set of characters and contribute another weekly 18,000 word story. Under the pen-name of Frank Richards he created Harry Wharton & Co. of Greyfriars School, a set of characters whose weekly exploits were soon being eagerly sought by half of the schoolboys in the country. When Charles Hamilton or rather Frank Richards as he preferred to be called, wrote "The Making of Harry Wharton" for the first issue of "The Magnet" in February, 1908, he could hardly have guessed at the popularity that the characters were to achieve over the years. "The Magnet" ran until May, 1940, and Hamilton wrote over 1,300 of the 1,683 Greyfriars stories that appeared within it's pages. After the Second World War he continued writing Greyfriars stories for hardback book publication and was still chronicling their exploits at the time of his death on Christmas Eve, 1961.

An irregular feature in some of the early "Magnets" was "The Greyfriar's Herald," the school newspaper supposedly written by the Greyfriars' boys and edited by Harry Wharton. The feature was so popular with readers, many of whom believed that they were reading extracts from an actual school newspaper, that it was decided to publish "The Greyfriar's Herald" as a separate publication. Charles Hamilton already had an extremely heavy weekly workload and could write only a small portion of the new publication. He chose to write "The Adventures of Herlock Sholmes."

Sholmes was not Hamilton's first sleuth. Early in the century he had written of detectives with such improbable

'SHEERLUCK COMBS' drawn by Murdoch Stimson for 'Slick Fun Album' 1949.

'SHERLOCK SLICK' from 'Smasher Comics' No. 1 drawn by Bob Monkhouse.

names as Denham Croft and Sedley Sharpe. In 1907 he had created a detective named Ferrers Locke who cropped up in his "Gem" and "Magnet" stories off and on for over thirty years. But Sholmes, the spoof detective, was something different and, after spending so much time writing school stories, Hamilton must have found it a refreshing change to write stories in a totally different vein. The humour in the stories was often barbed and much of it must have gone over the heads of the twelve to fifteen year olds who bought the weekly "Greyfriar's Herald."

The sixth story in the series, "The Death of Sholmes," parodied "The Adventure of the Final Problem." "It was at sunset one evening that we found ourselves pursuing a lonely track amid the rocky wastes and precipices of the wild Hill of Ludgate. Far below us flowed the dark waters of the Fleet river." The mood is so right, catching exactly the sombre feel of Doyle's original. At other times the tales contain rib tickling humour, passages that are impossible to read without bursting out with laughter. In many of the tales as in the "Case of the American Millionaire," Hamilton gleefully took a sidelong swipe at some of his own pet hates and petty bureaucracies.

The paper shortage of the First World War brought an end to "The Greyfriar's Herald" in March, 1916, after only eighteen issues. But Sholmes could not be kept down for long and in December, 1916, he bounced back in "Herlock Sholmes' Christmas Case" in "The Magnet." A further five Sholmes cases appeared in "The Magnet" early in 1917 before the detective changed his allegiance to "The Gem," where a further eight tales appeared. It was back to "The Magnet" in August, 1917, for another series of cases. Very few Sholmes adventures were published during 1918 and 1919, but in 1920 he began to feature quite regularly in the pages of the re-launched "Greyfriar's Herald" and thirty-two of his exploits appeared between June 1920 and February 1921, when the paper was re-christened "The Boys' Herald." Throughout the rest of 1921 there were few cases for Sholmes to solve. Two were published in "The Penny Popular," a paper that consisted mainly of reprinted Greyfriars and St. Jim's stories. Five cases also appeared in "The Magnet" and ten new Herlock Sholmes stories were published in "The Penny Popular" during 1924 and early 1925.

Controversy has long raged amongst collectors over the authorship of some of the Herlock Sholmes adventures. Charles Hamilton once claimed that he had written them all, but he was notorious for his poor memory concerning his output, hardly surprising when considering its huge volume! The early tales certainly bear all of the hallmarks of being his work, but some of the later ones lack his sparkle and may well have been the work of other hands. Some authorities claim that the twelve stories in "The Penny Popular" and the last series of five in "The Magnet" were not the work of Hamilton and some weight is given to the argument by the fact that most of the contested tales appeared under the 'Dr. Jotson' or 'Herlock Sholmes' byline.

The final two Herlock Sholmes stories, "The Missing Millionaire" and "The Case of the Perplexed Painter," were certainly the work of Hamilton. They appeared in the second and fourth issue of "Tom's Merry Own" in 1950 and 1952, respectively. Although it was a quarter of a century since he had last written of Sholmes and Jotson his vigorous dig at 'modern art' in the final story showed his readers that he still possessed a satirical wit ready to pan those institutions that he found ridiculous.

In all there were nearly one hundred Herlock Sholmes tales, most of them miniature gems of pastiche that have lain all but forgotten for over sixty years. Eighteen of them were published in the United States of America by The Mysterious Press in 1975, but this is the first attempt to collect the entire Herlock Sholmes cycle into one volume.

There was a desperate struggle. In the midst of it, the door was flung open, and Inspector Pinkeye rushed into the room.

THE ADVENTURE OF THE DIAMOND PINS

No. 1

Sholmes was examining attentively, under a powerful microscope, a leading article in the *Daily Mail,* when I came into our sitting-room at Shaker Street. He looked round with a lazy smile.

"I have surprised you, my dear Jotson," he remarked.

You are always surprising me, Sholmes," I replied. "May I ask what you hope to discover by a microscopical examination of a daily paper?"

He yawned slightly as he laid down the microscope.

"Merely an amusement, Jotson. It may not have occurred to you that by a careful examination of the type in which an article is printed, much may be learned of the man who wrote it; in fact, his age, form, and starting-price, with sufficient care and attention. A simple amusement for an idle moment, my dear Jotson."

"You amaze me, Sholmes."

"Not at all, my dear Jotson. I do not say that this theory is widely known. Scotland Yard would smile at the idea." Herlock Sholmes shrugged his shoulders, as he frequently did at the mention of Scotland Yard, and changed the subject. "I see that you have not shaved this morning, Jotson."

"Sholmes, how could you possibly know—"

He laughed.

"Is it not a fact?" he asked.

"It is a fact, certainly. But how you guessed—"

"It was not a guess, Jotson." Sholmes frowned a little. "I never guess. I leave guesswork to the police. It was a simple deduction, Jotson, simply explained. After shaving, your face presents a smooth and newly-mown appearance. I have observed this on innumerable occasions."

"True. But—"

"At the present moment it presents a rough and hairy appearance. To a trained eye, my dear Jotson, the conclusion is instant and obvious. You have not shaved."

"It is simple enough now that you explain it, Sholmes, but I confess it would not have occurred to me. Yet I have endeavoured to study your methods."

"Rome was not built in a day, my dear fellow," said Sholmes, with a smile. "You must take time. It would amuse me to test your progress. Look at this, and tell me what you deduce from it."

He took a large pistol from a drawer, and handed it to me. I examined it with great attention. I confess to a keen desire to prove to Herlock Sholmes that my progress in his peculiar art was greater than he supposed.

"Well, Jotson?" he said, a smile lurking round the corners of his mouth.

"In the first place, Sholmes, it is a firearm." I felt that I was upon safe ground so far. This much was, indeed, almost obvious.

He nodded.

"Go on, Jotson!"

"In the second place," I went on, encouraged by Sholmes' approval, "it is a revolver of the Colt pattern, which is manufactured in the United States."

"What do you deduce from that, Jotson?"

"That it is an American pistol," I said triumphantly.

"Bravo!" exclaimed Sholmes. You are indeed progressing, Jotson. I am interested now; pray continue."

He threw himself back in his chair, and put his feet on the mantelpiece, in his usual attitude of elegant ease.

"There is a dark stain upon the butt," I continued. "I conclude from that—that—"

"Courage, my dear fellow. Go on!"
"That the revolver has been used as a paperweight, and that ink has been spilled upon it," I suggested.
I was mortified to see Sholmes burst into a hearty laugh. I threw down the pistol somewhat pettishly.
"I suppose I am wrong?" I exclaimed.
"Excuse me, my dear Jotson." Sholmes checked his merriment. "I am afraid you are a little wide of the mark. That stain is not ink; it is blood."
"Good heavens!" I exclaimed.
"The revolver was found upon the scene of the Hornsey Rise murder," explained Sholmes. "You have heard of it? Seventeen of the most respected residents of Hornsey Rise were murdered on the night of the fourth. The peculiar circumstance is that each of them was robbed of a diamond pin. The police have concluded that the murders were committed for purposes of robbery. To that extent, Jotson, the intellect of Scotland Yard can go, but no further. They have no clue excepting this revolver, which has been handed to me. As a last resource," added Sholmes, shrugging his shoulders, "the police are willing to make use of my humble services."
"Better late than never," I remarked.
"Perhaps so." Sholmes glanced at the clock. "Nearly half-past nine. At half-past nine, Jotson, I expect a visitor."
I rose.
"Do not go, my dear fellow. I shall need you."
"You delight me, Sholmes. You wish me to observe and deduce—"
"I wish you to take the tongs, and station yourself behind the door," said Sholmes calmly. "You will prevent his escape if I do not succeed in handcuffing him. He will be desperate."
"Sholmes! Who is it, then, that you are expecting?"
"The Hornsey Rise murderer!" said Sholmes tranquilly.

CHAPTER 2

Before I could make any rejoinder to my friend's astounding remark the door was thrown open, and our landlady announced the visitor.
He was a man of powerful frame. My study of Sholmes' methods made it possible for me to observe that he was a man of dangerous character. The handles of several knives protruded from his pockets, and he carried a bayonet in the place of a walking-stick. These details did not escape me, though perhaps I ought to admit that, but for Sholmes' warning, I should have noticed nothing out of the ordinary.
Herlock Sholmes greeted him genially. But the fact that he picked up the poker showed me that he was upon his guard. I secured the tongs immediately, mindful of my friend's admonition.
"Good-morning!" said Sholmes. "You have only to establish your right to the property in question, and it will be handed over to you immediately. This way, please! Ah! Help, my dear Jotson!"
Sholmes was upon the ruffian with the spring of a tiger.
I rushed forward.
There was a desperate struggle. In the midst of it, the door was flung open, and Inspector Pinkeye rushed into the room.
A moment more, and the handcuffs snapped upon the wrists of the ruffian.
Herlock Sholmes rose, panting, to his feet. He lighted a cigarette.
"Quite an easy capture," he drawled. "You are welcome to him, Pinkeye."
"Much obliged to you, Mr. Sholmes," said the inspector, with a smile of satisfaction. "I don't know how you did it, but you've done it. A lucky fluke, I suppose—what?"

Sholmes smiled.
"Exactly—a lucky fluke, my dear Pinkeye!" he said, with a sarcasm that was lost upon the worthy inspector. "Good-morning, Pinkeye!"
Inspector Pinkeye marched the scowling ruffian from the room. Herlock Sholmes sank into his chair again, yawning.
"Twas ever thus, Jotson," he said, with a trifle of bitterness. "Scotland Yard will never understand my methods, and is content to call my success a lucky fluke. But for your generous appreciation, Jotson, I should be discouraged."
"You may always count upon my admiration, Sholmes," I said fervently. "You astound me more than ever. May I ask—"
"To you, Jotson, I will explain," said Sholmes. "It may help you on in your study of my methods. The capture was effected simply through the medium of an advertisement in the daily papers. The murderer left his revolver on the scene of the crime. You are aware that lost property, advertised in the papers, is very likely to be claimed."
"I have heard so," I assented. "But surely, Sholmes, the murderer would not have answered an advertisement of his lost revolver. Might he not have suspected that it was a trap of the police?"
"Undoubtedly, and therefore I did not advertise the revolver. I advertised a diamond pin."
"A – a what?" I exclaimed in amazement.
"A diamond pin, my dear Jotson. Look at this paragraph." I looked. The advertisement ran:
"FOUND, in the neighbourhood of Hornsey Rise, a valuable diamond pin. Owner can have same by applying to No. 101, Shaker Street."
I gazed at Herlock Sholmes in complete astonishment.
"Sholmes!" I ejaculated. "You had found a diamond pin?"
"Not at all."
"One was lost?"
"Certainly not!"
"Then, in the name of all that is wonderful—"
Sholmes smiled patiently.
"My dear Jotson, reason it out. Seventeen murders were committed in a single night, each for the purpose of stealing a diamond pin. Does this not argue that the criminal dealt specially in diamond pins? My advertisement stated, therefore, that a diamond pin had been found. Sooner or later it was certain to meet his eyes, and the rest was inevitable. To add one more diamond pin to his collection of ill-gotten gains would be an irresistible attraction for him."
"Most true!" I exclaimed. "But – forgive me, Sholmes – one more question: Suppose some ordinary member of the public had lost a diamond pin – such things happen – and suppose he had seen the advertisement, and come here—"
"My dear Jotson, you are supposing now, and my methods do not deal with suppositions." Herlock Sholmes yawned. "I leave suppositions to the police, my dear fellow. It is time you went to visit your patients, Jotson."

THE CASE OF THE BISCUIT TIN

No. 2

Sholmes was at breakfast when I came down. He was dressed with his usual negligence, in a dressing-gown, a bathing-towel, and a slipper of a curious Oriental design.
He threw down the morning paper with a gesture of impatience.
"Nothing doing, my dear Jotson," he said. "The criminal classes seem to have gone out of business for three years, or the duration of the war. I have had nothing since the case of the King of Spoofia's Crown Jewels and the case of the missing Duke of Hookeywalker. I am growing bored, my dear Jotson."

Bakenphat staggered back. The handcuffs were on his wrists. "There!" exclaimed Sholmes. "There is your prisoner, Inspector Pinkeye. You will find the duke's diamonds concealed in a German sausage in his watch-pocket."

"You are not losing your keenness, my dear Sholmes."
"I wonder," said Sholmes, absently knocking the ash from his eternal cigarette into my left ear— "I wonder, my dear Jotson! Shall I tell you what you had for breakfast this morning?"
I smiled.
"You cannot, Sholmes."
"Now, you have put me on my mettle, my dear Jotson. In the first place," said Sholmes dreamily, "you rose from that bed."
I started.
"It is true," I admitted. "But how—"
"You then took your morning bath."
"Sholmes!"
"And you breakfasted upon eggs and bacon."
"Marvellous!"
Sholmes smiled, with a slightly bored expression.
"Nothing at all, my dear boy. Deduction, that's all."
"But how—"
"Ah, if I explain you will no longer wonder at the accuracy of my deductions!" he said, with a smile. "Still, I will risk it with you, my dear Jotson. In the first place, you are now in a perpendicular attitude."
"True!"
"The observations of a lifetime have led me to conclude that in bed people generally – in fact, almost invariably – assume a horizontal attitude."
"True again!" I exclaimed. "I had not observed it, but, now that you point it out, I must admit that so far your deductions seem very simple."
"Did I not tell you so? But to proceed. Your present perpendicular attitude shows indubitably that you rose from your bed. As for your bath, I have observed your customs during the time we have been together at Shaker Street. Why should the habit of years be broken upon this especial morning? I admit that this was a venture, but it proved correct, as you admit."
"Perfectly correct. But the eggs and bacon?"
"Ah, there we go a little deeper!" smiled Sholmes. "First, I have observed that, contrary to modern custom, you wear a moustache."
"You astound me, Sholmes!"
"Upon your moustache remains a slight trace of the breakfast egg. *Voila tout!*" said Sholmes carelessly.
"But the bacon?" I urged.
"Ah, there I was obliged to call upon my very wide experience! Bacon and eggs frequently – in fact, almost invariably – are taken together. From the eggs I deduced the bacon."
"Marvellous!"
Before I could further express my admiration for the marvellous insight of my amazing friend the door was flung open, and Inspector Pinkeye, of Scotland Yard, rushed into the room.
"Sholmes!" he gasped. "Ah, thank goodness you are here! But—"
"You may speak freely before my friend, Dr. Jotson," said Sholmes. "Take a cigarette, my dear Pinkeye, and a gallon of cocaine."
"Sholmes, the Duke of Shepherd's Bush's diamonds have been stolen! There is no clue. The thieves left nothing behind them but a biscuit-tin!"
Herlock Sholmes was on his feet in a twinkling. All the laziness was gone from his manner. He was once more the keen, cool detective.
"Only a biscuit-tin!" he drawled. "That is hard upon you, my dear Pinkeye. What do you deduce from that?"

"Nothing!" said the inspector, with a despairing gesture.
Sholmes smiled.
"Then answer one question," he said: "Was the lid on the biscuit-tin?"
Inspector Pinkeye shook his head.
"It was not!" exclaimed Sholmes.
"No. But what has that—"
But Herlock Sholmes was gone.

CHAPTER 2

I did not see Sholmes again for some days. Although kept pretty busy by my medical practice, my thoughts were chiefly with my friend. The case of the stolen diamonds occupied my mind, and I wondered whether the Duke of Shepherd's Bush would ever see them again. To this preoccupation I attribute the fact that several of my patients died during those few anxious days. This was a considerable loss to me financially, but I gave it little thought in my concern for Sholmes.

At last he reappeared. When I found an Italian organ-grinder reposing on the couch in my consulting-room one morning I had little difficulty in guessing that this was my friend in one of his innumerable disguises.

"Saffron Hillo!" he said. "Greeko Streeto! Macaroni, vermicelli!" Herlock Sholmes spoke Italian like a native. "Organ-grindo! Soupo potato!"

"Sholmes!" I exclaimed.

"Right again, my dear Jotson!" he said, rubbing his hands. "Are you busy this morning, or would you like a little excitement?"

"My dear Sholmes, I am entirely at your service. I was about to visit a patient for a dangerous operation. Probably he will not survive if it is delayed. But what does that matter at a time like this? Lead on!"

"Good man, Jotson! What should I do without my faithful Jotson?" said Herlock Sholmes, with one of those rare touches of affection that endeared him so much to me. "But you must be disguised."

With a few touches of his skilful hand, he disguised me as a coal-heaver.

A few seconds later we were seated in a taxi-cab.

"Where are we going, my dear Sholmes?" I asked, as the taxi whizzed through the streets at breakneck speed, causing several unfortunate fatalities by the way.

"You will see in a moment, Jotson. Have you your revolver?"

I felt a thrill.

"It is in my pocket, Sholmes."

"Leave it there, my dear fellow. It is safer there."

Before I had time to reflect upon this cryptic remark the taxi drew up at the door of the Hotel d'Oof. I followed Herlock Sholmes into the gorgeous vestibule. We were shown at once into the spacious kitchens. I was amazed. What mystery was this? My amazement increased at the sight of Inspector Pinkeye and several special constables hiding behind a pat of butter in a corner of the kitchen. Evidently the climax was at hand.

The chef was busy, with his spotless apron about him, and his sleeves rolled up. A momentary frown appeared upon his fat face at the sight of Sholmes, but it vanished immediately, and he smiled.

"Good-morning, Mr. Bakenphat!" said Sholmes cheerily. "I have brought my friend, Jotson, to see that remarkable wrist-watch of yours."

The chef started, and turned deadly pale.

"You have no objection?" smiled Sholmes.

"None at all," stammered Mr. Bakenphat. "You are quite welcome—"

He held out his wrist. The watch was worn in a somewhat remarkable bracelet formed of dull metal. Sholmes appeared to examine it attentively. There was a sudden click.

Bakenphat staggered back.

The handcuffs were on his wrists.

"There!" exclaimed Sholmes, with an exultant note in his voice. "There is your prisoner, Pinkeye. You will find the duke's diamonds concealed in a German sausage in his watch-pocket."

"But – but how—" gasped Pinkeye, as he grasped his prisoner.

"And if you observe closely, my dear Pinkeye," said Sholmes, in a careless drawl, "you will find that watch-bracelet is made of tin—"

"Tin!"

"And is, in fact, the missing lid of the biscuit-tin. Come, my dear Jotson! We are finished here. The police can do the rest."

CHAPTER 3

In our rooms in Shaker Street, after the usual pint of cocaine and a hundred cigarettes, Herlock Sholmes explained.

"Quite simple, my dear Jotson," he said – "elementary, in fact. The thief left behind him an empty biscuit-tin. You must be aware that it is not usual for cracksmen to take tins of biscuits with them upon burgling expeditions. This peculiar taste on the part of the cracksman furnished the first clue. Observe, Jotson, that while leaving the empty tin upon the scene of crime, he had taken the lid away with him."

"But Inspector Pinkeye attached no importance—"

Sholmes made a gesture.

"Ah, these Scotland Yard men!" he murmured. "They tire me, Jotson! Cannot you see that, when the lid of the biscuit-tin was found, the thief was found? Where would he conceal it? And observe that, however cunningly he might hide the lid of the biscuit-tin, he could not hide the abnormal taste for biscuits which had caused him to leave this clue behind him."

"True!"

"Such was my task. Well, the chef at the Hotel d'Oof had an almost morbid affection for biscuits. I discovered that he had taken to wearing a wrist-watch instead of the usual time-keeper in the usual place. Aha! Disguised as a butcher's boy, I penetrated into the kitchens of the Hotel d'Oof. His watch-bracelet was made of beaten tin; his watch-pocket bulged. It was enough. It was a cunning scheme, which would have deceived the police. Who, my dear Jotson, would have suspected a cracksman of concealing the lid of a biscuit-tin under the form of a watch-bracelet?"

"Nobody but you, Sholmes," I said, with conviction. "It is wonderful!"

"Elementary, my dear Jotson."

"One more question, Sholmes. Why did not the thief throw the lid of the biscuit-tin into the nearest dustbin?"

Herlock Sholmes smiled his inscrutable smile.

"Ah, why, Jotson?" he replied. "The psychology of the habitual criminal presents many baffling peculiarities. This is one of them. Pass the cocaine."

THE BOUND OF THE HASKERVILLES

No. 3

The story of the disappearance of Sir Huckaback Haskerville, and the strange events that followed, has never been fully told. It is my privilege, as the faithful companion and chronicler of Herlock Sholmes, to give the story to the public for the first time.

A strong scent of frying fish came from the open window!

It was Sholmes, it is needless to say, who solved the mystery that had baffled the police for three weeks. It is only just that my amazing friend should be given, even at this late date, the credit that is his due.

The disappearance of Sir Huckaback, the head of one of the oldest families in Slopshire, had created a sensation. There were whispers of family dissensions that had preceded it. Society held that Lady Haskerville was to blame. What seemed certain was that the unhappy baronet, after hot words at the breakfast-table, had rushed forth from his ancestral halls, and plunged to his death in the deep chasm in the heart of Haskerville Park. From these gloomy depths he had never emerged.

Strange stories were told of that yawning chasm in Haskerville Park. Tradition had it that a certain ancestor of the Haskervilles, who had sided with King Charles in the Civil Wars, had escaped the soldiers of the Parliament by a desperate leap across the yawning gulf. From this tradition the place was known locally as "The Bound of the Haskervilles." A certain resemblance was given to the story by the fact that this ancient Haskerville had had a considerable reputation as a bounder in the Royal Court before the wars.

Be this as it may, there could be little doubt that his descendant had perished in those gloomy depths. His footsteps had been traced to the edge of the chasm, and there were no returning footprints. Where his ancestor, pursued by Cromwell's Ironsides, had bounded to safety, if local tradition was to be relied upon, Sir Huckaback had plunged to his doom.

The grief of Lady Haskerville was terrible. For several days she was not seen at the theatre or the cinema. I was not surprised when, one morning, as I sat at breakfast with Herlock Sholmes in our rooms at Shaker Street, Lady Haskerville was announced.

Sholmes made a slight gesture of impatience. He was very busy at this time upon the case of the missing Depaste diamonds, and had no mind for other work. But his face relaxed at the sight of Lady Haskerville. Even the clever work of her Bond Street complexion specialist could not hide the pallor of her beautiful face.

"Mr. Sholmes," she exclaimed, clasping her hands, "you will help me! I have come to you as a last resource. The police are helpless."

Sholmes smiled ironically.

"It is not uncommon for my aid to be called in when the police have proved to be helpless," he remarked. "But really, my dear Lady Haskerville—pray sit down—really, I cannot leave the case I am engaged upon."

"Mr. Sholmes, to save me from despair!"

I glanced at Sholmes, wondering whether his firmness would be proof against this appeal. My friend wavered.

"Well, well," he said. "Let us see what can be done. Pray give the details, Lady Haskerville. You may speak quite freely before my friend Jotson."

"I am convinced that Sir Huckaback still lives," said Lady Haskerville, weeping. "But he will not return. Mr. Sholmes, it was my fault; I admit it. Oh, to see him once more, and confess my fault upon my knees! The bloaters were burnt!"

"The bloaters?" queried Herlock Sholmes.

"It was a trifling quarrel," said Lady Haskerville tearfully. "Sir Huckaback's favourite breakfast dish was the succulent bloater. I have never cared for bloaters; my own taste ran rather in the direction of shrimps. Mr. Sholmes, we loved each other dearly; yet upon this subject there was frequently argument. On the morning of Sir Huckaback's disappearance there were words—high words. Sir Huckaback maintained that the bloaters were burnt. I maintained that they were done perfectly. Mr. Sholmes, to my shame I confess it, I knew that the bloaters were burnt!" She sobbed.

Sholmes' clear-cut face was very grave.

"And then?" he asked quietly.

"Then, Mr. Sholmes, Sir Huckaback rose in wrath, and declared that if he must eat burnt bloaters he would not remain at Haskerville Park. I was angry, too; I was not myself at that moment. In my haste I said that if he persisted in his obnoxious predilection for bloaters, I never desired to look upon him again. He gave me one terrible look, and vanished. Too late I called to him; he did not return. In spite of the difference in our tastes, I loved him dearly. But he did not come back. Search was made.

The police were called in. The track of his boots was found, leading down to the yawning abyss in the park known as the Bound of the Haskervilles. There he had disappeared."

Lady Haskerville trembled with emotion. My own eyes were not dry. The grief of this beautiful woman moved me deeply. Sholmes was unusually gentle.

"But I cannot believe he is dead," continued Lady Haskerville, controlling her emotion. "Mr. Sholmes, he is keeping away from me. He has taken my hasty words too, too seriously; and that he will never give up bloaters I know only too well. I feel that he is living yet, in some quiet and serene spot where he may be able to enjoy his favourite breakfast-dish undisturbed. He must be found, Mr. Sholmes, or my heart will be broken. This dreadful doubt must be set at rest."

"It is quite certain that the footprints leading to the chasm were really Sir Huckaback's!" asked Sholmes.

"Yes, that is certain; his footprints were well known. He took number eleven in boots."

Herlock Sholmes caressed his chin thoughtfully for a moment. Then he rose to his feet.

"Your car is outside, Lady Haskerville?"

"Yes, Mr. Sholmes, You will come with me?" she exclaimed eagerly.

"We will come," corrected Herlock Sholmes. "My friend Jotson will, I am sure, give up his patients for one day."

"Willingly!" I exclaimed.

Ten seconds later we were in the car, whirling away at top speed for the ancient home of the Haskervilles, in the heart of Slopshire.

CHAPTER 2

"So that is the celebrated Bound of the Haskervilles!" said Herlock Sholmes thoughtfully.

We arrived at Haskerville Park, and my friend had proceeded at once to the scene of the supposed suicide of the baronet. Following the tracks in the grassy sward, which had not been disturbed, we had arrived at the border of the yawning abyss.

Sholmes stood regarding it thoughtfully. I watched, in wonder, striving to guess the thoughts that were passing in that subtle brain. He had stopped for a few minutes in the house to use the telephone. Why? I could not guess. Now we were upon the scene of the disappearance. Three weeks had passed since Sir Huckaback had reached that fatal verge. What did Sholmes hope to discover there?

He turned to me at last with his inscrutable smile.

"Do you feel inclined for a stroll, Jotson!" he asked.

"Anything you like, Sholmes."

"Come, then."

We started off along the edge of the abyss. A quarter of a mile's walk brought us to the end, and we walked round it, and along the other side. Sholmes took a pair of powerful glasses from his pocket, and scanned the smiling countryside. In the distance the smoke of a cottage rose above the trees.

He started off again, and I followed him in wonder. When we reached the cottage it was easy to learn that the occupant was at a meal, for strong scent of frying fish came from the open window.

Sholmes knocked at the door.

It was opened by a man in rough attire, wearing very large heavy boots. He looked suspiciously at Sholmes.

"What's wanted?" he asked gruffly.

Sholmes smiled.

"You are Sir Huckaback Haskerville?" he replied tranquilly.

The man staggered back.

I could not repress a cry of astonishment.

"Sholmes!"

"It is false!" exclaimed the cottager. "Sir Huckaback Haskerville is dead."

"My dear Sir Huckaback," said Sholmes quietly, "it is useless to deny your identity. But I have come as a friend, not as an enemy. Her ladyship has repented. She confesses her fault. In future, I am assured, she will utter not a single word that could wound your feelings upon the subject of bloaters. Sir Huckaback, be generous. Return to her ladyship, and relieve her breaking heart.

He wavered.

"Come!" said Sholmes, with a smile. And, after a brief hesitation, the baronet assented.

"Sholmes, I am on tenterhooks!" I exclaimed, as the express bore us Londonwards. "You astonish me anew every day. But this——"

He laughed as he lighted a couple of cigarettes.

"The fact is, Jotson, I am pleased myself," he said. "Yet it was very simple."

"But the police——"

He shrugged his shoulders.

"The police knew that old story of the Bound of the Haskervilles," he said. "Yet they never thought of the obvious deduction. The baronet had determined to disappear. By leaving the unmistakable track of number eleven boots to the verge of the chasm he gave the desired impression. A certain ancestor of Sir Huckaback originated the tradition of the Bound of the Haskervilles by clearing that chasm at a single jump. Why should not that trait have descended to the present baronet? That was the theory I worked upon, Jotson. I was perfectly prepared to find that, instead of having fallen into the abyss, Sir Huckaback had repeated the performance of his ancestor by clearing it. Consequently, I searched for him on the other side."

"Wonderful!"

Sholmes smiled.

"I wished to ascertain, Jotson, whether Sir Huckaback had ever shown any trace of inheriting the peculiar bounding powers of his ancestor. I called up his college at Oxford. In five minutes I had learned all I wished to know, Sir Huckaback's reputation, in his college days, was that of the biggest bounder at Oxford. Have you any cocaine about you, Jotson? Thanks!"

And Herlock Sholmes remained in a comatose condition till we arrived at Shaker Street.

THE FRECKLED HAND

No. 4

In looking over the notes of this period of my residence at Shaker Street, with my friend, Herlock Sholmes, I find three cases of especial interest: "The Case of the Missing Dumb-bell," "The Adventure of the Prime Minister's Ear-trumpet," and the strange and tragic story of Dr. Grimey Pylott, which I have classified as "The Case of the Freckled Hand." It is the last-named that I propose to give here.

I was chatting with Sholmes one morning, when a young lady, deeply veiled, was shown into our sitting-room at Shaker Street. Sholmes removed his feet from the table at once, with his usual exquisite politeness where women were concerned. The visitor pushed back her veil, and revealed a beautiful and tear-stained face.

"Mr. Sholmes," she said, in an agitated voice, "I have come to you because I am in danger of my life. If my uncle should learn that I have come, he would blow out my brains upon the spot! He is accustomed to these ebullitions of violent temper. Mr. Sholmes, will you help me?"

"Pray give me some details!" said Sholmes. "You may speak quite freely before my friend, Dr. Jotson."

"I should tell you first that my name is Mary Jane Pylott. I live at Coke Pylott with my uncle, Dr. Grimey Pylott. My sister lived with us there till the time of the tragedy of two years ago. One never-to-be-forgotten night, Mr. Sholmes, she came into my room, and sank upon the floor. All she could utter was, 'It was the hand—the freckled hand!'" Mary Jane Pylott sobbed. "Some time before, she had told me of how she was disturbed in her sleep by the sound of a rattle. Mr. Sholmes, last night I woke up, and heard distinctly in my room the sound of a rattle."

Sholmes' eyes gleamed. I could see that he was deeply interested.

"What kind of a rattle?" he asked.

"That I cannot say. It was simply a rattle. As there are no children in the house, and my uncle is too old to play with a rattle, I cannot account for it. But—but I am sure, Mr. Sholmes, that it was the same rattle that my unhappy sister heard upon that fatal night. Without saying a word to my uncle, I came here by the first morning train. I fear that he has followed me. I dare not remain another moment!"

Our visitor departed hastily.

A few minutes later a gigantic man rushed into the room. Herlock Sholmes eyed him calmly, as he advanced with menacing gestures.

"You are Herlock Sholmes!" shouted he.

My friend nodded tranquilly.

"Good-morning, Dr. Grimey Pylott!" he replied.

"Sholmes, the detective! Sholmes, the meddler! Sholmes, the spy!" hissed Dr. Grimey Pylott.

"What beautiful weather we are having!" yawned Herlock Sholmes.

"If you dare to meddle in my affairs, I will break you as I break this vase!" shouted Pylott, as he seized a vase from the mantel-piece, and hurled it upon the floor, where it shattered into a thousand fragments.

"The sunflowers are coming on well," remarked Herlock Sholmes.

Dr. Grimey Pylott glared at him, and rushed from the room, slamming the door behind him with a noise like thunder.

Herlock Sholmes yawned.

"A pleasant visitor, Jotson. If he had tried conclusions with me, he might have found, perhaps, that he had met his match!" With scarcely an effort Sholmes tossed the fragments of the vase into the grate. "Jotson, there is work to do! Not a moment is to be lost! You may go and see your patients, my dear fellow."

He was gone before I could reply.

CHAPTER 2

Sholmes came in towards evening, looking somewhat tired. But he had not come in to rest.

"Come, my dear Jotson—that is, if you wish to be in at the finish!"

"Where are we going?" I asked.

"To Coke Pylott."

The express from Euston bore us away. My friend was silent and distrait during the whole journey. He smoked some hundreds of cigarettes, but I noticed that he did not take his usual swig of cocaine.

The dusk was falling as we approached the house. It was a rambling old-fashioned building. Miss Pylott met us at the door.

"My uncle is shut up in this room," she whispered.

"All the better," said Sholmes. "Miss Pylott, in this case you must trust us absolutely. Could you sleep in the coal-cellar, or some secluded spot, this night, and leave your room to my friend Jotson and myself?"

"I am entirely at your orders, Mr. Sholmes."

"Good!"

We were shown to Miss Pylott's room, and left there. Sholmes looked about him, and listened at the wall which adjoined Dr. Grimey Pylott's apartment. The doctor could be heard pacing to and fro. A gleam of light penetrated into the darkened room from the doctor's apartment.

"Hush!" whispered Sholmes. "Not a word, Jotson! Have you a revolver?"

"Here," I whispered back.

"Be on your guard, Jotson! We are taking our lives in our hands!"

I thrilled at the words.

We waited.

For what were we waiting? I did not know. But I felt that danger was in the air. The shadow of tragedy brooded over the house.

No sound was heard save our subdued breathing. The hours struck dully from the clock in the hall.

Midnight!

My heart was beating wildly. In the gloom I could scarcely discern Herlock Sholmes. I saw that he had gripped his walking stick hard. His eyes were glittering. The hour was at hand.

Suddenly, in the deep silence, I heard a faint rattle.

I started.

It was the sound that had been described to us. My heart beat almost to suffocation.

The rattle was repeated.

With startling suddenness Herlock Sholmes turned on his electric lamp. The light flashed upon a large freckled hand, and upon—— Before I could see further my friend had sprung forward, and was lashing our furiously with his stick.

The rattle ceased.

From the adjoining room came a sudden, fearful cry.

"Follow me!" panted Herlock Sholmes.

We rushed into the doctor's room. Stretched upon the floor was the gigantic form of Dr. Grimey Pylott. About it was coiled a huge rattlesnake. With a single blow, Sholmes stretched the reptile dead upon the floor. He threw himself beside the doctor. But it was too late!

Dr. Grimey Pylott, the last representative of the ancient race of the Pylotts of Coke Pylott, had paid for all his sins!

CHAPTER 3

I was still considerably shaken by the tragic events of the night when we returned to Shaker Street. Sholmes himself was unusually grave.

"You are puzzled, my dear Jotson," he said.

"I am astonished, Sholmes! I do not see how——"

"If you could see how, my dear Jotson, it would not be necessary for me to give my usual explanation," he said, with a slight smile. "It was the freckled hand that gave me the clue I needed. When Dr. Pylott visited us, you may have noticed his hands?"

"I confess that I did not. But you——"

"I observed that they were very large and freckled, my dear Jotson. But that was not all. You remember the rattle? How could that mysterious sound be accounted for? That Dr. Pylott was in the habit of playing with a toy rattle was scarcely an admissible theory. I deduced a rattlesnake. When I left you yesterday, Jotson, it was to consult the wills at Somerset House. I found that Dr. Pylott was heir to his nieces, and that in the case of their death he would take possession of all their furniture. That supplied the motive, Jotson. When we arrived at Coke Pylott I was perfectly prepared to find a means of communication between Dr. Pylott's room and that of Miss Mary Jane."

"You found it?" I exclaimed.

He smiled again.

"Did you not observe, Jotson, when we were waiting in the dark, that a ray of light came from the adjoining apartment?"

"I did. But——"

"From that, my dear Jotson, I deduced an opening in the wall. Light cannot penetrate a solid body. Had the wall been intact the light could not have come through. I deduced an opening."

"Wonderful!" I exclaimed.

"Why was the opening there, Jotson? And you remember that strange exclamation of the former victim—'It was the hand—the freckled hand!' Once I deduced the opening in the wall, Jotson, the rest was easy. Through that opening the villain had introduced the rattlesnake into the room. But this time, Jotson, we were there. The dastardly work was interrupted, and the reptile, excited perhaps by the blows I had rained upon it, turned upon its master, and bit the freckled hand that held him. I confess that I had not anticipated this, but I cannot say that I am sorry. You remember that saying of the wise Frenchman, Jotson, *'Il fait beau temps! Bonjour!'*?"

And Herlock Sholmes was silent.

"Shakey-Cakey," said Sholmes. "Wallop hookey snookey whoosh!" Before he could say more, a dagger glittered in the hand of the Hindu. But Sholmes was never taken by surprise. In an instant the handcuffs were upon the wrists of Bhang Bhung Whallop, and he was a prisoner!

THE SIGN OF FOURTY FOUR

No. 5

The mysterious murders of forty-four retired Indian colonels, on forty-four successive nights, had naturally attracted a good deal of public attention. Even in the record of crime of the great metropolis this was a little out of the common. The police, as usual, were helpless. The case, indeed, presented many difficulties. With the exception of footprints, finger-prints, and a number of Oriental daggers of curious design, the assassin had not left a single clue behind him. I wondered whether my friend Sholmes would take up the case, though he had not yet been approached officially on the subject. On this occasion the police seemed to have forgotten their well-known custom of appealing for aid to private detectives in cases of exceptional difficulty.

I was reading the latest reports of the strange mystery one morning in our rooms at Shaker Street, when I observed Sholmes regarding me with a quizzical smile.

"You are reading the *Daily Mail!*" he remarked.

"Sholmes!" I exclaimed.

Accustomed as I was to my friend's amazing gifts, I could not repress that exclamation of surprise.

"Is it not a fact?" he asked, with a smile.

"It is," I replied. "But how——"

He made a bored gesture.

"A mere nothing, my dear Jotson. From the side of the table I observe the paper in your hand. An untrained eye would not observe that the title of a daily paper is printed in large letters along the top of the page; yet, if you make the observation for yourself, you will see that what I state is the fact."

"You are right, Sholmes," I replied, "as, indeed you always are. And, truly, by this time I should cease to be surprised at anything on your part. Now, Sholmes, I am going to speak to you frankly. Why have you not taken up the case of the forty-four murdered colonels?"

Sholmes shrugged his shoulders.

"The police have not cared to avail themselves of my humble services, Jotson. I do not wish to intrude."

"I am sure that you have formed a theory, Sholmes."

"Theories, my dear Jotson, I leave to the police. My business is with facts. Perhaps if our friend, Inspector Pinkeye, chose to consult me, I could point out a few facts that have escaped his attention, but he has not chosen to do so."

"After the priceless aid you rendered in the case of the biscuit tin——"

"I am afraid, Jotson, that our friend Pinkeye is a little jealous. Even police-inspectors are only human. But I do not deny, Jotson, that the case presents certain aspects of interest. There is a wholesale characteristic about it which pleases me—in a professional sense, of course." He rose, and paced the room restlessly. "Jotson, as I have said, I do not care to offer my services unasked, yet it is now the forty-third day since the crimes were committed."

I looked at Sholmes in astonishment. His remark puzzled me.

"You mean that the assassin has had ample time to make his escape?" I asked.

"I mean nothing of the sort." He changed the subject abruptly. "Have you ever studied the science of numbers, Jotson?"

"Numbers, Sholmes?"

"Numbers," he replied. "You are aware, of course, that there are certain numbers that are regarded as sacred or of mysterious import in different countries. For instance, take the number two. In this country, for example, every man, and, indeed, every woman, has two hands and two eyes. There are two editions to a morning paper, there are two shillings to a florin, and two half-sovereigns to a pound; there were two Kings of Brentford. The number two constantly recurs."

"I had never observed it, Sholmes; but now that you point it out——"

"Exactly!" he interrupted. "Now that I point it out, even the police could see it. Take the number seven. There were seven Sleepers of Ephesus, seven ages of man, seven hills in Rome, and seven times seven in the number forty-nine!"

"True!"

"And now," said Sholmes, his look growing more serious, "take the number forty-four. Do you not see the connection between that mysterious number and the mysterious murders that have shocked the whole community? Forty-four Indian colonels were the victims of the unknown assassin on forty-four successive nights. Since then nothing has been heard of the ruthless assassin, and the remainder of the retired colonels in England have slept in peace. "But,—Herlock Sholmes spoke slowly and distinctly—"to-morrow, Jotson, it will be forty-four days since the last of the murders."

A strange thrill of apprehension came over me. In my mind's eye, I seemed to see a perspective of forty-four new crimes that threatened an equal number of as yet unsuspecting victims.

"That has not occurred to the police." Sholmes smiled. "Are you ready for an adventure to-day, Jotson?"

"I am entirely at your service, Sholmes."

"Your patients——"

"Most of my patients died while we were busy on the case of the biscuit-tin. For the remainder I care little in comparison with my interest in your work!"

"Faithful Jotson!" said Sholmes, with one of his rare pokes in the ribs. "Let us go!"

CHAPTER 2

"Where are we going?" I asked, as the taxicab whizzed through the busy streets.

"Hounslow Heath!" said Sholmes briefly.

"But why?"

"A fair is being held there."

"A fair?" I exclaimed.

He nodded.

"A fair, Jotson—with the merry roundabout, the exhilarating swing-boat, and the cheery circus. We are going to see the Indian juggler, Bhang Bhung Wallop, and his troupe of performing elephants."

"Sholmes!"

"A little relaxation will do us no harm, Jotson. By the way,"—he changed the subject abruptly—"you read the account of the crimes? On each occasion the victim was attacked in his bed-room, which was entered by the window."

"Undoubtedly."

"How did the assassin reach the window, Jotson?"

I shook my head.

"He must have had some visible means of support," remarked Sholmes.

"A ladder?" I suggested.

"A man carrying a ladder at night would excite remark, Jotson. The aim of this amazing assassin has been to shroud his movements in mystery. He did not use a ladder."

"You know what he did use, Sholmes?"

"Perhaps."

I could not extract another word from Sholmes until the taxi drew up at the heath. The entertainments were not yet in progress at that early hour, and the place was almost deserted. Outside the circus-tent a lithe, dark-skinned man was feeding a troupe of elephants. Sholmes approached him.

"Good-morning, Bhang Bhung Whallop!" he said genially.

The Hindu gave him a surly look.

"No speaky English," he said.

I think I have already mentioned in these memoirs that Sholmes was a master of every language, ancient and modern. I was not surprised to hear him address the Hindu in his own tongue.

"Hookey wookey dummy bang woop!" he said, with a smile.

The Hindu sprang to his feet.

The meaning of those strange-sounding words I could not fathom; the tongue was unknown to me. But their effect upon the Hindu was electrical. His dusky eyes rolled, and his dark face became livid.

"Shakey-cakey," said Sholmes. "Wallop hookey snookey whoosh!"
Before he could say more, a dagger glittered in the hand of the Hindu. But Sholmes was never taken by surprise. In an instant the handcuffs were upon the wrists of Bhang Bhung Whallop, and he was a prisoner!

CHAPTER 3

"Sholmes!" I exclaimed, when we had returned to Shaker Street, after handing over the sullen prisoner to the police. I am on tenterhooks——"
"As usual, Jotson," he said, with a smile.
"As usual, Sholmes. You will make your explanation as usual?"
"Is there anything to explain?" yawned Sholmes, as he lighted the eternal cigarette. "To me, the thing was obvious from the first. It all centred, Jotson, upon the sign of forty-four. As you doubtless know, in the deep and mysterious East, a magic import is attached to certain sacred numbers. It was not by chance, Jotson, that forty-four retired colonels were slain upon forty-four successive nights. It was evidently a dark plot of Oriental vengeance, and the clue was in the number forty-four. I have questioned our dark friend, Bhang Bhung Whallop, and he confessed that, long ago, in his native land, he was fined forty-four rupees. Something of the sort, Jotson, I had divined. The sign of forty-four gave me my clue."
"But how——"
"My dear fellow, I had to find the man to whom the number forty-four was a deep and mysterious symbol. I was aware that at the time of the murders Bhang Bhung Whallop was in London, giving performances with a troupe of forty-four elephants."
"Forty-four!" I ejaculated.
"Exactly. The sign of forty-four!" smiled Sholmes. "Had the police cared to avail themselves of my assistance, I could have pointed out our friend Bhang Bhung Whallop to them at once. But when forty-three days had elapsed since the crimes, Jotson I could hesitate no longer. On the forty-fourth day of the series of crimes would have recommenced, and forty-four fresh victims would have fallen. I acted in time. That mysterious number gave me my clue; but that was not all. How, my dear Jotson, had the assassin reached the windows? He could not have carried a ladder, and a steam crane was out of the question. Yet he must have mounted upon something to reach the windows. I deduced an elephant.
"One more question, Sholmes," I said. "You have observed that the carrying of a ladder to the scene of the crimes would have excited remark. Was not the presence of an elephant likely to be equally remarked?"
But Herlock Sholmes was already under the influence of cocaine, and he did not reply.

THE DEATH OF SHOLMES

No. 6

The case of Professor Hickorychicory—pronounced Hickychicky—is the next on my list at this period of our residence at Shaker Street, and it is the one I propose to give here. This case, which caused the disappearance and supposed death of Herlock Sholmes, proved the most tensely exciting of all in which I shared the work of my amazing friend.
Sholmes had been absent for several days, and I was growing somewhat uneasy on his account, when one morning a coal-heaver was shown into my rooms while I was at breakfast. I rose to my feet, somewhat surprised, but at once the well-known voice reassured me.
"Good-morning, Jotson!"
"Sholmes!" I exclaimed, in astonishment.
"Himself!" he replied, sinking into the armchair, and resting his feet on the mantelpiece in his old familiar way that I knew so well. "Give me something to eat, my dear fellow. I have eaten nothing for fourteen days. I am famished!"

Hardly had we reached the garden, when a terrific explosion shook the building to its foundations. "A bomb!" said Sholmes. "The work of Professor Hickorychicory!"

He devoured bacon and eggs ravenously. Through the grime on his face, he looked at me with his old smile.

"I see you have changed your habits, my dear Jotson."

"In what way, Sholmes?"

"You have taken to clean-shaving."

I started.

"My dear Sholmes," I protested, "you have been absent! How can you possibly be aware——"

"Deduction, my good fellow," said Sholmes carelessly. "When I left you, you were wearing a moustache. At the present moment there is no trace of hair on your upper lip. To the trained eye of a detective, Jotson, the inference is clear. You have shaved clean!"

"I see that you have not changed, at all events, Sholmes," I replied. "The same amazing insight—the same irresistible power of deduction——"

"You flatter me, Jotson. At the present moment," he said moodily, "my insight is at fault. I have met my match at last, Jotson."

"Impossible!"

"It is true. Have you ever heard of Professor Hickorychicory—pronounced Hickychicky?"

I shook my head.

"Naturally," said Sholmes. "Few have heard of him. The police know nothing of him. Even the fact that his name is Hickorychicory, and pronounced Hickychicky, has failed to put them on the track. Yet he is the most dangerous criminal in London—or in the world. Every crime that has been committed during the past seventy years has been planned by this man. His hand is everywhere—invisible, but powerful. It was he who stole the Crown Jewels of Spoofia; he who robbed the Princess of Ghammon; he, my dear Jotson, who kidnapped the young Duke of Shepherd's Bush, and assassinated the Marquis of Hornsey Rise; he who made away with the Depaste diamonds; he who administered the permanent sleeping-draught to Sir Tedward Bray; he who abstracted the Prime Minister's spectacles at a critical moment, and caused him to remain in ignorance of the existence of Vulgaria on the map at a very critical hour in European history!"

"Good heavens, Sholmes!"

"It is true, Jotson. With this unseen, invisible, indiscernible, and unspotted criminal I am now at the death-grapple!"

"My dear Sholmes!"

"Murder," said Sholmes quietly, "is nothing to him! I have had several narrow escapes. He has sworn my death! Ha, ha! Yesterday, in a fashionable restaurant, I detected a fragment of German sausage in my soup. It was a plot to poison me; he bribed the waiter. Last evening I received free tickets for the latest revue at the Giganteum Theatre; a cunning scheme to bore me to death. Last night a German band began to play under my window; I barely escaped with my life. This morning, as I came here, my taxi-cab was blown sky-high by a bomb cunningly placed in the taximeter, timed to go off when twopence had ticked away. I was blown into the air. Fortunately, I landed unharmed on top of the Monument, and descended safely by means of the steps.

"Jotson, you know that I have nerve, but I confess that this has shaken me."

He rose to his feet and tiptoed to the window. On the other side of the street a ragman was passing, uttering the familiar cry: "Rags and bones, bottles and jars!" Sholmes turned to me, his face blazing with excitement.

"Run, Jotson!"

"Sholmes!" I ejaculated.

"You see that ragman? It is Professor Hickorychicory—pronounced Hickychicky—in disguise! Bolt!"

We rushed to the door.

Hardly had we reached the garden, when a terrific explosion shook the building to its foundations. Sholmes looked at me, with a grim smile.

"Just in time, Jotson!"

"Sholmes!"

"A bomb!" he said. "The work of Professor Hickorychicory—prounounced Hickychicky. He sticks at nothing. The coils are closing round him, Jotson. Only my demise can save him." He set his teeth. "It is a struggle for life or death between Herlock Sholmes and Professor Hickorychicory—pronounced Hickychicky. Jotson, are you with me?"

"Hear me swear——" I began.

"Enough! Let us go!"

With a few magic touches of his hand, he disguised me as a fishmonger. Then he hurried me away.

CHAPTER 2

The next few weeks were crammed with excitement.

It was the hardest case Herlock Sholmes had undertaken, and he did not conceal from me that sometimes he feared that Professor Hickorychicory—pronounced Hickychicky—might yet escape him. Our narrow escapes were marvellous; we grew familiar with danger. The coils were closing round the hardened criminal, but he was fighting hard. The man who had ruled the criminal world for seventy years was not to be taken easily.

Why Sholmes did not cause the arrest of the man who was so deeply dyed with crime was a mystery to me. Sholmes did not explain. It was one of the secrets that were locked up in that inscrutable breast.

It was at sunset one evening that we found ourselves pursuing a lonely track amid the rocky waste and precipices of the wild Hill of Ludgate. Far below us flowed the dark water of the Fleet river. Sholmes had been silent for several minutes—a most unusual circumstance. He turned to me suddenly.

"Jotson!" he said. His voice was unusually gentle, and I could not help a rush of tears to my eyes. I blew my nose. "Jotson, I feel that the end is coming—the end for him, Jotson, and the end for me!"

"Sholmes!" I murmured.

"He is here," said Sholmes. "I have tracked him down. In the narrow pass leading to the Bridge of the Black Friars he is in hiding. Jotson, my old friend, good-bye!"

"You shall not go alone!" I exclaimed.

"I must, Jotson. At the finish we must be alone—Herlock Sholmes, the detective, and Professor Hickorychicory—pronounced Hickychicky—the master-criminal. Fear not for me, Jotson; I am armed. I have here a railway sandwich, and with one blow——"

"But——"

"If I fail, Jotson, I leave to you all my belongings. My account in the bank, amounting at the present moment to fourpence-halfpenny, will be paid to you in a lump sum. I have instructed my bankers. The furniture at Shaker Street is yours—on the sole condition that you pay the remainder of the instalments. Only the tabby cat I should like to be given to my Aunt Sempronia. You promise me this, Jotson?"

I promised, with tears in my eyes. Could I refuse him anything at that moment?

It was in vain to seek to change his resolution. The last scene of the tragedy was to be enacted between those two alone—Herlock Sholmes, my dear, amazing friend, and the dark and tortuous criminal, the spelling of whose name gave no clue to its pronunciation.

We parted, and Sholmes plunged into the dark and gloomy pass. I sat upon a rock and waited. My eyes were blinded with tears. Was I ever to see again my astonishing friend—ever again to behold those old familiar feet resting upon the mantelpiece in the old rooms at Shaker Street? I am not ashamed to say that I wept, and the lonely rocks around me echoed: "Boo-hoo! Boo-hoo! Boo-hoo!"

Suddenly there was a trampling of feet—a sound of voices. I recognised the voice of Herlock Sholmes.

"At last!"

"At last! Ha, ha!" echoed another voice, the deep and thrilling tones of Professor Hickorychicory—pronounced Hickychicky.

For a moment I saw them—locked in a deadly embrace, reeling upon the verge of the wildest precipice of the Hill of Ludgate. Then they disappeared from my sight—still locked in that deadly embrace as in a Chubb lock.

I stumbled away—I hardly know how. I had looked my last upon Herlock Sholmes—that marvellous man whose adventures I now present for the first time to the public (copyright in the U.S.). Far, far below, where the dark waters of the Fleet murmured beneath the frowning crags of Ludgate Hill, lay Herlock Sholmes, side by side with his deadly foe, Professor Hickorychicory—pronounced Hickychicky!

THE RETURN OF HERLOCK SHOLMES

No. 7

Herlock Sholmes having gone to his death in that last struggle with Professor Hickorychicory, it might be supposed that his remarkable career had come to a complete stop. That, however, was far from being the case.

Sholmes was no ordinary man. What happened would undoubtedly have put a period to the career of any other man. To Sholmes it was merely an incident.

I confess to feeling some surprise, however, when, a few weeks after that terrible fatality, Sholmes walked into our old rooms at Shaker Street. My feeling, I suppose, showed in my face, for Sholmes burst into a hearty laugh as he regarded me.

"I have surprised you, my dear Jotson," he remarked.

"Sholmes! It is really you?"

"Myself, in flesh and blood!" he replied. "You never expected to see me again, Jotson?"

"I should have known you better, Sholmes!" I said. "Even after all my amazing experiences with you, you never cease to surprise me!"

He looked anxious for a moment.

"I hope you have kept up the instalments on the furniture, Jotson?"

"I have."

"Good!" He sank into a seat, and rested his feet upon the table, in the old, easy, elegant manner that was so familiar to me. "Well, here I am again, Jotson, ready for work! Have any clients called during my absence?"

"Several. But, on hearing you were dead, Sholmes, they decided not to place their affairs in your hands. One, however, has persisted, and, indeed, he is calling again this morning. He has left his stick here."

"His stick?" said Sholmes. He took the walking-stick in his hands, and turned it over, regarding it with the old keen look. "Ah! A young man! Not over twenty-five, with a blonde moustache, and very strong teeth. It is curious that he should have black hair as well as a blond moustache. He must have made a long journey when he came here!"

I started.

"Sholmes, how can you know?"

"Because he lives in the country, Jotson, and we live in Shaker Street," smiled Sholmes. "A wealthy young man; money no object with him. Just the client I wish to see, if we are to keep those instalments paid, Jotson."

"Sholmes," I almost shouted, "do you seriously mean to tell me that you have deduced all this from the walking-stick?"

"Undoubtedly. Is not my description correct?"

"Perfectly correct! But how, in the name of wonder——"

Sholmes yawned slightly.

"My dear Jotson, look at the stick for yourself. Every picture tells a story, you know, and every story a gem. It is the same with walking-sticks. In the first place, as to wealth. You see that the stick has a silver top, which must have cost, at the lowest computation, eighteen pence. I deduce a wealthy man, careless with his money."

"Most true! But his blonde moustache, his black hair, his strong teeth. Oh, Sholmes——"

To my amazement, the butler seized the soup-tureen and rushed to the door. Sholmes was upon him with the spring of a tiger. Crash!

"If you examine the stick, Jotson, you will see by certain marks that the owner is in the habit of gnawing it. The wood is hard, the deep indentations argue very strong teeth. In one of those indentations, Jotson, is a short blond hair, evidently from his moustache. In another, a long black hair, equally evidently from his head."

"Marvellous!"

"Marvellous to you, my dear Jotson, but to me a very simple matter."

But his age, Sholmes. You stated——"

"Ah, there we are in deeper waters!" he smiled. "Yet it is obvious that if he were an old man, his hair would not have remained black."

"And how do you deduce that he comes from the country?"

"Look at the lower end of the stick, Jotson!"

"It is muddy," I said.

"Exactly. And that variety of mud, Jotson, is not found nearer than Slopshire. I have made a special study of varieties of mud, Jotson, and have, indeed, written a monograph on the subject, now in the collection at Hanwell. But here, I think, is our visitor himself."

The young man entered the room as he spoke, and Sholmes rose courteously.

"Herlock Sholmes?" exclaimed the visitor.

"Himself. You may speak quite freely before my friend, Dr. Jotson."

"Mr Sholmes, hear my story! My name is Hogg—you may have heard the name. I do not wish to boast, Mr. Sholmes, but since the beginning of history, there have been Hoggs in Slopshire. It is the oldest family in the county, connected at one time with the great Lord Bacon, and with the French family of Du Porc. I, sir, am the last of my race, I was reared in our ancient manor on the shores of the Wash. My grandfather, old Sir Pryze Hogg, cast me off. His sternness was due to my love of the cinema, which he held in abhorrence. He made a will, leaving the family estates to his butler, Pawker."

Sholmes nodded.

"Sir Pryze Hogg is dead," said the young man. "All the Hoggs have been rash, but Sir Pryze Hogg was rasher than the rest, and he was the victim of a fatality. Before he expired he sent for me, and whispered with his latest breath that he had made a new will. That will, Mr. Sholmes, cannot be found. Unless it is found, Pawker claims the estate under the old will. Mr. Sholmes, I have been accustomed to live in wealth and luxury——"

Sholmes shot me a triumphant glance. It was a verification of his infallible deductions.

"Unless the will is found I shall be reduced to poverty," said the young man moodily. "No more reckless expenditures of sixpences at the cinema, no more wild nights in the Mile End Road. For me, Woodbine cigarettes and fried fish will be things of the past. Save me, Mr. Sholmes!"

"I will save you!" said Herlock Sholmes quietly. "The will shall be found. As you are aware, where there is a will there's a way. Come, Jotson!"

CHAPTER 2

We arrived at the old Manor-house of Hogg, on the shores of the Wash, as night was falling. I glanced curiously at Pawker, the butler, as we were shown in. Unless the will was discovered, a Pawker would reign in the place of a Hogg. That Herlock Sholmes already suspected Pawker of concealing the will of the irascible old baronet, I knew. But where had he concealed it? That was the question. The mystery was, to me, impenetrable, but I had faith in my amazing friend.

For two days Herlock Sholmes appeared to be idle. Our young friend showed impatience, but I knew Sholmes too well. I knew that under the inscrutable exterior his marvellous brain was working at express speed. On the third day the young baronet could contain his impatience no longer.

"Mr. Sholmes, you have not been at work yet——"

Sholmes smiled.

"I have been at work," he yawned.

"You have made discoveries?"

"Yes."

"And what, pray?"

"I have discovered," said Sholmes calmly, "that your butler always serves the soup."

"What?"

"And that he always, with his own hands, carefully places the soup in the tureen before it is brought into the dining-room."

"Mr. Sholmes!"

"And that he never allows the tureen to be washed up with the other crockery," said Sholmes lazily.

"But I do not see——"

"Naturally!" said Sholmes. "If you could see, you would not require my services. But patience! Let us dine!"

We sat down, in great astonishment. That Sholmes was not speaking at random I knew. Yet I could not follow his line of reasoning.

The butler served us, as usual, with soup. I noticed that Sholmes did not taste his.

"There is something in the soup," he said, in a quiet, deliberate voice.

The butler started.

"Pray bring the tureen here," said Sholmes.

"The—the tureen?" stammered the butler.

"Certainly!"

Pawker stood rooted to the floor. His face was deadly pale.

"I am waiting," said Sholmes, smiling. "I remarked that there was something in the soup, Pawker. Ha! Stop him!"

To my amazement, the butler seized the soup-tureen, and rushed to the door. Sholmes was upon him with the spring of a tiger.

Crash!

The tureen fell to the floor, where it was shattered into a thousand fragments. Soup streamed over the polished floor. In the midst of the spilt soup lay a roll of parchment.

"What does this mean?" shouted the young baronet.

Sholmes yawned.

"It means the missing will is discovered, my young friend."

"Sholmes!'" I exclaimed. "You mean to say——"

"Pick it up, my dear Jotson, and see for yourself!"

I could no longer doubt. It was the missing will, discovered by the marvellous penetration of my extraordinary friend.

CHAPTER 3

Sholmes smiled as we stepped into the train for London. I knew that he was pleased with his success.

"You amaze me more and more, Sholmes!" I said, as he lighted a couple of pipes, and blew out two thick clouds of smoke. "May I ask——"

"The usual question, Jotson!" He laughed. "My dear fellow, it was child's play. The butler had concealed the will. The soup-tureen was never out of his hands. Covered with soup, the document was always invisible. I had discovered that Pawker always washed the tureen himself. It was enough. I had noticed a slight flavour in the soup; I was sure then. True, I could have descended to the kitchen, and demanded the missing document, but I preferred to spring a surprise upon our friend Pawker. You know that I have a touch of the dramatic, Jotson. I dearly love a striking *denouement*. A cunning rascal, Jotson. Who else would have dreamed of hiding a will in a soup-tureen?"

"And who but you would have divined it?" I could not help exclaiming. "I, too, had noticed a flavour in the soup, but I did not connect it with the missing will. Yet I have studied your methods."

"Ah, my dear Jotson!" said Sholmes, dropping into French, as he often did. "It is Montaigne who says, *"Vous etes drole, mon cher, vous etes tres drole. Passez les allumettes! Merci Allons!"*

THE MISSING MOTHER-IN-LAW

No. 8

Herlock Sholmes has frequently been the recipient of striking testimonials of gratitude from clients whom his wonderful abilities have served.

Clients of all classes have generally shown the same desire to testify their gratitude.

I need only refer to the splendid elephant, with howdah complete, presented the Rajah of Bunkumpore after Sholmes' amazing discovery of his fifteen missing wives; the magnificent set of artificial teeth, jewelled in every hole, which came as a reward for the solution of the mystery of the Duke's Dentist; and the humbler, but not less highly-prized, gift of kippered herrings from William Sikes, Esq., after Sholmes had elucidated the problem of the Missing Moke. That last gift, indeed, was long remembered by us, for its fragrance long haunted our rooms in Shaker Street.

But there have been occasions when Sholmes has been repaid with the blackest ingratitude. Such occasions have been rare, but they have occurred.

It is such a case that I find next upon my list. Even now, in speaking of the adventure of the Missing Mother-in-Law, Sholmes will pass his hand tenderly over his nose and his left eye. It is one of his least happy recollections, yet in no case in my long records did his amazing abilities shine forth so marvellously.

On referring to my notes at the time, I find that it was upon Monday, January 32nd, that the matter came under our notice.

Sholmes had been looking inexpressibly bored at breakfast. During the meal I had been entertaining him with some account of my former experiences in India.

The case of the Pawned Pickle-Jar had been wound up, and Sholmes was idle. Idleness did not agree with his active, energetic nature. That there were several cases at Scotland Yard requiring his amazing insight was very probably, but the police preferred to go on in their own blundering way.

The case of Mrs. Knagg came, therefore, as a relief. I had read the report in the paper, and I saw Sholmes glancing at it.

"After all, I must work, my dear Jotson," he remarked. "This is a very pretty little problem."

"You have not been approached upon the subject, Sholmes?"

He shook his head.

"No. Crouch, the son-in-law, appears content to leave it in the hands of the police." Sholmes shrugged his shoulders. "You know what that means. The bereaved man will probably never see his mother-in-law again."

He reflected a little.

"I am idle for the moment, Jotson. I can afford to take up the case; the instalments are paid on the furniture, and I can afford a little relaxation. Why should I not take up this case for nothing, and bring joy to a humble household?"

"My dear Sholmes," I said warmly. "that is like you! Any assistance I can render——"

"After all, the thanks of a good and worthy man are a sufficient reward to one who cares little for mere lucre," said Sholmes thoughtfully. "Besides, the case is interesting in itself. Mrs. Knagg, a widow lady, took up her residence with her married daughter six weeks ago. On Thursday morning she left the house in Larkhall Rise, taking with her a bag and an umbrella. From that moment she disappears from human ken. A very pretty problem!"

"You have already formed a theory, Sholmes?"

He frowned a little.

"I have already made deductions from the obvious facts," he replied. "Theories I leave to the police. The case centres round the umbrella."

"The umbrella, Sholmes!" I could not help exclaiming.

"Undoubtedly."

"From the reports in the newspapers, the police appear to attach no importance to the umbrella."

"Ah, the police!" smiled Sholmes. "Fortunately for Mrs. Knagg and her grief-stricken son-in-law,

Sholmes raised his hat. "Mrs. Knagg?" he said. The gaunt women started. "That is my name," she said. "For three days I have waited here for a train!"

we follow other methods. Mark, my dear Jotson, this good lady had no possible motive for disappearing of her own accord. She had been heard to declare that she intended to reside permanently with her son-in-law. It was her intention to wean him from such bad habits as smoking and consuming whisky-and-soda. Why, then, did she disappear so completely?"

"Foul play?" I suggested.

"Or accident?" said Sholmes.

"But, in the case of an accident, surely something would have been heard——"

"That depends upon the nature of the accident." Herlock Sholmes rose to his feet, and stretched himself. "Are you prepared for a little run to-day, Jotson?"

"I am entirely at your service, Sholmes."

"Then I will call a taxi."

I could not dissemble my astonishment as we stepped into the taxi, and I was still further amazed to hear Sholmes give the driver instructions to drive us to Winkle Bay.

"My dear Sholmes, are we going to the seaside?" I exclaimed.

"Why not, Jotson?"

"But Winkle Bay is on the South-Eastern line."

"Exactly!"

"Then why not take a train?"

He smiled in his inscrutable way.

"Undoubtedly we could take a train, Jotson. I have no doubt that, if we did so, we should ultimately arrive at our destination. But what length of time might elapse before we could return to London?"

"True?"

"No, Jotson; as I have only days, and not weeks, to spare we will not travel by the South-Eastern railway. A taxi will serve our turn."

"But what do you expect to find at Winkle Bay, Sholmes?" I exclaimed.

His answer astounded me.

"The missing mother-in-law!" he said calmly.

CHAPTER 2

Sholmes declined to speak another word as the taxi bore us to our distant destination. I sat in puzzled silence. What unknown clue had presented itself to the amazing brain of my gifted friend, while I remained completely in the dark? I had endeavoured to study Sholmes' methods. But I had to confess that I could not see a gleam of light. What was the mysterious connection between Winkle Bay, on the South Coast, and the disappearance of Mrs. Knagg from Larkhall Rise? Time alone could tell.

Winkle Bay came is sight at last. To my surprise, Sholmes directed the chauffeur to drive to the railway-station.

We soon reached a dreary, deserted building, with few signs of life about it. A train stood upon the metals with great masses of cobwebs festooned over the carriages. A thrush had built its nest in the tender.

Bidding the driver wait, Sholmes entered the station, and I followed him, greatly amazed. What were we to find there? The dust, seldom disturbed by human feet, rose in clouds as we advanced.

On the platform a gaunt woman, with a bag and an umbrella paced to and fro.

It was evidently a passenger waiting for a train.

Her thin face showed signs of exhaustion, and of a deadly, dull, persistent patience, of the hope deferred that maketh the heart sick.

Sholmes raised his hat.

"Mrs. Knagg?" he said.

The gaunt woman started.

"That is my name," she said.

"Sholmes!" I murmured.

"Madam, I am returning to London in my taxi," said Sholmes. "May I have the honour of offering you a lift?"

The gaunt face brightened up.

"For three days," said Mrs. Knagg hoarsely, "I have waited here for a train. Hope had almost died in my breast. And what may be happening in my absence, goodness alone knows. That George Crouch has resumed smoking in the drawing-room I have not the slightest doubt." Her hand tightened upon her umbrella. "I thank you from the bottom of my heart. Let us go."

A minute more, and we were whirling Londonwards.

I sat in amazement.

The taxi stopped at last in Shaker Street, and we alighted. Mrs. Knagg wrung my friend's hand, and the taxi bore her onwards to Larkhall Rise, to the bosom of her bereaved family.

It was not till Herlock Sholmes had consumed his usual quart of cocaine and gross of cigarettes, that I ventured to ask him for the usual explanation.

He smiled in a slightly bored fashion.

"My dear Jotson, it was very simple—elementary, in fact. I told you that the clue lay in the umbrella."

"But how——"

"Last Thursday, Jotson, was a fine day—the finest day we have had this year. For what reason, then, did Mrs. Knagg take with her an umbrella? It was not likely to rain in London. Evidently, my dear Jotson, because she was about to make a journey to some place where rain might be expected."

"True!"

"If you read the weather reports in last Thursday's paper, Jotson, you will see that, while fine weather reigned in London, there was a heavy rainfall at Winkle Bay. The conclusion was irresistible."

"Most true. But, having established that Mrs. Knagg left her home to spend a day at Winkle Bay, why did she not return? In the name of all that is wonderful, Sholmes, how did you trace her to the railway-station at Winkle Bay?"

"That was the simplest part of the problem, Jotson. The good lady intended to return—we knew that. To one who has travelled on the South-Eastern line, Jotson, the reason of her non-return was not difficult to guess. She was waiting for a train."

"Sholmes!"

"You see, my dear Jotson, it is no longer wonderful when it is explained. I had established that Mrs. Knagg paid a visit to Winkle Bay. I knew that Winkle Bay was on the South-Eastern. I looked for her, therefore, at the Winkle Bay station on that line. I found her, as I expected, waiting for a train. But for our intervention, the unfortunate lady might be waiting there still, perhaps for weeks, and her son-in-law would still be in doubt of her fate. I have no doubt that he will call to thank me. The thanks of a good and worthy man——"

Heavy footsteps on the stairs interrupted Sholmes.

The door was thrown open, and a little man, with a pale and harassed face, rushed into the room.

"Mr. Herlock Sholmes?" he exclaimed.

"I am he!" said Sholmes, rising. "You are Mr. Crouch?"

"I am. You found my mother-in-law, who was missing?"

"I am happy to say I did."

"But for you she might still be waiting for a train on the South-Eastern—for weeks, perhaps for years?"

"Undoubtedly."

"Then take that?"

To our amazement, the man hurled himself violently upon Herlock Sholmes, hitting out with indescribable fury. I was spellbound, and Sholmes, for once, was taken utterly by surprise. One terrible drive caught him on the nose, another in the left eye. He fell to the floor, and the visitor, whose rage was still unabated, danced upon his fallen form.

Then, shaking his fist at my amazing friend, Mr. Crouch quitted the room. Herlock Sholmes sat up, gasping.

"My dear Jotson—grooogh—oh, my eye! Oh, my nose—ow-ow-ow!"

His eye was already becoming black; his nose was streaming red. His famous dressing-gown was torn and rumpled, and both his pipes were broken. I helped my unfortunate friend into a chair.

"Jotson!" he gasped. "My dear Jotson—yow-ow-ow!—if ever I help a man to discover his missing mother-in-law again—groogh!—you may use my head for a football—wow-wow-wow!"

THE ADVENTURE OF THE BRIXTON BUILDER

No. 9

Herlock Sholmes took the cask from the corner, and the hypodermic syringe from the coal-box. With his long white fingers he adjusted the needle, and turned back his trouser-leg. For some little time his eyes rested dreamily upon the pink sock, all scored and spotted with innumerable darns. Finally, he pressed the sharp point into the fatted calf, and sank back into the armchair with a loud snort of satisfaction.

Many times I had witnessed this operation, but never had I found the courage to protest. But now I could contain myself no longer.

"What is it?" I asked. "Morphine or cocaine?"

He raised his eyes dreamily from the front page of *Chuckles.*

"Cocaine," he replied. "A seven-hundred-per-cent solution. Would care to try a gallon or so, my dear Jotson?"

"Sholmes," I said earnestly, "count the cost."

He shook his head.

"My dear Jotson, my chemist makes a reduction upon large quantities. He supplies my weekly cask at reasonable rates."

"I referred to the cost to your health, Sholmes. The continual use of cocaine may result in rendering permanent the state of mental idiocy which is now only intermittent."

"Perhaps you are right, my dear Jotson," he said thoughtfully. "But my powerful brain rebels at stagnation. Crime, my dear fellow, is on the down-grade. Since the death of Professor Hickorychicory—pronounced Hickychicky—really interesting crimes have been disgustingly rare. Give me a case which calls forth my transcendent abilities, and I am happy. Otherwise——" He made a gesture towards the cask of cocaine.

At this moment the door was flung violently open, and a young man rushed into the room.

"Mr. Sholmes," he exclaimed, "shave me—excuse my agitation—I mean save me. I am the unhappy Hector McWhusky."

"Indeed!" drawled Sholmes. "I do not think I have the honour of your acquaintance, Mr. McWhusky."

"You have not heard my name?"

"No."

"Then you have not seen the morning papers. Mr. Sholmes, even now the police are on my track. They believe me guilty of the murder of the Brixton builder."

"Calm yourself, Mr. McWhusky," said Sholmes. "If the police believe you guilty, the great probability is that you are innocent. Their methods are not mine."

"Bless you for those words, Mr. Sholmes. But Inspector Pinkeye is even now at the door. I saw him following me on the next motor-bus. Listen to my story."

"Take a swig at the cocaine, my dear fellow, and proceed."

"Look at the head-lines in the paper, Mr. Sholmes. 'Disappearance of a Brixton Builder! 'Murder and Incendiarism!' 'Arrest of the Criminal Hourly Expected!' Last night, Mr. Sholmes, I stayed at the house of Mr. Lathan Plasster, the Brixton builder. This man has always been the bitter enemy of our family. Judge of my astonishment, therefore, when he asked me to visit him, and showed me a will he had made in my favour, leaving a row of houses in Gerrybilt Street. I stayed with him till after midnight, and when I left, I left him alive and well. But you will see in the paper——"

The sound of snoring suddenly ceased, and a man, with a scarred face, sprang into view. "Good-evening, Mr. Lathan Plasster!" said Sholmes. "Pinkeye, there is a prisoner for you, to replace the one I have been compelled to deprive you of." "Alive!" yelled the inspector.

Herlock Sholmes glanced at the report. It stated briefly that Mr. Lathan Plasster, the well-known Brixton builder, had been murdered the previous night, and his body disposed of in a burning wood-pile in the backyard. His boots, partly burned, had been found, as well as several waistcoat-buttons, amid the charred embers. There were bloodstains in the house, proving beyond doubt that several pints had been shed.

"I left him alive and well," repeated Hector McWhusky. "But the police——"

There were heavy footsteps on the stairs. Inspector Pinkeye, of Scotland Yard, entered the room.

"Mr. Hector McWhusky," said Pinkeye, "I arrest you——"

"Save me, Mr. Sholmes."

The inspector smiled.

"A clear case this time, Mr. Sholmes—what!"

"Perhaps so," said my companion enigmatically. "Mr. McWhusky, rely upon me. I will do what I can for you."

"Ha, more theories?" said Inspector Pinkeye. "I think my facts will weigh more with a jury than your theories, friend Sholmes. But we shall see."

And Inspector Pinkeye led his unhappy prisoner from the room.

CHAPTER 2

Sholmes was silent for several minutes, during which I regarded him curiously. I confess that to my mind there appeared little doubt of the young man's guilt.

Sholmes rose at last and stretched his long neck.

"Would you care for a morning in the beautiful and salubrious suburb of Brixton, Jotson?" he asked.

"Certainly, my dear fellow."

"But your patients, Jotson——"

"The last of my patients died while we were busy upon the case of the Pawned Pickle-Jar," I replied. "I am quite at your service."

"Good!"

An hour later we were in Brixton. Mr. Plasster's house was in the possession of the police. Inspector Pinkeye was there, and he welcomed us with an ironical smile. It was evident that the worthy inspector was assured that he had found the right man, and that he was elated to think that Scotland Yard had succeeded, for once, without the assistance of Herlock Sholmes.

"You would like a look round, Mr. Sholmes," he said affably. "Pray go ahead. If you discover any clues I have missed, you are welcome to them. There is not the slightest doubt that young McWhusky murdered the old man, and cremated him in the wood-pile to cover up his tracks. His stick has been found, covered with blood."

"He left it behind specially to assist you in your case, doubtless!" said Herlock Sholmes, with a touch of sarcasm.

"He left it behind, at all events," said Inspector Pinkeye, nettled. "There is no room for wild theories here, Sholmes."

My friend did not reply, but he proceeded to a close examination of the building. While he was so engaged night fell, but Herlock Sholmes did not tire. The inspector watched him at work, with the same ironical smile. He was evidently enjoying his anticipated triumph over my amazing friend.

Suddenly the sound of a loud snore was heard, proceeding from a direction that could not be ascertained.

Herlock Sholmes smiled.

"What is that, Pinkeye?" he asked.

"A snore, I presume," said the inspector testily. "What importance do you attach to that common everyday sound, Sholmes?"

"That is what we shall see."

"It is probably the housekeeper snoring," said the inspector, with a stare. "Really, Sholmes, this approaches absurdity."

Sholmes smiled again his inscrutable smile. The sound of the snore was almost continuous. Inspector Pinkeye returned to the lower room with a gesture of impatience.

"Come, my dear Jotson!" said Sholmes, at last.

We descended the stairs.

Inspector Pinkeye greeted us with a mocking grim.

"You are finished, Sholmes?" he asked.

"Quite."

"You have come to the conclusion that there is nothing doing?"

"Not at all. I advise you, my dear Pinkeye, to effect the release of young McWhusky at the earliest possible moment."

"Sholmes"—I could see that the worthy inspector was a little staggered by my friend's confident manner—"what do you mean? Who is the man who murdered Mr. Plasster, if not the young man who was with him last night, and who benefits under his will?"

"No man at all, Pinkeye."

"A woman?" exclaimed the inspector.

"No?"

I regarded my friend in amazement. The inspector stared at him blankly.

"Who, then?" shouted Pinkeye.

Herlock Sholmes' reply astounded us.

"Nobody!"

"Sholmes! If this is a joke——"

"I never joke, my dear Pinkeye. There is one thing, and one thing only, that I need to conclude my case."

"And what is that?"

"A pick-axe."

"A—a—pick-axe?"

"Exactly."

I could see that the inspector believed that my amazing friend had taken leave of his senses. The same fear came into my own mind. But Herlock Sholmes, with the same inscrutable smile upon his face, took a pick-axe, and proceeded up the stairs. We followed him. Our amazement intensified when Sholmes raised the implement, and crashed it upon the wall of the upper passage.

There was a spattering of lath and plaster. A door, cunningly concealed, burst open.

The sound of snoring suddenly ceased, and a man with a scarred face sprang into view.

"Good-evening, Mr. Lathan Plasster?" said Sholmes calmly.

"Pinkeye, there is a prisoner for you, to replace the one I have been compelled to deprive you of."

"Alive!" yelled the inspector.

"Mr. Lathan Plasster, alive and well!" smiled Sholmes. "You will arrest him upon a charge of conspiracy, with intent to cause serious bodily injury. That would certainly have resulted, Pinkeye, if you had succeeded in hanging our friend McWhusky."

The handcuffs clinked upon the wrists of the Brixton builder. Leaving the astounded Pinkeye with his prisoner, we returned to our cab.

CHAPTER 3

"Sholmes! I am on tenterhooks——"

Herlock Sholmes smiled as he stretched himself in the old armchair, in our rooms at Shaker Street.

"Nothing could be simpler, my dear Jotson," he drawled. "It was a cunning scheme. The Brixton builder's object was, of course, revenge. He was the old and bitter enemy of the McWhuskys, as young McWhusky told us. He had, in former days, been the suitor of McWhusky's aunt, and she had accepted him—hence his hatred of the family. The will, the bloodstains, the buttons in the burnt wood-pile, were all in the game—yet I confess that even I might have been deceived but for the fact that the plotter betrayed himself."

"How, Sholmes? I am quite in the dark!"

"The snore, Jotson."

"The snore?" I exclaimed.

"Undoubtedly. He had built himself a secret recess, wherein to lie hidden while the police hanged McWhusky for his supposed murder. During the day he lay there silent and safe. But at night, Jotson, he slept—and he snored!"

"Then it was not the housekeeper who snored!"

"That, Jotson, was the most obvious theory, which was, accordingly, seized upon by Inspector Pinkeye, in the well-known Scotland Yard manner. I ascertained that, at that precise moment, the housekeeper was in the kitchen, frying bloaters. Evidently it was not the housekeeper who snored. Then, who was it? The conclusion was inevitable."

"To you, Sholmes," I said; "but to no other. It was fortunate, indeed, that young McWhusky came to you."

"Fortunate for him, and fortunate for me, my dear Jotson," said Herlock Sholmes. "This amazing case has supplied me with the stimulus I needed—and the cask of cocaine will now last me over the week-end."

THE CASE OF THE AMERICAN MILLIONAIRE

No. 10

The name of Ephraim Z. Squawk, the millionaire Beef King of Chicago, was, of course, well known to us. The enormous number of tins he exported yearly, and the mystery surrounding their contents, had made him an interesting figure. I could not help regarding him with some curiosity as he was shown into our sitting-room at Shaker Street.

Herlock Sholmes had been about to make one of his accustomed inroads upon the cask of cocaine. He rose, however, and yawned in the polished and courteous manner so characteristic of him.

The millionaire, who in features somewhat resembled a hatchet, was pale and agitated.

"Mr. Sholmes," he said, "I guess I want your help. I calculate if you work the riffle, you can count out your own spondulics. A gripful of greenbacks more or less cuts no ice with me. I guess I am up against it, and it's a regular cinch for that hoodlum who is after me!"

Sholmes, who speaks American like a native, nodded. As on so many occasions, his gifts as a linguist stood him in good stead.

"Pray give me a few details, Mr. Squawk," he remarked. "You may speak quite freely before my friend Dr. Jotson,"

The millionaire sat down and glared at the fender, and then under the table, and then into the fire, and told his story.

"I guess I wasn't always what I am now, Mr. Sholmes. Jest now, the name of Ephraim Z. Squawk is known throughout the world as the biggest exporter, sir, in all Chicawgo. Squawk's American beef is known wherever the American language is spoken. But at one time, sir, I was simply manager of a canning works in Chicawgo. It was then that it happened."

"What happened, Mr. Squawk?"

"The unfortunate death of Mike Mulligan, sir. He was a man at the canning works. I guess I hardly knew him by name. P'r'aps you know, Mr. Sholmes, suthing of the working of an American beef factory. The machines, sir, go on night and day. The steers are driven in one gate, and at another they come out in the form of Squawk's potted beef. Stopping the machinery means the loss of a heap of dollars, and a foreman who stopped for a minute, sir, would be fired before he could say 'No sugar in mine!' It sometimes happens, unfortunately, that a man falls into the machines and gets mixed up with the beef. Of course, it's unfortunate. But sich things, sir, can't be helped in a hustling town like Chacawgo. It doesn't happen often—not mor'n once in a week, I guess. Such a man, sir, disappears from human knowledge. When he comes out of the machinery, he comes out along with the beef, and is exported in tins to all parts of the world. One bit of him may go to England, another bit to Russia,

Sholmes, who speaks American like a native, nodded. As on many previous occasions, his gifts as a linguist stood him in good stead. "Pray give me a few details, Mr. Squawk," he remarked. "You may speak quite freely."

another bit to South America—it depends on the tins he's potted in."

Herlock Sholmes nodded.

"Well, sir," resumed the millionaire, "men have disappeared that way and nothing has happened, till it happened about Mike Mulligan. He got tipsy and pitched in, and vanished from the airth. His brother, sir, came to see me to have the machines stopped. Stopped, you know—a loss of p'r'aps five hundred dollars! It couldn't be did! Besides, by the time we'd got 'em stopped, Mike Mulligan would have been turned into canned beef, and it would have been a sheer waste of time. But, for some reason, Paddy Mulligan was wild, and he left the works swearing revenge."

The millionaire mopped his perspiring brow.

"Waal, Sir, now I come to the pint. This man, Paddy Mulligan, took it to heart. He wrote threatening letters, making the most unreasonable demands. He wanted the body of his brother Mike for burial, sir. Now, I put it to you, Mr. Sholmes, as a reasonable man, what could I do? If I had opened all the tins in the factory, what was left of Mike wouldn't have been recognisable. Besides, he was already exported. At that time we were working at pressure on contracts for London, and, while Paddy Mulligan was bothering me, his brother had already been distributed in fragments all over the Yewnited Kingdom. His own relations in Ireland, sir, may have received him, in parts, without knowing it."

"Certainly it would have been a very difficult task to collect him," Sholmes remarked.

"The only way to satisfy Paddy Mulligan, sir, would have been to hand him the whole week's output of the factory—beef and Mike and all—and let him bury it," said Mr. Squawk, "and you can bet your bottom dollar, sir, that I wasn't doing that. Besides, as I've said, Mike had already been exported. Since that date, Mr. Sholmes, Squawk's potted beef has achieved a worldwide reputation. Its peculiar flavor, sir, has recommended it far and wide, especially in the South Sea Islands. But, while I have piled up mountains of dollars, sir, I've been haunted by that guy's threats of revenge. Paddy Mulligan is still demanding his brother's body for burial, and threatening revenge if he doesn't get it. I confess, sir, that I came to this benighted island chiefly to get away from Paddy Mulligan. But he has followed me here, and I live in terror, sir, night and day, of having my brains knocked out with his shillelagh."

The millionaire paused, in great agitation.

"It's a regular cinch for him," he explained. "I guess I can't always dodge him. Mr. Sholmes, I want you to nail the hoodlum."

Herlock Sholmes looked thoughtful.

"You want this man captured?"

"Yep."

"And then?"

"Put where he can't do any harm!" said Mr. Squawk.

"But so far he has only written threatening letters," said Herlock Sholmes thoughtfully. "For that, he could only be given a term of imprisonment. When he came out, he would be as dangerous as ever."

"More dangerous, perhaps," I ventured to remark.

Mr. Squawk gave a groan.

"I reckon that's so," he said. "I guess I'm up against it. I want him nailed and kept safe somehow. Mr. Sholmes, give me your advice for making that man safe, and name your own figure."

"I am entirely at your service, Mr. Squawk. Fortunately, I am able to suggest a plan which would be thoroughly efficacious, if you carry out my instructions to the minutest detail."

"Go ahead, sir."

"So far, this man has threatened your death, and for that he could be imprisoned, but he would be subsequently released, when he would doubtless carry out his threat at once. The best thing you can do, Mr. Squawk, is to encounter him personally—"

"Eh?"

"He will then, doubtless, knock out your brains with his shillelagh as you have remarked."

"Wha-a-at?"

"And for that," explained Herlock Sholmes, "he can be hanged. He will then be safe from doing further harm."

I could not help giving my amazing friend a glance of admiration at this simple and the same time subtle suggestion. The millionaire, however, did not appear to be satisfied. Such a method of disposing of a dangerous character appeared to be admirable in its simplicity, and certainly would have been thought of by no one but Herlock Sholmes.

"Excellent!" I could not help exclaiming.

"Jerusalem crickets!" exclaimed Mr. Squawk. "I guess that cuts no ice with me, Mr. Sholmes. I calculate I'm not taking any."

Sholmes stiffened perceptibly.

"If you decline to follow my directions, Mr. Squawk, I can only decline to take up the case." he said. "I always insist upon my clients placing themselves unreservedly in my hands."

Mr. Squawk rose, and, after making several uncalled-for remarks of a personal character, quitted the room, closing the door behind him with a bang.

Herlock Sholmes elevated his eyebrows.

"A very peculiar client, Jotson," he remarked. "I can do nothing in this case, but I fear that he will have reason to repent of his obstinacy. By the way, Jotson, you might mention to Mrs. Spudson that under no circumstances whatever is she to make any use of American canned beef in our cuisine. It would be distinctly unpleasant to be served with any portion of the unfortunate Mike Mulligan which may still be in existence."

CHAPTER 2

I have not recorded this interesting case as one of the triumphs of Herlock Sholmes, but rather as an example of the disastrous results which followed in the rare instances where his professional advice was disregarded by a client. Such instances were very rare, and in every case Sholmes was justified by the results.

We did not see Mr. Squawk again.

I hoped that, for his own sake, he would return and place himself in the hands of my amazing friend for guidance.

But he was a man of obstinate character, extremely self-willed and pertinacious. We heard later that he gone to the police for protection, and naturally, we were not surprised to hear that the result was what might have been foreseen. The shillelagh of the revengeful Paddy Mulligan claimed his victim, and the man then disappeared without leaving a trace behind him—as completely as if he had fallen into the machines in the canning works at Chicago.

THE FOREIGN SPY

No. 11

In the course of his varied professional experiences, Herlock Sholmes has met, and mingled freely with, members of every rank in Society. His famous dressing-gown has been in the lounges of the titled and the wealthy as often as in the haunts of vice and the purlieus of crime. Kings and princes have visited our humble quarters in Shaker Street, rubbing shoulders with butchers, bakers, and candlestick-makers. But though accustomed to visits from personages of the highest station, I confess to feeling something of a thrill when, one morning, our landlady, Mrs. Spudson, announced the name of Sir Obviously Hardley-Sain.

For that name, at that moment, was in everybody's mouth. The great diplomat of the age, the untiring Minister, who was regarded with limitless admiration by everyone who did not judge merely by results, entered our apartment, and even Sholmes was a little impressed. At least, I judged so by the fact that he removed his feet from the table, and took both pipes from his mouth.

"You know me, Mr. Sholmes?" said the great Minister abruptly.

Herlock Sholmes nodded.

The Minister touched a bell, and a stout and florid gentleman, with a spiked blonde moustache, entered the room. "Mr. Speistein – Mr. Herlock Sholmes!" said Sir Obviously. The secretary bowed. Herlock Sholmes' next action was amazing.

"Everyone knows Sir Obviously Hardley-Sain!" he replied gracefully. "If my humble services can be of use to you——"

"That is why I have come to you, Mr. Sholmes. But——"

Sir Obviously paused, and glanced at me. I rose.

"Do not go, my dear Jotson," said Herlock Sholmes quietly. "You may speak quite freely before my friend Jotson, Sir Obviously. Dr. Jotson is kind enough to assist me in my work."

"Very well, Mr. Sholmes. But you will understand that the matter is of the first importance, and must be kept strictly secret. Mr. Sholmes, there is a spy in the Red-Tape and Sealing-Wax Department, of which I am the head."

Sholmes smiled.

"You have just discovered that, sir?"

"At least, I have the strongest suspicion that such is the case," replied Sir Obviously. "I do not understand that smile, Mr. Sholmes."

"Pray excuse me. But I could have given you the information you have just given me a considerable time ago," explained Sholmes. "The course of political events during the past year points indubitably to the conclusion that there is an enemy influence at work in the Red-Tape and Sealing-Wax Department."

Sir Obviously Hardley-Sain frowned. It was quite evident that he did not relish my friend's remark.

"I can hardly agree with you, Mr. Sholmes. Of course, as a Minister, I cannot be expected to see what is obvious to every man in the street, neither should I desire to do so—I trust I understand too well the traditions of my high office. It may, therefore, be as you say. However, to come to the point. Are you prepared to undertake to discover this secret and malign influence in the Red-Tape and Sealing-Wax Department?"

"Undoubtedly. Pray give me a few details." Herlock Sholmes stretched himself in the amrchair, scratching his left ear in a way I knew so well. "What has given rise to your suspicions?"

"The fact that every political move for some time past has been discounted in advance by our enemies. I have been attacked in some newspapers on that account, as if the conduct of the Red-Tape and Sealing-Wax Department was not my own particular business!" said the baronet, with a touch of natural indignation.

"Has any search been made for the supposed spy?"

"Certainly. Every morning I make it a point to look carefully into the coal-box, under the paper-weight on my desk, and into the receiver of the telephone. So far I have discovered nothing. The aid of the police was invoked, and plain-clothes officers have, for weeks, kept a careful watch upon the taxi-stand at the corner and upon the telegraph poles at a short distance from my official residence. But the result has been the same."

"You suspect no particular person?"

Sir Obviously Hardley-Sain made a haughty gesture.

"Personal suspicions would be scarcely becoming to the head of the Red-Tape and Sealing-Wax Department, Mr. Sholmes. I am surprised at the question!"

"Your pardon!" said Herlock Sholmes gracefully. "You have, probably, some confidential secretary in whom you repose the most absolute confidence?"

"Certainly; his name is Heinrich Speistein."

"One of our old British names!" said Sholmes musingly.

"A gentleman, sir, whom I trust implicitly!" said the baronet, with emphasis.

"Naturally. His name answers for him," said Sholmes. "the Red-Tape and Sealing-Wax Department would scarcely be expected to repose trust in a Smith, a Brown, or a Robinson. But a Speistein is above suspicion."

"Exactly!"

Sholmes appeared lost in thought.

"Well, Mr. Sholmes?"

"Pray leave the case in my hands," said Herlock Sholmes. "I will make my report in the course of a day or so."

Sir Obviously Hardley-Saine was shown out.

I looked at Sholmes inquiringly.
He lighted both his pipes, and rested his feet on the table, and seemed plunged in thought.
"You have formed a theory, Sholmes?" I asked, at last.
He made an irritated gesture.
"How often have I told you, Jotson, that I never form theories? My business is with the facts. But I confess, Jotson, that at present I see no clue. All is darkness. Sir Obviously's precautions are all very well, so far as they go, but I hardly believe that the spy and traitor will be found in the coal-box or in the telephone receiver, or even under the paper-weight on the honourable baronet's desk. The search must go deeper."
"But the police——"
"I admit, Jotson, that the police have shown unusually keen intuition. It was a cunning move to watch the taxi-stand. It was a clever stroke to set a watch upon the telegraph-poles. For it is extremely unlikely that the spy would hide under a taxi, which might be set in motion at any moment, and highly improbable that he would climb a telegraph-pole for concealment. Being unlikely, it was therefore the thing that was most probable to happen. You know my system, Jotson?"
"Quite so. But in this case——"
"In this case it has failed," Herlock Sholmes knitted his brows. "Jotson, I confess that I am quite at sea. If the most unlikely theory proves to be incorrect, how can I even grasp at a clue?"
"You will never be beaten, Sholmes," I said confidently.
"Am I permitted to make a suggestion?"
He laughed.
"Certainly, my faithful Jotson!"
"The most unlikely theory having proved incorrect, how would it do to test the most likely one?"
Sholmes started.
I saw a glitter come into his eyes. He rose and paced the room hurriedly, his dressing-gown whisking behind him.
"Jotson!" His voice trembled. "You have benefited by your study of my methods. Jotson, you have given me the clue to the mystery!"
"Sholmes!"
He grasped me by the shoulder.
"Come!" he exclaimed.
"But——"
"Not a word—come!"
A few minutes later we were seated in a taxi-cab, and whirling across London. Shaker Street was left behind.
"Where are we going, Sholmes?" I gasped.
"To the Red-Tape and Sealing-Wax Department."
"But—but for what——"
Herlock Sholmes' reply astounded me.
"To arrest the spy!"

CHAPTER 2

Sholmes did not speak another word till the taxi had stopped at the palatial official residence of Sir Obviously Hardley-Sain, and we were shown in to that great statesman's private office. The baronet was evidently surprised to see us, after taking leave of us so short a time before in Shaker Street. But his manner was courteous and polished as he greeted us.
"Mr. Sholmes, you have surely made no discovery, so far?"
"My visit, sir, is in connection with your confidential secretary, who can materially assist us in this case. Kindly send for him."
The Minister touched a bell, and a stout and florid gentleman, with a spiked blond moustache, entered the room.

"Mr. Speistein—Mr. Herlock Sholmes!" said Sir Obviously.

The secretary bowed.

Herlock Sholmes' next action was amazing. With the spring of a tiger he was upon Mr. Speistein; there was a click, and the handcuffs jingled upon the wrists of the confidential secretary of the Minister of the Red-Tape and Sealing-Wax Office.

The surprise was complete.

"Mr. Sholmes!" ejaculated the baronet.

Sholmes yawned.

"There is the spy, Sir Obviously. Look!"

He turned out the pockets of the shrinking scoundrel. German banknotes, plans of fortifications, and naval and military lists rolled upon the rich carpet.

Sir Obviously Hardley-Sain stood dumbfounded.

"Mein Gott!" murmured his secretary.

"You may call the police," said Herlock Sholmes, with a ring of exultation in his voice. "They may leave the taxi-stand, they may cease to watch the telegraph-poles. There is your prisoner."

"Sholmes, this is wonderful!"

Sholmes smiled as he leaned back in the taxi and hung his feet negligently out of the window.

"Elementary, my dear Jotson! The suggestion came from yourself, though you were hardly aware of it."

"From me, Sholmes?"

"Undoubtedly. Did you not suggest that, the unlikeliest theory having failed, the likeliest should be tried?"

"True, but——"

"It was all I needed, Jotson. For, granted that there was a foreign spy in a high and important office, where was he likeliest to be found? Evidently in a high position, and enjoying the fullest faith and confidence of the Minister concerned. *Voila tout!*"

I could not help but agree. And, proud as I was of having contributed, in ever so humble a degree, to the success of my amazing friend, I acknowledge that it was the simplest case Herlock Sholmes had ever handled.

THE CASE OF THE PIPE-CLAY DEPARTMENT

No. 12

Even Herlock Sholmes looked a little impressed when the Duke of Hookeywalker was shown into our apartment at Shaker Street. His Grace, Percy Augustus, second Duke of Hookeywalker, Earl of Bassbeer, Viscount Fourhalf, Knight of the Shoebuckle, Grand Chamberlain of the Backstairs, Lord Warden of the Royal Gluepot, A.S.S., P.O.T.T.Y., etc., had been one of the greatest figures in politics before the war. His rare gifts of debate, his telling speeches in which the keenest of reporters could discover no meaning, had naturally marked him out for a great place when war broke out. He had become the head of the Pipeclay Department, a position he filled with brilliance.

That this great and famous personage should require the services of Herlock Sholmes was a flattering tribute to my amazing friend.

Sholmes placed a chair for the distinguished visitor, and pushed a decanter of cocaine across the table. His Grace declined it, however, with a wave of his hand.

"Mr. Sholmes, I trust you will be able to help us. I may say that the result of the war with"—his Grace referred to a notebook—"with Germany may depend upon the result of your efforts."

"I am entirely at your Grace's service. Pray give me a few details. You may speak quite freely before my friend, Dr. Jotson."

"It is a curious affair, Mr. Sholmes. You are aware that I am the Secretary for the Pipeclay Department—the most important of Government Departments in time of war. Under my influence, a reform has been instituted in this Department. Usually the scene of peaceful slumber, it has changed its character entirely—until lately. You are, perhaps, aware of the regulations in the Pipelcay

With a crash the screen toppled over, and Herlock Sholmes sprang upon the traitor. There was a startled cry from the discovered villain!

Department?"
Sholmes shook his head.
"I will be more explicit. The usual routine was this. The officials arrived at eleven in the morning, and dozed gently in well-padded armchairs till lunch-time. Three hours were taken for lunch, but the whole body of officials were expected to return to their bureaux by four o'clock. They slumbered peacefully until five, when they left for their homes. This arrangement, excellent in peace time, was not, I felt, wholly adequate at a time when the British Empire was at grips with her mortal foe. Loath as I was to interfere with the honourable traditions of the Department, I felt that a change was necessary, at least during the period of the war with"—the Duke glanced at his notebook again—"with Germany. You are aware, Mr. Sholmes, that this country is at war with Germany?"
"I have seen it in the papers," assented Sholmes.
"Ah, I never read the papers! I was, however, officially informed of the fact, and there was no mistake about it. Having decided upon drastic reforms in the Pipeclay Department, I adopted the use of a very ingenious invention. Regarding it as imperative that the officials of my Department should remain awake at least one hour daily. I had this invention installed. It is an electrical apparatus, by means of which every official, on falling asleep in his chair, receives a slight shock, which awakens him in a few minutes. There is also a gramophone attachment to the apparatus, which repeats in a loud voice every half hour the sentence: 'WE ARE AT WAR!' This is a very useful reminder to the Department, the fact constantly escaping their memory."
"Excellent!" said Sholmes. "I no longer wonder at the distinction your Department has achieved during the war. This invention might be utilised with advantage in other Departments."
The Duke bowed.
"Unfortunately, Mr. Sholmes, some unscrupulous hand has been at work, and the apparatus has ceased to act. That is why I require your assistance. Every morning for the past week the apparatus has been deliberately disconnected, and has not worked. The result has been deplorable. The days have passed in peaceful slumber, as in pre-war times. Despatches have accumulated on the tables. Telegrams have remained unanswered. Armies despatched to distant corners of the earth have been forgotten, and have been cut up by the enemy. I felt that this could not be allowed to continue, Mr. Sholmes, and, as my social engagements have, fortunately, left me one half-hour free to-day, I determined to call upon you."
"I thank your Grace," said Herlock Sholmes. "I shall be glad to be of assistance. Evidently an emissary of Germany has been at work."
"I fear so, Mr. Sholmes. Spies have informed the plotters in Berlin of the existence of the electric awakener, and they have determined to cripple the efforts of this country by putting it out of action."
"Are any Germans employed in the Pipeclay Department?"
The Duke smiled slightly.
"Naturally!" he replied.
"You do not suspect——"
"My dear Mr. Sholmes, it is a maxim in the Pipeclay Department that Germans are above suspicion. We leave that kind of thing to the halfpenny papers."
"Is it possible for a stranger to penetrate into the Department?"
"Quite. The doorkeeper has received strict injunctions to remain awake at his post, but it is possible, or course, that these injunctions are neglected, owing to the general soporific atmosphere of the place."
Herlock Sholmes looked thoughtful.
"I had better make my investigations upon the spot," he said, rising. "Come, Jotson."
In a few minutes, the Duke's car was bearing us to Whitehall, where we were shown at once into the Pipeclay Office.

CHAPTER 2

The palatial department was buried in silent slumber.

From the various bureaux came only the soft sound of peaceful breathing.
Outside the newspapers were crying the latest news: "Magnificent Retreat!" "Heroic Retirement!" But their raucous voices did not penetrate into the peaceful depths of the Pipeclay Department.
There all was peace.
The Duke glanced at Herlock Sholmes.
"You see, Mr. Sholmes," he remarked, "the apparatus is out of action at this moment. Otherwise, instead of the sound of peaceful breathing, the whole building would throb with yawns."
Sholmes nodded.
"I must see it," he observed.
We were led into the Duke's private cabinet. It was there that the apparatus was installed. By the simple device of a switch in the wall, the electric awakener would be set in motion.
"Every morning," said the Duke, "I turn on the switch at eleven o'clock. Then I leave the Department, my daily labours ended. Observe!"
He pressed down the switch.
Immediately, from the adjoining apartments, came a sound of loud yawning. The awakener was at work. From the gramophone attachment a deep voice came, repeating the sentence: 'WE ARE AT WAR!' Thus reminded of the fact that had escaped their memory, the whole body of officials rubbed their eyes and set to work. I could scarcely repress an exclamation of admiration for this great invention, the installation of which in the Pipeclay Office proved that we are very little, if at all, behind the Germans in real efficiency.
The Duke turned off the switch again. The yawning died away, and once more the peaceful sound of deep breathing was heard. The Pipeclay Office had sunk one more into somnolence.
"You see," said the Duke, "how terribly we are handicapped in this war by the apparatus being tampered with. I look to you, Mr. Sholmes, to discover the villain who tampers with it!"
"I will do my best," said Herlock Sholmes. "Pray turn on the switch again! Exactly! Now retire behind this screen!"
We stepped behind the screen, and waited. Loud yawning was heard from various directions, showing that the awakener was in full action, and that the labours of the Department were proceeding. Important letters, neatly tied with red tape, were carefully stacked into pigeon-holes. Busy pens traced out "Observations upon the Remarks of the Forty-fourth Report of the Seventh Committee of Inquiry into the Alleged Lack of Waistcoat-buttons in the Patagonian Expeditionary Force." The Pipeclay Department was in full swing!
We waited in silence. Herlock Sholmes' face was inscrutable.
The Duke had sunk into an easy-chair, and his eyes had closed. But, in spite of the slumberous influence around, I did not think of sleep. I watched the inscrutable face of Herlock Sholmes.
There was a soft step upon the rich, thick carpet. We peered from behind the screen.
A fat and florid man, with a blonde spiked moustache, had entered the cabinet, and with a grin of fiendish cunning upon his face, was creeping towards the switch of the electric awakener.
His fat and podgy finger pressed the switch.
The inevitable result followed.
In a few moments the Pipeclay Office was buried in slumber. The awakener had ceased to act!
With a crash, the screen toppled over, and Herlock Sholmes sprang upon the traitor. There was a startled cry from the discovered villain, and he turned to flee. His feet, however, were entangled in Sholmes' dressing-gown, and he fell heavily to the floor. Before he could rise the handcuffs were on his wrists.
The Duke, awakened by the crash of the screen, started to his feet. Startled suddenly from slumber, he did not realise where he was.
"My Lords," he said, "I beg to assure your lordships that the prosecution of the war is proceeding as well as can be expected. The general average of wakefulness in my Department exceeds—"
His Grace evidently fancied for the moment that he had awakened from a nap in an "Exalted Place."
"Bless my soul!" he exclaimed. "What has happened, Mr. Sholmes?"
Herlock Sholmes smiled.

"There is the villain who turned off the switch, your Grace!"
The Duke stared at the handcuffed traitor in amazement.
"But—but he is a German!" he exclaimed. "One of my most faithful employees! Is it possible that I have been deceived in him? Call the police! Villain, imprisonment for a week awaits you for this treachery, and I shall consider very seriously whether to employ you again in the Pipeclay Department!"

CHAPTER 3

"Success again, Sholmes!" I remarked, as we walked homeward to Shaker Street. "But how did you know that the traitor would come—"
He smiled.
"I reasoned it out, Jotson. The rascal had turned off the electric awakener, and fancied that the Pipeclay Department was put of action for the day. But turning it on again, I drew him into the snare. Finding the officials awake at their desks, he would guess that someone had entered the Duke's private cabinet, and turned on the apparatus. He came at once to stop it, and plunge the Department into its usual slumber. Then we had him! I am glad, Jotson, that the Duke called me. With the electrical awakener in full action, it appears probably that the Patagonian Expeditionary Force will, in due time, receive the full supply of waistcoat-buttons—and, perhaps, even ammunition. Who knows? I think I have fairly earned the Duke's handsome cheque; and we will have kippers for tea, Jotson!"

THE CASE OF THE PAWNED PICKLE-JAR

No. 13

I have already mentioned, in the course of these memoirs, the curious case of the Pawned Pickle-Jar. In no case has the amazing insight of my remarakble friend Herlock Sholmes been displayed to greater advantage. How Sholmes, in a few hours, elucidated a mystery that had baffled Scotland Yard for several weeks, I now propose to describe.
Sholmes was lounging idly by the window of our sitting-room in Shaker Street, his hands thrust into the pockets of his celebrated dressing-gown—that somewhat shabby but still gorgeous dressing-gown which has become historic in the annals of crime. I looked up as he uttered a sudden ejaculation.
"Our friend Pinkeye!"
I joined him at the window. Inspector Pinkeye of Scotland Yard had just stopped at the door.
Sholmes smiled slightly.
"My assistance is required again, I fancy, Jotson," he remarked. "Once more the Criminal Investigation Department has realised its helplessness. Well, well, we must do our best to help friend Pinkeye out of his scrape."
A few minutes later our landlady, Mrs. Spudson, showed the inspector into our sitting-room.
"Good-morning, Pinkeye! Have the missing bonds come to light yet?" drawled Herlock Sholmes.
"It is about those bonds that I have come to consult you, Sholmes," said Inspector Pinkeye, sinking into a chair. "I admit, Sholmes, that we have been completely beaten so far. Messrs. Have & Hookit's War Bonds are still missing. We have the thief safe and sound, but the plunder—" The inspector made a gesture of despair. "Can you help us, Sholmes?"
Herlock Sholmes leaned back in his chair, his feet resting negligently on the mantelpiece, his dressing-gown draping carelessly about his knees.
"Pray let me have a few details, Pinkeye," he said. "You can speak quite freely before my friend Dr. Jotson."
"I dare say you have seen the case in the papers," said the inspector. "It beats us, Sholmes. Here is the matter in a nutshell. Mr. H. Walker, chief cashier to Messrs. Have & Hookit, was discovered to have been robbing the firm for years. He was arrested, but not till he had made away with a number of bonds belonging to his employers. These bonds have not been disposed of in the market, and they

Herlock Sholmes produced a small bundle of papers, and Inspector Pinkeye gazed upon them dumbfounded. “The - the bonds!” he stammered.

cannot be found. The prisoner declines to give information. Evidently he has concealed the bonds, as a nest-egg for his old age when he comes out of chokey. But where—that is the question."

"You have searched——"

"His lodgings have been searched, even the wallpaper being stripped off the walls, every inkpot emptied and examined under the microscope, and his bulldog subjected to Rontgen rays. No trace of the bonds has been discovered."

"And his person——"

"Subjected to the most thorough examination. Nothing was found upon him but a pawnticket."

"Ah," said Sholmes—"a pawnticket! An indication that Mr. Walker has been hard up for ready cash?"

"I suppose so, but it does not represent a large amount. The sum stated on the ticket is fourpence, and the article entrusted to the care of the pawnbroker was simply a pickle-jar."

Herlock Sholmes raised his eyebrows.

"A pickle-jar, Pinkeye?"

"Simply a pickle-jar. Quite unconnected with the case in hand, of course. The pickle-jar has been ascertained to be his own property."

Sholmes nodded.

"Certainly there seems no obvious connection between a pickle-jar and War Bonds to the value of a thousand pounds," he remarked. "And what is not obvious is of no use to Scotland Yard—eh, Pinkeye?"

"Really, Mr. Sholmes, I don't quite follow. Our department has attached no importance whatever to the pawned pickle-jar."

"Naturally!" said Sholmes. "Can I see the pawnticket?"

The inspector made a gesture of impatience.

"I came to you for advice, Mr. Sholmes. Your methods are not the same as ours, but I admit that, in some cases, you have had phenomenal luck. But——"

"Luck, my dear Pinkeye, is not a word in my vocabulary," said Herlock Sholmes, with some asperity. "My method is deduction. I repeat that I should like to see the pawnticket."

With evident impatience, Inspect Pinkeye drew the little slip of cardboard from his pocket, and passed it to Herlock Sholmes.

"Now tell me what you make of that!" he exclaimed, with unconcealed derision.

Sholmes did not reply.

He took the pawnticket and examined it minutely.

I watched my amazing friend with the keenest of interest. Knowing Herlock Sholmes as I did, I should not have been surprised if he had described minutely the hiding-place of the missing bonds, merely from an examination of the pawnticket referring to the pickle-jar. He did not speak for some minutes, but his brow was very thoughtful. Both his pipes went out, a proof of his concentration of mind. It was the official who broke the silence.

"Well, Mr. Sholmes?"

Herlock Sholmes yawned.

"May I keep this ticket for an hour or so?" he asked.

"Oh, certainly! It is of no use to Scotland Yard!" said the inspector. "Perhaps, Mr. Sholmes, you have already discovered the hiding-place of the bonds?"

"Exactly,"

"What!"

Sholmes laughed, and rose.

"My dear Pinkeye, as you have already remarked, my methods are not yours. Jotson, my dear fellow, may I trouble you to call a taxi?"

"Certainly, Sholmes."

"Will you do me the honour to remain here a little while, Pinkeye? I shall be absent an hour or so. You will find these cigarettes excellent, and the cask of cocaine is in the corner."

"But—but——" stammered the inspector.

But Herlock Sholmes was gone.

CHAPTER 2

"Bosh!" growled the inspector.

He stood at the window, watching the taxi as it sped away with Herlock Sholmes. The expression on his face was one of ironical impatience. It was evident that he believed that he was wasting time.

"You may rely on Sholmes," I ventured to remark. "His experience of pawntickets has been long and varied, extending over many years. At almost every period in his career he has had a large collection of them."

Inspector Pinkeye merely grunted. He did not share my faith in the amazing abilities of Herlock Sholmes. The hide-bound prejudice of the official mind was not so easily overcome.

We waited.

In less than an hour, the taxi was heard without, and then we heard the familiar tread of Herlock Sholmes on the stairs. He came in, smiling.

"Well?" snapped Inspector Pinkeye.

"I have had a very agreeable drive," smiled Herlock Sholmes.

"I trust you have not been bored by my friend Jotson, Pinkeye?"

"Mr. Sholmes, we are wasting time. Kindly return the pawnticket, and I will return to my duties," said the inspector gruffly.

"Too late!" smiled Herlock Sholmes. "I have parted with it."

"You have parted with it?"

"Yes; but I have something to hand you in exchange."

"And what may that be?"

"The missing bonds," drawled Herlock Sholmes.

He drew a small bundle from beneath his dressing-gown, and laid it upon the table, Inspector Pinkeye gazed upon it, dumbfounded.

"The—the bonds?" he stammered.

"Pray, examine them, Pinkeye, and I think you will find the numbers correct."

With trembling hands, the inspector examined the bonds.

"They are all here," he said. "In the name of wonder, Sholmes——"

Sholmes shrugged his shoulders.

"My dear Pinkeye, there are the bonds. Good-morning!"

"Sholmes!" I exclaimed, when the inspector was gone.

Herlock Sholmes did not reply for a moment. He was lighting a pipe with his usual methodical care.

"Sholmes, you amaze me more and more. You have discovered the missing bonds?"

"So it appears, Jotson."

"Merely from the clue of the pawnticket?"

"Evidently."

"You astound me, Sholmes!"

"My dear Jotson, you should be accustomed to being astounded by this time," said Sholmes chidingly.

"True. And yet——"

"A perfectly simple case, Jotson. Nothing was found on the prisoner but a pawnticket relating to a pickle-jar in the custody of a Mr. Solomons in security for a loan of fourpence. What would you, my dear Jotson, have deduced from that?"

"That H. Walker was extremely short of money, when it was worth his while to raise a loan of fourpence by pawning a pickle-jar," I replied.

"Exactly the conclusion that the police came to, Jotson," Sholmes smiled. "But I did not come to that conclusion, Jotson. Consider a moment, my dear fellow. Fourpence, certainly, is not a sum to be despised. But the purloiner of the bonds had a more powerful motive. If he had pawned a clock, or a walking-stick, or a parrot, the police theory might have held water. But have you not remarked upon the extraordinary circumstances that the article pawned was a pickle-jar?"

"I confess, Sholmes——"

"Not a jar of pickles, you observe, but a pickle-jar," resumed Sholmes. "Does that tell you nothing,

my dear Jotson?"
"Nothing, Sholmes."
"My dear fellow, you are fully qualified for a high position in Scotland Yard,' said Herlock Sholmes, with a smile. "Observe! The thief's object was to discover a safe hiding-place for the bonds. What securer place could he find than the interior of a pickle-jar placed in the keeping of a common, or garden, pawnbroker? His object was not to raise the useful, but far from lavish, sum of fourpence."
"Sholmes!"
"I presented the pawnticket to Mr. Solomons, Jotson, and claimed the pickle-jar, Inside it—somewhat stained with disused pickles, but still recognisable—reposed the missing bonds. *Voila tout*."
"Marvellous!" I could not help exclaiming.
Sholmes smiled.
"Elementary, my dear Jotson. But, until your valuable memoirs appear in the Press, Jotson, Inspector Pinkeye will remain mystified. The intellect of Scotland Yard is not equal to discerning the connection between the missing bonds and the Pawned Pickle-Jar."

THE MUNITION MYSTERY

No. 14

Herlock Sholmes was poring over a letter when I came into our sitting-room at Shaker Street. His feet rested upon the mantelpiece, and his famous dressing-gown hung in graceful folds about his waist. That he was deep in thought I could see at a glance, for he was smoking three pipes instead of the usual two—a habit of his when he had to deal with some problem that required intense concentration of mind.
He laid down the letter, however, and glanced at me with a smile.
"You are late down this morning, my dear Jotson," he remarked.
"Sholmes!" I exclaimed.
"It is a fact, is it not?"
"I admit it, Sholmes, but——"
He laughed.
"Your amazement is amusing, Jotson. Yet have you not told me that you have studied my methods?"
"To the best of my poor ability, Sholmes," I replied, somewhat nettled. "But in this instance I confess that I do not follow your reasoning. I should be glad to know how you made that deduction."
"I have no objection to explaining, my dear fellow. To you, at least, I do not desire to make a mystery. That you are down late this morning I deduced from a casual examination of the clock."
"The clock!" I could not help exclaiming.
"The clock, Jotson. Look at it yourself, and tell me what conclusion you draw."
"I confess that it tells me nothing."
Herlock Sholmes yawned.
"My dear Jotson, it is perfectly simple. The hour hand indicates nine, the minute hand rests at three. Taken in conjunction, these two facts indicate—as it is not an American clock—that it is now a quarterpast nine."
"True!"
"Your usual breakfast hour is half-past eight; you are, therefore, three-quarters of an hour past your usual time. From such simple facts, Jotson, I deduced that you were later than usual this morning."
I regarded my amazing friend with speechless admiration.
"But to come to more serious matters," said Sholmes, "I have received this letter—a most peculiar case, Jotson. I should be glad of your opinion."
"You flatter me, Sholmes."
"Not at all, my dear fellow. 'Out of the mouths of babes and sucklings,' you know! A very

As we left the munition works Mr. Milcoe stopped us, and shook hands with my amazing friend, with a look of the deepest gratitude. "I shall never forget this, Mr. Sholmes," he said, brokenly.

interesting case, Jotson. You are aware that a large number of munition factories have been established in the country. Our far-seeing statesmen, having consulted the very best expert military opinion, have now decided that cannons are more formidable to the enemy when supplied with shells. Naturally, there was some hesitation at first, but this opinion is now pretty generally adopted, and the result is that munition factories have sprung up all over the country. Gentlemen of all trades and professions—even engineers, as I hear—have been appointed as inspectors of munition works. The work is going on famously, but there appears to be trouble at this particular place"—he referred to the letter—"at Slowcome."

"What has happened, Sholmes?" I asked, keenly interested.

"The details are curious enough. It appears that the factory at Slowcome is turning out big shells. But of late a considerable number of these shells have been found to be filled with water."

"Water, Sholmes?"

"Water!" he replied. "I know little of engineering, Jotson, I admit—scarcely more, than a munition inspector—but it appears that a shell filled with water is useless for military purposes. The inspector in this especial factory is a very honest and reliable gentleman—a dairyman by profession. He passed the shells as satisfactory, unfortunately having had no training in the business. Now, my dear Jotson, what is your opinion?"

"German treachery!" I replied at once. 'Undoubtedly the Germans have discovered that our artillery is, at last, to be supplied with ammunition, and they have taken measures accordingly."

Sholmes smiled.

"Ah, Jotson, have I not warned you against obvious theories?" he said.

"True! But in this case——"

"You may be right, Jotson. *Nous verrons!*" said Sholmes, rising. "If you would care to come down to Slowcome with me to-day, we shall see. I must investigate on the spot."

Ten minutes later, the 7:63 from Euston was bearing us rapidly towards Slowcome.

CHAPTER 2

Herlock Sholmes was very thoughtful during the journey.

I could hardly extract a word from him.

As a matter of fact, I felt decidedly taken with my own theory, and I fancied, for once, that even Sholmes, in his contempt for the most obvious solution of a problem, had overlooked the explanation which had occurred to me. The filling of the shells with water rendered them useless for military purposes, and to whom could such an act be attributed save a German spy?

We alighted at Slowcome, and walked to the gigantic factory. Sholmes was still very thoughtful.

"You are satisfied with your theory, Jotson?" he asked me, with a smile.

"Quite!" I replied, with conviction.

"But the inspector!" he said.

"Perhaps a German, or in the pay of the enemy," I replied. "How can he be trustworthy, Sholmes, when he has passed as satisfactory, shells filled with water?"

"My dear Jotson, the inspector concerned is a milkman well known in Slowcome, and of the highest character."

"You have formed a theory, Sholmes?"

He frowned.

"I do not deal in theories, Jotson. I have, I believe, deduced the correct conclusion from the known facts. But we shall see."

We entered the factory. We were greeted cordially by the manager, who bore the old British name of Von Gollop. Machinery was at work on all sides turning out the shells that were to crush the Huns to the very dust—at some date at present unfixed. Sholmes looked round him with his usual inscrutable smile.

"I should be glad to see the inspector," he remarked.

"He is here," said Mr. Von Gollop. "I vill send for heem."

Sholmes shook hands with Mr. Milcoe, the munition inspector. I noted that he regarded Mr. Milcoe very keenly, and nodded as if satisfied.

"Kindly wait for me in the office, Jotson," he said.

Somewhat puzzled, I entered the manager's office and waited. Sholmes' whole interest seemed to be centred in Mr. Milcoe, the inspector, though he had himself told me that the gentleman was of the highest character. Indeed, as I learned later. Mr. Milcoe had a very wide connection in Slowcome as a family dairyman, and served the best families with milk.

Mr. Milcoe was making his tour of inspection, and, to my amazement, Herlock Sholmes was shadowing him through the munition factory. Did he, after all, suspect Milcoe of treachery? I was puzzled and impatient. I settled down at last to read the newspaper, perusing with great satisfaction the three hundred and seventy-fifth epoch-making speech of the great and revered Mr. Hashquick.

I had scarcely read more than the first ten thousand words, however, when Sholmes entered, smiling.

"We have time to catch our train, Jotson," he said.

"Sholmes, you are not finished?"

"I am finished."

"You have discovered——"

"I have."

"And it was not a German spy?"

He laughed.

"Nothing of the kind, my dear Jotson. Come!"

As we left the munition works Mr. Milcoe stopped us, and shook hands with my amazing friend, with a look of the deepest gratitude.

"I shall never forget this, Mr. Sholmes," he said brokenly. "It was, as you so wonderfully deduced, merely absent-mindedness."

"Exactly!" said Sholmes.

"In future every care shall be exercised," said Mr. Milcoe, wringing my friend's hand. "Mr. Sholmes, you have perhaps saved the Empire—not to mention the Alhambra and the Coliseum. For if the war should last more than seventy-nine years, the result may easily depend upon the supply of shells from Slowcome. Bless you, Mr. Sholmes."

I could scarcely contain my impatience till we were seated in the London express. Sholmes was elated, as I could see by the way he tossed off a swig of cocaine from his flask.

"Sholmes," I exclaimed, "in the name of wonder——"

"You are mystified, Jotson?"

"Unutterably! You have discovered who placed the water in the shells?"

"Assuredly."

"By whose hand, then, was the foul work done?"

"By Mr. Milcoe's."

"Sholmes! Then he is a traitor?"

"Nothing of the sort, my dear Jotson," smiled Sholmes.

"He is a milkman."

"Sholmes!"

"In forming your theory, my dear Jotson, you left out of consideration the cardinal fact that the munition inspector was a milkman by profession. It did not escape me, however. I shadowed Mr. Milcoe in the factory. He is a dairyman of the highest character—but slightly absent-minded. Old habits are strong, Jotson. Mr. Milcoe was a slave to habit. Taken suddenly from his business as a milkman, placed in a position of a munition inspector, his habits could not change so suddenly as his occupation. He had been accustomed to filling his milk-pails with water. Milk-pails were no longer at hand. But the shells were there. From force of habit, he filled the shells with water. Knowing nothing of the nature or manufacture of shells, he was naturally unaware that such an operation rendered them useless. Now that I have put him on his guard, however, he is not likely to make this error again."

"Wonderful!" I exclaimed. "But why, my dear Sholmes, should a milkman be appointed inspector of munition factory?"

"That is easily explained, my dear Jotson. It is probable that there were no butchers or bakers or candlestick-makers available!"

THE CAPTURED SUBMARINES

No. 15

The efficient manner in which our Navy has dealt with the submarine menace is well known. The part played in the affair by my amazing friend, Herlock Sholmes, has not, however, been communicated to the public in the official reports. It is not generally known that, as a matter of absolute fact, the failure of the German submarine campaign was largely due to my amazing friend. But honour must be given where honour is due.

I was reading the obituary notices of some of my patients one morning, in our sitting-room in Shaker Street, when Sholmes came in, and I could not help glancing at him in some surprise. He wore a skipper's cap, and his famous dressing-gown was tucked into high sea-boots.

"My dear Jotson," he said. "are you a good sailor?"

"I am quite at home upon the water, Sholmes. In those far-off peaceful days before the war, I frequently made the trip from London Bridge to Southend. On more than one occasion I have ventured upon the remotest recesses of the turbid Serpentine."

"Good! I require an experienced seaman as first mate of the Spoof Bird. You shall have the post, Jotson."

"Where are we going?" I asked.

"Hunting," he replied. "You are aware, Jotson, that the German submarines have caused a good deal of havoc among our shipping. The authorities, for reasons best known to themselves, have not cared to avail themselves of my services. I have, however, decided to step in. A trim craft, the Spoof Bird, lies ready. We have but to embark."

"You have formed a plan, Sholmes, for dealing with these pests?"

"Naturally, Jotson. But you will see."

I forbore to ask further, knowing my friend's dislike of questioning. I followed him. Shaker Street, with its old familiar motor-buses, and its familiar, haunting scent, was left behind, and we embarked upon the Spoof Bird, and ere long we were cleaving the wild water of the North Sea.

I admit that I was in some perplexity.

The Spoof Bird was a well-found craft, but I could observe no means aboard of dealing with submarines. There were no guns, and there was no ammunition. The absence of amunition I could have understood, on the supposition that Sholmes was acting upon expert advice from high quarters. But I had expected to see guns. No guns, however, were visible.

Several large packing-cases were piled on the deck, the contents of which Sholmes did not acquaint me with.

Sholmes was tireless. In the intervals of absorbing cocaine and smoking some thousands of cigarettes, he kept an intent watch upon the sea with a very large telescope. Towards evening, he turned to me with a smile of satisfaction.

"The enemy are in sight, Jotson."

I felt a thrill.

"A submarine, Sholmes?"

"A submarine," he replied.

A dark object appeared on the waters. Herlock Sholmes rapped out a rapid order. A large packing-case was immediately tossed over the side, and it floated between us and the submarine.

"Sholmes, in the name of wonder——"

Sholmes did not reply.

The submarine was approaching rapidly, and all his skill was needed to save the Spoof Bird from the treacherous torpedo.

Sholmes was an accomplished seaman. His voice rang out from the bridge, giving orders.

"Take a double reef in the propellor! Lower the topgallant sails into the engine-room! Hoist the main deck overboard!"

These orders were promptly obeyed.

Like a thing of life, the Spoof Bird flew over the wild waters, and the submarine and the floating packing-case vanished astern.

Herlock Sholmes rubbed his hands with satisfaction.

"One!" he said, with his inscrutable smile.

"But, Sholmes, I do not comprehend!"

"My dear Jotson, have you forgotten the old proverb, that little boys should not ask question?" said Sholmes.

"True. But——"

"Moreover, if I should explain it now, it would spoil our usual little explanation in the sitting-room at Shaker Street, which should properly come at the end of the story," added Sholmes.

"I submint to your judgment, Sholmes. But I am amazed."

"By this time, Jotson, you should be accustomed to amazement."

I felt the force of my friend's remark, and was silent.

Our cruise continued, and each time that an enemy submarine was sighted, a fresh packing-case was dropped overboard, and, owing to Sholmes' wonderful seamanship, the Spoof Bird eluded the enemy.

It was not until the last of the packing-cases had been disposed of that the prow of the Spoof Bird was turned for home.

When we arrived at Baker Street, I could contain my impatience no longer.

"Sholmes," I excliamied, "I am on tenterhooks."

"Remain, my dear Jotson, upon tenterhooks a little longer. I am awaiting for a report from the Admiralty."

"But——"

"Pass the cocaine!" said Herlock Sholmes.

I passed the cocaine, and was silent.

CHAPTER 2

I could not help wondering about this strange affair. That Herlock Sholmes' apparently mysterious action was based upon some amazing and far-reaching plan, I knew. But it was not till a week later that I learned the astounding facts.

One morning, when I came down to breakfast, I found Sholmes in high good-humour. He was reading a long report, but he looked up as I came in, with a smile.

"Well, Jotson, your curiosity is about to be satisfied," he said. "The submarine campaign has been an eminent success."

"I am overjoyed to hear it, Sholmes. And the result——"

"You remember that there were twelve packing cases on board the Spoof Bird, Jotson?"

"Exactly."

"Twelve submarines have been captured," said Sholmes, rubbing his hands. "The crews were in a helpless condition, and fell easily into our hands."

"But how—why? It was your work, Sholmes?"

"It was my work, Jotson, though I doubt whether my name will appear in the official communications. That, however, I do not desire. I derive my satisfaction from the knowledge that I have dished the enemy, and that Admiral Von Whiskerpitz will be tearing his hair."

"You promised me an explanation, Sholmes."

"I am ready to give it, my dear fellow. You did not know the contents of those packing-cases?"

"Some terrible explosive?"

"More dangerous than that, Jotson."

"Some deadly chemical?"

"More dangerous than that."

"Some poisonous gas?"

"Still more dangerous, my dear Jotson."

"In Heaven's name, Sholmes, what terrible secret did those packing-cases contain?"
Sholmes smiled.
"German sausages!" he replied.
"German sausages?" I exclaimed.
"Nothing more nor less, Jotson. Consider. The submarine crews were far away from land. For days and days they had not tasted German sausages. They examined the packing-cases left floating behind the Spoof Bird; they found them to contain German sausages. You can easily guess the result—an orgy in the submarine. Not one of the sausages, probably, was left undevoured."
"True. But still, you forget, Sholmes, that German sausages, though perhaps fatal to civilised stomachs, are an accustomed article of diet among the Huns."
"I do not forget, Jotson," said Sholmes coldly.
"Excuse me, Sholmes, then how——"
"I have not told you all. In each sausage were cunningly concealed a fragment of American potted beef, especially imported from Chicago for the purpose."
"Sholmes!"
"You will now comprehend, Jotson, The sausages they would have survived, their systems being inured to such diet. But the Chicago beef, Jotson, put the lid on it. That mysterious compound, the ingredients of which are known only to the American inventor, was too much for them. Completely overcome, they lay sick and feeble, at the mercy of wind and waves, and submarine after submarine was snapped up by our patrols before they could recover."
I could only gaze at my amazing friend in silent admiration.

THE SHAM HUNS

No. 16

During the latter part of 1915 a series of remarkable disappearances had attracted a great deal of public attention. It was natural that, after Scotland Yard had realised its helplessness in the matter, the assistance of my amazing friend, Herlock Sholmes, should be called in.
Sholmes, took up the case willingly enough. There were, as he explained to me, many points of quite unusual interest in it. On my return one morning from the funeral of an old friend and patient, I found him busily engaged with the papers relating to the case.
"Quite a remarkable case, Jotson," he said, looking up. "Needless to say, the police can make nothing of it. We must see if we can help them out a little—eh, Jotson? During the past few weeks, my dear fellow, two hundred persons have mysteriously disappeared from London. Strangest of all, the disappearances are continuing, so it is evident that the same mysterious agency is still at work."
"Extraordinary, Sholmes!"
He nodded, and blew out two large clouds of smoke from his pipe.
"A very extraordinary case, Jotson. Look over these papers, my dear fellow, and tell me your opinion. You have studied my methods."
"I will do my best, Sholmes."
I perused the pages eagerly. I should have been very willing to show that I had achieved some measure of success in my study of his amazing methods. I looked up at last with some degree of confidence.
"Foul play," I said.
"And by whom, Jotson?"
"The Germans."
"Such, I believe, is the police theory," said Sholmes, with a smile. "I do not deal in theories, but in facts, unfortunately. However, let us see upon what you base this theory, Jotson?"
I was somewhat nettled by his bantering tone, and I replied a little warmly:
"In each case some sign of German intervention has been discovered. Each of the men who have disappeared was in poor circumstances. Some of them had suffered losses and hardships. Yet, when

Sholmes was busy for an hour or more, and at the end of that time, two hundred downcast wretches had been turned from the gates of Jollyboys Hall.

their lodgings were searched by the police after their amazing disappearance, in most cases a German grammar was discovered. In many cases a German dictionary also came to light. Why should they have purchased these expensive volumes themselves, with their straitened means?"

"Ah! Why?" said Sholmes.

"Moreover, in many cases written sheets of German exercises were found, showing that the unfortunate victims had been studying the German language."

"True."

"In some cases neighbours have given that the victims were heard making guttural and animal-like sounds, evident proof that they were endeavouring to learn to speak in German."

"Quite correct."

"I deduce, therefore, Sholmes, that the German agency in the matter is clearly proved. For some reason, which I do not pretend to fathom, German agents supplied these unfortunate men with grammars and dictionaries. Their disappearance followed. In some cases it is possible—I speak as a medical man—that apoplexy may have supervened as a result of speaking too recklessly in German, and the unfortunate victims may have fallen and expired by the wayside. This, however, I admit, would hardly account for two hundred cases."

"Probably not, Jotson. There is no reason why a man of ordinary physical fitness, and with a well-developed larynx, should not speak German for many years, and, indeed, live to a good old age."

"I admit it, Sholmes. For the disappearances I cannot account, but the German agency in the matter appears to me proved beyond the shadow of doubt. Otherwise, why the German grammars, dictionaries, and exercises?"

I was considerably nettled to see Sholmes burst into a hearty laugh.

"My dear Jotson," he said, "you should really apply for a position in the official police."

"You do not, then, agree with my deductions, Sholmes?"

"I fear that I cannot, my dear fellow. You have overlooked the most important point in the case."

"And that?"

"That the victims were in very poor circumstances."

"I do not see how that affects the case."

"Naturally, Yet it is obvious. Allow me to draw your attention to this paragraph in the daily paper, Jotson."

I glanced at the paragraph. It had not, so far as I could see, anything whatever to do with the matter in hand. It gave a description of a concentration camp in which aliens were interned as follows:

"The fitting up of the Jollyboys Hall for interned Germans is now completed. There was some dissatisfaction expressed at first, owing to the lack of marble baths, but this has now been supplied. A seven-course dinner is now provided, the former dinner of five courses having caused discontent. Some ill-natured critics of the administration have found fault with the circumstance that guns and game-licences are supplied to the interned aliens, but we are assured that without these concessions their comfort would not have been complete. We are happy to say that now their only dread is that the war may come to an end, and that they may be sent back to their own country."

I looked at Sholmes in amazement.

"In Heaven's name, Sholmes, what connection has this paragraph, relating to internment camps, with the disappearance of two hundred inhabitants of London in poor circumstances?"

Sholmes did not reply. He yawned, and rose to his feet, and drew his dressing-gown about him. He knocked out the ashes from his pipe absently on the back of my head.

"Would you care for a little run to-day, Jotson?"

"Certainly, my dear Sholmes! But where?"

"To find the two hundred men in poor circumstances who have disappeared," he replied, with a twinkle in his eyes.

"My dear Sholmes——"

"Come!"

We descended to the street. I was lost in amazement. I could not fathom what mysterious clue Herlock Sholmes had discovered, yet it was certain that he was not directed by chance. His deductions were always dictated by a cold, clear logic, and the unravelling of a mystery placed in his hands was a mathematical certainty.

We stepped into a taxi, and sped away through Shaker Street.

Herlock Sholmes sat silent. I asked no questions. For the directions he had given to the driver completed my amazement. It was:

"Jollyboys Hall!"

CHAPTER 2

Herlock Sholmes did not speak during our journey to Jollyboys Hall. He was examining with care a number of photographs, evidently those of the missing men whose strange disappearance had so startled and mystified the authorities. To a brain like Sholmes,' it was nothing to remember every trait in two hundred photographs.

We arrived at Jollyboys Hall.

It was a handsome building, surrounded by sumptuous gardens. The soft strains of a band proceeded from the lofty dining-hall, where the interned aliens were sitting down to the first of the usual seven courses. From the deep woods came occasionally the crack of a gun, showing that the shooting-parties had not yet left all the coverts. The whole scene told of a luxurious comfort that spoke well for the sportsmanlike qualities of the British people, who, in the midst of a great war, could provide for their enemies regardless of expense.

"A happy scene!" said Herlock Sholmes, as we entered the dining-hall. "But I fear, Jotson, that our visit will cast a shadow upon the general bliss."

"But why, Sholmes?"

"I fear, Jotson, that there are some here who are not entitled to share in these luxuries. Duty is sometimes painful, but duty must be done."

Most of the diners glanced at us as we came in. Most of them seemed very contented, though a few were complaining of the soup, which, it appeared, was not a real turtle. The waiters apologised humbly, and assured them that mock-turtle should never be served again at Jollyboys Hall. Sholmes stopped beside one of the diners, who seemed to shrink from his eye, and spoke to him in German:

"Hack, hock!" said Sholmes quietly. "Donnerblitzen sauerkraut. Gug-gug-gooch. Grooh-grooh-grooh!" Sholmes speaks German like a native. "Bub-bub—hack—shack—gerrrrrrgh!"

"Das der dem, ja wohl!" stammered the man.

Sholmes smiled.

"I am afraid your German will not pass muster, William Jones," he said. "Leave this establishment at once, and return to your home. You are sharing in a splendour that was never intended for such as you."

I stood rooted to the floor.

Sholmes was busy for an hour or more, and at the end of that time two hundred downcast wretches had been turned from the gates of Jollyboys Hall. Then Sholmes touched me lightly on the arm.

"Come, Jotson!"

We returned to the taxi. As we drove away the merry strains of the band followed us, and hundreds of guttural German voices merrily raised in singing the "Hymn of Hate."

CHAPTER 3

Sholmes did not speak till we were in our sitting-room at Shaker Street once more, and he had written out his report for the authorities. Then he consented to explain. I was, as usual, on tenterhooks.

"You are surprised, Jotson?"

"I am astounded, Sholmes. You have discovered the hundreds of men in poor circumstances who were missing——"

"Every one, Jotson."

"At Jollyboys Hall?"

"Exactly!"
"But how—why—what clue?"
Sholmes laughed.
"The clue was obvious, Jotson. Did I not observe that the most important point in the case was that the missing men were in poor circumstances? That, added to the fact that it was clear that they have been learning German, supplied all the evidence I needed. My dear Jotson, put yourself in their place. As Britishers they might have perished of starvation, but once they had succeeded in passing themselves off as German aliens, they were assured of every comfort and care. I do not defend their conduct, Jotson, but it was a strong temptation. The idea undoubtedly originated with the first man who disappeared—naturally, without leaving a trace behind him, for had the imposition been discovered, he would have been cast out of the lap of luxury, back into the sordid penury of his ordinary existence. But finding himself a happy dweller in the splendours of Jollyboys Hall, every want provided, every wish anticipated, doubtless he decided to let his friends into such a good thing, and they, in turn, communicated the good news to their friends, so that the number of disappearances increased week by week. Had I not been called in, Jotson, the number of pretended German aliens might have run into millions in the long run, and the accommodation of the internment camps strained to breaking point; indeed, it might even have been necessary to cut down the luxuries supplied to the genuine Germans, which would have caused our great State a very real grief. The scheme, however, has been nipped in the bud, owing to my intervention; and the public may rest assured that in future the splendours of Jollyboys Hall will be wholly preserved for genuine Germans."

THE KAISER'S CODE

No. 17

I have often referred to the fact that my amazing friend, Herlock Sholmes, has frequently placed his marvellous talents at the service of the police. Inspector Pinkeye, of Scotland Yard, has reason to be grateful to him, notably in the famous case of the Pawned Pickle-Jar. It is much to be regretted that Sholmes has never been given full credit for his inestimable services. Indeed, it is painful to relate that, upon more than one occasion the authorities have preferred their own facts to Sholmes' theories. Such an instance occurred in the case of the Kaiser's Code.

I am perfectly well aware that Inspector Pinkeye does not believe in the Kaiser's Code. Needless to say, I take Sholmes' view of the matter. After my amazing experiences with him at Shaker Street I am not likely to lose faith in the judgment of my astounding friend.

Herlock Sholmes was smoking a pipe and several cigarettes one morning after breakfast in our room at Shaker Street, when Inspector Pinkeye was shown in. Sholmes gave him a friendly nod.

"What is it this time, Pinkeye?" he asked. "Help yourself to the cocaine, my dear fellow. You can speak quite freely before my friend Dr. Jotson."

"A very curious case, Mr. Sholmes," said the inspector. "Of course, we are quite capable of dealing with it ourselves——"

Herlock Sholmes smiled ironically.

"But I admit that I should like to have your opinion," said the inspector. "Kindly look at that postcard."

He laid a postcard on the table, and Sholmes glanced at it carelessly. I followed his glance, and could not repress a start of surprise.

For this is what was written on the card:

"Kt. to K 2.
W.J."

I could see that Sholmes was interested, for he allowed several of his cigarettes to go out.

"And now this," said the inspector, producing another card. It contained the following:

"P takes R. Ch.
W.J."

As Sholmes and I looked out of the window we saw Inspector Pinkeye hurrying away.

Herlock Sholmes' eyes glistened.

He turned over the cards, and found that both of them were addressed to "George Wopps, Esq., Forest View, Sluggs' Road, Peckham."

"Well," said the inspector, "what do you make of that, Mr. Sholmes?"

Herlock Sholmes yawned.

"Nothing; excepting that these cards were posted by a man about six feet high, with a sandy moustache and a cast in the left eye, dressed in a brown ulster, and wearing a fancy waistcoat," he said.

The inspector started.

"How did you discover that, Mr. Sholmes?"

"My dear Pinkeye," drawled Sholmes, "your methods are not mine, and it would be useless for me to explain. Let us get to business. What is it you wish me to do?"

"For some time past, Mr. Wopps, of Peckham, has been receiving these mysterious communications, and it has come under the notice of my department," explained the inspector. "Evidently it is a secret code. At least, it appears as such."

"It is such," said Sholmes calmly.

"I am glad you agree with me, Mr. Sholmes," said the inspector, evidently relieved. "In war time one cannot be too careful. The efficiency of the German spy system is well known, and if we had the time, we should certainly keep a watch upon the Germans now living in England."

"What steps have you taken, inspector?"

"I have made enquiries concerning this man Wopps. He is a retired grocer, and lives a very quiet life, chiefly amusing his leisure time in playing chess."

"Probably a blind."

"Possibly," assented the inspector.

"I said probably!"

"I do not dispute your judgment, Mr. Sholmes. The house has been watched, and all visitors carefully scrutinised. Nothing of a suspicious character has been observed; but, remembering your methods, Mr. Sholmes, I have come to the conclusion that that fact alone is very significant."

"Extremely so," said Sholmes drily. "How did you obtain possession of the cards?"

"They were discovered in the sanitary dustbin by one of my men."

"That is remarkable," I ventured to observe. "It looks as if Mr. Wopps attaches little importance to them."

Herlock Sholmes smiled.

"My dear Jotson," he said, "how often have I told you that the obvious is necessarily incorrect? If Mr. Wopps appears to attach no importance to these postcards, that is a direct proof that he attaches the greatest importance to them."

And indeed I could not help being astounded at this fresh proof of the perspicacity of my amazing friend.

"You want me to decipher this, I presume," said Sholmes carelessly.

"Exactly," said the inspector. "once the cipher is read, we have evidence in our hands, and can proceed to action. But I fear that even you, Sholmes, may fail."

Sholmes made a gesture, and the inspector was silent.

My friend's eye were fixed upon the mysterious cipher. We watched him anxiously—the inspector with doubt, myself with perfect confidence. I felt, however deep the mystery, Sholmes would not fail. I was right.

Herlock Sholmes looked up at last.

"The first card reads 'Kt. to K 2,'" he said calmly. "K evidently stands for Kaiser."

The inspector drew a deep breath.

"And the 2?" he asked.

"You are probably aware that the present Kaiser is William II."

"True. But the 'Kt.'"

"Evidently an abbreviation of 'Kraut,'" explained Sholmes. "You know that Germans subsist largely upon a dish known as sauer-kraut. Deciphered, the message means simply this: 'Sauer-kraut to Kaiser William II.' Evidently it refers to some attempt to baffle the British blockade of Germany, and hints that sauer-kraut is the article of which they are most in need."

"By Jove!" said the inspector. "And the second card, Mr. Sholmes?"

"'P takes R. Ch.'" said Sholmes musingly. "It is perfectly clear. Prussia takes risks—meaning that the Kaiser takes the risk of the shipment being seized by the British Fleet, so that no loss will fall upon the traitor who is trading with the enemy."

"And the 'Ch'?"

"'Ch' are the second two letters of the German word 'schnell.' Schnell means quick. It means that there is no time to be lost."

"Thank you, Mr. Sholmes." The inspector rose to his feet. "With this evidence in our hands, we can obtain a search-warrant. Good-morning.

"I advise you to search the house, and secure the incriminating evidence which is undoubtedly there," said Sholmes. "Let me know your success on the telephone."

"Certainly."

The inspector hurried away.

CHAPTER 2

Buzzzzz!

It was about two hours later that the telephone bell rang. Sholmes took up one receiver, and I the other. Sholmes was looking somewhat elated. Only his powerful brain could have penetrated the secret of the Kaiser's secret code, and he knew it. The glory of the capture of the man who was trading with the enemy would fall to Inspector Pinkeye, but for that my friend cared little.

"Is that 'Mr. Sholmes?" came the inspector's voice over the wires.

"Yes, inspector. Have you been to Mr. Wopps'?"

"I am 'phoning from there," replied the inspector.

"You have made the arrest?"

"Nunno."

"Then what has happened?"

"Mr. Wopps has explained the matter satisfactorily."

Sholmes gave a somewhat bitter smile.

"Oh, the police?" he murmured.

"It is quite all right, Mr. Sholmes," went on the inspector's voice. "Mr. Wopps is a chess player."

"That is a blind, my dear fellow."

"Not at all. He is in the habit of playing chess by correspondence with a friend at a distance, named William Jones. Mr. Jones' initials are signed on the cards, you will remember."

"And what is Mr. Wopps' valuable explanation of the cipher?" asked Herlock Sholmes, with a smile of sarcasm.

"On the first card, 'Kt. to K 2' stands for 'Knight to King's second square.' It was Mr. Jones' move in the game then under progress."

"Egregious!" murmured Sholmes. "And the second card?"

"'P takes R—ch,'" said the inspector. "That stands for 'Pawn takes Rook—check!'"

"My dear Sholmes," I ventured to remark, "the explanation is most plausible."

Sholmes smiled.

"The fact that the explanation is plausible, Jotson, is convincing proof that there is nothing in it."

"Most true!"

"And you are satisfied, inspector?" asked Sholmes.

"Quite."

Herlock Sholmes laughed.

"Then if you are satisfied, inspector, I have no more to say. Good-bye!"

Sholmes rang off.

"What will you do in the matter now, Sholmes?" I asked.

"Nothing!" said Sholmes firmly. "Unless the authorities call me in, I shall make no move in the matter at all. Importation of sauer-kraut into Germany is undoubtedly going on, on a large scale, but I cannot move in the matter. Doubtless the inspector will realise his egregious mistake, and return later to ask my aid. I shall not refuse it."

It is with deep regret that I record that Inspector Pinkeye did not return to ask for further aid in the matter. Whether he realised his egregious blunder, even, I am unable to state. So far as my knowledge extends, no further step has been taken in the case of the Kaiser's Code. The fault is not Sholmes'.

THE YELLOW PHIZ

No. 18

Herlock Sholmes was examining a series of pawntickets, of which he had a large and interesting collection, when a visitor was shown into our sitting-room at Shaker Street.

He was a young man with a somewhat pale and harassed face. It was evidently some deep-seated trouble which had brought him to consult my amazing friend.

"Mr. Sholmes!" he began eagerly.

"One moment!" said Sholmes. He finished his examination of the tickets. "Jotson, three of these are nearly up. Perhaps you will be good enough to see our friend Mr. Solomons in the morning. Now, sir, I am quite at your service!"

The young man plunged eagerly into his story.

"My name is Green," he said. "I live in the salubrious suburb of Peckham. I am sorely troubled, Mr. Sholmes, by a mystery that weighs upon my spirits and disturbs my domestic peace. I have recently——"

"Married," said Herlock Sholmes quietly.

Mr. Green started.

"How did you know?" he gasped.

Sholmes smiled.

"To a trained eye it is obvious," he replied. "A button is missing from your waistcoat, and your coat-collar requires brushing. It is quite evident that you have no longer the advantage of possessing a careful landlady."

"It is true, Mr. Sholmes. I have married—and when I was united with my dear Sempronia Whilks, I deemed myself the happiest man living! She had every charm that the most sensitive lover could desire or dream of—a comfortable balance at the bank, a large house standing in its own grounds, two motor-cars, and a relation in the peerage. She was a widow, Mr. Sholmes, the late Alderman Whilks having died suddenly after a dinner at the Mansion House. For three months, sir, I was deliriously happy. But now"—he made a tragic gesture—"now, Mr. Sholmes, my happiness is dashed—perhaps for ever."

"The bank has failed?" I asked sympathetically.

"No, it is not that."

"The motor-cars have broken down?"

"No, no!"

"The mortgagees have foreclosed on the house?"

"No, no! In all those respects, Sempronia is as charming as ever. But a hidden mystery preys upon my peace of mind."

"Pray give us some details, Mr. Green!" said Sholmes. "You may speak quite freely before my friend, Dr. Jotson."

"From the first week at Whilks Hall, Mr. Sholmes, I became aware that Sempronia was concealing something from me. One wing of that imposing mansion was never opened to me. Sempronia kept the key, and sometimes she would disappear into those deserted rooms alone, and remain for hours. After a time I grew curious on the subject. I asked for an explanation. To my surprise, Sempronia burst into tears, and begged me to trust her. Mr. Sholmes, I would have trusted her with my fortune, if I had possessed one; but I was uneasy and alarmed. That closed wing of the house became an obsession in my mind. I could not find it in my heart to force an entrance there against Sempronia'a wish, but I prowled round the place occasionally, looking at the windows. On several occasions I heard cries proceeding from the rooms, yet it is supposed to be untenanted."

"Cries! Of what nature?" asked Sholmes, interested.

"It was somewhat like the crying of infants, Mr. Sholmes. But when I asked Sempronia for an explanation, she trembled and was silent. Mr. Sholmes, I know well that Sempronia loves me. Only this morning she stroked my hair and called me her dusky little Charley. Yet she keeps this weird secret from me. She tells me that if I knew it I should love her no longer. Mr. Sholmes, I can bear no more. You must help me to penetrate this mystery, for Sempronia's sake and my own."

"I am quite at your service, Mr. Green," said Herlock Sholmes, rising. "We will proceed at once to Whilks Hall. Come, Jotson, unless you have another engagement."

"My dear Sholmes, I had intended to attend the funeral of one of my patients, but I will come with you with pleasure!"

"You have no more details to give me, Mr. Green?"

The young man hesitated.

"I have, Mr. Sholmes, yet it so extraordinary I almost fear to relate it."

"Pray proceed!"

"In prowling around the ruined wing, a prey to uneasiness and curiosity, I happened to glance at the windows, and I saw"—Mr. Green shuddered "I saw a face, Mr. Sholmes. It was a terrible-looking face—yellow in colour, and marked with what appeared to be daubs of black and blue paint. A grocer's boy, who was passing on his way to the kitchen door, saw it too, and ejaculated: 'What a chivvy!' It was indeed an extraordinary and alarming chivvy. Mr. Sholmes! It disappeared at once!"

"Extraordinary!" I exclaimed.

"Since then," said Mr. Green hoarsely, "I have seen it again and others. In all, I have counted fifteen—every chivvy of them a hideous-looking phiz, as ugly and ferocious in expression as the masks used by boys on the fifth of November. Mr. Sholmes, I am not dreaming. Extraordinary as it appears, it is the fact!"

Sholmes smiled.

"The improbability of your story, Mr. Green, renders it all the more likely to be correct, in my opinion. My system, as you are perhaps aware, is not that of Scotland Yard. But let us go."

And, in a few minutes more, a motor-bus was bearing us to Peckham.

CHAPTER 2

We arrived at Whilks Hall, one of the finest of the great fashionable mansions of Peckham. As we crossed the extensive grounds, Mr. Green pointed out to us the deserted wing. He gripped Sholmes' arm suddenly.

"Look!" he breathed.

At a large window a face suddenly appeared. I could not help a thrill of horror as I saw it. It was a face that, once seen, could never be forgotten—yellow in hue, with strange marks of red and blue and black—a huge misshapen nose, and wide, curling, grinning mouth. As we gazed, it was joined by a crowd more, all looking at us as we stood. Then suddenly a blind was drawn, and the yellow phizzes vanished from our sight.

"You saw them?" said Mr. Green huskily.

Sholmes' look was sombre.

"Let us proceed," he said.

A door opened, and a lady came forth, and Mr. Green ran towards her. It was evidently Mrs. Green, late Whilks. I turned to Sholmes.

"Sholmes, what does this dreadful mystery mean?" I murmured.

He shook his head.

"Jotson, I confess I am puzzled. Let us go on."

We hurried after Mr. Green. The beautiful Sempronia was endeavouring to prevent him from entering the door of the deserted wing. She threw herself on her knees.

"It is useless, Sempronia!" said the young man. "Let me pass with my friends who have come to investigate this mystery. Otherwise, I leave this house to-day, and return to my humble but happy lodgings in Camden Town."

"Then I will tell you all!" sobbed Sempronia. "but do not forsake your little Sempy! Follow me!"

She swept into the house. We followed, amazed. What strange mystery was about to be revealed?

"Bobby! Tommy! called out the beautiful Sempronia. Gladys! Mary Ann! Willy! Herbert! Charley! Frank! Fred! Wilhelmina! Francesca! Rupert! Cecilia! Ethel! Johnny!"

There was a rush of feet. The hideous faces we had seen at the window surrounded us. Even Sholmes stood dumbfounded. But in a moment more the secret was revealed. With a sweep of her hand, Sempronia removed the fifteen Guy Fawkes' masks from the fifteen faces, and fifteen boys and girls of varying ages stood revealed.

"In mercy's name, Sempronia, what means this?" gasped Mr. Green. "Is this place an orphanage?"

Sempronia drew herself up proudly.

"Nothing of the kind, Charles Green! Forgive me! I have always intended to reveal the truth, but always I have put it off, even as one puts off a visit to the dentist's. When you met me, you knew that I was a widow, but did know that I had fifteen children. I dared not tell you; I feared that it would diminish your love, that it would outweigh, in the balance, the bank-account, the freehold house and the motor-cars for which you adored me. Forgive me, Charles, and take them to your heart!"

"Sempronia!"

"In my dread that you would see them, and discover my fatal secret, I disguised them with Guy Fawkes' masks," murmured Mrs. Green, "otherwise, the resemblance would have betrayed the secret; but in these masks there is little or no resemblance to my features!"

"None!" said Mr. Green.

His face had cleared, and he drew Sempronia to his heart.

Sholmes and I slipped away quietly. We felt that we should be *de trop* at that tender scene of reconciliation. As we glanced back from the gate, we saw Mr. Green taking the merry fifteen to his heart, as requested by Sempronia; but, owing to their number, he was taking them on the instalment system!

Here ends the original set of eighteen 'Herlock Sholmes' adventures originally published between November 1915 and March 1916 in 'The Greyfriars Herald.'

The Herlock Sholmes series was relaunched in February 1917 in 'The Magnet' and continued in a spasmodic run in other magazines such as 'The Gem' and 'Penny Popular' until 1925 and a further two stories were published in 'Tom Merry's Own Annual' as late as 1950 and 1952. This 'second series' of stories are now presented for your amusement.

1917

THE CASE OF HIS LORDSHIP'S ENGAGEMENT

No. 19

The amazing flight of Lord Stony de Broke was a nine days' wonder.

As all the world knew, his lordship had been in considerable financial difficulties for some time, and his disappearance at any earlier period would not have occasioned surprise.

But it was when his financial difficulties came to an end, on his engagement to the daughter and heiress of Ebenezer K. Sprouts of New York, that the young nobleman vanished from the aristocratic circles that knew him.

The engagement had been announced in the Society papers, and his lordship's creditors were rubbing their hands with satisfaction, when the news of his inexplicable flight burst upon an astonished West End.

Scotland Yard having proved, as usual, helpless in the matter, I was not surprised when Mr. Sprouts called upon my amazing friend Herlock Sholmes to enlist his services. His lordship's prospective father-in-law was greatly distressed by the extraordinary conduct of the young man.

I was somewhat interested to see Mr. Sprouts, of whose sudden and giddy rise to fortune, due to the war, everyone was talking. In 1914 Mr. Sprouts had been a paper manufacturer on a small scale in New York. Then the war had come, and all was changed. The enormous export of Notes by the American President had caused a run on paper products of all kinds, and Mr. Sprouts' fortune was made. At the present hour he owned a line of steamers exclusively employed in the conveyance of wood-pulp to his factories, and the factories themselves, working in shifts night and day, poisoned the atmosphere of his native city for scores of miles.

With the immense increase in the export of Notes Mr. Sprouts' business expanded, till now he hardly knew how many millions of dollars he was worth. His daughter and heiress, Miss Seleucia Sprouts, was sought by the scions of the oldest families in New York, men whose names had been known for months, and even years; some of whom, indeed, even knew who their grandfathers were. But, like many gentlemen of his kind, Mr. Ebenezer K. Sprouts had decided to invest his money in a peerage.

For this purpose he had visited London, where he had made the acquaintance of Lord Stony de Broke. An agreement, naturally, was soon arrived at. His lordship was in need of dollars, and Mr. Sprouts was in need of a son-in-law, and Lord Stony de Broke consented to accept the dollars with Seleucia thrown in. Seleucia who was still in New York, signified her consent by cable, and the engagement was announced, much to the satisfaction of his lordship's tailor and hatter and jeweller and wine-merchant. Miss Sprouts had taken the next steamer for Europe, and then——

Then the unexpected had happened! His lordship had called at the Hotel d'Oof, where the Sprouts were staying, to be presented to his fiancee. He had been presented, and had been noticed to turn suddenly pale. He had made an excuse for quitting the room, and had—vanished!

"Clean vamoosed!" said Mr. Sprouts, detailing the strange affair to Herlock Sholmes. "Absquatulated—lit out—simply mizzled! Not a word, and not a line since! All we yeerd about him was that he had jumped into a taxi, and told the driver to drive like thunder. I guess it beats me, Mr. Sholmes, and I calculate I want you to find his lordship."

Herlock Sholmes rubbed his nose thoughtfully.

"His lordship is staying away of his own accord?" he remarked.

"I guess so."

"He has given no reason?"

"Nope! It simply stumps me," said Mr. Sprouts. "That morning he was looking jest the same as usual till I introduced him to Seleucia. Then he absquatulated—went off on his ear, I guess. I reckon, Mr. Sholmes, that I'm not letting him clear off like that. I want him found."

"And the engagement —"

"That engagement still goes!" said Mr. Sprouts emphatically. "So far as I'm concerned, or Seleucia, any old lord would answer the purpose. But, you see, I've already paid out cash. I've settled with that young man's tailor to stop an action, and I've paid his wine-merchant—a tidy bill, sir! All that was before he met Seleucia. Then, sir, he bolts—leaving me and Seleucia stranded. I guess, sir, that young man's got to be found, and he's going to marry Seleucia right away, sir!"

"If you place the case in my hands, Mr. Sprouts, I will do my best to find him," said Herlock Sholmes. "I promise no more than that."

"I guess that's a deal, Mr. Sholmes. You trot that young jay back to be married to Seleucia, and name your figure. I guess, sir, that Ebenezer K. Sprouts will never be short of spondulicks as long as Woodrow Wilson keeps on sending Notes."

And Mr. Sprouts was shown out.

Herlock Sholmes lighted his pipe in a thoughtful way.

"A peculiar case, Jotson!" he remarked. "How would you account for the sudden flight of Lord Stony de Broke on meeting his fiancee?"

I shook my head.

"I cannot account for it, Sholmes. Unless, perhaps, he may have heard a rumour that the American President is no longer too proud to fight; in which case, of course, the Notes will cease to be sent, and Mr. Sprouts' contract will fall through and his huge profits cease."

"That is hardly likely, Jotson. This export of Notes has now grown into a confirmed habit, and it is not likely to cease even when peace breaks out. Probably it will be continued by subsequent Presidents, with an ever-increasing demand upon the resources of the United States for the supply of paper. No; Mr. Sprouts' fortune is secure. It is not that."

"Then what motive, Mr. Sholmes, can the unfortunate young man have had? Although his tailor and his wine-merchant have been paid, there are many other creditors still unsatisfied, so he cannot be supposed to have any objection to the match."

"It is a mystery at present, Jotson, but we shall unravel it. We shall find the fugitive nobleman, and then——"

"You will hand him over to his fiancee?"

Sholmes reflected.

"I shall judge by circumstances," he said. "His lordship may have an explanation to make. We shall see! But now, Jotson, the search begins!"

CHAPTER 2

I need not give the details of the search for the fugitive nobleman. The tale would be too lengthy. Lord Stony de Broke was doing his utmost to keep concealed, Herlock Sholmes was doing his utmost to find him. But the contest was not long; Sholmes was not to be denied. Within a fortnight he called for me in Shaker Street, and I knew by his expression that he had succeeded.

"You have found him, Sholmes?"

He nodded.

"Yes. Come, Jotson. You shall be in at the death, my dear fellow. Not a new experience for you, doctor—what?"

We walked down Shaker Street and turned into Oxford Street. After a walk of some duration Sholmes halted at a public-house.

"We have arrived, Jotson."

"Here, Sholmes?"

"Here," he replied, with a smile. "We shall find his lordship, I fancy, in the billiard-room. You see, my dear fellow, the unfortunate man was thrown quite upon his uppers by mizzling out of his engagement with the American heiress. He was compelled to turn to work to support himself. His training at the public school and the University, Jotson, had fitted him for only one possible profession—that of a billiard-marker. Come!"

I followed Sholmes into the billiard-room. It was untenanted save by the marker. The marker came towards us, and Sholmes fixed his eyes upon the noble, aristocratic features, the striking hooked nose, which, at the first glance to a trained eye, betrayed the young man as a member of the nobility.

"Good-evenin', gentlemen!" said the marker.

"Good-evening, Lord Stony de Broke!" said Herlock Sholmes calmly.

His lordship staggered back.

Then, recovering himself, he grasped a cue and stood at bay.

"You have found me!" he said hoarsely. "Ha? I see here the hand of Ebenezer K. Sprouts! But I will not be taken alive! Let Seleucia Sprouts return whence she came—or let Ebenezer K. seek a blind nobleman to become his son-in-law! Though her dollars were as numerous as President Wilson's Notes, I would not return!"

"Calm yourself!" said Sholmes soothingly. "I am prepared to hear the reason of your flight. I shall not necessarily hand you over to the tender mercies of Seleucia Sprouts. Explain!"

Lord Stony de Broke thrust his hand into his pocket, and drew out a photograph.

"I have her photograph here," he said. "She handed it to me that—that fatal day when I first looked upon her face! I have kept it, and when my courage has failed at the thought of doing honest work for the rest of my days, and I have allowed my mind to linger upon the dollars of Ebenezer K. Sprouts. I have looked at this picture, and have been strengthened. Look at it, Mr. Sholmes—one look will be enough—and you will know why I fled like a madman from the Hotel d'Oof on that fatal day!"

He held up the photograph.

Sholmes sank feebly into a chair as he gazed upon the pictured features of the heiress of Ebenezer K. Sprouts.

"Enough!" he said faintly. "Take it away!"

CHAPTER 3

It was some time before Herlock Sholmes recovered sufficiently to leave the billiard-room, and he leaned heavily upon my arm as we walked home to Shaker Street. Needless to say, he threw up the case, and Lord Stony de Broke remained concealed, in fear and trembling, but safe. A few weeks later a fresh diplomatic crisis in Washington led to an immense increase in the export of Notes, and Ebenezer K. Sprouts was called home to superintend the erection of gigantic new paper mills to meet the Presidential demand. Then—and not till then—was Lord Stony de Broke seen once more by his anxious friends and creditors!

THE MISSING MINISTER

No. 20

It was not generally known that at a certain period of the war Government circles were thrown into a state of consternation and dismay by the disappearance of the great Minister whose firm hand upon the helm had so long guided the ship of State safely through seas of Parliamentary eloquence. His name (deleted by the Censor) is known wherever the art of rhetoric is prized, and even his opponents admit that he had no equal at waiting or at seeing. That the whole Empire was not thrown into dismay and confusion at this crisis was entirely due to my amazing friend, Herlock Sholmes.

Dismay, almost paralysis, had fallen upon this great Minister's colleagues. The fount of eloquence had dried up. The stirring speeches with which he had met the cannon salvoes of the Huns, had ceased. The enemy guns still thundered, but no flow of epoch-making oratory was there to answer them.

Fortunately, Herlock Sholmes was available.

A telegram from the Red Tape Office apprised him of the news. In three seconds he had thrown aside his pipes, buttoned his dressing-gown, thrust a flask of cocaine into his pocket, and was descending the stairs four at a time. I dashed after him, and a taxi bore us at breakneck speed to the Red Tape Office.

All was dismay when we arrived there.

The news had been kept secret, as may be guessed. The Empire, hitherto held together by the eloquence of this great Minister, would have fallen asunder had it known that his stirring voice was stilled. A secretary, in a state of great agitation, met us in the private cabinet of the missing Minister.

"Kindly give us a few details," said Sholmes. "You may speak quite freely before my friend Dr. Jotson."

The secretary passed his hand over his perspiring brow.

"The Minister has disappeared?" Sholmes asked.

"Utterly!"

"When was he last seen!"

"Yesterday afternoon. He was seen leaving his private residence, with a bag of golf-clubs under his arm."

"Golf-clubs?" repeated Sholmes.

"Exactly! Since then he has not been seen or heard of!" the secretary gasped. "It must be foul play! He has vanished. If the news becomes public, I tremble for the results. Three hundred and fifty speeches are due to be made this week, and not one of them can be uttered unless he is found!"

"In what direction was he proceeding when he was last seen?"

"Towards the railway-station."

Herlock Sholmes knitted his brows.

"Foul play?" he murmured. "Perhaps. But it is possible that he may have become intoxicated with the super-abundance of his own verbosity, and in that state may have wandered away."

"It is possible. But what is to be done? We are in your hands, Mr. Sholmes."

Sholmes smiled.

"You are in safe hands," he said. "The secret must be kept. No one outside the Red Tape Office must suspect that the great man has vanished. Rely upon me. I ask but one hour. If he is not found, he must be replaced."

"Replaced!" gasped the secretary.

"Yes, until he is found. But there is no time for words. Leave it to me!"

Leaving the dismayed secretary in a state of astonishment, Sholmes rushed back to the taxi. I followed him in amazement.

"Shaker Street!" he rapped out to the chauffeur.

"We are going home, Sholmes?" I asked.

"No."

"Where, then?"

"To Madame Trousseau's."

I sat amazed. The taxi stopped at Madame Trousseau's, and Herlock Sholmes alighted and rushed into the building. In ten minutes he returned, with a bundle as large as himself, which he placed carefully in the cab.

"Sholmes!" I gasped.

"No time for words now, Jotson! Back to the Red Tape Office, chauffeur, as fast as you can go!"

The taxi whirled through the streets.

At the Red Tape Office Sholmes alighted with the large bundle, leaving me in the cab, too astonished to move.

He returned in a few minutes, his face full of satisfaction.

"Home!" he said.

When we arrived in Shaker Street I expected an explanation, but none was forthcoming. Sholmes was busy. I asked no questions, but I watched him with increasing astonishment.

His first action was to rush to the telephone. Then he paced to and fro in the room, his dressing-gown whisking behind him, his brows corrugated with thought. He muttered to himself as if composing a speech, and I caught detached sentences such as "Wait and see!" and "Everything is proceeding upon the most satisfactory basis, and all depends upon the rigid enforcement of the economy by everyone but myself and my colleagues." And so on.

A little later a man arrived, with a large black bag. In stupefied silence I watched him unpack it, and watched Sholmes as he started work. To my intense amazement, he was making phonograph records.

I retired from the room, wondering—in fact, amazed.

CHAPTER 2

The next day I watched the newspapers anxiously to ascertain whether there had been any leakages of the dread secret.

But there was no hint of it.

The Ministers disappearance remained a secret with the Red Tape Office, Sholmes, and myself. The habits of secrecy long practised by the officials stood them in good stead now. After making for so long deep mysteries of unimportant trifles, they were well fitted to keep this great and tremendous secret.

But my amazement increased at the report of a speech by the very Minister who, I knew, was missing and untraced.

I rubbed my eyes.

But there it was:

"Report of the Great Speech of Mr. —— to a Deputation from the Shylock Shipping Company."

I felt that I was dreaming. Sholmes was watching me across the breakfast-table, with a quiet smile. I held up the paper.

"Sholmes," I gasped, "what does this mean?"

"It means what it says, Jotson?"

"But—but he has disappeared?"

"Exactly!"

"He has not returned?"

"No."

"Yet here is his speech!"

"As you see, my dear Jotson."

"I am amazed, Sholmes!"

"Naturally."

He vouchsafed no further explanation.

On the following day there were the reports of nineteen further epoch-making speeches delivered by the great Minister. The next day there were seventeen more. The Minister was missing, yet he was seen daily by deputations, and his epoch-making speeches reeled off as usual from his august lips. What was the explanation of this?

Whatever was the explanation, the public remained in a state of tranquility. To every salvo of the German guns the usual stirring speech relied; for every shell fired by the enemy a winged word was hurled back by the great Minister. All was going well. Outside the Red Tape Office not the slightest suspicion existed that the great Minister had been spirited away.

Meanwhile Sholmes was busy in the search. But this search for the missing Minister came to a sudden end by the time a fortnight had elapsed. A message arrived from the Red Tape Department, and Sholmes smiled as he read it.

"The Minister is found, Jotson," he remarked carelessly.

"You have found him, Sholmes?"

"At least, I divined his place of retirement, and set the secretary on the track," smiled Sholmes. "Pass the cocaine, Jotson. I think I deserve an extra swig after this."

I passed the cocaine.

CHAPTER 3

Herlock Sholmes took a deep draught of his favourite beverage, and smiled. He could see that I was upon tenterhooks.

"I will not tantalise you, Jotson," he said good-humouredly. "The matter is very simply explained."

"To me all is dark, Sholmes. You have found the missing Minister, yet you have not stirred from Shaker Street! Where was he found?"

"In Scotland."

"Sholmes! And how?"

"You forget the clue, Jotson. Do you not remember that when the Minister disappeared he was seen going towards the railway-station with a bag of golf-clubs? At this period of the year in peace-time, he is accustomed to playing golf. The conclusion, to a trained mind, was obvious. He had forgotten that we were at war, and had started off as usual for golf. My course of action was simple. I caused inquiries to be made at every golf-links in Great Britain. Upon a Scottish links the great Minister was discovered, deeply engrossed in his game, and quite oblivious of the thunder of the German guns, fortunately out of hearing. Reminded of the fact that the war was not yet over, he returned to town immediately—an example of the patriotic self-sacrifice, Jotson, which we have learned to expect from our statesmen."

I nodded. The explanation was simple. I wondered, indeed, that it had not occurred to my own mind.

"That much, Sholmes, I can understand. But during the fortnight of the great Minister's absence, how is it that he has received deputations, made speeches——"

Sholmes smiled.

"That was due to me. You remember our visit to Madame Trousseau's. In that celebrated waxwork establishment there was a life-size figure of the great Minister; you are aware of the perfection to which modern waxworks have been carried, Jotson. This wax figure was installed in the great Minister's cabinet to act as his substitute."

"But the speeches, Sholmes?"

"You saw me making records, Jotson? Really, after your study of my methods you should have guessed! In the cabinet, behind the waxwork Minister, a phonograph was installed, which, when set in motion, reeled off the expected speeches. The speeches were composed by myself on the lines laid down by that great orator, and passed muster excellently, as you have yourself seen in the newspaper reports."

"My dear Sholmes——"

"A simple device," smiled Sholmes, "which kept the public tranquil and saved the whole Empire from the keenest anxiety. It has earned me the undying gratitude of the great Minister. For, as you have observed, everything went on very well during the great man's absence; and on future occasions, when the interest of the State conflict with those of golf, the same device may be used. The Minister has purchased the waxwork figure and the phonograph, and they are permanently installed in the Red Tape Office, to be used as occasion demands. And in the future, Jotson, strange as it may seem, not even I shall be able to guess whether we are being governed by the great Minister or by his waxwork representative!"

THE CLUE OF THE CHANTING CHEESE

No. 21

Clang, clang, clang!

The latest up-to-date telephone arrangement in our room informed me that someone desired a communication with either myself or Sholmes.

"Jotson, my dear fellow," said Sholmes, languidly pushing his shapely feet further up the chimney, "that is our patent telephone-bell ringing."

"Sholmes," I exclaimed, "how——"

"Merely deduction, my dear Jotson," he said modestly. "The telephone is on the table near my elbow, the bell of the telephone, I perceive, is vibrating, and the sound comes from that direction, therefore"—he shrugged his powerful shoulders—"the conclusion is obvious."

Clang, clang, clang, clang!

"It was a wonderful idea of mine, Jotson!" murmured Sholmes dreamily. "Who would have thought of having a church-bell attached to a telephone instead of the commonplace little toy ones which everyone uses? The police would laugh at the idea." He smiled scornfully, and threw a handful of margarine at me to show his contempt for the police force in general.

Clang, clang, clang!

"Ah, the bell is ringing yet, my dear Jotson!" remarked Sholmes, glancing up at the huge church-bell proudly. "Any of my enemies listening outside would never dream that someone was ringing me up on the telephone. Even if they looked in they would probably not notice a church-bell, whereas a telephone——"

Clang, clang, clang!

"The person at the other end seems to be in a hurry, my dear Jotson. Do not look surprised. I deduced that from the number of clangs there are per half-second. In that invaluable penny ready-reckoner you see in the wastepaper-basket——"

Clang, clangty, clang!

"I wonder why they are ringing so hard?" murmured Sholmes, placing his right thumb against his nose and extending his fingers—his usual attitude when thinking deeply.

"Perhaps they want someone to answer the telephone," I ventured.

"An excellent suggestion, Jotson!" exclaimed my friend, jabbing a fork into my ribs approvingly.

He took up the receiver, which was made to represent a grandfather's clock, so as not to attract attention—another of Sholmes' ingenious ideas—and called down.

"Hallo! Did you ring?"

"Is that that idiotic imbecile of a Sholmes speaking?" raved a voice.

"It is," replied Sholmes, raising his hat.

"Don't go out, pothead! I'll be around in a brace of shakes. Infernal mystery to be cleared up. Coming round in my aeroplane. Pip, pip!"

Clang, clang, clang!

The amiable gentleman had rung off.

"I am expecting a visitor—from somewhere in the vicinity of Colney Hatch, I believe," yawned Sholmes, by way of explanation.

A few minutes later there came a crash as the door downstairs was flung open, closely followed by a loud bump and a feminine shriek.

"Our visitor is using violence, and quite possibly strong language," remarked Sholmes.

I could not help giving vent to a gasp of astonishment at this marvellous piece of reasoning on my friend's part.

Before Sholmes had time to utter another chapter, the sound of heavy, hobnailed boots could be distinctly heard ascending the stairs. Even to my untrained ears the sound was evident, but perhaps my study of Sholmes' methods accounted for this.

Sholmes lazily took a pair of handcuffs from behind his ear.

"They may be needed," he said.

A moment later a gentleman burst into the room.

"Take a seat, my dear sir!" said Sholmes, waving his hand towards the coal-scuttle.

Our visitor did not seem to hear. He appeared to be in a rather uneasy frame of mind.

"You are the chap who answered the 'phone, eh?" he inquired.

"I ham! Name, please!" said Sholmes, jotting down on his shirt-cuff the man's size, age, appearance, and bank balance.

"U. R. H. Ump," answered the visitor, lighting a Wild West Woodbine with an imitation five-pound note.

"I am a what?" exclaimed Sholmes, picking up the fender, and wiggling his ears in a warlike manner.

"Uglyface Rottenfizze Harebrayne Ump," repeated the gentleman, stirring the fire with the hobnailed end of his expensive canary-wood walking-stick, and at the same time carefully wiping his boots on the tablecloth, which could boast of never having been washed since Sholmes rescued it from a dustheap. "I am the Marquis of Mudville."

"Please to meet you, m' lord," warbled Sholmes, rubbing his hands together, and purring his satisfaction.

"There is still a chance of keeping the instalments going, my dear Jotson—what!"

"Look here, Sholmes!" began the marquis. "And don't shade your eyes, either. The famous Mudville Emerald has been stolen! It is worth two-and-sixpence-halfpenny if it is worth a penny, which is doubtful. We can't afford such a loss, although we are exceedingly rich—five millions a year or less. My grandmother is dreadfully cut up. She fears that if the thief gets away, the stone will soon be cut up, too! That's a pun!" And he glared round threateningly, raising the teapot aloft, prepared to shy it if we did not appreciate his witty effort.

"Ho, ho, ho!" I bellowed.

"He, he, he!" smiled Sholmes musically. "I will take my fee in advance, if you don't mind, Lord Frump."

"Ump, my name is!" scowled the marquis, handing him a cheque for one shilling.

The fee was not exorbitant, however, as the marquis had nothing but an overdraft at the bank.

"I shall expect you to recover that emerald or leave me the equivalent in your will," snorted the Marquis of Mudville. "You had better make your will before you come to my house to investigate. Ha, ha! You see, I want to be married before the century is out, and I'm rather short of cash."

"I understand," said Sholmes, who was in the same position.

"You know the way to Mudville, I suppose?" growled the marquis. "It's on the outskirts of Mudville. Don't fail to turn up between now and the end of the war. So-long!"

"Hoh reservoir!" returned Sholmes in perfect French, and our client had gone. Sholmes' fountain-pen had gone also.

"Rather an appetising case," commented Sholmes, starting upon his tea, which Mrs. Spudson had just brought in.

He had hardly eaten three pounds of ham, a tin of sardines, a couple of loaves, a jar of jam, a bottle of pickles, and a dozen jam-tarts when a lady was shown into the room.

Sholmes calculated she could boast of being a centenarian, but her modesty intervened.

"Mr. Sholmes," she sobbed. "I am seventeen."

Sholmes nearly swallowed his clay pipe.

"Oh, crikey!" I gasped.

"A sad case!" my friend murmured. He told me afterwards that the good lady had probably lost the flight of time for the last ninety years.

"My name is Emmeline Ayrloome," she said, breaking into a flood of tears which soon covered the floor.

We were compelled to rest our feet on the table, and Sholmes had the pleasure of seeing his new washtub sailing out of the door.

The tears subsided at last, and the lady resumed.

"Mr. Sholmes," she said, in a loud voice, "I have been shamefully treated! I have been the maid-of-all-work at the Marquis Of Mudville's for sixty—ahem!—a year at least, and now I am discharged! Boo-hoo!"

"Hush, Emmeline!" said Sholmes softly.

He had a tender heart had Sholmes, especially where women were concerned.

Miss Ayrloome dried her tears on the tablecloth.

"I will tell you all about the terrible affair," she exclaimed. "My mistress—the grandmother of the terrible marquis—had just received an emerald by parcel-post from Mr. Folstone Fakem, the great diamond dealer of Paste Court. 'Twas he who made the Depaste Diamonds."

"I have heard of him," put in Sholmes. "He was invited to stay at a certain abode in Dartmoor for a couple of years by Yearshard, the magistrate, after having been bowled out by Inspector Pinkeye."

"Yes, that is he," agreed the young lady. "Well, my mistress placed the stone upon the table whilst she swept the floor and washed the crockery—she did not leave the room once, and was sure no one entered—and when she went to the table the stone had gone! She flew out of the room in terror and dismay, and while she was out, I, knowing nothing of the theft, entered the room to tidy it up a little. I had just commenced when in rushed my lady, her grandson, and the butler. They could not find the stone, and the rascally marquis said she must have dropped it and I must have picked it up.

"So I"—she emphasised her statement by breaking a plate over Sholmes' head—"I am accused of the theft, and I have been dismissed!"

Sholmes woke up.

"Pray calm yourself, my dear lady!" he said soothingly, tossing the broken crockery down the back of my neck. "I will go to Mudville immediately, and I am sure my friend Jotson will accompany me."

"Most assuredly!" I replied promptly. A visit to the house of a marquis appealed to my aristocratic instincts.

"I had decided upon going out, whether or no," yawned Sholmes, when our lady client had gone. "I am expecting the gentleman for the instalments any minute now, and unless my deductions are at fault, that is he knocking at the door. Let us depart by the back way, my dear Jotson."

CHAPTER 2

"Here we are, my dear Jotson! This gallant craft will take us across to Mudville, so, as you are paying the fare, we may as well step in."

How Sholmes discovered that I was paying the fare across I am at a loss to imagine. But, as Sholmes had predicted, I did pay, for he had left all his spare change in our room.

"I don't trust that fellow," murmured Sholmes, eyeing the ferryman suspiciously. "Lend me the money. I will pay him."

I handed my friend half-a-crown, the the ferryman gave Sholmes the change. Sholmes counted it carefully and slipped it into his pocket.

"Now, get across as quickly as you can!" my friend ordered.

We were about half-way across when the boat sprang a leak.

The ferryman, by way of encouragement, informed us that the ship would be at the bottom of the ocean in five minutes.

Sholmes, who was a good hand at cheering people up, remarked that the engine might burst at any minute.

And Sholmes, as usual, was right.

I first became aware of the catastrophe when we were about twenty feet in the air, and my head cannoned violently against the learned cranium of Sholmes. Then I felt my ears caught in a vicelike grip, and Sholmes muttered, as he gritted his back teeth:

"Jotson, never mind the weather!
If we die, we die together!"

The next moment we were swimming for our lives in fully four feet of unfiltered water.

After swimming for about a dozen miles by the side of Sholmes, I was almost exhausted. But Sholmes, who had won his third-class swimming certificate at school, adopted the famous overheel stroke, and held me up, and after another score miles or so we reached the shore.

Later we discovered we had been swimming in circles; but as we had no time to waste in language, we entered a neighbouring farmhouse and obtained a change of attire.

The well-knit figure of Sholmes was seen to advantage in the kilts of a Highlander, and he spoke highly of my appearance in the garb of a cowboy.

"We'll visit our friend the marquis now," said Sholmes precisely. "Put on your top-hat, my dear Jotson, and keep this backfire blunderbuss—the wonderful work of the great German inventor, Karl Krackt—within easy reach of your trusty hand."

We reached Owte House, and were greeted profusely by the marquis. Sholmes, however, did not appear to trust him. There also seemed some reason to fear that the marquis did not trust Sholmes.

"This, I presume, is your fat-headed friend and dotty disciple, Shotson?" he said genially, scowling at me the while.

I bowed low. Fortunately the sound of rending cloth from the rear passed unnoticed.

"Have a cigar, Sholmes?" said the marquis, holding out the box to Sholmes.

"Certainly!" replied Sholmes, condescendingly taking a handful.

"A famous and noteworthy brand, these," said the marquis, grinning devilishly. "My butler tried one this morning, and is now seriously ill in bed. They are the wonderful Dan-de-Lion leaf brand. Ever heard of them?"

Sholmes nodded, but I noticed that for some reason, he did not place a couple in his mouth, as was his custom.

The marquis offered me one, but I informed him that liquid refreshment was more in my line. However, I ignored the muddy water he brought me. The bottle I drew from my inside pocket contained something more to my taste.

"I will show you your bed-room now," remarked the marquis. "Stay a moment, thought! I will ring up the undertaker. We may need him to-morrow."

And he chuckled again.

I observed that Sholmes gave the marquis a suspicious look, although I must confess that the time I saw no cause for it.

We passed along a corridor, and suddenly from a passage on the right there came a humming sound, accompanied by the unmistakable odour of antique cheese.

"Don't go down there!" exclaimed the marquis suddenly, catching Sholmes by the hair and me by the collar. "It is only some cheese we have placed in the cellar to asphyxiate the mice!"

He showed us to our bed-room, which contained only one narrow bed.

It was still only afternoon, but the marquis said he liked plenty of sleep, and five o'clock was his bedtime.

"I'm off to bed!" he announced. "I don't suppose you will retire yet. Good-night, or, to be more appropriate, good-bye!"

And, with a brutal guffaw, he left the room.

"I have my suspicions of that man," remarked Sholmes. "The cigars he gave me are the most notorious brand on the market, and the fact that he rang for an undertaker does not suggest real hospitality. I will make a thorough search of this room."

He produced from his pocket a pair of powerful spectacles which he had discovered in the foot of his stocking after hanging it up on Christmas Eve.

He donned them and peered under the bed.

"As I thought, Jotson!" he murmured, drawing from beneath the bed an infernal machine timed to go off at eleven o'clock in the morning. The marquis evidently knew Sholmes' habits. At that hour he would be sound asleep.

The villian had laid his schemes well. Even if we failed to smoke the poisonous cigars, we should go up in unpleasant fragments at 11 a.m. precisely. That was why he summoned an undertaker, so Sholmes deduced.

Sholmes tossed the villainous contrivance out of the window, and looked at me with a smile.

"Let us go downstairs, my dear Jotson," he said. "I have already formed a deduction."

"Sholmes!" I exclaimed. "In this short time, with absolutely nothing to go upon——"

Sholmes held up his hand warningly.

"'Sh, my dear Jotson!" he murmured. "The marquis may hear you, and we don't want him to suspect anything. But I may say, Jotson, in strict confidence, that I suspect him of trying to take our lives. Do not express your admiration in words, Jotson. To a trained, deductive mind, my dear Jotson, that is the obvious conclusion to be derived from the facts."

We descended the stairs, and a sound like the sawing of wood cause me to believe that the scheming marquis was asleep.

"We will now make inquiries in the city," proposed Sholmes, and ten-minutes later found us in the heart of Mudville.

CHAPTER 3

"My questioning will begin at this shop," remarked Sholmes. "I notice they sell cheese, although I cannot see it."

I was aware of the fact, too, although the sense which led him to this conclusion was not as highly trained in me as in the great Sholmes.

That genius entered the establishment.

"One halfpennyworth of Spanish telephones," he ordered briskly.

The old lady handed him the goods and the bill, and as she was rather shortsighted he paid her with a bad halfpenny.

"Has the Marquis of Mudville made any purchases here lately?" asked Sholmes, in mysterious tones.

"Oh, the mad marquis! He gets madder the longer he lives. A few days ago he came for a pennyworth of cheese, and bought the oldest I had in the shop. He said he wanted it as a memento of the days before the Flood. Goodness knows how he keeps it in captivity—I don't. I had to hold it down with a huge anchor-chain and cover it with a thick glass dish."

"Excellent!" murmured Sholmes, rubbing his hands together. "Good-afternoon, my good woman!"

We left the shop, and Sholmes made a bee-line for the establishment of Mr. Popshop, the pawnbroker of Mudville.

Good-afternoon, Mr. Popshop!" greeted Sholmes. "I see you deal in secondhand respirators. Have you sold one to the marquis recently?"

"Yes, the mad marquis bought one, and, as usual, he did not pay for it."

"Let me have one, please."

Sholmes took the respirator, and started to leave the shop.

"Here, I want three shillings for that!" roared the pawnbroker.

"Oh, quite so!" agreed Sholmes, taking the hint and handing the man three halfpennies.

Sholmes hurriedly retired, heedless of any thanks or words of praise the pawnbroker might wish to utter.

"Jotson," said Sholmes, when we were safely within the walls of Owte House, "the marquis is rapidly nearing the end of his tether. To-night will be his downfall."

That night Sholmes, unlike myself, stayed awake.

He did not need much sleep, and if he had, he would not have been able to get it, for I am slightly addicted to snoring.

I slept soundly all night, and during that time the mystery was solved.

When I got down the next morning I was astounded to find Sholmes seated in a chair, and in another chair the marquis, handcuffed.

"No need to ask the usual question, Jotson," he said, on observing me. "I will explain. The odour from the cheese aroused my suspicions in the first place. A piece of cheese which possessed a perfume like that one does is a safe hiding-place for an emerald. To approach it a hero's heart—or a deaf nose—is needed. The question was: How could the thief get at the cheese? I deduced a respirator.

"The marquis and his butler were in league together. The emerald is insured in twenty different companies against theft, and the marquis is heavily in debt; therefore"—he shrugged his shoulders—"he succumbed to the temptation. He deliberately tried to kill the butler by giving him one of these cigars, in order to keep his ill-gotten gains to himself."

"You are the devil himself, Sholmes!" snarled the marquis.

Sholmes did not blush. He had long been proof against compliments.

"He wanted me out of the way as well, for while I lived he felt himself insecure. That is why he asked me to look into the case. But he did not know that thereby he was scaling his own doom! He scuttled the ferryboat, but did not reckon on my marvellous swimming prowess.

"I have called in a vet to the butler, and he is rapidly recovering. He confessed that he was hiding under the table and stole the mistress' emerald, and the marquis here embedded it in the cheese, Miss Ayrloome, as I surmised all along, is innocent.

"The marquis went to bed early last night so that he could remove the emerald from the cheese and disappear. He intended, doubtless, to return when the commotion caused by three deaths—yours, mine, and the butler's—had died down, and to deceive the bungling police with some plausible excuse. Ha! Here is Pinkeye! Take your man, inspector!"

"You excel yourself, my dear Sholmes!" I exclaimed. "But why did the marquis not dispose——"

"Enough!" interrupted Sholmes imperatively. "Pass the cocaine-barrel!"

THE MISSING MOKE

No. 22

I have already referred in these chronicles to the case of the Missing Moke, the masterly handling by which Herlock Sholmes earned my amazing friend the undying gratitude of William Sikes, Esq.

Truly, in few of the cases handled by Sholmes has his genius shone more conspicuously. It has caused a prejudice against my amazing friend to exist in the Knackers' Department of the Pipeclay Office, but to that Sholmes is indifferent. The recover of the much-prized animal brought joy to a humble home, and that was enough for Sholmes.

Mr. William Sikes was shown into our sitting-room at Shaker Street one morning during the early months of the war. He was looking deeply troubled.

"Which I 'ope you'll hexcuse me, Mr. Sholmes," he said, "but I'll take my davy you're the only cove wot can 'elp me in this 'ere fix."

"Pray be seated," said Sholmes. "Let me have a few details. You can speak freely before my friend Dr. Jotson."

"It's about the moke, sir," said Mr. Sikes almost tearfully. "Neddy, I calls 'im. The best friend I've got, sir. He pulls the barrer, and wot I shall do without 'im beats me."

"Your donkey has disappeared?"

"That's it, sir. It 'appened like this 'ere. I'd been on a long round, and I stopped at Slushey. I'd sold all the bananas, and I stopped there for a rest, and I let Neddy loose on the common. When I came out of the Peal o' Bells there was the barrer safe and sound, but Neddy had wanished. 'Igh and low I 'unted for Neddy, sir, but he had wanished. He'd been stolen."

Herlock Sholmes made pencil notes on his cuff.

"Did you observe any suspicious characters in the neighbourhood?"

Mr. Sikes shook his head.

"Not as I knows on, sir. There's a camp, close at 'and, and the gents of the Knackers' Department 'ave their 'eadquarters there. They're there to buy up 'orses for the Knackers' Department, you see."

"The common is an unfrequented spot?"

"Nothin' there exceptin' the 'orses bought up for the Pipeclay Office, Mr. Sholmes. There was lots of them lyin' about till they could be carried away."

"Are the horses still there, Mr. Sikes?"

"No, sir. They've been took into the camp now to be doctored."

"At what time did your moke disappear. Mr. Sikes?"

"Yesterday afternoon, sir."

"H'm!" Herlock Sholmes took a draught of cocaine, and lighted his pipe. "Have you a photograph of the missing animal, Mr. Sikes?"

"'Ere you are, sir. Took on Derby Day a year ago," said Mr. Sikes, with a sigh.

Sholmes glanced scrutinisingly at the photograph. It represented a donkey attached to a barrow in which several ladies and gentlemen were seated. The donkey's head was adorned with flowers, and its forelegs with a pair of somewhat shabby trousers. The photograph had evidently been taken upon a festive occasion.

"I shall know this donkey again," said Herlock Sholmes thoughtfully. "You may leave the case in my hands, Mr. Sikes. Call here again this afternoon, and I may have news for you."

Mr. Sikes left us, and I looked curiously at Herlock Sholmes.

"A strange case, Jotson," he remarked. "I hope we be able to recover the missing moke—what?"

"It does not seem an easy task,' I replied. "There appears to be no clue to the animal's whereabouts."

Sholmes smiled.

"You have heard the details Mr. Sikes gave me, Jotson. You have studied my methods, yet you do not see a clue?"

"I confess I do not, Sholmes. The donkey has undoubtedly been stolen——"

"Very probably."

"I see no clue to the thief, Sholmes."

"A clue to the thief, Jotson, is not so important as a clue to the donkey." said Herlock Sholmes. "It is the missing moke that Mr. Sikes wishes to find."

"True! But I do not see——"

"Neither would Scotland Yard see, if Mr. Sikes had taken the case there," smiled Sholmes. "My dear fellow, the officials of the Knackers' Department of the Pipeclay Office were on the spot buying horses for the troops."

"I do not see the connection, Sholmes."

Herlock Sholmes rose.

"I must leave you now, Jotson. No, don't trouble to come with me. Go and see your patients, my dear fellow."

"You are going——"

"To Slushey——"

"To the common——"

"No; to the headquarters of the buyer for the Pipeclay Office."

Without another word Herlock Sholmes hurried away, leaving me in a state of profound astonishment.

CHAPTER 2

Mr. Sikes returned early in the afternoon, while I was still waiting for Herlock Sholmes.

"Sholmes is still absent," I said. "But you may rely upon my amazing friend, Mr. Sikes. He has had great and varied experience in dealing with asses. His profession had led him into every Government department in the kingdom."

A little later there was a sound of clattering hoofs, and loud cheering came from the street. We rushed to the window.

A crowd had gathered, and we soon saw the reason. Herlock Sholmes had returned. He was mounted upon a donkey, and with that playful humour which was one of the outstanding traits of his remarkable character, he was seated with his face to the tail. His arrival caused intense interest among the more youthful habitues of Shaker Street.

Mr. Sikes gasped.

"Neddy!" he exclaimed.

Mr. Sikes rushed from the room, dropping, unheeded, his clay pipe in his delight.

Sholmes dismounted at the door, and it was pleasant to see the satisfaction in Mr. Sikes' honest, if somewhat grubby, countenance as he led away the moke.

I turned to the door as Sholmes entered smiling.

"Sholmes! You have found the missing moke!"

"So it appears, Jotson," said Sholmes. "Rather a dramatic climax, my dear fellow—what? You know my love of effect."

He rolled the cask of cocaine from the corner, and sank into his chair.

"Sholmes," I exclaimed, "I am amazed!"
"As usual, Jotson!"
"As usual, Sholmes. Before you reduce yourself to a comatose condition, my dear Sholmes, pray explain."
Sholmes smiled, and laid down the hypodermic syringe. He lighted a couple of pipes, and blew out two clouds of smoke.
"My dear Jotson, it was simple—elementary, in fact. Mr. Sikes, as he told us, let loose his donkey on Slushey Common. It was purloined as it fed on the herbage amid the equine wrecks purchased for the Pipeclay Department."
"But how——"
"Consider, my dear Jotson, the probable motive of the thief. Naturally he would wish to dispose of his plunder as quickly as possible, at a profit."
"True. But——"
"For that reason, Jotson, I paid my visit to the office of the Knackers' Department at Slushey. Upon showing my card, I was permitted to look over the horses now undergoing renovation.
"I do not see——"
Herlock Sholmes smiled.
"Among them I found Neddy, as I expected. Having his photograph, I was easily able to identify him, even to the satisfaction of Mr. Evidently Greene, the buyer for the Pipeclay Office. As I suspected, he had been palmed off as a horse upon the professional buyer for the Pipeclay Office."
"Sholmes!"
"Mr. Evidently Greene, of course, is very slightly acquainted with animals; and his vision, too, is somewhat obstructed by his eyeglass," explained Sholmes. "His usual system, in buying a horse for the Pipeclay Department, is to count its legs in order to assure himself that it is a horse. When Neddy was brought to him he followed his usual system, and, having ascertained that there was a leg at each corner, he did not doubt that the animal was a suitable purchase for the Kanckers' Department of the Pipeclay Office. It was with some difficulty that I convinced him that Neddy was, in point of fact, a donkey; and he parted with the animal very unwillingly. However, I gained my point, though I fear," added Sholmes, with a smile, "that after this I shall not be *'persona grata'* at the Pipeclay Office!"

THE VANISHED ALIENS

No. 23

Among the ever-glorious deeds of Sholmes' triumphs, the case which was perhaps of the most vital importance to the British nation was the case of the Vanished Aliens.
The War Office staff were even troubled in their sleep to such an extent that it is said they dreamed we were at war with the Orkney Islands instead of Germany, and our troops were accordingly sent to Inverness under the impression that that town was the capital of the Orkneys!
To such a pass had the state of affairs arrived when the case was placed in Sholmes' hands—at three-thirty precisely on the thirty-fifth of March, nineteen hundred and nineteen.
We were seated in our own rooms in Shaker Street. I was busily making notes on the Affair of the Lost Sardine, and Sholmes was contentedly swigging cocaine by the gallon. He was still wearing his famous well-patched dressing-gown. The door was thrown open suddenly, and an inky boy, very red in the face, with ruffled hair flying in all possible directions, and panting energetically, made us aware that he had entered the room.
Sholmes removed from my shoulder a large and shapely boot, through which five elegant toes were peeping. He took another of the same kind from the fireplace. He turned his head, and gave the boy a piercing look.
"Boy, you have been hurrying!" he said, with his usual miraculous deduction.
The boy started perceptibly.
"Sir, how could you know that?" he gasped.
Sholmes scowled, and filled a bucket with cocaine.
"Deduction!" he grunted, drinking it off at one gulp.
The boy looked surprised, but hurriedly explained his interview with us.
"Mr. Sholmes," he said, "I am the office-boy at the War Office!"
He looked doubtfully at me, probably wondering whether I was a rhinoceros or a chimpanzee.
"You may speak freely before my friend Jotson," said Sholmes airily. "He may be considered in the same light as a gatepost."
The boy, readily believing him, went on:
"There have been heard lately many strange and unaccountable sounds from beneath the office. They are rumbling and gurgling noises, most irritating to the nerves. The staff cannot sleep for them! I remember one of our brightest clerks staying awake for an hour at a stretch, unable to continue his daily sleep. I fear he has insomnia. We despatched one of our most trusty men up here to you in a taxi; but he must have fallen asleep inside, and may now be somewhere in the north of Scotland. Of course, the taximeter will have ticked off a considerable amount by now; but we can easily remedy that by having a tax put on tomatoes or treacle."

"I will look into this case," said Sholmes. "Have you brought my fee? Thanks! Have a swig of cocaine, and get out!"

When the boy had departed, Sholmes walked up and down the room, talking.

"Jotson," he said, speaking between draughts of cocaine, "this is rather a perplexing mystery. I noticed in the 'Daily Dummkopf' during my stay in Germany the day before the war broke out, that the Germans expected the War Office to be attacked somewhere about this date. We must work quickly, Jotson!"

There was a thoughtful silence for some moments.

Then Sholmes began:

"My dear Jot——"

"My dear Sho——"

"Enough! Let us go!"

Once outside, Sholmes started talking again.

"I had read in the paper all about the affair before the boy arrived," he remarked. "He must have taken a few rests on his way to our rooms. The War Office staff, as he said, have been greatly disturbed by these strange sounds. They seem to emanate from beneath the office. The police, understudying my methods, searched the place from which the sounds were not likely to come. The roof has been thoroughly overhauled, and one keen police-inspector even looked up the chimney, but nothing was discovered.

"The sounds seem to come from the cellar, therefore it is hardly likely that anything will be discovered there. Still, that remains a remote possibility.

"It was stated in the papers that two men were heard speaking in German just outside the establishment of another German at the corner of War Office Street.

"Perhaps you are not aware, my dear Jotson, that when two men of foreign appearance are conversing privately with each other in German they are very likely to be of German nationality."

"Is that so, Sholmes?" I exclaimed involuntarily.

"Decidedly so!" said Sholmes, bringing his hand heavily down, by way of emphasis, upon my new top-hat. "I made the discovery during my visit to Germany in the Irrenhaus at which I stayed. What hour have you, Jot?"

Sholmes of late had developed the habit of calling me Jot.

I drew my watch from my pocket.

"Jot," remarked Sholmes, with a smile, "I will tell you the exact time without looking at your watch!"

"Sholmes, are you serious?"

"Of course!" he answered.

I accepted his word without question, though one would not have thought so after looking at his face.

"Well, my dear Jot, it is exactly four o'clock!"

I started, as if stung by a caterpillar.

"Sholmes, without looking at your watch——"

He smiled sadly.

"All that I have to remember my watch by," he murmured, "is a ticket signed by man whom I prefer to designate as an avuncular relative."

I nodded sympathetically. My cigarette-case was in the same hands.

"But how——" I began.

"Oh, the deduction is simple," he said indifferently. A moment ago the bell in the tower yonder pealed forth four times. Did you not hear it, Jot?"

"Yes, now I come to think of it, dear Sholmes, I did."

"But, of course, you did not connect it with anything. For many years—in fact, ever since I was parted from my watch—I have noted that when the bell strikes four times it is four o'clock. When it strikes once, it is one o'clock. When it strikes twelve time it is twelve o'clock, and so forth. A little thinking——"

"Marvellous!" I ejaculated. "Your powers of observation, my dear Sholmes, are tremendous, not to say terrific!"

"What is more," Sholmes continued, "I perceive that the small hand of the clock is pointing to four, and the large to twelve. That also tells me it is four o'clock!"

For not for the first in my chequered career I was amazed.

We walked on, Sholmes resting his elbow on my head, and I making notes in abbreviated shorthand as fast as I could.

Sholmes placed a pipe in either corner of his mouth, and a cigarette between his lips, and commenced to talk again.

"Jotson," he said, stopping a moment to wipe the mud off his boots with my handkerchief, "my spies tell me there have been several disappearances of Germans lately!"

Sholmes had spies everywhere, and confided to me that the majority of them were domiciled at Bedlam.

"There is Herr Zozzidge, the pork-butcher, whose disappearance is as mysterious as the contents of the pork-pies he used to sell. Von Tusch, another wealthy German, has completely disappeared, but I have got a good idea of his whereabouts. There is a secret coal-grate just outside the War Office, Jot,

"I must confess I did not," I admitted.

"The traitors in our midst must have informed the Germans of it. His footprints were traced up to there, but no further. He left his boots on the War Office doorstep, but they were thrown into a dustbin by a policeman. Now, what does this point to?"

"That the boots were worn-out," I ventured.

"It proves," said Sholmes triumphantly, "that the German went down the coal-hole! I have given Scotland Yard this explanation, but Inspector Snooze pooh-poohed the idea, and Chief Constable Snoak had just time to say 'Piffle!' before he fell asleep."

"The police were ever bunglers!" I murmured.

"Herr Popstein, the pawnbroker, who reminds me so clearly of my watch, will shortly disappear, I firmly believe.

And Sholmes' foresight proved correct, for, as we afterwards discovered, Herr Popstein disappeared that day.

"See, that is the place outside of which those two men were heard speaking in German!" indicated Sholmes, pointing with a long and bony forefinger to a huge Empire Sausage manufacturing works controlled by a German gentleman named Herr Blitzen. "We must watch that to-night! The food manufactured there which is now called Empire Sausage, is really German sausage cleverly disguised. The police, of course, know nothing of this valuable clue.

"Herr Blitzen, when going on a journey, invariably travels by means of a Zeppelin. As you know, I have made a great study of the British nation, Jot, and this mode of travelling is not at all natural for a Briton. Now, think carefully, Jot. Have you ever seen an Englishman go from one place to another in a Zeppelin?"

I thought long and hard, my somewhat rusted brains making such a creaking, jarring noise in this unusual exercise as would have disturbed less metallic nerves than those of Herlock Sholmes.

"No, of course not!" I cried at last.

"That minute detail is enough to arouse my suspicions," said Sholmes.

Even then, I must confess that I thought Sholmes was on the wrong track. The police were sure that Herr Blitzen was a most respectable and patriotic Briton, for thousands of people had seen him publicly drop eighteen-pence in the War-box.

And there was nothing to suggest his being a spy, save for the fact that occasionally plans for fortifications and naval constructions were seen protruding from his pockets.

Besides, he was naturalised! What greater proof of patriotism could possibly be required?

Sholmes, however, had formed a deduction, and as that deduction led him to suspect Herr Blitzen, guilty or not guilty, the German must pay the penalty of any crime he may or may not have committed.

Sholmes looked at his nose with one eye and at the setting sun with the other—a sure proof that he was hungry—and addressed me:

"Let us seek a harbourage, Jot, where we can obtain a morsel of something digestible!"

CHAPTER 2

It was common knowledge that Sholmes was acquainted with every street, every house, every person, and, last, but not least, every public-house in London.

We decided to find shelter in some obscure building, for Sholmes was in danger all the while he was out. He was Germany's greatest stumbling block. In fact, the Germans had dropped bombs on both Colney Hatch and Hanwell, in the mistaken assumption that he must be in one of these residences; but luckily he was not, being still at large.

We adjourned to a restaurant, where Sholmes partook of a light repast, consisting merely of a quart of shrimps, a battalion of oysters, an army corps of kippers and bloaters, topped with two or three filleted lobsters. Sholmes firmly believed in moderation in eating.

From the restaurant window, which had no panes, we had a very good view of the War Office.

"Jot," said Sholmes, thoughtfully chewing the head of a bloater, "there are spies everywhere nowadays. Only the other day a person of decidedly foreign appearance was discovered on Maniac Moor, flashing a powerful electric lamp of German design. He repeated; 'Mein Gott!' nineteen times before he arrived at the police station.

"There he explained in the German language that he had been looking for buttercups with the aid of a flash-lamp. He was then, of course, immediately released.

"Personally I believe that man to be a spy in the pay of Germany, and his explanation was merely a clever excuse!"

"Sholmes!" I murmured in expostulation.

"It is common knowledge," went on Sholmes, heedlessly starting on another bloater-head, "that the German Spy Association is willing to pay anyone up to the exorbitant sum of ten shillings per annum to spy upon the War Office for them. They have approached me on the subject!"

"And you refused?" I asked.

"Certainly!" heatedly replied Sholmes, who was patriotic to his finger-tips. "It was not good enough for me! I demanded twelve-and-sixpence per annum; but they would not pay it, so, as a true patriot, I utterly refused to have anything to do with them!"

"Bravo, Sholmes!" I exclaimed. "You share my patriotism! I wish they would ask for my services though!"

Sholmes smiled, and fell asleep, with his head hanging out of the window. I also fell asleep, and rolled under the table, where I dreamed I was making notes on the Case of the Kidnapped Kipper—one of Sholmes' greatest triumphs.

Dusk fell, and still we snored on in a sweet harmony, which had the effect of setting all the dogs in the neighbourhood barking their objections.

Suddenly I was awakened by a dig in the ribs, and had the satisfaction of feeling Sholmes' boot collide forcibly with my left eye.

"Jotson, take up your notebook and write!" I heard Sholmes command. "Mine hour hath come!"

I rose to my feet fearing that the full moon had had its usual effect on Sholmes.

At that moment the old—exceedingly old—clock in the distance struck fifteen times.

"Ten minutes to twelve!" announced Sholmes, "In ten minutes' time it will be midnight!"

Before I had time to applaud this clever piece of deduction, he held up a warning hand.

"Look out of the window, Jot, and tell me what you see!"

I placed my notebook behind my ear and looked keenly out of the window.

"Sho," I exclaimed—when I was excited I always called him Sho—"there are two men outside Herr Blitzen's works! I hear them speaking gutturally to each other in German!"

Sholmes nodded.

"That is what awoke me, Jot." he said. "I knew there must be something wrong, and, as you know, I always look very closely into things that are wrong. You may have noticed me regarding you keenly at times, Jot?"

I said that I had noticed him, and remarked, further, that on several occasions I had observed him looking into a mirror with his usual piercing gaze, sadly shaking his head the while.

"As it is a high jump from this window to the ground, you had better leap first, Jot," he said. "When you reach the ground, lie prostrate, so that I may alight upon you. That may help to break my fall a little."

"An excellent suggestion!" I approved, willingly carrying out his instruction.

"Regardez! The men have received a heavy box from Herr Blitzen!" exclaimed Sholmes, after his leap. "They are making for the War Office. I perceive! We must shadow them!"

Sholmes followed the two men at a respectable distance, and I crawled after Sholmes with a pain in every part of my body.

Still, as Sholmes afterwards agreed, anything, was better than for him to be hurt, for then mystery upon mystery would be left in the hands of the police, and, of course, remain unsolved until Sholmes recovered.

The two suspects stopped abruptly outside the War Office, and in less time than it takes to recite "The Lay of the Last Minstrel" they had disappeared, taking the box with them.

"Now they are trapped!" said Sholmes exultantly.

He drew a mouth-organ from his pocket, and upon it commenced to play what he afterwards told me was a new variant of "The Death of Nelson."

Instantly two thousand Metropolitan Police, headed by Inspector Pinkeye, marched up to discover the cause of the disturbance.

"Follow me, men!" cried Sholmes, donning a policeman's helmet, and keeping in step.

Sholmes located the secret coal-grate, and hopped down the hole out of sight, Inspector Pinkeye did the same, and, one by one, the men followed.

I peered down the hole and had a birds eye-view of all that happened.

"Where does this lead to?" demanded Sholmes, pointing to a rusty iron door in the wall of the coal-cellar.

No one knew.

Guzzling, gurgling, grunting, and rumbling sounds came from within, and Sholmes ordered the men to break open the door.

That was soon done, and a startling scene met the astonished gaze of Inspector Pinkeye and his men.

Sholmes, however, merely smiled. He had anticipated this.

The room was packed with Germans, some of them eating German sausage and drinking lager, and others, snoring loudly on the floor.

Herr Popstein was there, and so were many other rascally Germans with whom Sholmes was acquainted.

They were thrown into the utmost confusion when the police entered.

"At them, men!" came Sholmes' voice from the rear.

"Mein Gott!" gasped a big, blonde German, laying about him with a piece of sauerkraut.

"Mein sauerkraut!" grunted another.

The aliens were soon all captured, and Inspector Pinkeye severely told them to go to the nearest police-station.

The box which the two aliens had been carrying was found to contain innumerable rolls of German sausage—the curse of the age.

When we arrived at our own rooms Sholmes explained the mystery.

"When I learned that rumbling sounds had been heard from beneath the War Office," he said, "I easily deducted that they were caused by German snores. This chief characteristic of a German is his snore, which is almost as loud as your own, Jot."

"Never!" I ejaculated.

"The guzzling sounds were made by the aliens eating and drinking. They wanted food, of course, and the two spies obtained it nightly from Herr Blitzen, who is now under arrest. The Germans' scheme was to band together and attack the War Office in their sleep. The War would then soon be at an end—probably in our favour, I, however, frustrated their villainous scheme, and the police have told them not to do it again!"

Thus, once more had Sholmes' wonderful detective powers come to the rescue of his country, and Germany's latest scheme had ended in smoke!

THE RED TAPE MYSTERY

No. 24

I find on consulting my notes, that at this period of our residence in Shaker Street, Herlock Sholmes was engaged upon three cases of the first importance. First and foremost was the Case of the Premier's Spectacles, which, involving as it does, the State secrets of the deepest import, must be reserved until after the war.

Then, there was the Mystery of the Tinned Tongue, which caused Sholmes to undertake a trip to Chicago, and which his wonderful knowledge of chemistry enabled him to solve. It may truly be said that Sholmes was the only man who had ever succeeded in tracing out the various ingredients used in this product. Then there was the Red Tape Mystery, the solution of which stands as a lasting monument to the perspicacity of my amazing friend.

The case came under his notice immediately after his return from Chicago. Sholmes was somewhat feeble in health at this time. In his keenness to solve the Mystery of the Tinned Tongue, he had not hesitated to taste that curious product of modern American science. Danger never deterred Sholmes. In the course of an investigation his courage was equal to the most crucial test. But his health had naturally suffered from his devotion, and as his medical adviser, I suggested a long rest. But duty called him, and Sholmes was never slow to obey the call. I could not blame him—for the Red Tape Mystery was a case in which the fate of the whole Empire was involved.

Sholmes had been deep in thought for some time, and I had not ventured to interrupt him. He had consumed gallons of cocaine over his usual allowance, and he had let both his pipes go out, which proved that his astonishing brain was working at high pressure.

"It must be there!" he exclaimed at last. "Yet——

"Sholmes!" I remonstrated. "You are not fit really to undertake a new case until you have recovered from the effects of your visit to Chicago."

He made an impatient gesture.

"You do not realise what hangs upon this, Jotson! It is a matter of imperial importance. The whole administration is paralysed until I can discover the clue to the mystery."

"You amaze me, Sholmes! What has happened."

He rose to his feet and paced the room hurriedly, his dressing-gown whisking behind them.

"It is a case of mysterious theft in the Circumlocution Department," he explained. "A quantity of red tape—the whole supply available at the present moment—has been mysteriously abstracted. You are aware, Jotson, of the great importance of the part played by red tape in this war. Without a constant supply of this article the administration cannot move. Every important letter must be tied in red tape before it can be stacked away in a pigeon-hole. Volumes of reports, observations, remarks, annotations, etc., must be bound up in red tape, in order to be forwarded from the Circumlocution Department to the Sealing-Wax Office, and from there to the Pipeclay Department thence again to the Lead-Pencil Office, and again to the Permanent Consideration officials, before they find a final resting-place in the Waste Paper Department. Without the usual supply of red tape nothing can be set in motion. The Germans, of course, are well aware of this, and a German agent is at work."

He paused for a drink.

"For a week past, Jotson, the supply of red tape, as fast as it has arrived at the Circumlocution Department has been abstracted! It is under the charge of an old, experienced official, a gentleman named Slack Karr, who is responsible for it. It is delivered daily, in large quantities, in Mr. Slack Karr's office, and then—it vanishes!"

"Good Heavens, Sholmes!"

"The public, Jotson, unreasonable as the public generally are, complain of slackness on part of the administration. The public, of course, are not in the secret. Deprived of red tape, the officials are helpless, like asses deprived of their thistles. It must be found, Jotson, and I must find it. But where?"

"There is no clue——"

"None! A watch is kept in the Circumlocution Office, and it is impossible that the thief can have escaped with his valuable plunder. Everyone employed there, even German employees, is searched on leaving the building. Not an inch of red tape has been discovered on any of them. The priceless plunder is evidently still within the walls of the Circumlocution Department. But where—where? I have searched the Department, Jotson, and failed to find it."

They swamped the floor, and rose around us in piles.

"You are not in your usual form, Sholmes. The lingering effects of the American tinned tongue——"

"I suppose that is it, Jotson," he said, passing his hand across his brow. "But the mystery must be solved. Everything is at a standstill. Orders for shells cannot be despatched until they are tied in red tape. Directions to commanding officers are accumulating on the desks—impossible to forward to the various fronts till this mystery is solved. It is not too much to say, Jotson, that the fate of this great war hangs trembling in the balance, Come, Jotson!"

I had never seen Sholmes so agitated.

I endeavoured to console him as we walked down Shaker Street, and turned out steps in the direction of Whitehall.

But Sholmes was silent and moody. The mystery which as yet he had been unable to solve, lay heavily upon his mind, and indeed, I could not help realising the terrible importance of the matter. After a long struggle, after so much gallantry by land and sea, was the Empire to be robbed of victory by this base design of the enemy—this last desperate device of the plotters of Berlin? All depended on Herlock Sholmes!

CHAPTER 2

Mr. Slack Karr received us at the Circumlocution Department. He adjusted his glasses and ear-trumpet, and greeted us very cordially, in spite of the fact that we had awakened him from a nap. He acceded to Herlock Sholmes' request to leave us alone in the Bureau, and retired to finish his nap in an adjoining apartment.

"Here, Jotson, we are on the scene of the mystery," said Sholmes, gazing round the Bureau, at the innumerable shelves, wall-cases, and pigeon-holes stacked with important communications. "As you see, the work of the department has been arrested in full time. Thousands of important documents have been tied in red tape and stacked away—but thousands remain to be dealt with, and cannot be touched till this mystery is solved. In this apartment, Jotson, the thefts are committed daily, but where and oh where, Jotson, is the priceless loot?"

I shook my head.

The problem was beyond my powers.

Herlock Sholmes moved restlessly to and fro, It had been proved that it was impossible for the loot to be removed from the Circumlocution Department. On Sholmes' masterly system of reasoning, that the least likely was the most probable, it seemed only natural to conclude that it had been removed, in spite of the impossibility. Yet, though search had been made in the most unlikely places, and even in likely places, no trace of the missing red tape had been found. For once in his amazing career Sholmes seemed at a loss.

But, as every reader of these memoirs will have noted, it was impossible for that amazing brain to be at a loss for long.

A sudden gleam darted into Sholmes' eyes. He was scanning the immense array of pigeon-holes, only half-filled with documents tied with red tape.

"Jotson!" he ejaculated.

"Sholmes!"

He smote his forehead.

"Fool!" he exclaimed. "Jotson, it was the Chicago tinned tongue. I am sure of it. It has affected me more than I supposed, or I should have guessed it before! The loot is here!"

"Here?" I exclaimed, in amazement.

"In this room, Jotson."

"But—the search——"

He smiled.

"There is one portion of this apartment, Jotson, that is safe from research. These thousand of pigeon-holes, in which documents are stacked after being tied in red tape, are never touched by a human hand. Once the documents are stowed away, there is no reason for disturbing them again. The work of the Circumlocution Department finishes there. Jotson look!"

Sholmes dragged out from the pigeon-holes a vast pile of bundles, all neatly tied in red tape. They swamped the floor, and rose around us in piles. There were documents of all kinds, in myriads, which, but for Sholmes, would never have been disturbed till the end of time.

Behind them, in the recesses of the pigeon-holes, should have been empty, dusty space. But the space was filled! With an ejaculation of triumph, Sholmes drew out bale after bale of red tape, which had lain concealed there since the moment when it had been hidden by the cunning thief!

"Jotson! Call Mr. Slack Karr."

I rushed into the adjoining room, and awakened the official.

"Found!" he ejaculated, as he entered the bureau.

"Found!" said Sholmes carelessly. "And I have no doubt, sir, that if a search is made in the rest of the pigeon-holes, some thousands more bales will come to light."

Mr. Slack Karr grasped his hand.

"Mr. Sholmes," he said, his voice trembling with emotion, "you have saved the Empire!"

CHAPTER 3

Herlock Sholmes smiled as we walked homeward. Success had a wonderfully renovating effect upon Sholmes, and he looked fully equal to new. He had recovered at last from the dire effects of his visit to Chicago, and his perilous investigations there. I could not find words to express my admiration. Mr. Slack Karr had not, in his gratitude and relief, over-stated the case. Herlock Sholmes had saved the Empire! Once more abundantly supplied with red tape, all the department were working at full pressure—and even before we had shaken the dust of Whitehall from our feet matters were taking their old course—volumes of reports, observations, minutes, remarks, despatches, annotations, etc., were being tied in red tape, and forwarded from the Circumlocution Department to the Sealing-Wax Office, thence to the Pipeclay Department, to the Lead-Pencil Office, then to the Permanent Consideration officials, to reach their last resting-place in the Waste-Paper Department!

THE CASE OF THE ESCAPED HUN

No. 25

Inspector Pinkeye rushed breathlessly into our room at Shaker Street.

"Sholmes!" he gasped.

We were at breakfast. Herlock Sholmes had carved the kipper generously passing me the tail. Sholmes glanced up carelessly at the excited face of the inspector. Calmness is Sholmes' distinguishing trait. I have seen him face unmoved the man who calls for the instalments on the furniture.

"Calm yourself, my dear Pinkeye," drawled Herlock Sholmes. "Scotland Yard in difficulties again—what?"

"Yes, yes."
Sholmes stirred his tea, helping himself absently to my allowance of sugar.
"Pray give me details, inspector," he said, taking his pipe, and knocking out the ashes upon my chin in the old familiar way that was so delightful in Herlock Sholmes. "You can, of course, speak quite freely before my friend Dr. Jotson. I believe I have mentioned that before."
The inspector sank into a chair.
"Sholmes, you have heard of Von Porkstein——"
"The German who escaped a week ago from the internment camp?" said Sholmes, with a nod.
"Exactly. He has not been recaptured."
"The official police were given the task of hunting him down?" asked Sholmes.
"That is so."
"Then you need not mention that he has not been recaptured," said Herlock Sholmes drily.
"Sholmes, this is a serious matter! The villain has been at large for over a week, and there is simply no clue. We have searched everywhere, but he has vanished into thin air. All his old haunts have been searched. His relatives in Government departments have been questioned. But nothing can be discovered. I have not forgotten how you helped us in the case of the biscuit-tin, Sholmes. Help us again!"
Sholmes thought for a few moments.
"I have several important cases on hand," he remarked. "There is the case of the Purloined Potato, and the mystery of the disappearance of August de Vere's watch after a visit to his uncle. However, I am at your service, Pinkeye.
"Bless you, Sholmes!"
"Von Porkstein was interned in Jollyboys' Hall," explained the inspector. "For some time he appears to have been quite happy there. The rumour that civilian prisoners were to be sent home to Germany appears to have alarmed him. Moreover, since the food regulations have come into force, the allowance of turtle soup has been cut down at Jollyboys' Hall. These two causes, taken together, determined him to escape, from what we can ascertain. The guards appear to have suspected nothing when he telephoned for a taxi-cab. The taxi has been traced, and it is ascertained that Von Porkstein alighted in Trafalgar Square."
"Trafalgar Square!" repeated Sholmes thoughtfully.
"From that moment all trace of him had been lost.
"And what do you deduce from that, my dear Pinkeye?"
The inspector made a despairing gesture.
"Nothing, Mr. Sholmes."
"Trafalgar is very near Whitehall!" he remarked.
"Undoubtedly," said the inspector. "It pleases you to speak slightingly of Scotland Yard, Mr. Sholmes, but I assure you that that fact is known to the police. I myself have been well aware of it for some time."
"You are getting on, Pinkeye," said Sholmes admiringly. "But from this fact, well known to you, as you remark, you deduce nothing?"
"What is there to deduce?"
Sholmes laughed lightly.
But evidently he did not intend to explain. Sholmes' explanations were invariably reserved for my ear alone at the end of the story.
"Come, Mr. Sholmes! Can you help us?" asked the inspector.
"I can."
"My dear Jotson, if you have finished dissecting the tail of the kipper——"
"Certainly!" I replied.
"Then we will go. You have a taxi outside, Pinkeye?"
The inspector started.
"How did you know that, Mr. Sholmes?" he asked, evidently impressed.
"Merely a deduction, my dear fellow," said Herlock Sholmes negligently. "I heard the taxi draw up to the door. I have not heard it drive away. Putting two and two together Pinkeye, I deduce that the taxi is still outside."
"You were always too much for us, Mr. Sholmes," said the inspector, with reluctant admiration. "I admit that you are right."
"Come!" said Sholmes.
We descended the stairs together. Inspector Pinkeye entered the taxi with us. I could see that he was puzzled.
"Whitehall!" said Herlock Sholmes to the taxi-driver.
The taxi buzzed off.
"We are going to Whitehall?" said Inspector Pinkeye.
"Undoubtedly."
"But why?"
"Wait and see, my dear fellow!"
And with that statesman-like reply Herlock Sholmes relapsed into silence.

CHAPTER 2

The taxi drew up at last, and Herlock Sholmes alighted, signing to me to follow. Inspector Pinkeye was left in the cab.

"Follow me, Jotson," said Sholmes.

I followed him, in a perplexed frame of mind.

My astonishment increased as he led me into the Circumlocution Department of the Sealing-Wax Office.

Here reigned a stillness, very pleasant, after the noise of the streets without. The silence was broken only by the sound of deep breathing and an occasional snore.

Officials, stretched comfortably in easy chairs, slumbered peacefully till the time should arrive to leave their offices.

Sholmes passed from apartment to apartment, scanning the features of the slumberers.

"Not here!" I heard him murmur.

"My dear Sholmes——"

"Come, Jotson!"

To my amazement, our steps led us next to the Red-Tape Department. Here the same examination was gone through. One or two officials woke up as Sholmes made his inspection, but they dozed off again as we left.

"Where next, Sholmes?" I asked.

"To the Unanswered Letters Department," said Sholmes.

We proceeded to make a tour of the Unanswered Letters Department, but apparently without result. Sholmes knitted his brows.

"My dear Sholmes——"

"Come, Jotson, there is still the Pipeclay Office!"

We turned our steps in the direction of the Pipeclay Office, and entered the Chin-wag Department.

Here the same aspect of peaceful slumber greeted us.

But suddenly Sholmes gave a start.

"Have you your revolver, Jotson?" he whispered.

"I left it at Shaker Street," I replied.

Sholmes drew a breath of relief.

"Good! Come on!"

He strode towards a bureau, where a stout man with a waxed moustache, was seated. He was devouring a succulent dish of sauer-kraut. I looked at him with some interest, for, although office hours were not yet over, he was wide awake.

Sholmes touched him on the shoulder.

"Kindly come with me, Herr von Porkstein," he said calmly.

The detected villain bounded to his feet.

"Mein Gott!" he ejaculated. "Who vas you?"

"I am Herlock Sholmes."

The German groaned.

"Der game is oop!" he gasped.

The next moment the handcuffs clinked upon his wrists.

CHAPTER 3

Herlock Sholmes smiled expansively as we walked back to Shaker Street, the astounded Pinkeye having taken his prisoner away in the taxi.

I could not contain my impatience.

"Sholmes," I exclaimed, "I am on tenterhooks."

"As usual, Jotson," smiled Sholmes.

"You astound me, Sholmes. You have solved in an hour a case that has baffled the police for a week!" I exclaimed. "Of course, that is not at all unusual. But how did you know that Herr von Porkstein was to be found in the Chin-wag Department of the Pipeclay Office?"

"My dear Jotson, it was perfectly simple—elementary, in fact. Consider the facts of the case. The German had escaped from the internment camp, and it was absolutely necessary for him to find concealment in a spot where his true character would not be suspected. Only a spot where the most guileless simplicity reigned would suit his purpose. What better place, my dear Jotson, could he have chosen than a Government department?"

"True!" I exclaimed.

"Every day, Jotson, some ten thousand new officials are added to those already in existence. Indeed, statistics on the subject prove that if the war should last two years longer, every individual in these islands will be an official at the present rate of increase. Among such numbers the addition of more was certain not to be noticed. The cunning German calculated upon this.

"The fact that he alighted from the taxi-cab in Trafalgar Square was the clue. That given, his whole scheme was clear to me. A few steps carried him to Whitehall, where he vanished from human ken amid hordes of officials. No wonder the police searched for him in vain." Sholmes smiled. "They did not think of looking for him among the seventy-seven thousand officials of the Chin-wag Department."

I gazed at my amazing friend in specchless admiration.

THE CASE OF THE CURRANT BUN

No. 26

I found Herlock Sholmes in a very thoughtful mood when I came down to breakfast in our rooms at Shaker Street.

He was sitting in his usual graceful attitude, with his feet on the mantel-piece, and his hands driven deep into the pockets of his celebrated dressing-gown, which hung in elegant folds about his knees.

"You are busy, Sholmes?" I asked.

He glanced up, and absently knocked the ashes of his pipe out on the back of my neck.

"Yes, Jotson. A curious case. Have you come down to breakfast?"

I nodded.

"From certain facts within my knowledge, Jotson, I deduce that you will have no breakfast this morning," said Sholmes.

I started.

"Sholmes!" I murmured.

"I think you will find it will prove to be so, Jotson."

"From what data, Sholmes, do you draw this very remarkable deduction?" I could not help inquiring.

Sholmes smiled.

"I do not mind explaining, my dear fellow. The food restrictions cause only a certain amount of provender to be placed upon the breakfast-table——"

"True!"

"The portion allotted to me did not satisfy my appetite, Jotson, and I therefore ate your breakfast as well as my own. There is nothing left for you, my dear fellow. To the trained mind the conclusion is obvious. You will have no breakfast this morning."

I could only gaze at my amazing friend in silent admiration. I need not say that Sholmes' deduction proved to be perfectly correct.

"However, to come to more important matters," resumed Sholmes. "A very curious case has been placed in my hands. I am requested to take up the defence of the Honourable Algernon de Smythe, now under arrest for a breach of the Expense-to-the-Realm Act. His guilt appears to be established, but I could not resist the entreaties of Lady Gloxiana Whiffkins, his betrothed. For Lady Gloxiana's sake, I must see what can be done."

Sholmes knitted his brows, and lighted a couple of pipes.

The facts, Jotson are these. Since the appointment of the Muffin Controller, you are aware that it is verboten—I mean forbidden—to consume muffins, crumpets, buns, or doughnuts, without a special permit signed by the Muffin Controller, countersigned by the secretary of the Crumpet Department, and passed for publication by the Censor. Anyone found in possession of a currant bun without this permit, is guilty of a summary offence under Regulation 101,111,888, Section 223,479, Schedule 457,692, of the Expense-to-the-Realm Act. The Hon. Algernon de Smythe was seen by several witnesses in possession of a bun containing, according to the evidence, at least one currant. He was arrested at his dentist's shortly afterwards."

Sholmes paused.

"The case seems to be clear," I remarked. "Does the Hon. Algernon deny the possession of the bun?"

"It was found in his possession, Jotson. The marks of a chisel were found upon the bun itself, and a chisel was discovered in De Smythe's pocket."

I was silent.

I could understand how my friend's tender heart had been moved by the tears and entreaties of the beautiful Lady Gloxiana. But it seemed to me that even Sholmes had been set a task beyond his powers. The guilt of the unhappy young man appeared to be established beyond doubt.

"However, I am not wholly without hope," went on Sholmes. "There are certain peculiar aspects in the case which have escaped the notice of the regular police."

"Naturally!" I said.

"Naturally!" assented Sholmes. "Scotland Yard, as usual, is satisfied with the superficial facts of the case. What strikes you most about the matter, Jotson? Come, let us see with what result you have studied my methods!"

I reflectled deeply.

"The bun must have been an exceedingly stale one, Sholmes," I replied, after a pause.

Sholmes nodded approval.

"You are improving, Jotson. But your reasons?"

"The fact that De Smythe was forced to use a chisel upon it, Sholmes. His object can only have been to dismember the bun."

The Hon. Algernon's Visitors.

"True."

"The circumstances, too, that he was arrested at his dentist's," I went on, encouraged by Sholmes' evident approval. "This seems to my mind, to indicate that he had attempted, in the first place, to dissect the bun in the usual way, with disastrous results to his teeth."

"My dear fellow, you have not studied my methods in vain!" exclaimed Sholmes, "I shall be proud of you, Jotson, if you keep on like this."

Praise from Herlock Sholmes was praise indeed. I could not help purring with satisfaction.

"You have, in fact, hit upon the kernel of the matter," said Sholmes. "Upon the outstanding fact of the staleness of the bun depends De Smythe's chance of acquittal."

"My dear Sholmes!"

"You do not follow me, Jotson?"

"I confess that I do not see the connection."

"Natural enough, my dear fellow," smiled Sholmes. "In the deductions you have already made you have exhausted your mental powers. It would be advisable to give your brain a rest, Jotson."

"My dear Sholmes," I replied, somewhat nettled, "I fail entirely to see how the staleness of the currant bun affects the matter one way or the other."

Sholmes smiled indulgently.

"Upon that circumstance, however, Jotson, depends whether the Hon. Algernon de Smythe is restored to the arms of Lady Gloxiana without a stain upon his character, or whether he is dragged before a stony-hearted magistrate, and sentenced to the maximum penalty of ninepence three-farthings. Come Jotson, I have permission from the Secretary of the Stone-jug Department to visit the Hon. Algernon in his cell. If you can neglect your patients this morning——"

I smiled sadly.

"My patients no longer require my care, Sholmes. The general shortness of cash caused them to dispense with my services for a time, with the result that they recovered from their maladies. I am entirely at your service."

"Then come, my dear fellow!"

A few minutes later a taxi-cab was bearing us away from Shaker Street.

CHAPTER 2

Herlock Sholmes was shown into the cell of the Hon. Algernon de Smythe, and I followed at his heels. The Hon. Algernon rose from his plank bed to greet us. I gazed with silent sympathy at the extensive mouth, the strikingly-hooked nose, the wandering and unmeaning eye, that were so plainly indicative of the most noble descent. The noble youth gave a watery smile as Herlock Sholmes introduced himself. He seemed slightly surprised when Sholmes knocked out the ashes of his pipe upon the bridge of his nose. He was not so well acquainted as myself with Sholmes' somewhat eccentric habits.

"You will kindly give me the details of the case," said Sholmes. "You may speak quite freely before my friend, Dr. Jotson."

"Save me, Mr. Sholmes," said De Smythe hoarsely. "To you, I will tell all. In a moment of reckless indulgence, I purchased a currant bun. It was but the act of a thoughtless youth. At the moment I had forgotten Regulation 101,111,888, Section 223,479, Schedule 457,692, of the Expense-to-the-Realm Act. I was never good at mathematics."

"Where did you purchase the bun?" asked Herlock Sholmes.

"At a railway buffet."

I gazed at my friend inquiringly. It was evident that Sholmes attached the greatest importance to this circumstance. He did not, however, explain.

"Save me!" implored the Hon. Algernon. "If the maximum penalty is inflicted, Mr. Sholmes, it means ruin to an ancient and noble house. Already the financial resources of the De Smythes have been strained to the uttermost by the rise in the price of margarine. Save me!"

"Rely upon me," said Herlock Sholmes reassuringly.

Herlock Sholmes was very thoughtful as we returned to Shaker Street.

But I could see by the glimmer in his eyes, and by the fact that he executed a hornpipe on the doorstep, that he was satisfied with the result of the interview.

He was absent for the rest of the morning, and had not come in at lunchtime. Mrs. Spudson brought in the lunch, and as Sholmes was not present, I decided to dispose of his lunch as well as my own. Following Sholmes' own methods of deduction, I deduced from this that my amazing friend would have no lunch.

Sholmes returned later in the afternoon in great spirits. He smilingly threw his hat at me, and hooked his umbrella upon my left ear, in the playful way I knew so well.

"Success, my dear Jtoson!" he said. "The Hon. Algernon has been restored to his friends and creditors, without a stain upon his character."

"My dear Sholmes! And you——"

"Alone I did it, Jotson."

"But—but you amaze me, Sholmes! You will furnish the usual explanation, of course?"

"Certainly, Jotson. The whole case depended upon the staleness of the bun," Sholmes explained. "The fact that the Hon. Algernon had damaged his teeth upon the bun and attempted to dissect it with a chisel, put me on the track. I elicited from him that he had purchased it at a railway buffet. The rest was simple."

"Sholmes!" I murmured.

"You are aware, my dear Jotson, that Regulation 101,111,888, Section 223,479, Schedule 457,692, of the Expenses-to-the-Realm Act, refers only to muffins, crumpets, buns, and doughnuts, manufactured since August, 1914."

"True!"

"The bun was purchased at a railway buffet. The inference was, therefore, that it was more than three years old," explained Sholmes. "On investigation this proved to be the case. The actual bun purchased by the Hon. Algernon proved to date from the year 1912, as a matter of fact long before the way, Jotson. The purchase does not therefore, come within the scope of the expense-to-the-Realm Act. The Hon. Algernon is therefore cleared, and his marriage with Lady Gloxiana will take place as soon as the necessary seven-and-sixpence can be raised."

"Wonderful!" I ejaculated.

"Merely elementary, my dear Jotson. And now," added Herlock Sholmes, "I will have lunch."

I explained to Sholmes that the lunch had been disposed of, and the deductions I drew from this circumstance. So far as I could see, my deductions were framed absolutely upon his own methods of reasoning. But, from some cause not apparent to me, Sholmes did not seem satisfied.

THE CASE OF THE RUSSIAN REVOLUTION

No. 27

The great part played by my amazing friend, Herlock Sholmes, in the glorious Russian Revolution is not generally not known.

Few, if any, of the newspapers have mentioned the fact the he was in Petrograd the whole time, disguised as an officer of the Prjklmnopqrstuxyz Regiment.

It is time that the facts were given to the public, and that all should know that, but for Sholmes' masterly conduct of the Revolution a weak and tyrannic Tsar might yet be reigning over our noble Ally.

It was some days before the startling outbreak of the revolution that Sholmes came into our rooms at Shaker Street with some slight trace of excitement in his face—usually calm and impassive as a Guy Fawkes mask, which, indeed, it resembled in other respects.

"Are you ready to undertake a journey, Jotson?" he asked.

"Certainly, my dear Sholmes!"

"You can leave your patients for week or so, my dear doctor?"

For one moment I hesitated.

Although I never cared to mention the circumstances to Sholmes, my enthusiastic interest in his cases had caused a somewhat severe strain upon my finances.

During my frequent absences with him on the track of crime, my patients were deprived of my professional care, and but too often I had found on my return that they were so far advanced in recovery as to have no further occasion for my services.

But my hesitation was brief. I would not have refused to follow my amazing friend if it had cost me the whole of my practice.

"I am ready, Sholmes!" I said firmly.

"Good dog, Jotty!" said Sholmes, patting me on the ear in the old, affectionate way I knew so well, and absently abstracting my tobacco-pouch. "Then you shall come with me. We are going abroad, Jotson. Where do you think?"

"I should prefer not to go to Germany at the present moment, Sholmes," I remarked. "But I will follow you, even if you got to Jericho."

"What do you think of Petrograd, Jotson?" smiled Sholmes.

I started.

"The submarines, Sholmes——"

"I hope, Jotson, that you do not think that Hun submarines would stop me?" said Sholmes severely.

"But——"

"Moreover, as we shall go by airship, there will be relatively small danger from German submarines," Sholmes added.

I said no more, and we proceeded to pack. Sholmes took little besides his trusty revolver, a Russian dictionary, and a cask of cocaine.

Ten minutes later there was a tap on the window.

The airship was ready.

A few minutes more, and we were speeding through the clouds.

CHAPTER 2

Petrograd was in a state of fervid excitement when we reached the city.

We alighted in Xzytrkljhadz Street, and walked to the Jubjihgighgug Hotel, where we were to stay.

The streets were crowded with mujiks, droshkys, ukases, vodkas, and samovars. Among them jostled soldiers in the uniforms of the Pbvmzghkz, Xzxzrdg, and Jaklhgfds Regiments.

From the hotel windows we looked out on the surging crowds.

They were shouting:

"Xzdfght! Hjgftyuiolkj! Rtghfdy!"

Sholmes referred to his dictionary.

"There is trouble brewing, Jotson," he remarked. "I deduce that fighting is going on."

"Your reasons, Sholmes?" I asked.

Sholmes smiled.

"You can hear the machine-guns, Jotson?"

"Yes."

"You can see the police charging with bayonets?"

"True."

"You have already observed the fact that there are a large number of dead bodies?"

"Most true."

"To the trained mind, Jotson, the inference is obvious. There is fighting going on."

"Now that you point it out, Sholmes, I see that you are perfectly correct, as, indeed, you always are," I admitted. "I should not have observed it, but undoubtedly you are right."

"I must leave you for the time, Jotson. If you want anything, call out to the samovar. There is also a vodka in attendance."

With a few magic touches of his hands Sholmes disguised himself as a droshky, and disappeared.

I waited anxiously for his return.

The firing was continuous, and from Sholmes' masterly deduction I knew that fighting was proceeding.

Sholmes, as usual, had not acquainted me with his intentions. I did not know what master-stroke required our presence in the city of revolution.

I could only wait and hope for the success of the popular cause, and for the triumph of my amazing friend.

It was twenty-four hours before Sholmes returned to the Jubjibgighgug Hotel.

His return was dramatic.

Loud and enthusiastic shouts drew me to the window. I distinguished the words:

"Bnghfdghj! Hxzsdevb jklhgy, Iolkjhg lojhgfd lazxyrgh!"

"Sholmes!" I exclaimed.

Bore high on the shoulders of the enthusiastic revolutionists, Herlock Sholmes approached.

Among them I recognised many prominent members of the popular party, such as Pabghrfghfski, Fgrtdhsfgoff, and Jkahgrgrski.

Sholmes smiled genially as the enthusiastic Russians set him down.

He made a short speech, which I did not follow, owing to my ignorance of the language, but which I give for the benefit of my readers who are acquainted with Russian.

"Xrghty! Yuioptrew hjkgfy! Thevbno kjhgf ikj jkjhgfd! Uh lkjh ghfds iou. Jk! Jkhgfd rty lkj gh azbnxe!"

The crowd roared applause.

"Xkjhl! Xjkhgfd! Zxbtrj!"

Then Sholmes rejoined me.

"Sholmes," I cried. "you have——"

He smiled in a somewhat bored way.

"The revolution is over, Jotson."

"And you——"

"You are right. It was my work! But let us go. The airship is at the window."

And we went. And from the street below a cheer followed us:

"Xzghf! Xzsdfgh! Jkhg!"

CHAPTER 3

It was not till we were esconced once more in the old rooms at Shaker Street that Sholmes furnished his usual explanation. He seated himself with his accustomed elegance, his feet resting upon the mantelpiece, and helped himself to a liberal draught from the cocaine-cask.

"Sholmes," I exclaimed, "I am on tenterhooks. We arrived in Petrograd to find the city in the throes of revolution, and in twenty-four hours all was calm and bright. How did you affect this, Sholmes?"

Sholmes yawned slightly.

"It was perfectly simple, Jotson. The abdication of the Tsar settled the matter. Disguised as an officer of the Prjklmnopqrstuxyz Regiment, I penetrated to his presence in the palace of Tzarskoe Selo. The despot was at first obdurate. I whispered one sentence in his ear, Jotson, and he turned deadly pale, and his imperial knees knocked together. Then, in an expiring voice, he called for a pen, and signed the deed of abdication. It was done, Jotson!"

"But the words you whispered in his ear, Sholmes, which producCd this remarkable effect?"

"It was but a sentence, Jotson."

"And it was——"

Sholmes shook his head gravely.

"That Jotson, must remain a secret until the end of the war! Pass the cocaine!"

And Sholmes said no more.

THE LAST OF THE POTATOES

No. 28

Herlock Sholmes was looking very thoughtful. I did not venture to interrupt his reflections, but I watched him with keen interest, wondering what great thoughts were stirring in that mighty brain.

He looked up at last, and knocked out his pipe in the sugar-basin. Since the Government assumed control of the sugar supply, we have used the sugar-basin as an ash-try, having no further use for it.

"Another case, Sholmes?" I ventured to inquire.

He nodded.

"Yes, my dear Jotson—a case that will interest you, as you are of an antiquarian taste. Do you remember, Jotson, that before the war there was a vegetable well known in this country called the potato?"

"I have some rememberance of it, Sholmes. I have, however, almost forgotten its appearance," I confessed.

"A succulent vegetable," said Sholmes. "It was introduced into this country in the sixteenth century, and flourished here till quite a late period. In earlier, happier days I have feasted upon it. Ah, Jotson, those were great times! It seems scarcely credible at the present day that a few short years ago one could stroll carelessly down to the greengrocer's, and order potatoes by the pound, or even stone, without being requested to purchase also a trainload of swedes, radishes, turnips, parsnips, and brussels sprouts. Yet such was the case!"

I sighed.

Sholmes' words recalled memories of my own wild youth, when I feasted without restraint upon fried fish and chips in the genteel neighbourhood of the Mile End Road. Fried fish, indeed, I still knew; but where were the chips of other days?

Sholmes echoed my sigh.

"The poet asks, Jotson, where are the roses of yester-year?" he said. "A modern poet should rather ask, where are the potatoes of yester-year? Gone, Jotson—gone from our gaze like a beautiful dream! Since the maximum price was fixed at seven-tenths of a penny for a pound and three-quarters, they have vanished. However, to come to business. You have heard of Messrs. Slipton's, the London firm who have become famous as the possessors of the last potato on the market?"

I nodded.

"Messrs. Slipton's naturally refused to sell the potato," resumed Sholmes. "It drew vast crowds to their establishement, and made their name celebrated throughout the country. War-profiteers, bulging with wealth, drove up in their gilt-edged motor-cars, and offered fabulous sums; but Messrs. Slipton's stood firm. Fair women begged on their knees, society beauties used all the arts of persuasion; but the potato remained in Messrs. Slipton's establishement, guarded night an day by a corps of commissionaires. It was suspected that Messrs. Slipton were waiting for the ultimate removal of the maximum price, when the potato would undoubtedly fetch a larger sum that was raised in the last War Loan!"

"Very probably, Sholmes. It would have been a more patriotic act, however, to present the potato to the British Museum," I remarked.

Sholmes smiled.

"Messrs. Slipton are not likely to part with the prospect of becoming rich beyond the dreams of avarice, Jotson. However, they have now been deprived of this prospect. The potato has been stolen!'

"Good heavens, Sholmes!"

"Naturally, I have been called in," said Sholmes. "The official police were not likely to be entrusted with a matter of so much importance. Jotson, it is up to us to track down that potato!"

"A quite unique case, Sholmes. If you succeed——"

"If!" interjected Sholmes drily.

"I mean, when you succeed, Sholmes, your fame will ring throughout the land! The name of Herlock Sholmes will be associated for ever with that of the last potato existing in this kingdom! My dear Sholmes——"

"Moderate your enthusiasm, my dear fellow," said Sholmes. "The potato is not yet found. Even in case of success, Jotson, I doubt whether I shall allow my masterly conduct of the case to become generally known. In fact, I rather think that in this case I shall hide my light under a bushel!"

"Sholmes!" I protested.

"Enough, Jotson!" I have my reasons. Now for the facts of the case," continued Sholmes. "The person under suspicion is the Duchess of Peckham Rise. It appears that her Grace visited Messrs. Slipton's, and entreated with tears to be allowed to purchase the potato. She offered her diamonds, her ducal coronet, and a 'bus-load of War Bonds in exchange; but Messrs. Slipton were adamant. They might have been tempted to accede to the prayers of the beautiful duchess, but they dared not disregard the ukase of the Vegetable Controller. The duchess wept and pleaded in vain; but after she had departed the potato was missed!"

Sholmes paused.

"Apparently the attention of the guards had strayed, Jotson, and the duchess had boldy purloined the potato. Hardly had the sound of her car died away when the potato was missed; and Messrs. Slipton, in absolute consternation, called me up on the telephone."

"It seems clear, Sholmes. The duchess is the thief!"

"The difficulty in this case, Jotson, is not to find the thief, but to find the potato," explained Sholmes. "That is the crux of the matter. The question arises, did the duchess devour the potato immediately upon her return to her ducal mansion, or is she hoarding it? Ah, there is the taxi!" Sholmes rose. "Come, Jotson!"

I followed Sholmes to the taxi.

"Peckham Rise!" commanded Sholmes.

"Is the potato still in existence?" said Sholmes dreamily. "As Shakespeare remarked of old, Jotson, that is the question! On the one hand, it would be difficult for her Grace to resist the temptation to indulge in an immediate feast. On the other hand, there is the question of the cooking of the potato. Dared she confide it into the hands of her servants? Impossible? Yet to make arrangements for cooking the potato with her own hands in deep secret, must take time, Jotson. That her plans were not laid beforehand is evidenced by her desperate attempt to purchase the potato—in which case it would have been sent to the kitchen staff for treatment in the usual way. No, Jotson! The duchess yielded to the sudden temptation. She purloined the potato; she hurried home with the prize; and at this moment, Jotson, she is scheming to find an opportunity of cooking it unknown to her servants who would immediately betray her if they learned of the theft. Jotson, I trust we shall be in time!"

I felt my heart throb with excitement as the taxi rushed on through the busy streets.

Success or failure might depend upon minutes!

CHAPTER 2

The taxi stopped at last outside a mansion in the most aristocratic quarter of the Peckham Rise.

We were admitted, and waited in an antechamber while Sholmes' name was taken in to the duchess.

I gazed at my amazing friend inquiringly.

That Sholmes had formed a plan for regaining possession of the purloined potato was certain. But the secret was hidden behind that inscrutable smile.

"Jotson," he whispered, "listen to my instructions!"

"Yes, Sholmes."

"When I am shown in to the duchess, you will remain outside the door——"

"Eh?"

"You will allow one minute to elapse, and then you will rush in——"

"Sholmes!"

"And shout 'Fire! fire!'"

"My dear Sholmes——"

I had no time to say more. The footman returned, and we were conducted to the duchess's drawing-room.

Amazed as I was by Sholmes' instructions, I did not dream of disregarding them. Sholmes was shown in, and I remained outside, somewhat to the surprise of the footman, who eyed me suspiciously. Possibly he suspected me of designs upon the umbrellas in the hall.

I saw the duchess rise to greet Sholmes. From the fact that she was deadly pale, and trembled in every limb, Sholmes deduced—as he afterwards explained to me—that she was ill at ease.

Doubtless the name of Herlock Sholmes had roused forebodings in the guilty woman's heart.

"Pray excuse this intrusion, duchess?" said Sholmes, seating himself upon the corner of a table, and resting his feet upon the piano, with the easy well-bred elegance so natural to him when in high society. "I have called——"

The minute had elapsed.

Faithful to my instructions, I threw the door wide open and rushed in.

"Fire! Fire!"

The duchess started to her feet with a cry of affright.

She dashed to the piano, wrenched open the top, and groped down among the wires with a hurried hand.

As she withdrew her hand, Sholmes' grasp closed upon her wrist in a grip of iron.

"I will trouble you for that potato, madam!" drawled Sholmes.

With a despairing cry the duchess fainted.

CHAPTER 3

"Sholmes," I exclaimed, as the taxi bore us away, "explain——"

"Perfectly simple, me dear Jotson." smiled Sholmes. "It was certain, of course, that the duchess would have concealed the purloined potato in some safe recess, secure from search. I calculated, with my usual astuteness, Jotson, that when the cry of 'Fire!' was raised she would rush to the hiding-place, to save at least the one article that was dearer to her than diamonds, coronets, or War Bonds. My anticipations were reliased. The potato was concealed in the wires of the piano, as it proved. She drew it forth to flee into safety with it, and the next moment it was in my hands!"

I gazed at Sholmes in breathless admiration.

"Wonderful!" I ejaculated.

"Not at all, my dear fellow" drawled Sholmes. "Deduction, Jotson, that is all!"

"And we are now going to Messrs. Slipton?" I asked.

"Wrong again, Jotson. We are going to Shaker Street."

"But the potato——"

"Have you never heard the proverb, Jotson, that little boys should not ask question?" said Sholmes.

"True!" I exclaimed.

I said no more.

Of the ultimate fate of the potato I can give no further particulars. That evening, however, we had potato with our supper—an unlooked-for treat, which reminded us vividly of the dear dead days beyond recall. Sholmes had provided this addition to our frugal board; but when I inquired whence he had obtained this supply of the almost forgotten vegetable, he only smiled his inscrutable smile.

ON THE SCENT

No. 29

The case I now deal with was not a triumph for Herlock Sholmes. But this, as I shall show, was entirely due to the incompetence of the official police.

Sholmes had been absent for some days, and I was beginning to wonder what had become of him, when one evening he hurriedly entered our rooms at Shaker Street. He took a hasty swig from the cocaine-cask, and turned to me.

"All goes well, Jotson! I have called for you, my dear fellow, so that you may be in at the death—not a new experience for you, eh, doctor?"

"Not at all," I assented. "But what——"

"I will explain as we go, Jotson. There is no time to lose."

In the old, affectionate manner I knew so well, and which so endeared Herlock Sholmes to those who knew him best, he took me by the ear, and hurried me down the stairs. A taxicab was waiting without, and we entered it. Sholmes rested his boots upon my knees as the cab rolled away, and leaned back thoughtfully.

"A remarkable case, Jotson!" he said dreamily; "very remarkable! But the villain is booked—the dastard is about to be placed under lock and key! That is, if the police do not blunder!"

He shrugged his shoulders.

"My dear Sholmes, who—what——"

"You remember I left you somewhat suddenly last week, Jotson. I was called to the Cheese and Margarine Department, to take up an important case at the request of the Cheese Dictator. Since then I have been on the track. You are aware of the latest order of the Cheese Dictator."

I looked doubtful.

"I am not sure, Sholmes. I make it a rule to commit every new order, regulation, and prohibition to memory, but I confess that since the number has exceeded seven thousand, I am liable to forget a hundred or two. To which order do you refer?"

"Jotson, surely you are aware that cheese may now be purchased only in two pennyworths at a time. Anyone purchasing more than two pennyworth is liable to be imprisoned without the option of a fine; while anyone purchasing less than two pennyworth is liable to be fined without the option of imprisonment."

"True!"

"Well, this order of the Cheese Dictator has been eluded by unpatriotic persons, Jotson, and their heinous conduct has called forth a new order—Number 7157. Unscrupulous persons have been going about from cheesemonger to cheesemonger, purchasing two pennyworth at each place, until in some cases, they have accumulated a secret hoard of nearly a pound of cheese."

"Sholmes!" I exclaimed, in horror.

He smiled sadly.

"Even in war-time, Jotson, and even in our own country, such persons are found. It is incredible, and, therefore, true. You know my methods. Order 7157 forbids any person to have more than two pennyworth of cheese in his or her possession at any one time. Thus, Jotson, the cheese-hoarders are baffled. In short, the Cheese Dictator has compelled them to cheese it."

I made a mental note of the order and the number.

"A certain person, Jotson, has braved Order 7157, but I am on his track. Suspicion fell upon him owing to a powerful aroma which was noticed to linger about his premises in the Clapham Road. The policeman on the beat noticed it, but was put off by an explanation that Mr. Whiffley—the owner of the house—had been using a large quantity of fertilizer in his potato-patch. It could not, however, be concealed. The aroma spread across the street, and reached the nose of a neighbour—a retired cheesemonger. He immediately recognised the familiar scent of gorgonzola, and reported the matter to the Cheese Dictator. The guilt of Mr. Whiffley was, in fact, manifest."

"But, my dear Sholmes——"

"The fact was established, Jotson, that there was gorgonzola in the house. Two pennyworth could not possibly have spread to such a distance so exceedingly powerful an aroma. There was not the slightest doubt that the base, unpatriotic Whiffley had at least a pound of gorgonzola on his premises. A pound; Jotson—a pound of gorgonzola in the third year of the war!"

"Horrible!"

"The police were called in—our old friend Pinkeye." Sholmes smiled. "But you know the police, Jotson. Pinkeye was fobbed off with an explanation that the drains were out of order. Whiffley with fiendish cunning had called in the plumbers to keep up appearances."

"Good heavens, Sholmes!"

"Fortunately the matter was reported to me, and at the request of the Cheese Dictator I investigated the matter. A stroll past Mr. Whiffley's house convinced me that it was indeed gorgonzola that was in question, and that it was not a matter of the drains, as Mr. Whiffley pretended. To the trained nose, Jotson, there is a distinct difference between the aroma of gorgonzola cheese and that of a neglected drainage system."

"I have never observed it, Sholmes, but I have no doubt you are right."

"Quite so, Jotson. Without proof, however, the police were loth to stir in the matter. I cannot help suspecting that Inspector Pinkeye was not unwilling to avoid an encounter with the gorgonzloa at close quarters. It had not occurred to him to use a gas-mask; the police think of nothing. Proof, however, I obtained. I penetrated into the house."

"Splendid!" I exclaimed. "I presume that the house is lighted by gas, and therefore——"

Sholmes replied pityingly.

"The house is lighted by electricity, Jotson. There is no gas."

"Yet you——"

"My dear Jotson, is it necessary for me to explain my methods to you at this time of day? As Mr.

Whiffley does not use gas, he could not possibly be on his guard against the call of a gas-collector. Had I gone with a bill for electric light, he might have been prepared. As it was, I took him completely by surprise."

"Wonderful!"

"I traced the gorgonzola, Jotson, to the pantry. To the trained nose, that was not difficult. I left, convinced that the case was clear, and that nothing remained but to arrest the criminal. There is, however, no time to waste, for it is barely possible that the villian Whiffley suspected that I was not what I appeared, and may have taken the alarm. He might baffle us at the last moment by opening the pantry window, and allowing the gorgonzola to escape. But here we are, Jotson!"

The taxi stopped.

CHAPTER 2

Inspector Pinkeye greeted us warmly. But Herlock Sholmes wasted little time in words. He was undoubtedly on the scent.

"Your men are here, Pinkeye?"

"The house is surrounded," said the inspector. "Every precaution, of course, has been taken to prevent the villain suspecting that he is being watched. Two of my men are in the front garden, concealed behind a hollyhock. Two are in the backyard, carefully hidden in the sanitary dustbin. Three are on the roof. I confess, Mr. Sholmes, that I should not have known how to place them there without exciting remark, but for your suggestion of dropping them from an aeroplane."

"Good!" said Sholmes. "And the chimneys?"

"According to your instructions, Mr. Sholmes, they are sitting on the chimneys. The gorgonzola cannot escape that way."

"My dear Pinkeye, you are improving," said Herlock Sholmes cordially. "You see, Jotson, we cannot afford to take chances. If the gorgonzola should get clear away, the case would fall to the ground as there would be no evidence to convict Whiffley. To judge by the aroma, it is in a very active state, and I suspect that Whiffley keeps it chained in the pantry. You have given your men instructions to use their truncheons if necessary, inspector?"

"Yes, Mr. Sholmes."

"Good! Follow me."

We reached the door of Mr. Whiffley's residence.

Although my nose had not been trained to the same extent as Herlock Sholmes,' the powerful aroma that hung around the premises would have certainly warned me that considerably more than two pennyworth of gorgonzola was kept captive in the house. I confess, however, that I might have been deceived by Whiffley's cunning assertion that the drains were out of order. Sholmes, however, was not deceived.

We gained admittance.

Mr. Whiffley met us with an ill-assumed air of bravado.

"The game is up!" said Herlock Sholmes sternly. "There is your prisoner, Pinkeye. And now for the gorgonzola!"

Crash!

The pantry door flew open.

Sholmes uttered a cry.

"Gone!"

I rushed to his side.

Before our eyes lay a huge dish—empty? The window was wide open! There was no trace of the gorgonzola, save in the scent that hung lovingly about the pantry. Sholmes gritted his teeth, and rushed out of the house.

"Have you seen it?" he shouted.

The police, as usual, had seen nothing.

Sholmes smiled bitterly as he returned.

"You may release your prisoner, Pinkeye." he said curtly. "The gorgonzola has fled. Your men outside allowed it to pass, apparently. Perhaps they were too carefully concealed in the sanitary dustbin," he added sarcastically. "Come, Jotson, we have finished here."

I followed him to the taxi.

Herlock Sholmes' brow was moody as we returned to Shaker Street. I could see that he was disappointed.

"It was ever thus, Jotson!" he said bitterly. "As usual, I worked up the case to a triumphant conclusion, and handed it to the police—and the police, as usual, blundered. the house was surrounded by Pinkeye's men, yet the gorgonzola fled unhindered! The miscreant escapes; my labour has been in vain. And now—shall I receive my cheque from the Cheese Dictator? That is the question. And if I do not, what are we to say, Jotson, to the man when he calls on Saturday for the instalment on the furniture?"

And Sholmes remained plunged in a gloomy reverie from which I did not venture to arouse him.

THE CASE OF THE TEUTON'S TROUSERS

No. 30

During the spring of 1917, Herlock Sholmes was busy upon very many important cases. A Government pledged to efficiency could scarcely fail to avail itself of the services of my amazing friend. To Sholmes was due the discovery of the dastardly plot to assassinate a prominent Minister by introducing ear-wigs into his ear-trumpet. It was Sholmes who tracked down the miscreant afterwards sentenced to ninety-seven years' penal servitude, who was convicted of consuming three sardines upon a fishless day. It was Sholmes' eagle eye that detected the huge hoarding in Trafalgar Square, under the very nose of the Food Controller.

So far as money went, these were prosperous days in Shaker Street. The fees received by Sholmes for solving the mystery of the Substitute Sausage were very considerable. For the first time for many years my amazing friend was able to face without flinching the gentleman who called for the instalments on the furniture.

In my notebook for this period I find many cases of the first importance. Some of these must be held over till the end of the war, but will doubtless be read with the greatest interest by our great-great-grandchildren. There can be no harm, however, in giving here, the details of the celebrated case of the Teuton's Trousers.

The shortage of trousers had been very severely felt, especially during the winter. The matter was however promptly and efficiently taken in hand by the Bags Department, and a Kecks Controller appointed. A trouserless day once a week had been suggested, but the suggestion was dismissed owing to opposition in every part of the kingdom except the Highlands of Scotland. The order of the Kecks Controller, prohibiting the extravagant use of these articles—except in the case of railway trucks—was obeyed promptly by all patriotic citizens. Even the "knuts" of Whitehall cheerfully submitted to a decree which debarred them from renewing their elegant casements till after the close of hostilities. But the pro-German element in our midst was, as usual, busy; and it was soon suspected that these miscreants were making a deliberate attempt to cause a trousers' famine. By this traitorous means, a breach was made in the national defences—in fact, more than one breach; but Herlock Sholmes, as usual, was ready to throw himself into the breaches.

Indeed, it is not too much to say that Sholmes in these days of stress saved the nation from being compelled to resort to the universal use of knickerbockers.

I found him one morning in our sitting-room at Shaker Street, standing before the glass. He was endeavouring to compose his features into an expression of complete vacancy, approaching idiocy. This was not a difficult task for Herlock Sholmes.

He turned to me with a smile.

"A new disguise, Jotson," he remarked.

"What character, Sholmes, do you intend to assume?" I asked.

"That of a Government official, Jotson. In that character I shall be able to keep an eye upon the miscreants without risk of exciting their suspicion."

"True!" I exclaimed.

"I am already on the track, Jotson," said Sholmes. "If you care to accompany me to-day, I have no doubt I shall be able to show you a very interesting denouement."

"I am at your service, Sholmes. I had arranged to attend the funeral of one of my patients, but when duty calls——"

"Exactly, my dear doctor. There is no doubt," continued Sholmes, "that huge quantities of trousers have been bought up and hoarded by pro-Germans, for the sake of causing embarrassment at this critical time. But where are they concealed, Jotson? That is the question." He knitted his brows. "That problem, Jotson, I think I shall be able to solve. But you must be disguised.

With a few magic touches of his hand, he disguised me as a Member of Parliament, and we quitted the house together. We were on the track.

CHAPTER 2

"Hush!" said Sholmes.

I hushed.

Sholmes' eyes gleamed as they were fixed upon a stout gentleman who was walking before us.

His blond face, his expansive smile, and his well-fed appearance, indicated that he was a German:

"Is that the miscreant, Sholmes?" I whispered.

"That, Jotson, is the miscreant."

I felt in my pocket for my revolver.

"Hush, Jotson! We must use strategy," said Sholmes. "He must be shadowed. Take care that he does not observe you."

By the simple process—suggest by Sholmes—of dodging behind one another, we screened ourselves from the miscreant's observation, as we shadowed him.

The fat man entered a tailor's shop.

"Sholmes," I whispered, thrilling with excitement, "he has gone to buy trousers!"

"Undoubtedly."
"We will seize him as he comes forth——" "He may come third or second," said Sholmes, with his usual swift astuteness.
"True!"
"Moreover, as every citizen is allowed two pairs of trousers, Jotson, there is no proof against him so far."
"But——"
"Shut up, Jotson!"
I obeyed my amazing friend's injunction without question.
In a short time the fat Teuton came out of the shop. To my surprise, he was carrying no parcel.
"Sholmes, he has not, after all, purchased trousers——"
"Follow me, Jotson!"
We shadowed the Teuton along the street, keeping out of sight by the same simple device as before.
In a few minutes he entered another tailor's establishment.
When he came out again he was carrying no parcel. I was beginning to feel disappointed with this fruitless quest.
But Sholmes appeared satisfied.
For the third time the fat gentleman disappeared into a tailor's shop.
"Sholmes,' I murmured, "the man is undoubtedly simply looking at the goods, and making no purchases."
Sholmes only smiled his inscrutable smile.
For several hours we shadowed the fat Teuton successfully, and watched him enter tailors's shop after tailor's shop, but on each occasion he came out empty-handed.
At last he hailed a passing taxi.
"Aha!" said Sholmes. "Our friend's morn-expedition is finished. It is time for the denouement, Jotson."
Sholmes uttered a sharp whistle.
Inspector Pinkeye and half a dozen special constables immediately appeared from behind a lamp-post.
"There is your man, inspector!" drawled Sholmes. "Arrest him!"
A moment more and the handcuffs clinked on the wrists of the Teuton. He was bundled into the taxi, and Sholmes followed him, leaving me in profound amazement.

CHAPTER 3

Herlock Sholmes was in great spirits when he returned to Shaker Street, where I was anxiously awaiting him.
"Success, Jotson!" he announced. He laid a bundle on the table. "I have received my fee from the Kecks Controller, Jotson, and we are going to have kippers for supper. Call Mrs. Spudson!
The kippers having been handed over to Mrs. Spudson for treatment, Sholmes sat down, carelessly resting his feet on the back of my neck, and lighted a pipe.
"Ah, you are in your usual state of astonishment, Jotson!" said Herlock Sholmes genially.
"Exactly! So far as I was able to observe, the Teuton made no purchases at the tailors' establishments he visited."
"Yet, you have studied my methods, Jotson."
"True. But——"
"On the contrary, Jotson, at each of the tailors' shops the miscreant purchased a pair of trousers," said Sholmes.
"Yet he came out empty-handed——"
"I did not look at his hands, Jotson."
"You did not, Sholmes?"
"Certainly not! On each occasion that he visited a tailors' shop, Jotson, the scoundrel was a little stouter when he came out."
"I did not observe it, Sholmes."
"Naturally. But to the trained eye, Jotson, there is a distinct difference in the appearance of a man who is wearing a large number of pairs of trousers from that of a man with the usual supply."
"But——"
"The rascal's method was this. Under the order of the Keck's Controller the possession of these articles is limited to two pairs for every citizen. When he purchased trousers he donned the garments upon the spot."
"Sholmes!"
"By representing himself to the tailor as a Dutchman, Jotson, he avoided exciting suspicion. You are aware of the Dutch custom of wearing several pairs of nether garments at the same time?"
"True!"
"Each tailor, utterly unsuspicious of the trick, sold him one pair of trousers," explained Sholmes. "By donning the garments upon the spot, he concealed those he was already wearing, and at the next shop, of course, only his latest purchase was in sight. Jotson, and no fewer than two hundred and

seventy-seven pairs of trousers came to light."

"Sholmes!"

"And this game has been played under the eyes of the official police for a long time," smiled Sholmes. "Inspector Pinkeye would never have noticed the trifling detail that put me on the track—the fact that after each visit to a shop the rascally Teuton's circumference had increased. But it is upon such apparently trifling and unimportant details, Jotson, that the trained mind found its deduction."

"Wonderful!"

"Elementary, my dear Jotson! But here come the kippers!"

THE MISSING MARGARINE

No. 31

I was returning from the funeral of one of my patients when I met Herlock Sholmes on the steps of our house in Shaker Street.

"Just in time, my dear Jotson!" he exclaimed. "Come!"

"I have not had my lunch, Sholmes," I remarked.

"That is all right, my dear doctor—I have had it," said Sholmes, with one of his rare smiles. "Now, as in the well-known case of Mrs. Hubbard, the cupboard is bare. Did you not lunch with the relatives of your late victim—I should say, patient?"

"Unfortunately." I replied sadly, "they did not bury him with ham. But——"

"We may dine with the marquis," remarked Herlock Sholmes, "Come!"

He took me playfully by the ear, and lifted me into the waiting taxi. A moment more, and we were speeding through the streets in a westward direction.

"Where are we going, Sholmes?" I asked.

"To Hammersmith Hall, Jotson. I have been called up on the telephone by the Marquis of Hammersmith," explained Sholmes. "A serious case—a robbery at the Hall."

"The family jewels?" I inquired.

"More serious than that, Jotson. The marchioness' supply of margarine has been purloined."

"Good heavens!"

"Her ladyship is distracted with the loss," said Sholmes. "The marquis urged me to come at once. There may still be some hope of recovering the plunder. Unless it is recovered, he fears for her ladyship's reason. The marquis, who is immensely wealthy, could replace the margarine, but for the recent ordinance of the Grease Controller. As you are aware, Jotson, the purchase of margarine is now restricted to seven-eighths of a pound every three months. Even to obtain that somewhat meagre supply, it is necessary to wait in the margarine-queue for forty-eight hours. You see that the matter is serious—indeed, tragic."

And Sholmes was silent.

My amazing friend did not speak again till we arrived at Hammersmith Hall, and were shown into the library of that palatial residence, where the marquis received us.

His lordship was pale and agitated.

"Than Heaven you have come, Mr. Sholmes!" he exclaimed, grasping my amazing friend's hand. "You may save us yet!"

"Kindly give a few details," said Herlock Sholmes. "You may speak freely before my friend Dr. Jotson."

The marquis sank into a seat.

"There is little to tell, Mr. Sholmes. At twelve o'clock, her ladyship returned home with the margarine, exhausted by her long vigil in the queue outside Messrs. Welshem's establishment. She carried the margarine in her attache case——"

"You are sure that the margarine was there?" interrupted Herlock Sholmes.

"Absolutely! Her ladyship always brings home the margarine in precisely the same manner. I was, naturally, anxious upon the subject, and immediately upon her ladyship's arrival I looked at the margarine—I may say that I feasted my eyes upon it. There is no doubt that it was in the attache case. A moment later I was called away to the telephone, to receive a message from Mrs. Smythe-Porkins, a friend of the marchioness. When I returned to her ladyship the margarine had vanished."

"In what manner?"

"That is the mystery I wish you to solve, Mr. Sholmes. Her ladyship had left the attache case, still containing the margarine, on the dining-table for a few minutes. She returned, she assures me, in three minutes at the most, and that the attache case was still there, but the margarine had disappeared. In those three minutes, Mr. Sholmes, a dastardly thief had purloined the margarine!"

The marquis paused, and wiped his brow with his handkerchief. In spite of his aristocratic reserve and the icy calm that was the stamp of his noble race, he was almost overcome.

Herlock Sholmes pursed his lips thoughfully.

"Lead me to the scene of the crime!" he said abruptly.

We followed the marquis to the dining-room. Upon the vast mahogany table her ladyship's attache case lay. It needed but a glance to ascertain that it was empty, though several glimmering spots betrayed the recent presence of the margarine.

Herlock Sholmes was very busy during the next few minutes.

He examined the polished floor with a microscope, the marquis watching him with hopeful eyes. He then disappeared up the chimney for some time. But when he reappeared in a somewhat sooty condition, he shook his head.

For some time he stood deep in thought.

"You have a clue, Mr. Sholmes?" asked the Marquis of Hammersmith at last.

Herlock Sholmes smiled inscrutably.

"Allons donc! Il fait beau temps! Passez le sel!" he said, dropping into French, as he often did.

The marquis looked perplexed. He could not follow the working of the mighty brain of my amazing friend.

"You were called to the telephone by Mrs. Smythe-Porkins?" asked Sholmes suddenly.

The marquis inclined his head.

"For what purpose?"

"Mrs. Smythe-Porkins proposes to call upon her ladyship this afternoon," explained the marquis. "Doubtless she is aware that we shall be provided with margarine to-day, and proposes to stay to tea."

Sholmes smiled.

"Exactly. It will be necessary for me to be concealed in the drawing-room when Mrs. Smythe-Porkins calls," he remarked.

"As you wish, Mr. Sholmes."

"Not a word to her ladyship," added Herlock Sholmes.

"I am at your orders, Mr. Sholmes, but I do not understand——"

"As a member of the House of Lords, you are not expected to understand anything," explained Sholmes.

"True. It shall be as you desire."

I looked inquiringly at Sholmes. I could see that my amazing friend was on the track; but, diligently as I had studied his methods, I could not guess what thoughts were passing in that tremendous brain.

"You will wait here with his lordship, Jotson," said Sholmes.

"As you will, Sholmes. But——"

But Herlock Sholmes did not stay to listen. It was evident that, engrossed by the strange mystery, he had completely forgotten that I had not lunched.

CHAPTER 2

I waited in the dining-room with the Marquis of Hammersmith for a considerable time. The marquis, nobly as he strove to preserve the wooden impassiveness of his caste, was evidently a prey to deep emotion. He started to his feet in uncontrollable anxiety as Sholmes entered at last.

"Mr. Sholmes," he exclaimed hoarsely, "I can endure the suspense no longer! Have you, or have you not, discovered a clue to the missing margarine?"

Herlock Sholmes smiled.

"Better than that, my dear marquis. I have discovered the margarine."

"Mr. Sholmes!"

His lordship staggered, as Sholmes held out a small packet. A hoarse cry left his lips as he grasped it. There was no doubt—it was the missing margarine!

"Bless you, Mr. Sholmes!" he said brokenly.

We left his lordship still holding the margarine, and gazing at it with ecstatic eyes. I was, as usual, on tenterhooks, and as we stepped into the waiting taxi I could not contain my impatience.

"Sholmes!" I exclaimed, "you amaze me more and more! You have penetrated, in a few hours, this terrible mystery——"

Sholmes yawned.

"Elementary, my dear Jotson. The matter was simple."

"But the thief——"

"There was no thief, Jotson. The margarine had never left Hammersmith Hall. You observed me making my investigations in the dining-room. That the thief had entered by the door or window I knew could not be the case——"

"But how——"

"Have you forgotten my methods, my dear Jotson? It was most likely that a thief would enter by the door or the window. On my usual theory, that the most likely is the least probable, I ruled out the door and window as inadmissable. There remained the chimney. I made a thorough examination of the chimney, and satisfied myself that the thief had not entered by that method of ingress. It was clear, therefore, that the margarine had not been purloined at all, but had been abstracted from the attache case by her ladyship herself."

"Marvellous!"

"Marvellous to you, Jotson, but to a brain like mine, mere child's play," said Sholmes negligently. "It remained to discover her ladyship's motive, and to unearth the hidden margarine. I was aware, Jotson, that her ladyship belonged to a fast, bridge-playing set, of which Mrs. Smythe-Porkins was also a member. That the marchioness had abstracted the margarine, intending to consume it all on her own, and deprive the marquis of his fair share, I did not believe—such conduct would have been unworthy of a member of the British aristocracy, Jotson. I deduced a more deep and desperate motive. For that reason I concealed myself behind a Japanese fan in the drawing-room, and, unseen, watched the interview between the marchioness and Mrs. Smythe-Porkins. A few words were sufficient to prove the correctness of my deductions. The marchioness, deeply in debt to Mrs. Smythe-Porkins for losses at bridge, handed her the packet of margarine in full settlement. Despairing of raising money to pay her debt, she had taken the desperate resolution of parting with the family supply of margarine. One more example, my dear Jotson, of the ravages of the bridge-mania among our upper classes."

He paused.

"The rest was simple, Jotson. At the psychological moment, I stepped from behind the Japanese fan, and seized the margarine. Her ladyship fell upon her knees. I admonished her to confess all to the marquis, who, in the joy of recovering the margarine, would be sure to forgive her. She promised to follow my advice. The rest you know, Jotson. If her ladyship tackles the marquis while the first flush of joy at the recovery of the margarine still exercises its softening effect upon him, I have no doubt that all will be well."

I could only gaze at my amazing friend in the silent admiration.

THE MYSTERY OF THE DUSTBIN

No. 32

Sholmes and I were at lunch in our room at Shaker Street when the door was suddenly thrown open, and a young man rushed excitedly into the room.

"Herlock Sholmes!" he exclaimed breathlessly.

Sholmes, who was about to cut the war-bread, laid down his pickaxe.

"At your service!" he drawled.

"Save me, Mr. Sholmes!"

I gazed at the young man. From the fact that he was gasping for breath, that he had forgotten his hat, and that his eyes were staring wildly, I deduced that he was in a state of excitement. I had not studied the methods of Herlock Sholmes in vain.

"Even now the police are on my track!" he panted. "Inspector Pinkeye is following me as fast as the size of his feet allows. Any moment I may be dragged off to prison, and I am innocent—I swear it!"

"Quite so," said Herlock Sholmes.

"Mr. Sholmes. You believe that I am innocent?"

"I know it," said Sholmes calmly.

"Bless you, Mr. Sholmes! But how did you know it, may I ask?"

"Because the police are on your track," explained Herlock Sholmes. "If you were guilty, that would be an extremely unlikely contingency!"

"True!"

"Kindly give me a few details," said Sholmes reassuringly. "You may speak quite freely before my friend Dr. Jotson!"

"My good name has been threatened by a fearful accusation!" groaned the young man, as he sank into a chair. "Mr. Sholmes, my name is Horatio Smiff, and I live in Peckham! Beloved by my dear Amelia Ann, provided with potatoes from my own allotment, exempted from service because my services are indispensable in the Unanswered Letters Department, my life has been one dream of happiness. The only cloud on the horizon was the emnity of my next-door neighbour, the envious and iniquitous Montgomery Smuggins. He hated me, Mr. Sholmes; he envied my happiness; and Mrs. Smuggins entertained a deadly animosity towards my dear Amelia Ann, whose bonnets were always more fashionable than her own. Now that this terrible blow has fallen, the Smugginses gloat over my misery. I am accused"—his voice faltered—"Mr. Sholmes, I am accused of wasting a winkle, in direct contravention of the fifteenth-millionth regulation of the Preservation-of-Foodstuffs-during-the-Duration-of-the-War-and-the-Prevention-of-Waste-and-Extravagance-in-all-Articles-of-Diet-on-the-part-of-the-Public Act!"

He gasped for breath.

Sholmes' face was very serious now.

"You know the penalty, Mr. Sholmes—imprisonment for a hundred and twenty-five years, without the option of a fine!" resumed Mr. Smiff, in agitated tones. "I am innocent! I swear it! Even in peace-time I have never wasted a winkle! And in war-time, Mr. Sholmes, when the victory of the Allies may depend in the long run on the supply of winkles, only the most degraded criminal could dream of such an act! But the local dustman has discovered a winkle in my sanitary dustbin, and I am lost!"

He covered his face with his hands.

"Courage!" said Herlock Sholmes tranquilly. "The winkle was actually discovered in your dustbin?"

"I cannot deny it. The winkle was there." Mr. Smiff looked at my amazing friend with haggard eyes. "It was there, Mr. Sholmes. As you are aware, the dustmen have now been invested with the powers of the Spanish Inquisition, and it is their chief business to track down those who infringe the regulations of the Preservation-of-Foodstuffs-during-the-Duration-of-the-War-and-the-Prevention-of-Waste-and-Extravagance-on-all-Articles-of-Diet-on-the-part-of-Public Act. The removal of refuse is a seconday consideration. Every dustman is now provided with a microscope, with which he examines the premises in search of cabbage leaves, cherry-stones, or cheese-mites that may have been recklessly thrown away by extravagant householders. And—I cannot deny it—the winkle was in the dustbin! Imagine my feelings, Mr. Sholmes! I was about to start for the office, and had kissed Amelia Ann good-bye at the door, when the dustman, in a voice of thunder, called my attention to the winkle. Distracted with terror, I fled. I thought of you, Mr. Sholmes; you were my only hope. The police were at once on the track! Inspector Pinkeye is close behind me! You alone can save me, Mr. Sholmes, by clearing up the mystery of the winkle!"

There was a heavy step on the stairs. From the fact that the building shook as if in the throes of an earthquake, I deduced that the footsteps were those of a policeman, Inspector Pinkeye strode in.

"Aha! Run to earth!" he ejaculated, as his glance fell upon the shrinking form of Horatio Smiff. "Nothing for you to do here, Mr. Sholmes—what? A clear case—direct contravention of the fifteenth-million regulation of the——"

"Exactly!" interrupted Sholmes. "You need not recite the name of the Act, inspector; life is too short. You are sure of your case?"

The inspector smiled.

"Quite clear, Mr. Sholmes! The winkle found in this man's dustbin is now in the possession of the police. The matter is all the more serious because I have discovered that Mr. Smiff has made no purchases of winkles for a month, which looks as if the winkle has been hoarded. By the recklessly wasteful act of consigning it to the dustbin he had endangered the cause of the Allies, and perhaps rendered vain our efforts to defeat Prussian militarism. If the sun sets of the British Empire, it may be directly due to this man's heinous act in deliberately wasting a winkle!"

The handcuffs clinked on the wrists of Horatio Smiff.

"Herlock Sholmes," said the accused man hoarsely, "I rely upon you! The winkle was not mine; I never wasted it!"

"A likely story!" said the inspector. "Come my man! You can tell that yarn to the magistrate!"

And the unhappy culprit was led away.

CHAPTER 2

Herlock Sholmes was silent and thoughtful for some time. In an absent-minded way he chopped at the war-bread, causing splinters to fly off in various directions. At last he rose.

Come, Jotson!" he said. "We must see into this! Horatio Smiff is innocent, and while he is detained by the unthinking police the national cause suffers. You heard him remark he is employed in the Unanswered Letters Department. In his absence from his post letters may be recklessly answered by someone new to the work. Heaven only knows what the result might be!"

"Let us not lose a moment, Sholmes!" I exclaimed anxiously.

We lost no time. In an hour we were at Laburnum Villa. We found Mrs. Smiff in tears. The prospect of being separated from her beloved Horatio for a period of a hundred and twenty-five years had completely overcome her. Sholmes comforted the poor woman as best he could, and then we proceeded to make an examination of the sanitary dustbin.

I watched Sholmes' actions with keen interest. Deeply as I had studied his wonderful methods, there was always something new to be learned from Herlock Sholmes.

His eyes gleamed under his knitted brows as he sounded the dustbin with a stethoscope. He then produced a microscope, and examined the fence which separated Mr. Smiff's garden from that of his neighbour, Mr. Smuggins.

"Sholmes!" I exclaimed at last.

He yawned.

"Come, Jotson!"

We left the garden.

"Where are we going, Sholmes?"

"To call upon Mr. Smuggins, Jotson!"

"You desire to see Montgomery Smuggins?"

"Not at all. The whole case hangs, Jotson, upon Mr. Smuggins' trousers. If he wears grey trousers, Horatio Smiff will be restored to the bosom of his family. If his trousers are of any other colour, Jotson, the unhappy Smiff will be consigned to the company of Suffragettes and conscientious objectors for a period not exceeding a hundred and twenty-five years!"

"Good heavens, Sholmes!"

My amazing friend knocked at Mr. Smuggins' door.

It was opened by that gentleman himself.

"Mr. Smuggins?" asked Herlock Sholmes genially.

"Yes."

"Thank-you! Good-afternoon!"

Sholmes walked promptly away, possibly leaving Mr. Smuggins in a state of some surprise. He smiled as we stepped into the taxi.

"You noticed his trousers, Jotson?"

"They were grey, Sholmes."
"Exactly. Justice will be done!"
We stopped at a post-office, where Herlock Sholmes used the telephone. Then we returned to Shaker Street.
An hour later I was surprised to see Horatio Smiff enter. He grasped Herlock Sholmes' hand with deep emotion.
"Mr. Sholmes, you have saved me! How can I thank you?"
Sholmes smiled.
"By returning at once, Mr. Smiff, to your duties at the Unanswered Letters Department!" he replied. "Lose no time!" In your absence important letters may be answered!"
"True!"
And Horatio Smiff dashed away.

CHAPTER 3

"Sholmes!" I exclaimed, in amazement.
"Well, Jotson!"
"I am astounded——"
"Naturally," said Herlock Sholmes, with a smile. "But it was very simple, Jotson. Having ascertained the facts during our visit to Laburnum Villa, I telephoned the result to Inspector Pinkeye. Mr. Smiff was accordingly released, and Montgomery Smuggins has taken his place, on the charge of conspiracy!"
"Montgomery Smuggins?"
"Precisely!"
"Then he was guilty!"
"Evidently, Jotson!"
"You astound me, Sholmes! How did you discover——"
"My dear Jotson, the matter was simple—elementary, in fact. The winkle was placed in Mr. Smiff's sanitary dustbin by a felon hand. It was placed there to be discovered by the dustman when making his round. You observed me making an examination of the garden fence?"
"True!"
"Upon the palings, Jotson, was a fragment of grey rag, evidently torn from a pair of trousers worn by a person engaged in surreptitiously climbing over the garden fence. The case was clear. In the dead of night Horatio Smiff's enemy had climbed the fence, and deposited the winkle in the dustbin. It only remained to interview Montgomery Smuggins, and ascertain the colour of his trousers. Had this clue failed me, there were seventy-seven other details, Jotson, which I need not enumerate, which would have provided me with fresh clues. But, as a matter of fact, the matter was settled at once. Mr. Smuggins wore grey trousers!"
"Marvellous!"
"Not at all, Jotson. Elementary!"
"But suppose, Sholmes," I remarked, after some thought—"suppose—what if Mr. Smuggins had changed his trousers?"
But Herlock Sholmes was busy sharpening a saw, preparatory to an attack on the war-bread, and he did not reply.

THE CASE OF THE AMERICAN CLOCK

No. 33

Herlock Sholmes was pacing to and fro in our sitting-room at Shaker Street, the folds of his dressing-gown whisking behind him as he moved.
His face was deeply corrugated with thought. He was smoking several cigarettes at once—a sign of the deep concentration of that powerful brain.
I did not venture to interrupt his thoughts.
I knew that some terrific problem was exercising his mind, and only feared lest, perchance, something should crack under the strain.
He turned to me at last.
"Ah, you are there, Jotson?"
"I am here, my dear Sholmes. Can I be of any use?"
Sholmes smiled.
"It is scarcely likely, Jotson, that your tenth-rate brain would be able to grapple with a problem that baffles mine."
"True!"
"But I will tell you the facts, Jotson. My services have been enlisted for the defence of Adolphus de Jones, nephew and heir of the Duke of Shepherd's Bush. You have heard of the attempt upon the life of his Grace?"

I nodded.

I had read in the newspapers of the attempt, and of the arrest of Adolphus de Jones on the charge of firing the almost fatal shot. His prompt arrest at a cinema within a few hours of the crime was a triumph of Inspector Pinkeye of Scotland Yard.

"The noble family of De Jones, Jotson, have begged me to take up the case and prove the innocence of Adolphus. Yet——"

"The evidence seems clear, Sholmes," I remarked. "Inspector Pinkeye has no doubt of his guilt."

"Exactly! And for that reason, Jotson, I entertain a hope that the unhappy young man may be innocent. The facts are these: On the evening preceding the crime De Jones visited his uncle, requesting the loan of sixpence to pay for admission at the local cinema. This the duke refused. High words followed, and the duke's butler bears witness that De Jones addressed his elderly relative as an 'old Hun.' Owing to the key being in the keyhole, he was unable to hear more. They parted in anger. De Jones denies this, asserting that he was simply calling his uncle 'old 'un,' an affectionate title he bore in the family circle.

"In the small hours of the morning the duke was discovered upon the floor, the servants having been aroused by the sound of a pistol-shot. The window was open. The bullet had glanced from the duke's head, and struck the clock on the mantelpiece, which was stopped at exactly half-past twelve. His grace, fortunately, was not seriously injured, and was immediately attended by his panel doctor; but he has not yet recovered consciousness. His evidence, therefore, cannot be taken.

"Inspector Pinkeye was called in at once, and early in the morning he arrested Adolphus de Jones at the neighbouring cinema palace, where he was attending the first performance of the day. De Jones had paid sixpence for admission, and it was proved that sixpence was missing from the duke's supply of cash, the duchess testifying that, to her knowledge, his Grace had had three-and-ninepence in his possession the previous day, of which only three-and-threepence was found upon his unconscious form."

Sholmes paused to refresh himself with swig of cocaine from the cask. He struck a match upon my left ear, lighted his pipe, and resumed:

"According to De Jones' statement, the duke handed him the sixpence after considerable demur, and he had parted from his relative on amicable terms. The stopping of the clock fixed the hour of the crime. Where was Adolphus de Jones at half-past twelve? Friends testified that at twelve o'clock they saw him outside the Red Lion trying to induce the landlord to open and serve him. This the landlord refused to do, and De Jones went away to seek to quench his thirst elsewhere. At a quarter to one he entered his lodgings in Smiff Street. But from twelve to a quarter to one, Jotson, he cannot account for his movements; and that was the period in which the crime was was committed."

I was silent.

"The stopping of the clock by the bullet, Jotson, is the fatal circumstance in the case. At first I considered whether perhaps it was Inspector Pinkeye's face that had stopped the clock. This theory is excluded, however, by the evidence of the servants, who testify positively that the clock was stopped before the inspector's arrival. According to De Jones, he spent the time from twelve till a quarter to one in visiting a succession of places of refreshment in the hope of finding one open; in which he failed. This, however, he cannot prove. If the clock had been stopped at twelve, or at one, he would be cleared. But——"

Sholmes knocked out his pipe on the bridge of my nose in his absent-minded way.

"What do you think, Jotson?"

"I think that the young man's guilt is established, Sholmes."

"You feel sure of that?"

"Absolutely!"

"You encourage me, Jotson."

"Ah! Then you agree with my deduction, Sholmes?" I asked, somewhat flattered.

"Not at all, my dear Jotson. If you think the young man is guilty, the probability is that he is innocent!"

"Sholmes!"

"You must take into account, my dear fellow, the fact that you are very obtuse—in fact, wooden-headed!"

"True!"

Sholmes rubbed his hands.

"We may learn more upon the scene of the crime, Jotson," he remarked. "Come! At Shepherd's Bush Hall we may get on the track."

A minute later and we were on our way.

CHAPTER 2

There was a hushed silence in Shepherd's Bush Hall when we arrived.

The duke still lay unconscious in his bed-chamber.

The butler showed us to the library, the apartment where the attempted crime had taken place.

I noticed that Sholmes scanned the butler's face intently, and sounded him with a stethoscope, and took careful measurements of his feet with a tape-measure. The butler, I am convinced, noticed it also.

"Ah!" he ejaculated.
"Sholmes!" I murmured.
"Look at the clock dial, Jotson."
I looked.
"What do you see there?" he asked.
"Merely an inscription, Sholmes, to the effect that the clock was made in New York," I replied.
"I will wager you, Jotson, that Inspector Pinkeye never thought of noting that clue!"
I gazed at my amazing friend in astonishment.
"But, Sholmes——"
"Ring off, my dear Jotson!"
And I was silent.
I could see by Herlock Sholmes' expression that he was in a satisfied mood as we returned to Shaker Street. He executed several double-shuffles as he walked along, an infallible sign that he was satisfied with the progress of his case.
At Shaker Street he left me, and did not return for several hours.
I regarded him anxiously as he came in.
As he cake-walked into the room I could see that he was in a triumphant mood. He hooked his umbrella on my ear in the kind, playful way I knew so well.
"Sholmes," I exclaimed, "you have succeeded?"
"Need you ask, Jotson?"
"True! But——"
"I fear that I have disappointed our friend Pinkeye," said Herlock Sholmes, with a smile.
"De Jones——"
"He is free as air. His alibi is proved."
"But how——"
"My dear Jotson, it was perfectly simple. Inspector Pinkeye had noted the fact that the clock was stopped at half-past twelve. He had not, however, noted the fact that it was an American clock. If a clock of American manufacture, my dear Jotson, indicates the hour of half-past twelve, the inference is that it is twelve o'clock, or one o'clock, or any hour you please excepting half-past twelve o'clock.
"Most true!" I exclaimed.
"It is certain, therefore, that whatever time it may have been when the bullet struck the clock, it was not half-past twelve, resumed Sholmes. "As De Jones was able to account for every hour of the night excepting half-past twelve, it follows that his alibi is incontestable. Inspector Pinkeye was not willing to part with his prisoner, but he could not resist the evidence. De Jones was released."
"Wonderful!"
"However, I have compensated our friend Pinkeye," yawned Herlock Sholmes. "I have examined the duke's will, Jotson, and find that he left the sum of twelve shilling and sixpence and his old trousers to his butler. This supplies a motive for the crime. There were footprints in the garden—and you saw me measure the butler's feet, Jotson. The footprints were sixes in size; the butler's boots were eights. This was conclusive. Of course, he had changed his boots. Had his boots been the same size as the footprints, his guilt would have been so probable that I should have dismissed it as impossible. But the size was different——"
"Amazing!"
"Merely elementary, my dear fellow. I left Pinkeye on his way to Shepherd's Bush to arrest the butler. I have received my fee from De Jones' grateful family, Jotson, and this evening"—he gave me one of his rare pokes in the ribs—"this evening, Jotson, we shall have tripe for supper!"

THE CASE OF THE HIDDEN HUN

No. 34

Buzzzzzz!
With a bored look Herlock Sholmes took up the receiver.
He made me a sign to be silent, and I laid down the breakfast loaf and the pickaxe.
From the fact that he ejaculated "Oh, jiminy! Strike me pink!" I concluded that Sholmes was receiving a startling communication over the wires.
I was right.
He laid down the receiver at last, and turned to me with a grave expression upon his face.
"A serious matter, Sholmes?" I ventured to ask.
"Very serious, Jotson. The call was from the Red Tape Department of the Circumlocution Office. Fortunately, I shall be able to deal with the matter—perhaps sooner than they think at the Red Tape Department." He smiled. "The Baron Pikkald Unyunz is in England, Jotson."
I started.
"The German diplomatist, Sholmes?"
"The same!"
"Good heavens!"

I gazed at Herlock Sholmes in amazement and consternation.

Wherever German intrigue and treachery had been at work—that is to say, in every corner of the earth from Peru to Peckham Rye—the name of Pikkald Unyunz was known.

"In England, Sholmes?" I faltered.

"Such is my information from the Red Tape Department. They have just learned of it."

"How long has he been in the country, Sholmes?"

"From the fact that the Red Tape Department has just learned of his presence, Jotson, I deduce that he has been here a considerable time."

"No doubt," I assented. "He must be in disguise, Sholmes."

"Probably. However, he will be run to earth. His business here, Jotson, is to confer with the pro-Germans, and perhaps to cause a rising of the German bakers."

"Sholmes!"

"Some such scheme, Jotson, is undoubtedly working in that cunning brain. If the plot should be a success, think of the result. London, perhaps, suddenly attacked in the dead of night by hordes of ferocious bakers and confectioners, aided by the savage, untamed Conscientious Objector!"

I shuddered.

"However, I am here! said Sholmes reassuringly.

I breathed again.

After all, with Herlock Sholmes upon the spot, even the machinations of the Baron Pikkald Unyunz, cunning as he was, would be foiled, diddled, dished, and done.

"I am requested," drawled Sholmes, "to track down the scoundrel. The official police, of course, are useless. The villain's presence is known—that is all. Already he has been at work. I have not the slightest doubt that he was at the bottom of the recent plot to assassinate the Secretary of the Chinwag Office by putting war-bread into his soup, Jotson. He has attempted to tamper with Labour—with the engineer and the engine there!"

"Good heavens!"

"He is at the bottom of the war-profiteering which has caused so much unrest," continued Sholmes. "But for German intrigue, Jotson, no one would think of charging more for his goods that they are actually worth."

"I am sure of it, Sholmes. Let us start at once!" I exclaimed, springing to my feet. "Do not let the foul Hun remain at liberty a moment longer!"

"Back pedal, my dear fellow!" drawled Sholmes. "He has to be found before he can be arrested."

"True!" I exclaimed.

"However, I have a clue."

I gazed at Sholmes in amazement.

"But it is only a few minutes, Sholmes since you learned that the Baron Pikkald Unyunz was in this country at all."

Sholmes shrugged his shoulders carelessly.

"Excuse me, Sholmes," I said. "I should not be surprised at anything you say, knowing you as I do. I had forgotten, for the moment, the remarkable powers of your terrific non-stop brain. But the clue?"

"Hand me the 'Chronic Daily,' Jotson."

I passed the newspaper to Herlock Sholmes.

"With the assistance of this journal, Jotson, I hope to track the villain down," observed Sholmes.

"My dear Sholmes!" I murmured.

"You do not see how, Jotson?"

"Surely, Sholmes, a German diplomatist cannot be laid low, like a house-fly, by means of a newspaper!" I exclaimed.

"That is not my method, Jotson. Listen!"

Sholmes read aloud a paragraph from the 'Chronic Daily.'

It ran:

"'A state of considerable alarm exists in the neighbourhood of Snooker Street. For a considerable time past strange and unearthly odours have been noticed in this quarter. The drainage system has been completely overhauled, but the evil cannot be traced to this source. It is a mystery which baffles the sanitary authorities, and occupants of the houses are beginning to move away. There have been as yet no deaths, but illness is prevalent, evidently owing to the strange and terrible scent which pervades the vicinity. The medical profession is quite at a loss.'"

I listened in silence.

As a medical man, I was interested in the peculiar case reported in the "Chronic Daily." But I failed to see any connection between the epidemic of strange odours in Snooker Street and the secret mission of the Hun intriguer.

Sholmes laid down the paper.

"An interesting matter, Jotson!" he remarked.

"Extremely so," I replied.

"As a medical man, Jotson, to what would you attribute this strange and apparently unaccountable outbreak of weird smells in the Snooker Street district?"

I shook my head.

"Unless someone in the neighbourhood has been hoarding Chicago beef, Sholmes, and has carelessly allowed it to escape from the tins, I cannot account for it."

"Well, we shall see!" remarked Sholmes, with his inscrutable smile. "Come!"

"Where are we going, Sholmes?"

"To Snooker Street."

"But the German diplomatist!" I exclaimed. "Surely, Sholmes, the first business in hand is to track down the iniquitous Pikkald Unyunz!"

"Wait and see!" replied Sholmes.

He took me gently by the nose and led me from the room.

CHAPTER 2

I was amazed.

This, however, was my usual state when engaged with Herlock Sholmes upon one of his remarkable cases. I was, therefore, becoming accustomed to it.

We took the motor-'bus at the corner of Shaker Street. Here Herlock Sholmes' well-known skill as a boxer was very useful. After a successful engagement we boarded the motor-'bus, and were carried away in the direction of Snooker Street.

"Here we are, Jotson," said Sholmes, at last, when the 'bus stopped, and we alighted, fighting our way shoulder to shoulder to the pavement.

As we walked down Snooker Street, we became aware of the strange and terrible odour described in the "Chronic Daily,"

Sholmes sniffed at it, and nodded, as if satisfied.

"You notice it, Jotson?" he inquired.

"It is terrible, Sholmes!"

"Like many fearful things, Jotson, it may served a useful purpose."

"Sholmes," I murmured faintly, "why are we here? I feel that I shall be overcome—I am not so strong as I once was. I have never smelt anything so terrible as this, since I was in a German restaurant in Hamburg before the war."

"Exactly!" said Sholmes. "Follow the scent with me, Jotson, and when we have ascertained where it is most powerful"—he smiled —"then, Jotson, we shall see!"

"But how will you discover——"

"Perfectly simple, my dear fellow. Where the scent is strongest, we shall find that the odour is most powerful."

"Marvellous!" I exclaimed, amazed once more by the masterly reasoning of my astounding friend.

We pursued our way, Herlock Sholmes with his nose stretched out in advance, sniffing incessantly. Sholmes' nose was an unfailing guide.

As we proceeded the scent grew stronger and stronger, and I could only hope that my strength would hold out to the finish. Even Sholmes, man of iron as he was, was a little pale.

We stopped at last at a door, and Sholmes opened it with a skeleton-key. We rushed into the house.

A man was seated at a table before a strongly-smelling dish, from which he was eating with evident relish.

He sprang to his feet as we rushed in.

"Surrender!" exclaimed Sholmes.

"Mein Gott! Vas is das?"

Clink!

The handcuffs were on his wrists in the twinkling of an eye.

"Sholmes!" I exclaimed. "Who is this man?"

My amazing friend smiled.

"I arrest you in the name of the Red Tape Department, Baron Pikkald Unyunze!" he said distinctly.

"Pikkald Unyunz!" I exclaimed.

"The same, Jotson! Take his other ear and bring him along, my dear fellow!"

The discovered scoundrel fell upon his knees.

"Mein Herr—kamerad! I am your prisoner. But mercy! Permit me to take mein luffly sauerkraut with me!"

"There is no mercy for such as you, Baron Pikkald Unyunz!" said Herlock Sholmes sternly. And the dastard was led away.

CHAPTER 3

We returned to Shaker Street after the German had been safely lodged under lock and key.

I was, needless to state, amazed.

"The usual explanation, Jotson—what?" said Sholmes, with a smile. "My dear fellow, it was one of the simplest of my cases. The Baron Pikkald Unyunz came secretly to England in deep disguise. His identity disappeared; like a mole or a politician, he worked in the dark. But there was one thing, Jotson, that he could not part from—the succulent dish that Germans love—that dish so strange and fearsome to all but Germans—"

"Sauerkraut!" I exclaimed.
"Exactly! The paragraph in the 'Chronic Daily' gave me this clue. That strange and terrible odour, which drove forth the inhabitants from the vicinity of Snooker Street, could only have been caused by the German national dish. I have followed the scent, Jotson, and found the hidden intriguer," Sholmes, shrugged his shoulders. "A simple case, Jotson—hardly worthy of my powers!

THE SECRETARY'S DOUBLE!

No. 35

Herlock Sholmes had been on a visit to Hanwell, where he had many friends. He was looking unusually grave when he returned to our rooms in Shaker Street.
I could see that something had occurred to disturb the tranquility of my amazing friend.
He did not hook his umbrella upon my ear, or knock the ashes of his pipe down the back of my neck, in the usual playful manner that so endeared him to me.
He sat silent and thoughtful at lunch, and absent-mindedly consumed my kipper as well as his own. I did not venture to interrupt him.
"My dear Jotson!" said Sholmes, at last.
"Something has happened during your visit to Hanwell, Sholmes?" I asked.
"Yes." He lighted several cigarettes at once, a proof of extreme concentration of thought. "A most puzzling problem, Jotson. You have heard of Lord Loosetop."
"The Secretary of the Chinwag Department?" I asked.
"The same."
"I have heard of him, Sholmes."
"But you are probably now aware, Jotson, that this great statesman has a double; a relation who resembles him very closely, and has, indeed, been mistaken for him. A very awkward position for his lordship, Jotson, as his relation, the Honourable Loonie Loosetop, is an incurable lunatic."
Sholmes knitted his brows.
"The Hon. Loonie, Jotson, was confined at Hanwell for his own good. Naturally, he did not like it, and on more than one occasion he attempted to escape from the asylum. It was, however, a great relief to Lord Loosetop. Being, however, a humane nobleman, he sometimes visited his unfortunate cousin at Hanwell. Now, Jotson, this is where the problem arises. During my visit to-day I saw the Hon. Loonie—the idiot of the family. He told me a most remarkable story."
"Go on, Sholmes!" I murmured, deeply interested.
"According to the statement made to me, the man now confined in Hanwell is not the Hon. Loonie at all, but Lord Loosetop himself."
"Sholmes!"
"His story is that, visiting his cousin in his room, he was suddenly seized by him. The lunatic changed clothes with him, and left—leaving his lordship in his place.
"Good heavens!"
"A terrible blow for his lordship, if true," resumed Sholmes. "The change of quarters was not a severe hardship, for after many years passed in a Government department his lordship was naturally fitted, to a certain extent, to take his place with distinction in a lunatic asylum. But he has been kept away from his important work in the Chinwag Department—in war-time, too, Jotson, when chinwag is playing so great a part in the nation's affairs. Worst of all, the escaped lunatic, relying upon his resemblance to his lordship, has taken his place as Secretary and Member of the Cabinet. A very serious position, Jotson."
"But surely, Sholmes, the asylum warders must have noticed a difference——"
Sholmes shook his head.
"To the trained eye of a detective, Jotson, there is a distinct difference between a Cabinet Minister and an ordinary lunatic. But the asylum warders are not accustomed to taking note of fine distinctions of this kind."
"True!"
"If I saw them together, Jotson, I could doubtless pick out the Government official from the lunatic. There are many shades of difference which would not escape an experienced eye. But of late the Secretary of the Chinwag Department has carefully avoided visiting his relation in Hanwell. Jotson, this seems to hint that the story I have heard to-day may be well founded. It looks like a lunatic's cunning."
"Most true!"
Sholmes rose, and began to pace the room, his dressing-gown whisking behind him. My amazing friend was evidently much disturbed.
"Consider the position, Jotson. If this story is true, and it is Lord Loosetop himself who is confined in the asylum, and a lunatic who has taken his place at the Chinwag Department, the matter is serious. The Honourable Loonie may make alarming mistakes in the management of the department. There

may be an interruption of the steady flow of chinwag the nation expects from its rulers. There is no telling what absurd freak the man may not commit, unused to the routines of Whithall as he is. It may be said, in a general way, that there is little to choose between the denizens of Hanwell and those of Whitehall, and this is doubtless true. But there are limits, Jotson. Inspired by maniacal energy, the unfortunate man may answer letters by return of post—he may see callers without keeping them waiting twelve hours in the ante-rooms—he may place black sealing-wax upon documents that require to be sealed with red sealing-wax—he may even use ordinary tape instead of red tape——"

"Good heavens, Sholmes!"

"Such are the possibilities of the situation, Jotson, if the story I have heard to-day is true."

I sprang to my feet.

"Sholmes? Something must be done!"

"Undoubtedly. The traditions of the Chinwag Department may be totally revolutionised, otherwise. The fate of the war may even tremble in the balance. By some act of mad energy it may be brought to an end in our own lifetime, instead of being continued to the thirtieth or fortieth generation."

"Sholmes!"

"It is up to me, Jotson," said Herlock Sholmes resolutely. "Come my dear fellow! Let us proceed to the Chinwag Department at once!"

He took me by the coat-tails and led me from the room.

CHAPTER 2

Sholmes was silent and thoughtful as we walked rapidly towards Whitehall.

It was a problem that seemed likely to tax even the astounding intellectual powers of my amazing friend.

There was no clue, so far as I could see, to follow.

The personal resemblance between Lord Loosetop and his cousin was complete. It was only in their actions that Sholmes could hope to detect a difference which would indicate which was the lunatic and which was the Cabinet Minister. Placed together, Sholmes' eagle eye would doubtless have discerned subtle distinctions which escaped the ordinary view. But Sholmes could not see them together; the places they occupied, though familiar, were far apart. I confess that I could not see upon what grounds Sholmes hoped to detect the genuineness, or otherwise of the man who claimed to be the Secretary of the Chinwag Department.

But my faith in my amazing friend never faltered.

Difficult as the task was, impossible to any other man, I never doubted that Sholmes would accomplish it.

We arrived at the Chinwag Department, and Sholmes sent in his card.

We were admitted to the Minister's bureau.

He rose to greet us courteously.

I saw Sholmes' eyes gleam as he exchanged greeting with the secretary. Had he discerned some clue already?

For my own part, I confess that I was wholly at a loss. I scanned the Minister with intent interest, but I could perceive no sign that he was any weaker in the head than is usual in gentlemen of his high position.

Sholmes sat down, in his usual elegant attitude, with his feet resting upon the table.

He conversed genially with the Minister.

He touched upon many subjects; and I could guess that he was testing the man, to ascertain by his replies whether he was what he represented himself as being.

But if the secretary was playing a part, he sustained it well.

He showed a statesmanlike ignorance of every subject broached by Sholmes; and though he had evidently heard of the war, he manifested very little interest in it.

The conversation was interrupted by the arrival of a messenger.

He carried an important letter, which required the immediate attention of the Secretary of the Chinwag Department.

"Excuse me, Mr. Sholmes," said the Minister. "Business first, you know."

He took the letter.

Herlock Sholmes drew a deep breath.

There was a clink as he thrust his hand into his pocket and drew out a pair of handcuffs.

The next moment they clinked upon the wrists of the pretended secretary.

"I am sorry, Loonie Loosetop," said Herlock Sholmes ironically. "I am afraid I must ask you to accompany me. Your place in Hanwell is waiting for you; and your cousin, Lord Loosetop, is ready to resume his duties here."

CHAPTER 3

I was in my usual state of amazement when we returned to Shaker Street.

The unfortunate lunatic had already been despatched to Hanwell, and Lord Loosetop recalled to his duties at the Chinwag Department.

Sholmes was in a very satisfied mood.

He gave me a smile as we sat down to our winkles at tea.

"You are surprised, Jotson?" he remarked.

"I am astounded, Sholmes, I do not doubt, of course, that you are right, but I confess that I see no grounds——"

"Yet you have studied my methods, Jotson," said Sholmes. "My dear fellow, the moment I entered the secretary's bureau in the Chinwag Department I was certain that it was the Minister's double I had to deal with. His utter want of acquaintance with the manners and customs of Whitehall was the clue."

"But——"

"You surely noted, Jotson, that he was wide awake when we entered?"

"True!"

"That was the clue, Jotson. However, proof was necessary. I had already arranged for the messenger to bring in the letter of importance from the Red Tape Office. That was the test; and that test, Jotson, was too much for the insane impostor. He stopped an agreeable conversation, Jotson, with the remark that he must attend to business first. No one acquainted with the routine of the Chinwag Department, Jotson, would have made so deplorable an error. Lord Loosetop, trained in diplomatic and Ministerial circles, would have never made so egregious a blunder. It was clear, therefore, that the man before me was not the genuine Secretary of the Chinwag Department." Herlock Sholmes shrugged his shoulders. "Your amazement is out of place, Jotson. So far from being a difficult problem, it is one of the simplest cases I have handled. Pass the winkles!"

THE LOTTERY TICKET

No. 36

"Another case, Jotson!" remarked Herlock Sholmes.

We were looking out of window at our rooms in Shaker Street when my amazing friend made that remark.

"A case, Sholmes?" I inquired.

He pointed carelessly with the stem of his pipe to a man who was coming along, scanning each door as he passed.

"You think he is coming here, Sholmes?"

"I do not think, Jotson. I never think. I know!"

"True! But your reasons?"

Sholmes smiled.

"The man is evidently in a very disturbed frame of mind, Jotson. From the fact that he is wearing only one boot, and that he has put on a bath-towel instead of a hat, I deduce that he left home in a hurry!"

"True!"

"From the further fact that his eyes are rolling like those of a mechanical doll, Jotson, and that he is foaming at the mouth, I deduce that he is in a state of considerable excitement!"

"Marvellous!"

"Not at all, my dear fellow! Deduction that is all! As he is looking at the number on each door, Jotson, I deduce that he is searching for a particular house——"

"Sholmes, you amaze me more and more!"

"My dear Jotson, these deductions are child's play to a brain like mine!"

"But how do you deduce, Sholmes, that he intends to visit this building?" I could not help inquiring.

Sholmes smiled again, in rather a bored way.

"I deduce it from the fact that he has stopped at our door and rung the bell, Jotson. It is quite simple—elementary, in fact. Had you trained your intellect to the observation of detail, Jotson, you would be able to deduce from such an act a desire on the part of the individual under discussion to enter the house!"

I could only gaze at my amazing friend in speechless admiration.

I was still doing so, and presenting somewhat of the appearance of a newly-landed fish, when our visitor was shown in—thus triumphantly proving the correctness of Herlock Sholmes' marvellous deductions.

"Mr. Sholmes?" he exclaimed.

"Good-morning!" said Herlock Sholmes calmly. "What can I do for you? You may speak quite freely before my friend Dr. Jotson, as I have had several occasions to remark before!"

"Mr. Sholmes, I have lost it!" He struggled for breath. "A fortune is at stake, Mr. Sholmes! You must save me! I have heard of your reputation, Mr. Sholmes; I have heard how you tracked down the missing margarine, and followed the scent of the hoarded Gorgonzola. You—and you alone—can help me!"

"Kindly give me a few details," yawned Herlock Sholmes, as he motioned the visitor to a seat.

"My name is Aubrey Baggs," faltered our visitor. "My life, Mr. Sholmes, has been one of humble usefulness. I am billiard-marker at the Pink Pigeon. A month ago I was induced to invest the sum of five shillings in a ticket in the Grand Continental Lottery, held at Spoofersdam, in Holland. It was in a careless moment that I made the investment, and I attached little importance to it, Mr. Sholmes—till yesterday——"

"Till yesterday?" said Sholmes.

"Then I learned, Mr. Sholmes, that I held the winning number," said Mr. Baggs, in tones of great agitation. "Ticket No. 100001 was the winner, Mr. Sholmes, and I held ticket No. 100001. I was entitled to the first prize in the Grand Continental Lottery!"

"I congratulate you, Mr. Baggs!" said Herlock Sholmes drily.

Mr. Baggs made a gesture of despair.

"I have lost the ticket, Mr. Sholmes! Without the ticket I cannot claim the prize! Mr. Sholmes, find the missing ticket for me, and name your own reward—one half of the prize if you like!"

Sholmes shook his head.

"I cannot work on those terms, Mr. Baggs! Even if the ticket is recovered, by the time you receive your prize from a Continental lottery I shall be getting my Old Age Pension!"

"True!" I remarked.

"Shut up, Jotson! Now. Mr. Baggs, when was the lottery-ticket in your possession?"

"Yesterday afternoon!" groaned Mr. Baggs. "I kept it in the pocket where I keep my chalk, safe as houses. When I heard the great news I took it out and looked at it, to make sure. There it was, Mr. Sholmes—No. 100001!"

"You replaced it in your pocket?"

"Yes."

"Your next proceeding?"

"I thought, as I was going to get the first prize, Mr. Sholmes, I would go to Houndsditch and see Mr. Montague Isaacs. That gentleman had kindly taken charge of my Sunday trousers a short time before, handing me a ticket and the sum of two shilling and ninepence in exchange."

Sholmes smiled.

"I deduce from this that Mr. Montague Isaacs is a pawnbroker?" he remarked.

"That is correct! I see that you merit your marvellous reputation, Mr. Sholmes!"

"You withdrew your Sunday trousers from the spout, Mr. Baggs?"

"I did, Mr. Sholmes!"

"And then?"

"On the 'bus home I missed the ticket—No. 100001. I may have given it in mistake for a tram-ticket," groaned Mr. Baggs. "I may have dropped it. Find it, Mr. Sholmes, and name your own reward!"

"You visited no one but Mr. Isaacs before you missed the ticket?"

"No one."

Sholmes looked very thoughtful.

I gazed silently at my amazing friend. I could not imagine how he would deal with this baffling case. A lottery-ticket, lost in the wide spaces of the London streets, was not easily to be found—unless by Herlock Sholmes. But I remembered his marvellous gifts, and my confidence returned. Only recently Herlock Sholmes had succeeded in solving the long-standing mystery of who killed Cock Robin, and had proved that A. Sparrow was not guilty of the crime, as was generally supposed until Sholmes took the case in hand. After that amazing example of my friend's perspicacity, nothing could shake my faith in him.

I was quite prepared for the inscrutable smile that crossed his features.

"You will find the ticket, Sholmes?" I exclaimed.

"I trust so, Jotson."

"Bless you, Mr. Sholmes!" said Mr. Baggs brokenly.

"Call again this evening, Mr. Baggs, and I may have news for you," said Herlock Sholmes reassuringly.

And our visitor took his leave.

CHAPTER 2

I was alone when Mr. Baggs was shown in that evening. Sholmes had been absent, and had not returned. Whether he was busily engaged on the case of the lottery-ticket, or whether he desired to leave me to interview the gentleman who called concerning the instalment due on the furniture, I could not determine.

Sholmes came in in a few minutes, however, and I augured success from the playful manner in which he hooked his umbrella upon my left ear.

Mr. Baggs regarded him anxiously.

"The ticket, Mr. Sholmes?" he exclaimed.

Herlock Sholmes smiled.

He slipped his fingers into his waistcoat-pocket and drew out a slip of pasteboard.

"No. 100001!" gasped Mr. Baggs.

"The lottery-ticket," said Sholmes negligently.

Mr. Baggs gazed at the recovered lottery-ticket in amazement and elation.

"Mr. Sholmes, you have saved me!" Name your own reward!"

"Two shillings and sixpence, with the addition of twopence for the 'bus fare," said Sholmes, in his staccato, businesslike tones.

He clinked the coins pleasantly in the pocket of his dressing-gown when Mr. Baggs had taken his leave.

"Sprats for supper this evening, Jotson!" he remarked, with one of his rare digs in the ribs.

"As you will, Sholmes. But——"

"Let us defer the usual explanation, my dear Jotson, until the sprats have been purchased."

"You are right, Sholmes."

It was not until the sprats were sizzling in Mrs. Spudson's frying-pan that Herlock Sholmes' consented to enlighten my devouring curiosity.

"It was simple enough, Jotson. Mr. Baggs, on hearing that he had won the first prize in the Grand Continental Lottery, rushed off to Mr. Isaacs' establishement to redeem his Sunday garments, reposing there up the spout. In the excitement of the moment Jotson, he handed Mr. Isaacs the lottery-ticket instead of the pawnticket. This I deduced immediately. From the fact that Mr. Montague Isaacs did not return the lottery-ticket to him, I deduced that Mr. Isaacs had kept it."

"Sholmes!"

"A simple deduction, Jotson; simple, I mean, to a detective's trained intellect."

"Simple to you, Sholmes," I remarked. "It would not have occurred to me. But pray continue."

"Mr. Isaacs must have had a reason for keeping it," resumed Sholmes. "My long acquaintance with the habits and customs of pawnbrokers, Jotson, made it quite well known to me that these gentry do not, as a rule, retain lottery-tickets which are handed to them in mistake for pawntickets. It could only be, Jotson, that Mr. Isaacs knew that the ticket held the winning number in the Grand Continental Lottery. It was his intention to diddle the unsuspecting Baggs."

"It is quite clear, Sholmes—but to recover the ticket———"

"That was easy, Jotson."

"I confess I do not see——"

"Naturally," said Sholmes calmly.

"True!" I exclaimed. "But how, Sholmes, did you recover the lottery-ticket?"

"By a simple method. Disguised as an official of the Pop-Shop Controller's Department, I entered Mr. Isaac's establishment and searched for it. Voila toot!" said Sholmes, dropping carelessly into French, as he often did.

"Amazing!" I exclaimed.

"Not at all, Jotson. But here are the sprats."

And Sholmes' active jaws were soon busy, to such an extent that he could not hear my exclamations of admiration. Once more my amazing friend's efforts had been crowned with success; and Aubrey Baggs, in his humble abode at the Pink Pigeon, waited in joyful anticipation of receiving the handsome prize from the Grand Metropolitan Lottery. He is still waiting!

1918

HERLOCK SHOLMES AT MONTE CARLO

No. 37

"The weather is very hot, Jotson."

I stared at Herlock Sholmes across the breakfast-table.

My amazing friend, well as I knew him, was always astounding me with some remark displaying his marvellous penetration.

"My dear Sholmes!" I murmured.

"It is a fact, Jotson."

"But from what premises, Sholmes, did you deduce this?" I could not help inquiring. "I do not deny the fact, but I am interested to know by what means you reached this conclusion. You know, I am studying your methods."

Sholmes smiled.

"It is very simple, Jotson—I may say elementary. We are now in the dog days——"

"True!"

"The sun is shining from a cloudless sky——"

"Undoubtedly!"

"And the thermometer registers a hundred and ten degrees in the shade. From these circumstances, Jotson, I deduce that the weather is hot."

"Wonderful!"

"Not at all. A simple deduction like that, Jotson, is nothing to what I could do if really roused."

"I am sure of it, Sholmes," I said, gazing at my amazing friend in admiration.

"However, returnong noose ah neutral mutton," said Sholmes, dropping into French, as he often did. "I think it is time we had a holiday, Jotson."

"My dear Sholmes, I quite agree with you, I had thought of postponing all holidays till after the war. But, speaking as a medical man, I do not think a holiday would be quite so beneficial to us when we have become centenarians. Where shall we go, Sholmes? Blackpool, I believe, is still safe from bombardment by the unspeakable Hun."

"On the contrary, Jotson, I have the surest information that at Blackpool the beach is simply covered with shells."

"Good heavens!"

"Look at this advertisement, my dear Jotson, and tell me what you think," said Sholmes, passing me his copy of the "Upper Circle Post."

I glanced at the paper, and read the advertisement aloud:

"'Enrol for National Service! Every man wanted——'"

"Not that one, Jotson—farther down the page!" exclaimed Sholmes sharply.

"Sorry, Sholmes!"

I looked further down the page, and read:

"'Monte Carlo for the winter! The finest climate in the world! Casino open all the year round!'"

I looked at Sholmes inquiringly.

"You are thinking of Monte Carlo?" I asked.

"I am."

"A good idea!" I said heartily. "I have often wished to break the bank at Monte Carlo, Sholmes, as has so often been done in newspaper advertisements. A very healthy climate, Sholmes; the visitor is likely to suffer from nothing but shock to the system."

"Exactly. I fear, Jotson, that your mental powers are hardly equal to the strain of breaking the bank, however."

"True!"

"I shall be there, however."

"My dear Sholmes, it is your intention to break the bank at Monte Carlo?" I exclaimed.

"Precisely."

"I have not the slightest doubt that you will accomplish that difficult task, Sholmes. The man who solved the baffling mystery of who killed Cock Robin is equal to any task."

"You are right, Jotson. Pack our bags, my dear fellow, and I will call at the Somnolent Office for our passports."

Sholmes, buttoned his dressing-gown and left me, returning in an hour with a trunk full of official papers required for our journey. We started for the railway-station, enjoying en route the mild excitement of an air raid. The same evening we were speeding southward for the delightful land of romance and roulette.

CHAPTER 2

"Monte Carlo! said Sholmes, yawning.

I stepped from the train, and fell headlong upon the platform. I was unaccustomed to French trains, and unaware that there was a three-foot drop outside the carriage.

Sholmes' masterly mind, however, saved him from a similar disaster.

He landed carefully upon my neck, and sat there for a few moments to recover himself.

"My dear Sholmes," I murmured, "far be it from me, your faithful follower, to wish to incommode you in any way, but that is my neck."

"True, my dear fellow!" remarked Sholmes.

"If you could find something else to rest upon, Sholmes——"

"Really, Jotson, it is somewhat inconsiderate to interrupt my mental aberrations with irrevalent remarks!" said Sholmes sharply.

"True!" I admitted.

"Little boys, Jotson, should be seen and not heard," added Sholmes.

I felt the truth of this remark, and was silent.

After a time Sholmes rose, took me gently by the ear, and lifted me to my feet.

"Proceedong noose ah neuter hotel, Jotson," he said in French.

"C'est vrai! Allong dong!" I replied in the same language. "J'ai boko de swiff."

We proceeded.

Monte Carlo was crowded by a gay and fashionable crowd.

Amid the aristocratic throng I observed grand dukes, marquises, company promoters, pickpockets, Cabinet Ministers, and many other representatives of the luxurious classes.

In fact, the elite of the whole world had been drawn to the beautiful resort by the shores of the blue Mediterranean, where riches cease from troubling and the occupants of the Suicide's Cemetary are at rest.

We reached our hotel, and sat down to a luxurious repast of cheval a la Froggee, chien a la mode, and chatte a discretion, followed by biscuits de chien and eau froid.

Sholmes leaned back in his chair and lighted a Flor de Cabbagio with an air of contentment.

"Try the cigars, my dear fellow," he said. "The Cabbagios are very good, and Chouxfleur are excellent."

"And now the casino," I said, as I lighted my cigar after a busy quarter of an hour with the French matches.

"The casino, Jotson, closes at twelve," said Sholmes. "It is now only ten."

"Then we have two hours."
"Three!" said Sholmes calmly.
"In three hours, Sholmes," I remarked, "the casino will have been closed for an hour."
"Exactly!"
"I do not quite understand you, Sholmes. Did you not come here to break the bank at Monte Carlo?"
"Certainly."
"To deprive the croupier's, Sholmes, of their tons of ill-gotten wealth?"
"Precisely!"
"Yet you do not propose to visit the casino until after it is closed!" I exclaimed.
"Correct!"
"I confess that I am quite in the dark, Sholmes."
"My dear Jotson," said Sholmes, with a somewhat bored look, "leave the matter to me. Your mentality, my dear fellow, is hardly equal to the strain.
"True! But——"
"There are two ways of visiting the casino," Sholmes explained. "If you wish the bank to break you, you visit it when it is open. If you wish to break the bank, you visit it after it is closed."
"Sholmes!"
"Wait and see, my dear fellow. Noose verrong!" said Sholmes. "Pass me another Cabbagio, and explode a match for me—thanks!"
And Sholmes smoked on, and refused to enlighten me further.

CHAPTER 3

It was not till an hour past midnight that Sholmes moved. Then he finished the bottle of red Stummackakeo wine, and rose.
"Time, Jotson!"
I followed him from the Hotel de Fleece.
"And now, Sholmes——"
"We are going to break the bank, Jotson." He paused under the shadow of a palm-tree, and took a jemmy from his pocket, and examined it carefully. "Right!"
"Have you brought your money, Sholmes?"
"My dear Jotson, it is an old rule of casino punters to play with the bank's money whenever possible. That is my system."
"Ah! Have you a system, Sholmes?"
"Undoubtedly!"
"By which you will win against the bank?"
"Without doubt!"
"And break the bank?" I exclaimed.
"Indubitably!"
"I do not doubt your assurance, Sholmes, but how can you work this system, no doubt excellent, after the casino is closed?"
"I could not work it while the casino was open, Jotson. However, wait for me under the palm-trees here, and whistle if you see a policeman."
"A policeman!" I ejaculated.
"Yes. The police, Jotson, in this delightful place, are paid their wages by the casino authorities, and they would undoubtedly interfere to prevent me from breaking the bank by my infallible system."
Before I could reply, he left me.
I waited anxiously.
Great as was my faith in the remarkable powers of Herlock Sholmes, I could not fathom how he hoped to contrive to break the bank at Monte Carlo after the casino was closed for the night.
However, I knew Sholmes too well to doubt.
I waited.
In half an hour he rejoined me. He was carrying a sack, which clinked musically as he moved, and his jemmy was under his arm. He smiled.
"Success, my dear Jotson!"
"Sholmes!" I exclaimed. "You have broken the bank?"
"I have!"
"Wonderful!"
"Not at all, my dear fellow. But now let us make for the railway-station, and we shall catch the night express."
"Without returning to our hotel, Sholmes?"
"Decidedly!"
"But we cannot pay our bills unless we return!"
"That is why it is not necessary to return, Jotson."
"True, I exclaimed, struck by this masterly reasoning of my amazing friend.
"Come!" said Sholmes.
And we departed.

CHAPTER 4

Home once more amid the familiar sights and sounds and smells of Shaker Street, I asked Herlock Sholmes for the usual explanation. But Sholmes shook his head. The system by means of which he had succeeded in breaking the bank at Monte Carlo was a secret he did not care to impart, even to his faithful Jotson.

"Enough, my dear fellow, that we have been successful," he said, with a smile. "Enough that we can now settle Mrs. Spudson's bill, and face the man, when he calls for the instalments on the furniture, without fear. That is enough—or, as the French say, c'est asinine."

And Herlock Sholmes turned to the cocaine-cask, and said no more.

THE CASE OF THE FINANCIER

No. 38

Even Herlock Sholmes looked a little impressed when Mr. Goldgrind, the celebrated financier, was shown into our rooms at Shaker Street.

Kings, princes, and even emperors had visited Shaker Street to consult my amazing friend, but such small fry paled into insignificance beside our present visitor.

Mr. Goldgrind was a power behind thrones, his nod was sufficient to make many a powerful potentate shake in his gilded palace.

That Sholmes was impressed I could see by the fact that he removed his feet from the mantelpiece and rose to greet the visitor.

"Mr. Sholmes?" asked the financial magnate, as he seated himself, with a musical clink of many articles of expensive jewellery, in the chair I at once placed for him.

"Quite so!" said Herlock Sholmes. "You may speak freely before my friend Dr. Jotson."

"I have been swindled, Mr. Sholmes!"

"My hat!" ejaculated Herlock Sholmes.

For once in his life Sholmes was surprised.

"You have been swindled?" he repeated.

The millionaire frowned.

"Yes, Mr. Sholmes."

"You have perhaps invested in one of your own companies by mistake?" asked Sholmes.

"I am not likely to make such mistakes!" said Mr. Goldgrind, frowning. "Nothing of the sort!"

"In what way, then, have you been swindled?"

I shared Sholmes' surprise. Knowing the great financier's reputation well, I was prepared to hear that he had swindled, but not that he had been swindled. So far as swindling was concerned, Mr. Goldgrind was supposed to be always in the active, and never in the passive, voice.

"You have heard of Smelowiski?" asked Mr. Goldgrind.

"The Russian Anarchist?"

"The same."

"I have of course heard of him," said Sholmes. "It was Smelowiski who blew up several Tsars and Tzaritsas before the Russian Revolution. Since the Revolution he has been inactive, either because there are no more Tsars to blow up, or because of a shortage of explosives. He is in London at the present time, I believe."

"That is the man I want you to find, Mr. Sholmes. Smelowiski has swindled me—me! I will explain the circumstances. You are aware that the uncertainty of affairs in Russia has caused a general fall in the value of Russian securities?"

Sholmes nodded.

"Russian Fives, for instance, fell from eighty-three to seventy-three," pursued Mr. Goldgrind. "Other securities in proportion. Every fresh rumour from Petrograd caused a further fall. If you read the financial news in your morning paper, Mr. Sholmes, you must have observed the fluctuations of Poppemoff Oil shares. The one pound shares were at ten shillings premium before the Revolution, and they are now marked at only five shillings for the one pound share. Poppemoff Oil, of course, is a first-rate proposition, and when the Russian Exchange recovers, big dividends will be paid. It was my intention to mop up all the Poppemoff shares on the market."

Sholmes nodded again.

"Having decided on this operation, I made my plans as usual," continued Mr. Goldgrind.

"It was necessary, of course, for affairs in Petrograd to take a very bad turn, so that the price would fall to the lowest possible mark, enabling me to scoop in Poppemoff Oil at next to nothing. After I secured the shares, it would then be necessary for reassuring news to arrive from Petrograd, causing the price to rise again, enabling me to sell out at a handsome profit. But you are probably acquainted with the methods of high finance?"

"Quite so."

"Well, sir, as this Anarchist Smelowiski, has great influence with the Red Flag party in his native country, I approached him with a business offer, and he agreed to arrange an Anarchist outbreak in Petrograd, the news of which would make Poppemoff shareholders uneasy, and anxious to sell for anything they could get. Later, his friends were to be reconciled to the Provisional Government, and declare themselves in favour of a great offensive on the Eastern Front, which, of course, would have the effect of steadying the market and raising prices all round. Naturally, this cost money. Anarchist outbreaks are not arranged free of charge, as you are doubtless aware. Bombs are expensive, to mention only one item."

"And Smelowiski failed to carry out the arrangement?" asked Sholmes.

"Exactly. Having pocketed the sum advanced for expenses, he failed to keep faith with me. The Anarchist rising has not taken place in Petrograd, and Popemoff shares, instead of falling to a shilling, have actually risen to seven-and-sixpence! The operation, which would have netted me a hundred thousand pounds or so, has been rendered impossible!" Mr. Goldgrind's voice thrilled with indignation. "I have been swindled—I, sir, who have been accustomed to skinning the public for fifty years or more, have been skinned! Smelowiski has disappeared, with the considerable sum advanced to him; and you, Mr. Sholmes, must track him down and bring him to justice!"

"Rely upon me," said Herlock Sholmes.

And Mr. Goldgrind took his leave.

CHAPTER 2

Herlock Sholmes wore a thoughtful expression after the millionaire financier had gone.

I did not venture to interrupt his meditations.

He looked up at last, and took a swig from the cocaine flask.

"A very serious case, Jotson," he remarked.

I nodded.

"I sympathise with Dr. Goldgrind," I observed. "A most promising stock operation has been nipped in the bud by Smelowiski's fraud. The man must be brought to justice."

"Undoubtedly. I shall take up the trail at once, and never rest till Smelowiski has paid the penalty. You may go and attend your patients, Jotson, if any of them are still living."

And Sholmes left me.

I did not see Herlock Sholmes again for some days.

I knew that he was very busy, however, and I waited with perfect confidence to hear the result.

He came into our rooms at Shaker Street one afternoon, in the following week, and from the smile that wreathed his expansive mouth I deduced that he had been successful.

"You have found him, Sholmes?"

He nodded.

"I have found him, Jotson."

"And the rascal is safe under lock and key?"

"As it happens, no," said Sholmes. "It appears that Mr. Goldgrind was labouring under a slight misapprehension. I found Semlowiski engaged upon the construction of a new bomb. Engrossed in his congenial task, he had forgotten the instructions of Mr. Goldgrind, and had omitted to communicate with his friends in Petrograd. However, it is not too late. Immediately upon my acquainting him with the state of affairs he thrust the unfinished bomb into his pocket and took a taxi to Mr. Goldgrind's office, in order to reassure him at once. All will be well."

"Good!" I exclaimed. "Then the operation will be a success after all?"

"Undoubtedly. The Anarchist outbreak will take place, and Poppemoff shares will fall to a mere song, and Mr. Goldgrind will scoop them in. The Anarchists will then submit to law and order, the market will be reassured, and the prices will rise, and Mr. Goldgrind will sell out and secure his hundred thousand pounds. Upon the whole, Jotson," added Sholmes thoughtfully. "I am glad I am not a shareholder in the Poppemoff Oil Company. I am glad I have invested my life's savings in a War Savings Certificate."

"True!" I exclaimed.

"However, come with me, Jotson," added Sholmes. "I have a cheque to collect from Mr. Goldgrind for my services, and we shall not only be able to pay the instalment on the furniture this week, but I think it will run to fish and chips for supper."

Sholmes took me by the nose in his playful manner and led me down to the waiting taxi.

A minute more and we were buzzing away for Mr. Goldgrind's office in Spoofem Street, in the City.

We stopped outside the palatial block of buildings.

We were about to alight when a terrific report rent the air.

Sholmes caught me by the shoulder.

"Wait, Jotson."

"Why, my dear Sholmes?"

"I fancy, Jotson, that an explosion has taken place."

"Sholmes! From what do you draw this deduction?"

Herlock Sholmes smiled.

"It is quite simple, Jotson. there was, a moment ago, a terrific report——"

"True!"

"Mr. Goldgrind's office had been blown sky-high——"

"Most true!"
"And is now descending in fragments on the pavement. From the circumstances, Jotson, I deduce that an explosion has taken place."
"Wonderful!" I ejaculated.
"Not at all, my dear fellow! Elementary."
Needless to say, Sholmes' deduction proved absolutely correct.
The bomb in Smelowiski's pocket had exploded at an inopportune moment, and the palatial office had been blown to fragments, and both Mr. Goldgrind and the Anarchist had disappeared skyward.
Whether they ever came down again cannot be said with certainty, as Herlock Sholmes' connection with the case ended at this point.

A MURDER MYSTERY

No. 39

The sudden and startling death of Mr. Skinflint Skinnem, the great shipowner, had caused a widespread sensation, and it was natural that my amazing friend, Herlock Sholmes, should have been called in to solve the mystery.

I was reading the latest report of the crime at our breakfast-table in our rooms at Shaker Street one morning, when Inspector Pinkeye was announced.

Sholmes smiled with a rather bored expression.

"Our old friend Pinkeye finds the Skinnem case a little above his weight, Jotson," he remarked. "I expected this."

"You will take up the case, Sholmes?"

"Undoubtedly." Herlock Sholmes nodded genially to the inspector as he entered, without removing his feet from the table. "Good-morning, inspector! Scotland Yard at its wits' end again—what?"

"It's the Skinnem case, Mr. Sholmes," said Inspector Pinkeye, sinking into a chair. "If you care to help us——"

"Certainly, my dear fellow! Pray give me a few details. You can speak quite freely before my friend, Dr. Jotson."

"An extraordinary case, Mr. Sholmes," said the inspector. "Mr. Skinnem, the managing director of Messrs. Skull & Krossbones, the shipowners, was found dead in his private office. There was no sign of violence about the body, and death had apparently been instantaneous. The medical evidence is that Mr. Skinnem had been the victim of a sudden shock—how adminstered, it is for the police to discover."

"He was alone in the office?"

"Quite alone, seated at the telephone, with the receiver in his hand. Apparently he had just taken a call."

"When was he last seen alive?"

"His confidential clerk, Samuel Smiff, had been with him ten minutes before, taking his instructions. Mr. Smiff's evidence is that Mr. Skinnem was in perfect health and spirits. He had, in fact, been particularly cheered that morning by good news, freights having risen considerably owing to the destruction of shipping by the German submarines. He remarked jokingly to Smiff that the Hun submarines were an excellent bull point for shipping shares—a Stock Exchange expression, Mr. Sholmes. Smiff left him, and shortly afterwards heard the telephone-bell ring. As it rang again and again, Smiff ventured to enter the private office, and discovered Mr. Skinnem dead at the telephone. That, of course, is Smiff's story, but he has been placed under arrest on suspicion.

Sholmes nodded thoughtfully.

"There is nothing against Smiff, except from the fact that he was the last to see Mr. Skinnem alive. He is a young man, exempted as indispensable, and paid the princely wage of seventeen shillings weekly—doubtless on account of his indispensability. So far as we can ascertain, he was properly grateful and devoted to his employer. Yet——"

"Suicide?" suggested Sholmes.

The inspector shook his head.

"There was no motive for suicide. Mr. Sholmes. Mr. Skinnem was enjoying unexampled prosperity. The Skull & Krossbones line had recently paid a dividend of three hundred per cent., and Mr. Skinnem's only worry was the difficulty of disposing of his huge accumulations of wealth. This trouble, however, he was facing with great equanimity. He was done to death. But by whom?" The inspector made a despairing gesture. "He had no enemies, so far as we have discovered. Among certain unthinking persons, of course, he had a degree of unpopularity. A gentleman in Mr. Skinnem's position could not escape slander and misunderstanding."

"And the cause of death——"

"A sudden, terrible shock, Mr. Sholmes—how administered is a mystery, unless by Samuel Smiff. Even if Smiff is guilty, it is not clear what means he used. You must help us, Mr. Sholmes."

Herlock Sholmes smiled.

"Rely upon me, inspector."

I gazed inquiringly at my amazing friend. Well I knew the inscrutable smile that played over Sholmes' expressive countenance.

"Sholmes," I ejaculated, "you have a clue?"
"Naturally," yawned Sholmes. "The clue of the telephone-call."
"Really, Mr. Sholmes——" murmured the inspector.
"You do not see it, inspector," smiled Herlock Sholmes. "These clues, indeed, are only discerned in Shaker Street. However, I will enlighten you. The shock that killed Mr. Skinflint Skinnem was administered by means of the telephone."
Inspector Pinkeye started.
"Mr. Sholmes!" You suggest an electric current, powerful enough to electrocute Mr. Skinnem——"
"Not at all."
"There was no sign of electrocution, Mr. Sholmes——"
"I did not say an electric shock, inspector."
"But—what other shock——"
Sholmes shrugged his shoulders.
"That is what we shall see, inspector. I shall proceed to work upon the clue of the telephone-call."
Inspector Pinkeye rose to his feet, with an impatient look.
"I came here for assistance," he said stiffly. "I fear that I have wasted my time, Mr. Sholmes."
And Inspector Pinkeye retired.
"'Twas ever thus, as the poet remarks, Jotson," smiled Herlock Sholmes. "Perhaps I shall surprise our good friend Pinkeye shortly."
"I have no doubt of it, Sholmes. Yet I confess that I do not understand——"
"The things you do not understand, my dear fellow, would fill large volumes," remarked Sholmes.
"True!" I exclaimed.
Sholmes removed his feet from the table, and rose.
"To work, Jotson!" he said. "The assassin is still at large. Are you disengaged this morning?"
"Quite!"
"Then remain disengaged, my dear fellow."
And Herlock Sholmes was gone.

CHAPTER 2

I was busy that afternoon, having several operations to perform, and the subsequent death-certificates to sign. I did not see Sholmes again till the evening. When he came into our rooms at Shaker Street I could see by the fact that he was executing a cake-walk that he was in a satisfied mood.
Inspector Pinkeye followed him in.
The inspector was looking somewhat glum as he sat down.
"Sholmes——" I exclaimed.
"We are expecting a visitor, my dear Jotson," drawled Sholmes. "The inspector has been kind enough to come to wait for him."
"I am here at your request, Sholmes!" said Inspector Pinkeye gruffly. "But I do not see——"
"Naturally!"
"For whom are we waiting?" demanded the inspector, as Sholmes filled both his pipes and lighted them negligently.
"Wait and see!" said Sholmes genially.
We waited.
Half an hour later Mrs. Spudson showed a visitor up.
He started a little at the sight of the inspector.
Sholmes strolled carelessly to the door, and placed his back against it.
"Mr. Whiffles?" he asked politely.
"That is my name. I have called to see Dr. Jotson——"
"To see me!" I exclaimed.
Sholmes laughed.
"Pray excuse me for using your name, Jotson. Mr. Whiffles would scarcely have called here to meet the inspector."
"What does this mean?" exclaimed Whiffles fiercely. "I was informed that Dr. Jotson had a job for me."
"Exactly! You are Montgomery Whiffles?"
"Yes."
"Lately in the employ of Mr. Skinflint Skinnem?"
"That is so."
"Discharged for having the audacity to ask for a rise in wages from sixteen shillings to sixteen-and-six weekly?"
Whiffles was silent.
"And wanted," continued Sholmes calmly, "on the charge of having caused the death of Mr. Skinnem by means of a shock administered through the telephone."
The man grew deadly pale.
"How do you know?" he gasped. "I—I was alone in the telephone-box! I was not seen——"

Sholmes smiled.

"There is your man, inspector!"

And the iniquitous Whiffles was led away with handcuffs on his wrist.

CHAPTER 3

"Sholmes!" I exclaimed breathlessly.

Sholmes carelessly tossed off a bumper of cocaine, and smiled.

"I have surprised you, Jotson?"

"You astound me, Sholmes. How——"

"It was simple enough," drawled Sholmes. "As I mentioned to the inspector, the clue was in the telephone-call. Naturally, an official detective could not see it. However, I followed up the clue. By inquiry at the telephone-exchange I learned whence that telephone-call had come. I traced it to a telephone-box in Grub Street Post Office. The rest was simple. The finger-marks on the receiver were an unfailing clue. I suspected revenge on the part of the discharged employee. Whiffles was the man. With fiendish cunning, Jotson, he had called up Mr. Skinnem in his private office on the telephone that morning, and administered the shock that killed him as if by a bullet from a rifle."

"But in what manner, Sholmes? By means of a powerful current——"

"Not at all!"

"Then by what means, Sholmes, could the assassin have conveyed a fatal shock to Mr. Skinnem along the telephone-wires?"

"By means of a message, Jotson. As that was the only possible method it was obviously the one used by Whiffles."

"Good heavens, Sholmes! And what message of terrible import could the man have breathed into the telephone to have this instantaneously fatal effect?"

"Ah! There we enter into the realms of theory, Jotson. But unless I am mistaken——"

"Impossible, Sholmes!"

"Quite so! The assassin breathed three words only—three words of dread import to a man in Mr. Skinnem's position."

"And those fatal words, Sholmes?"

"Consider, Jotson. The managing director of the Skull and Krossbones Line was reeking with prosperity, his dividends piled up mountainously around him. If the war should continue for another year, or two years, he had every reason to hope that the total wealth of the Kingdom would be accumulated in the hands of himself and his friends. He had only one thing to fear, Jotson—only one dread possibly clouded his happy horizon—the fearful possibility that the war would come to an end, and peace be declared. But for this haunting dread Mr. Skinnem would have been completely happy. But that dread, Jotson, must always have been in his mind, poisoning his prosperity, sapping away the satisfaction afforded even by dividends of three hundred per cent. With a cunning that approaches the diabolical the assassin breathed over the telephone the three terrible words: 'Peace is declared!'"

"Good heavens, Sholmes!"

"It was too much, Jotson. In that fearful moment the unhappy Mr. Skinnem saw his dividends dwindle away, his prospects of unlimited wealth shattered at a blow, his rosy dreams clouded for ever. And it slew him, Jotson—under the merciless blow he sank down, the victim of a terrible revenge!"

Tears stood in the eyes of Herlock Sholmes, and his voice faltered. It was not till he finished the cask of cocaine that he was himself again.

Needless to say, the subsequent confession of the heinous assassin fully bore out the masterly deductions of Herlock Sholmes. Once more one of the deepest, darkest mysteries in the annals of crime had been solved by my amazing friend.

THE CASE OF THE MISSING WIFE

No. 40

"Life is tame! observed Herlock Sholmes, grating his feet upon the mantelpiece in his private-room at Shaker Street. "Almost as tame as you are, my dear Jotson!"

"True!" I rejoined, marvelling at my friend's amazing philosophy.

"If the mountain will not come to Mahomet, then Mahomet must go to the mountain," continued Sholmes. "In other words, if clients will not come here to send me upon missions of peril, I must go forth and seek those missions of peril myself."

The light of battle was in my friend's eye as he drained the cocaine-cask at a gulp and strode to the door.

I was wondering whether to accompany him on his quest for adventure, or to go and tend those of my patients who were still living, when the sound of a loud concussion rent the air.

I rushed to the door, and found a portly gentleman of middle age in the act of descending the stairs head-foremost, having collided with the great detective at the top.

Having made the discovery that the bottom step was the lowest, our client—for such I presumed him to be—bounced up again with the velocity of an india-rubber ball. Sholmes took him by the nose

in his playful way and whisked him into the room.
"Proceed," he said, "if you have the necessary breath. You may speak quite freely before my friend Dr. Jotson."
Our visitor adjusted the back of his neck to his satisfaction, and glanced wildly at the great detective.
"Mr. Sholmes," he said dramatically, "my wife is missing!"
Sholmes beamed.
"A thousand congratulations, my dear fellow!" he exclaimed. "That is indeed a stroke of good fortune for you!"
"On the contrary, Mr. Sholmes, it is a matter for considerable alarm. She has in her possession our Post Office Saving Bank book!"
"Ah!"
"My name is Hennessy-Pethwick—pronounced Henpeck—and my wife's disappearance dates from Saturday of last week. I have advertised in the colums of 'Punch' and 'The Fishing Gazette,' but without result. Upon you, Sholmes, I hurl myself in my extremity!"
And our amazing visitor leapt at Sholmes, clutching him frantically round the neck.
"Pray remember whom you have the honour of addressing!" said Sholmes, in the cold, forbidding tones he reserved for these occasions. "How can I proceed with the case if you throttle me beforehand?"
Mr. Hennessy-Pethwick disentangled himself at the expense of bursting my friend's shirt-front.
"You will find my wife?" he asked eagerly. Shomes nodded.
"She will be on your doorstep at seven o'clock this evening," he said.
"But how—what——" gasped out client.
"I do not make my methods the subject of vulgar discussion. Leave it to me."
And Mr. Hennessy-Pethwick was ushered to the door. Judging by the detonation which smote our ears the next moment, he had again taken the line of least resistance with regard to the stairs.
Sholmes lit a Flor de Cabbagio with an abstracted air.
"This is quite in accord with a smiling world, Jotson. I foresee half the contents of that Post Office Savings Bank book transferred to my own pocket. I foresee a complete settlement of arrears with Mrs. Spudson. I foresee high revels this evening at the fried-fish shop!"
"But how do you propose to run Mrs. Hennessy-Pethwick to earth?" I asked. "It is impossible!"
"Nothing is impossible—except to Scotland Yard. Our friend left his address, did he not?"
"Yes; here is his card. 27, Ragtime Alley."
"Very well, Jotson. If you will saunter round to No. 27 at the time I specified, you will see Mrs. Hennessy-Pethwick restored to the bosom of her family. Did you get me, Steve, as they say in Persia?"
So saying, my wonderful friend tilted up the empty cocaine-cask with a gesture of annoyance, and proceeded to leave the house, donning his carpet-slippers lest Mrs. Spudson should hear him.

CHAPTER 2

Firm as was my faith in Herlock Sholmes, I confess I could not quite see how, without a single clue to guide him, he was to be successful in bringing Mrs. Hennessy-Pethwick back to the fold. Besides, the good lady had been missing since the previous Saturday, and in the interval which followed her disappearance she might have placed a gulf of hundreds of miles between herself and civilisation.
Yet my friend had so many brilliant achievements to his credit that I was impelled by instinct and curiosity to visit No. 27, Ragtime Alley, that evening.
I arrived at five minutes to seven.
Seated on the front gate, kicking his legs with agitated violence against the poodle which hovered there, was the distracted husband.
"Ah, Dr. Jotson!" he exclaimed on my approach. "You have come to report that there is nothing doing with regard to my wife?"
"On the contrary," I observed. "I have every reason to believe that my friend Sholmes will add yet again to his list of triumphs. Listen!"
Above the roar of the traffic and the booming of the anti-aircraft guns—for a mild aerial bombardment was in progress—we distinctly heard the rustle of a skirt.
The next moment the missing wife was locked in the embrace of her husband, who feverishly seized the Savings Bank book from her bag.
I turned away to hide my emotion, when Herlock Sholmes loomed up out of the shadows.
"A very happy climax, Jotson!" he said, rubbing his hands. "Mr. Hennessy-Pethwick once more breathes freely. His wife is restored to him complete, and—what is more important—his Post Office Savings Bank book. I think we have every reason to congratulate ourselves."
"Indeed we have, Sholmes!"
"Excuse me a moment, Jotson. I must secure my commission from the happy husband, or our dream of fried cod and chipped potatoes, may not materialise."
My friend stepped into the house, whither the couple had retired; and when he returned a moment later I distinctly heard the rustle of a shilling postal-order.
"Lead on, Macduff!" said Sholmes, prodding me in the ribs in his affectionate manner. "In addition

to our fish and chips, I fancy we shall be able to sport a bottle of strong ginger-beer.
We walked away, and I waited for my friend to give the usual explanation.
He remained silent, however, until after the first course. Then he turned to me with one of his rare guffaws.
"You are wondering how I found Mrs. Hennessy-Pethwick, Jotson?"
"My wonder increases each moment, Sholmes!"
"The thing," said my friend, mopping up his ginger-beer, with a smile, "was dead easy. The good woman was first absent on Saturday."
"True!"
"Why are women absent from their homes on Saturday, Jotson?"
"The lure of the cinema?" I suggested.
"Wrong, Jotson. From wide experience of this subject I have deduced that the majority of women are absent on Saturday in order to do their weekly shopping."
"Marvellous!" I exclaimed.
"Not at all. Granted, then, that Mrs. Hennessy-Pethwick had got to do her shopping, what commodity would she have gone chiefly to purchase?"
I shook my head.
"Why, margarine, of course! Margarine is a national necessity. Very well. And where can margarine be purchased cheaper than anywhere else?"
Again I shook my head.
"In Wapping, Jotson. There are many things that are cheap at Wapping, and margarine is one of them. My course, then was clear. I proceeded to Wapping, and found Mrs. Hennessy-Pethwick in the margarine queue. She had been waiting there since last Saturday!"
"Sholmes!" I exclaimed. "There are moments when my admiration for you knows no bounds! Only a master-mind such as yours could have deduced——"
"Enough!" said Sholmes, rising to his feet with a yawn. "This is neither the time nor the place to indulge in heroics. Pay the bill, Jotson, and we will travel."
We travelled.

THE CASE OF THE MISSING MANUSCRIPT

No. 41

Sholmes and I sat at breakfast in our apartments in Shaker Street. My amazing friend was reading for the tenth time a letter which had come by that morning's post. As he read he frowned thoughtfully.
At length Sholmes looked up.
"Jotson, I have an interesting case in hand. Will you come with me?" he said.
"But, my dear Sholmes, I have an engagement!" I ventured to remark.
"Pshaw! Bernard Pshaw! What is it?"
"I am attending the funeral of one of my patients, Sholmes."
"You can do that any day, Jotson."
"That is true, Sholmes. I shall have pleasure in accompanying you."
"That surely goes without saying, Jotson!"
"Yes, Sholmes. But I did not see why I should go without saying."
Sholmes did not appear to see the joke.
"You have heard of St. James' School, Jotson?" he said. "Even you must have heard ot that famous scholastic establishment."
"Yes, Sholmes. Are we going there?"
"That you will see presently, Jotson."
We took a taxi to Victoria, and went thence by train to Rylcombe. Here an antiquated growler conveyed us to the school gates, and we were admitted by a porter who seemed to have a peculiar sense of humour, for he sniggered at Sholmes, and laughed outright at me. But that may have been due to the fact that Sholmes, after his playful fashion, had made use of my collar as a pipe-rack.
Inside the gates we saw a thin youth with a large and bumpy forehead. He very politely conducted us to Study No. 6 on the Fourth Form passage, for which Sholmes inquired. On the way there he discoursed in a most philosophic strain.
"Come in, fathead!" yelled a youthful voice as Sholmes tapped at the door of the study indicated by our guide.
There were four boys in the apartment. One of them at once apologised for the term of endearment used in giving permission to enter. But Sholmes waved aside the apology in his usual airy fashion.
"Which of you answers to the name of D'Arcy?" he asked.
"Depends a good deal on what D'Arcy's wanted for," said the shortest of the four. "But it ain't often for any good, so——"
"Weally, Dig! I am D'Arcy, sir, an' I pwesume you are Mr. Herlock Sholmes?"
"At your service, my young friend."
"Pway take seats, gentlemen! I will welate bwiefly the twouble which caused me to w'ite to Mr.

Sholmes."

D'Arcy struck me as a very engaging young gentleman, but his ideas as to brevity were scarcely on all fours with mine.

Boiled down to about a tenth of the length at which he told it, his story practically amounted to this.

He and his youtful companions were all in a state which he described, by a picturesque phrase new to me, as "stonay." A visitor whom they desired to treat with honour was expected; and D'Arcy—as I gather, without the approval of the other three—hit upon what he regarded as an excellent method of "raisin' the wind"—another of his picturesque phrases.

He wrote a story entitled "Lord Topper's Trousers," and had intended to send it to a well-known London paper which is rumoured to pay high prices for really first-class contributions as there is no doubt this was—no doubt in the mind of D'Arcy, that is.

But this story mysteriously disappeared on the very day on which he had meant to post it. So he wrote to Sholmes.

CHAPTER 2

Sholmes sat wrinkling his thumbs and twirling his brows, after his usual fashion when deep in thought.

"May I ask, D'Arcy," he said at length, "whether your friends entertained a high opinion of your story?"

D'Arcy was not suffered to answer that question.

"It was utter piffle!" said the fresh-faced athletic youth.

"Beastly rot!" growled the burly one.

"Bilge-water and tripe!" said the short one, grinning.

Sholmes sat staring in an absent-minded sort of way at a large big-toe which peeped coyly from his right boot. I fancy he was deducing the fact that the boot needed repair.

"May I see your frying-pan?" he asked, after a few minutes.

"Fwyin'-pan? Of course, Mr. Sholmes! But weally——"

Blake dragged the required utensil from the cupboard. By the way, I deduced the fact that his name was Blake from the other three addressing him by that name, which shows that I am making progress in the deductive methods of my great chief.

"You used this pan of the same day on which D'Arcy missed his story, my young friends," said Sholmes.

"So we did, sir!" said the short youth.

"Ah! Before using it you wiped it out?"

"That's so, sir. We always do," said Blake. "Lots of things get cooked in that pan, and we don't like the flavours too mixed."

"Where do you usually throw any paper used to wipe out the pan?"

"Into the wastepaper-basket, sir."

"You will find your story in the wastepaper-basket, D'Arcy," said my wonderful friend. "Part of it will be greasy. The other part will be dusty, for I observe that the bookshelves have recently been dusted, and that it was done with something other than the article commonly employed for that purpose."

Blake upset the wastepaper-basket, and the correctness of Sholmes' deduction was at once made clear.

It was really one of the most amazing cases in which Herlock Sholmes was ever concerned, for who could have dreamed that that great mind would descend to the minutiae of schoolboy methods in such matters as cleaning a frying-pan and dusting bookshelves?

But it cannot be said that the fee was in proportion to the genius shown. Sholmes, in fact, refused to accept any fee at all, and we had to travel back under the seat, and to dodge the ticket-inspectors at both ends by a method which I am not at liberty to disclose.

1919

THE CASE OF THE AIRMAN'S MEDAL

No. 42

Herlock Sholmes emptied the cocaine-cask at a gulp, and assumed his favourite attitude by dangling his feet over the mantelpiece.

"Life is tame, Jotson!" he observed. "Since the signing of the Armistice I have found the tasks suited to my peculiar powers. I have successfully solved the Mystery of the Stolen Ration-book, and have smoothed out the complicated affairs of Professor Gotsuchakoff. My rooms here in Shaker Street are not, unfortunately, rent-free. Unless wealthy clients continue to solicit my assistance, I fear Mrs. Spudson will resort to forcible ejectment——"

"Hush!" I interrupted. "someone is coming!"

Herlock Sholmes sprang to his feet.

"If the brokers are here, Jotson," said he, "they shall only enter this room over my dead body!"

Our visitor, however, was nothing more harmful than a young flying officer who, having made a forced landing on the upturned carpet, addressed himself to Sholmes in tones of great agitation.

"You are Mr. Herlock Sholmes?" he cried.

"The same!" said Sholmes. "Pray be seated!"

Our visitor sank limply on to the coal-scuttle. Sholmes, drumming his fingers on the cocaine-cask, eyed him keenly.

"You are Second-Lieutenant Flapwing, of the Air Force?" he said.

The visitor started.

"Really, Mr. Sholmes! Is it possible that my identity is already an open book to you?"

Sholmes nodded.

"I remember to have seen your photograph in the 'Daily Monocle' at the time of your marriage," he said. "Features like yours are not easily forgotten. In what way can I be of service to you? You may speak quite freely before my friend Dr. Jotson'!"

"Mr. Sholmes," said the young officer, '"mine is a tragic story. My Distinguished Stunting Medal—which was presented to me at Buckingham Palace for killing two cows during a forced landing—has disappeared!"

"Ah!"

"Unless it is found, Mr. Sholmes, I am a ruined man! Now that the war is over, I intend to become the pilot of a passenger-airship plying between London and Colney Hatch. If I wore my medal, would-be passengers would at once realise that they were in safe and experienced hands. If I wear no medal, they will say, 'Ah, he is not a qualified pilot! He will send us crashing to destruction from ten thousand feet!' Such a prospect, Mr. Sholmes, is distracting!"

"Set your mind at rest, my dear fellow!" said Sholmes. "This case presents few difficulties to a master-mind, though it would undoubtedly baffle the obtuse brains of Scotland Yard. What is your address, Mr. Flapwing?"

"The Fledglings Club, Piccadilly."

"Very good! Your medal will be restored to you this evening at seven o'clock!"

"But how on earth——"

Sholmes raised his hand.

"My methods are not to be made the subject of vulgar cusiosity!" he said. "I wish you a good-morning, Mr. Flapwing!"

With that our visitor was ushered out. A subsequent crash from the hall below showed that he had taken the line of least resistance with regard to the stairs.

Accustomed as I was to the marvellous ingenuity of my friend, I must confess that I was surprised at the ease with which he confronted this colossal task. He had promised to bring the Distinguished Stunting Medal back to its owner at a specified hour—and he had not even a clue!

"I know what you are thinking, Jotson!" said Sholmes. "You imagine I have bitten off more than I can conveniently masticate. If your faith in my powers is shaken, you had better go and attend to your patients!"

"They are all dead, Sholmes!" I said sadly. "Whilst I have been engrossed with your exploits, I fear they have gone untimely to their graves. But that is neither here nor there. I am curious to see if you will prove successful in the present enterprise."

"In that case, Jotson, you had better be outside the Fledglings Club at seven o'clock precisely!"

And my companion, having assured him that the landlady was nowhere in sight, slipped out by the back door.

CHAPTER 2

When I arrived at the Fledglings Club shortly before seven, I found Second-Lieutenant Flapwing seated without.

"I fear, Dr. Jotson," said he, "that your friend's investigations will for once, end in smoke!"

"Nonsense!" I retorted. "Your medal will be restored to you at the stipulated time."

"If not" said the distracted airman, "I shall be compelled to suffocate myself in the nearest Tube station!"

At that instant the neighbouring clocks began to chime seven, and simultaneously came the purr of an automobile.

I turned to my companion with a smile of triumph.

"Sholmes has once more stepped in where Scotland Yard would fear to tread!" I observed. "And he has been, as usual, successful!"

Even as I spoke the great detective alighted from the car. He gripped a hard and heavy piece of metal in his hand.

"Ha, Mr. Flapwing!" said Sholmes, with one of his rare guffaws. "My quest was not in vain. Here is the medal which you won under such noble and destructive circumstances!"

"Mr. Sholmes! How can I ever thank you——"

"Don't try, my dear fellow!" said Sholmes genially. Then, turning to me, he muttered: "I will rejoin you, Jotson, as soon as I have drawn my commission!"

Sholmes followed the delighted airman up the steps, and a moment later I distinctly heard the rustle of a shilling postal-order.

"This evening, Jotson," he said, as we drove off to his rooms in Shaker Street, "we shall not only be able to indulge in the unusual luxury of fried fish for supper, but funds will probably run to a strong lemonade in addition."

"Really, Sholmes!" I exclaimed. "I can scarcely contain myself! I am bursting to learn some facts from you——"

"You know my methods in these cases, Jotson. From the first I was able to account for the disappearacne of the medal. It appears that only yesterday a collector of old iron called at the Fledglings Club."

"Sholmes!"

"The flunkey who opened the door to him," continued Sholmes, "ransacked all the rooms in quest of old iron. Seeing Mr. Flapwing's medal on the matelpiece he gathered it up with the rest, and handed it to the old-iron merchant.

"The rest was easy, Jotson. I tracked the itinerant vendor of ancient iron to his lair in Peckham. When I explained to him the value of the medal—at the same time covering him with two of my revolvers—he promptly handed it over."

"Marvellous!" I exclaimed.

"Not at all!" said Sholmes as we re-entered his room. "To a man of my illimitable deductive powers such work is child's play!"

And he buried his head in the cocaine-cask.

1920

HERLOCK SHOLMES COLOUR PLATE SECTION

Herlock Sholmes

Stretched upon the floor was the gigantic form of Dr. Grimey Pilott. About it was coiled a huge rattlesnake. (See 'The Freckled Hand').

Sholmes was an accomplished seaman. His voice rang out from the bridge, giving orders. "Take a double reef in the propellor! Lower the topgallant sails into the engine-room! Hoist the main deck overboard!" These orders were promptly obeyed. (See 'The Captured Submarines').

At a large window a face suddenly appeared, then as we gazed, it was joined by a crowd more, all looking at us as we stood. (See 'The Yellow Phiz').

A wax figure was installed to act as the great Minister's substitute. (See 'The Missing Minister').

As she withdrew her hand, Sholmes grasped it in a grip of iron. (See 'The Last of the Potatoes').

Sholmes opened with a beautiful right swing to the wicket-keeper's nose. (See 'The Missing Cricketer').

A gentleman with rather wild eyes' and a remarkable head of hair, came into the sitting-room. (See 'The Case of the Musician').

Sholmes followed the bloodhound, and Jotson followed Sholmes. (See 'The Case of the Sinn Feiners').

Sholmes neatly tripped the Bolshevik in passing. (See 'The Case of the Bolshevik!').

Sholmes was under the influence of some strange fear. (See 'The Disappearance of Dr. Jotson').

Sholmes swarmed up the telegraph-pole. (See 'The Case of the Lost Chord').

There was the ancient baboon cracking nuts with a pair of forceps. (See 'The Case of the Dentist').

"Mr. Sholmes!" gasped the newcomer. "Thank 'eavins you're hin!". (See 'The Case of the Lost Sapphire').

The pointed boot of steel shot out, and caught the ghostly knight on a tender spot. "Yoop! Yow-ow!" "Quick, Jotson!" shouted Herlock Sholmes. "Fetch a tin opener!". (See 'That Ghostly Xmas Knight').

Sholmes stood on his head on the lid of the cocaine cask and kicked his slippers to the ceiling. (See 'The Mystery of the Green Crab').

THE MISSING CRICKETER

No. 43

Shakespeare—a well-known playwright—has very truly observed that one man in his time plays many parts. This is particularly true of my amazing friend, Mr. Herlock Sholmes. During our residence together at Shaker Street I had the opportunity of witnessing many of his roles—indeed, I have even seen him lunch upon a roll. But the case of the missing cricketer brought to light a fresh side of his variegated character, to my increasing astonishment and admiration.

Sholmes was glancing over the morning paper when Sir Filbert Duxegg, the captain of Dudshire County, was shown in by Mrs. Spudson. The strange disappearance of Mr. H. Walker, the champion bat of Dudshire, was then absorbing public attention.

Sholmes, I knew. was interested in sport. He was an expert at shove ha'penny, and at marbles he had few equals. On horses his opinion was final; he knew why Squared Jim had won the Swindleton Handicap, and why Nobbled Nick had lost. With his usual judgment, he had backed Welsh Rabbit for the War Stakes. But I had yet to learn that his knowledge of cricket was equally extensive and peculiar.

He glanced over his paper at our visitor, with his penetrating glance.

"Good-morning, Sir Filbert," he said affably.

Our visitor gave a start.

"You know my name!"

"Evidently," said Sholmes, carelessly turning over the newspaper page, upon which a photograph of the Dudshire captain appeared. "Pray be seated. I am Herlock Sholmes. You may speak quite freely before my friend Dr. Jotson."

I gazed at Herlock Sholmes with silent admiration. With no clue but the photograph under his eyes, he had recognised the captain of Dudshire at a glance.

I could see that our visitor was also impressed. This nonchalant display by my amazing friend's powers had given him confidence in Herlock Sholmes.

"You have called in reference to your missing batsman, I presume?" continued Sholmes.

"That is the case," Sir Filbert leaned forward eagerly. "To-day we play Slopshire, and if Walker is not found we shall never pull through. Yesterday he disappeared——"

"Without leaving a clue?"

"He was last seen in the dressing-room. Nothing was found there but an empty bottle——"

"Ah!" I could see that Sholmes was interested. "Was there any distinguishing mark upon the bottle?"

"A label bore the name 'Johnnie Walker.' The police surmise that it may have contained some intoxicating fluid."

"It is possible."

"Mr. Sholmes, our only hope is in you."

Sholmes glanced at his watch.

"At what time does the match begin to-day, Sir Filbert?"

"Ten-thirty."

"And it is now half-past nine. You have not been in a hurry to call in my services," said Herlock Sholmes, with a touch of irony. "You relied on the official police, no doubt. However, if your only hope is in me, it is up to me to justify your faith. Dudshire will win the match to-day, Sir Filbert."

"Then you think——" exclaimed the baronet eagerly.

"I do not think; I know. By the aroma that floats in at the window, I judge that your car is waiting below. Let us be off. Rely upon me, Sir Filbert. I have, as a matter of fact, backed Dudshire to the extent of eightpence, and if they should be beaten to-day the financial results to me will be serious. Allons!"

We hurried down to the car.

In a few minutes we were whizzing through the busy streets, en route for the Dudshire County ground. It had been my intention that morning to attend the funeral of one of my patients, but I was too keenly interested in Sholmes' work to think of it now.

The Dudshire ground was already crowded when we arrived.

The visiting eleven undoubtedly counted upon an easy victory, in the absence of Dudshire's champion bat. But they reckoned without Herlock Sholmes.

The bottle was produced. Sholmes examined it attentively, and his expression showed that the scent emanating from it was familiar to him.

Sir Filbert watched him anxiously.

Sholmes spoke at last.

"This bottle contained spirits," he said. "Walker has been spirited away."

"The stumps are already pitched!" exclaimed Sir Filbert, in despair. "Mr. Sholmes, can you do nothing for us?"

"Everything," answered Herlock Sholmes quietly. "I have said that Dudshire shall win. Play me."

"You!" ejaculated the Dudshire captain. "Come, then! There is no time to be lost!"

I could scarcely believe my own eyes when Herlock Sholmes ran lightly into the field, bat in hand, to open the innings for Dudshire. Accustomed as I was to the versatility of my amazing friend, I was not prepared for this development.

But I watched with confidence. And my confidence was soon justified.

It is safe to say that such cricket had never been played before on the Dudshire County ground.

From the first ball of the first over Sholmes was the master of the situation.

He opened brilliantly, with a beautiful right swing to the wicket-keeper's nose, and there was a cheer from the Dudshire crowd. Then he gave a miss in baulk, modulated rapidly into C minor, and potted the red, amid growing enthusiasm.

Eager eyes followed him as he charged square-leg, boxed the compass, and, with an obligato entirely on the G string, took a header, and scored a bull's-eye on the pavilion clock.

Dismay fell upon Slopshire, utterly unaccustomed to play of this quality.

But Sholmes was not finished yet.

Without stopping to take rest, he huffed his opponent's king, and in less time than it would take to recite "The Charge of the Gas Company" he had beaten the opposing ranks, reached high-water mark, and put the lid on. Then there was enthusiastic clapping, as he jazzed with amazing velocity and cannoned off the cush.

Little more remains to be told. Nonchalant as ever, Herlock Sholmes checked with the knight, and trumped the ace, amid thunderous cheers.

He was borne shoulder-high from the field.

"Well, Jotson?" he said, with a smile, a few hours later, as we took our seats in the train for London.

"Sholmes!" I gasped.

It was all I could say. There were no words in which I could express my admiration for my friend's astounding abilities.

THE BACON MYSTERY

No. 44

Herlock Sholmes was standing at the telephone when I came in from visiting my patients. He put up the receiver, and glanced at me with a slightly bored expression.

"Another case, Sholmes!"

"Another case, Jotson," he answered. "I am wanted at the docks. A cargo of foodstuffs from Chicago was landed yesterday, and some foolhardy individual has stolen a side of bacon. At all events, so I am assured. The official who rung me up declares that it could not have wandered away, as the dock-gates were watched. If you care to come——"

"Certainly me dear Sholmes,"

"Then get your gas-mask at once, and let us start."

"My gas-mask?" I repeated.

"Undoubtedly. We are going among the newly landed cargo——"

"But——"

"You are aware, my dear Jotson, that in the United States everything moves on a higher plane than in this country. The ideals are high, the prices are high, and the bacon is most decidedly high. All things considered, it will be safer to take our gas-masks. Why run unnecessary risks?"

"You are right, Sholmes, as, indeed, you always are."

In a few minutes we were on our way to the docks.

We arrived there, and were received by the official in charge, and, having donned our gas-masks,

Having donned their gas-masks, Sholmes and Jotson entered the bacon storage department.

were taken to the bacon storage department.

There Herlock Sholmes made a very brief examination. As a rule Sholmes was very thorough-going in his methods. But on this occasion he seemed somewhat hurried.

"Have your suspicions fallen upon anyone?" he inquired, as we emerged.

"One of the casual workers has not turned up to-day, Mr. Sholmes. We have inquired at his home, and find that he is missing."

"Ah! What steps have been taken?"

"We have circulated his description among all the provision-dealers."

"For what reason?" inquired Sholmes.

The official stared.

"Naturally, to prevent him from disposing of the side of bacon, as it seems clear that he is the person who purloined it," he answered tartly.

"Really, Mr. Sholmes——"

Herlock Sholmes smiled his inscrutable smile.

"Any other steps?" he asked.

"None."

"Very good. I will take up the case, and I hope to place the man in your hands in a few hours. Give me his description.

We breathed more freely when we had taken our leave.

In Shaker Street once more, we separated.

"I shall be busy this afternoon, Jotson," said Herlock Sholmes. "You may go and see your patients, my dear fellow. The case is hardly worthy of my powers, but I will see it through."

"On the contrary, my dear Sholmes, you seem to have set yourself a difficult task," I remarked. "You have no clue——"
"I have the description of the man who bagged the bacon, Jotson."
"True; but——"
"I am now about to make a round, and look for him."
"But in so large a city as London, Sholmes!" I exclaimed in amazement. "Surely——"
"My visits will be confined to the places where it is probable that he will be found, Jotson."
"At the provision-dealers?"
"Not at all, But I will explain when we meeet again, my dear fellow, at the end of the story as usual.
And we separated.

CHAPTER 2

I was thinking of Herlock Sholmes a good deal during the remainder of the day.
My faith in my amazing friend was great, but I was perplexed.
With simply the description of the missing docker to aid him, how was he to find the man in the vast wilderness of London?
Certainly the man was not likely to return to the docks, and it had already been ascertained that he was missing from his lodgings. And Sholmes evidently did not believe that he would be found attempting to dispose of his plunder at a provision-dealer's.
What clue, then, existed to his possible whereabouts was a mystery to me.
I was eager to see Herlock Sholmes that evening, for, as I was, I did not doubt that he would be successful, as usual, and would furnish me with the usual explanation over our evening kipper.
I had to perform an important operation that afternoon. When it was over, and I had signed the death certificate, I returned to our rooms at Shaker Street. A grateful and comforting aroma of kippers greeted me as I entered. Sholmes, already seated at the table, looked up with a smile.
"My dear Sholmes," I exclaimed, "you are back already!"
"As you see, Jotson."
"And the case of the missing side of bacon——"
"Is finished."
"And the thief——"
"Is found."
"My dear Sholmes! You amaze me more and more."
Sholmes smiled, with a rather bored expression.
"My dear Jotson, the case was, as I remarked to you, hardly worthy of my powers. However, I will explain."
"I am all ears, Sholmes."
"Not all—though, perhaps, nearly all," smiled Sholmes. "However, to explain. What do you suppose the man's object was in stealing a side of bacon newly landed from an American ship?"
"For profit, I presume—to dispose of it to a dealer."
"Impossible. No dealer would have taken it off his hands. Even in a time of scarcity, Jotson, there is a limit. Moreover, the man could not have taken it about the streets for long without risk of detection. He might have been stopped at any moment by a policeman, for leading it about unmuzzled."
"True."
"No, Jotson; it was evidently a genuine case of hunger," said Sholmes. "The man bagged the bacon with the intention of eating it——"
"Poor, poor fellow!" I explained involuntarily. "He must indeed have been in severe want."
"Undoubtedly. The bacon was stolen yesterday, and I judged that he had had some of it, at least, for his supper—on the theory that he must have been very hungry indeed to take it at all. I took his description, therefore, and made a round in search of him——"
"Where, Sholmes?"
"Naturally, at the hospitals," he replied. "Convinced that he had eaten part of his plunder, where else should I look for him?"
"Most true!"
"At the third hospital I visited I found him. He had been admitted overnight, suffering from a complication of severe internal problems. I telephoned his present address to the docks, and—voila tout! Child's-play, my dear Jotson," said Sholmes, with a yawn. "But the kippers are getting cold; let us dine."

THE CHOPSTEIN VENUS

No. 45

Herlock Sholmes was drawing his usual quart of cocaine from the cask, after breakfast one morning, in our rooms at Shaker Street, when the door was flung suddenly open, and a man, hatless, breathless, and wide-eyed, rushed in.
"Mr. Sholmes!" he gasped, sinking upon a chair. "I—I—"

"Calm yourself Mr. Chopstein," said Herlock Sholmes.
I looked at our visitor with great interest. I had, of course, often heard of Chopstein, the celebrated sculptor, whose latest work had caused so much commotion in artistic circles.
"My latest, greatest work," he sobbed, "lost, stolen or strayed! Oh, Mr. Sholmes, if you cannot find my masterpiece——"
"Herlock Sholmes can find anything, from a German indemnity to a needle in a haystack," I interrupted severely. "Only this morning he found a pin which had been left by accident in the armchair——"
"Let us have a few details, Mr. Chopstein," said Sholmes quietly. "You may speak quite freely before——"
"You have heard of the statue, of course," said Mr. Chopstein, calming himself with an effort. "It was my celebrated statue of Venus. I am the leader of the Neo-Sculptors, My methods are ultra-modern. I used a pick-axe for my work—the results are atonishing. This statue—this masterpiece—was a miracle of art. I intended, at first to call it 'The Riven Oak'; later I thought that 'The Fallen Zeppelin' would be a better title; but I finally decide upon 'Venus.'"
He wept.
"And now?" said Herlock Sholmes.
"It was removed from the gallery, where it was exhibited, and left standing on the pavement for a short time. The road was up. The street in which the gallery stands is a very busy one, so naturally the road had been up for several days. It was necessary to procure a trolley to convey it to the corner, where a car was waiting to carry it away. While they were fetching the trolley, the statue vanished."
"Extraordinary!" I exclaimed.
"Very!" said Herlock Sholmes drily. "The theft must have been observed——"
"That is the extraordinary part of the story," exclaimed Mr. Chopstein. "There were a number of workmen on the spot, engaged in laying the paving-stones, but no one appears to have seen the statue removed. They have been questioned, but they do not seem to have observed the statue at all. Yet it vanished.
Sholmes looked very thoughtful.
"We will proceed at once to the spot. Take courage, Mr. Chopstein."
In a very short time we arrived at the Balmycrumpet Art Gallery.
The pavement was still up outside the building.
Workmen were laying paving-stones at a rate of speed which indicated that they did not desire to put the country to the cost of providing them with old-age pensions. A number of blocks stood about, with men sitting on them, discussing Ruskin and Joe Beckett. The foreman did not venture to interrupt. On a cart close at hand, laden with fresh paving-blocks, was the name, "John William Robinson, Contractor, Clapham."
Sholmes glanced at it, and addressed the foreman.
To my surprise, and that of Mr. Chopstein, his questions did not refer to the missing statue.
"You have a fresh lot of paving-blocks there?" he remarked casually.
The foreman nodded.
"Have you sent any away?" asked Sholmes carelessly.
"One was sent back to the yard this morning," answered the foreman, with a stare, evidently surprised at the question.
"Ah, why?"
"It had not been squared properly; it must have been sent on by mistake, as it was quite unfit for laying. I really don't see how you know anything about it," added the foreman.
"Mr. Sholmes," gasped the sculptor, "you are wasting time! Can you—will you—find the missing statue——"
"I trust so," answered Herlock Sholmes tranquilly. "It will be necessary for me to take a taxi; kindly advance me ten pounds off my fee, as I shall have to go several miles!"
Mr. Chopstein obeyed in silence, and Sholmes hailed a taxi.
"Wait for me at this corner," he said.
He stepped into the taxi, and I was still amazed when I heard him give the directions to the driver: "Clapham!"

CHAPTER 2

We waited.
Mr. Chopstein fumed with impatience and anxiety. It was evident that his faith in my amazing friend had received a shock.
It was with great relief that I saw, at last, the taxi returning. It stopped at the corner, and Sholmes jumped out.
"Look!" said Herlock Sholmes calmly.
He pointed to the vehicle. We looked, and Mr. Chopstein uttered a cry of joy. For a moment I could not understand his transports. What appeared to me a shapeless chunk of stone lay on the seat of the taxi. But a word from Herlock Sholmes enlightened me.
"The missing Venus!" he said quietly.

"Sholmes, you have found it——"

"Evidently!"

Leaving Mr. Chopstein weeping tears of joy over his recovered masterpiece, we walked back to Shaker Street. It was not till Sholmes was in his armchair, with his feet on the table, and a tankard of cocaine, at his elbow, that he consented to satisfy my curiosity.

"A very simple matter, me dear Jotson," he said. "You heard the question I put to the foreman?"

"Undoubtedly; but I did not see any connection between a paving-block, and the missing statue of Venus."

Sholmes smiled slightly.

"You forget, Jotson, that Mr. Chopstein is an exponent of the new art. The Chopstein Venus was left standing on the pavement. A number of paving-blocks were standing there also. The foreman's eye fell upon it. Not being a Neo-Sculptor he did not recognise it as a statue. So far from supposing that it was a masterpiece of the new art, he took it for a paving block that had been carelessly cut. As it was too irregularly shaped for using to repair the pavement, he sent it back to the contractor's yard at Clapham—where I found it, Jotson. That is all."

"Sholmes!"

"It was a natural mistake on the part of the foreman, and no harm is done," yawned Sholmes; "But had the foreman been a little less careful, the statue would have undoubtedly been used in repairing the pavement, and the world of art would have mourned for ever the loss of the Chopstein Venus!"

THE CASE OF THE MISSING HEIR

No. 46

I had been absent that morning, attending the inquest upon one of my patients, and when I returned I found that Herlock Sholmes was not alone. Mr. Pinch, of the well-known firm of Pinch and Pluckem, solicitors, was with my amazing friend. I would have retired, but Sholmes signed to me, in his genial way, to enter.

"Pray come in, my dear Jotson," he said. "Mr. Pinch is giving me the details of a very interesting, if simple case——"

"Simple, Mr. Sholmes!" exclaimed the solicitor.

Sholmes smiled.

"Simple to me," he explained. "Extremely puzzling to any ordinary intellect, such as that of my friend Dr. Jotson, of course. Sit down, Jotty, and help yourself to the cocaine. Pray continue, Mr. Pinch."

"The case appears to me a most difficult one," said Mr. Pinch. "I have come to you, Mr. Sholmes, as a last resource, to find the missing heir."

"Ah, the case of a missing heir?" I remarked with interest.

"Yes. Six years ago our former client, Mr. Boodle, disinherited his only son. He was a coal-miner in South Wales, of immense wealth. He has died without making a will, and unless his son can be found his fortune will go into Chancery. The young man has been missing for years, and no clue exists as to his whereabouts. All that is known of his intentions, when he left home, is that he declared his resolution to run away and become a pirate. This, from what we have been able to ascertain, had been his desire from his earliest years. I really do not see, Mr. Sholmes, how you can regard this case as a simple one."

I glanced at Sholmes.

I confess that I agreed with Mr. Pinch, and considered that my amazing friend had been set a very difficult task.

Sholmes smiled his inscrutable smile.

"The young man was traced to London, I think?" he said.

"That is the case, but there all trace of him was lost," said Mr. Pinch. "If he has carried out his intention, and become a pirate, he certainly will not be found in London, Mr. Sholmes.

"No doubt. But there are certain difficulties in the way of becoming a pirate, in these days," said Herlock Sholmes. "Piracy, of course, flourishes as much as in former days, but under altered and more legal forms. The clue, however, is one that even the police might be able to follow, if you had applied to them."

"I fail to see——"

"Naturally. If you could see, you would not come to me for aid," smiled Sholmes. "The case is, as I have said, simple. I take it that what you require now is the present address of the missing heir."

"Precisely."

Sholmes rose to his feet.

"Pray remain here till my return," he said. "I shall not be long, and I hope to bring with me the address you require."

"Mr. Sholmes!"

But Herlock Sholmes was gone.

"The missing heir is found," said Sholmes calmly. "Here is his address."

My amazing friend was absent an hour or more.
Mr. Pinch waited, with evident signs of impatience, though I endeavoured to reassure him.
Herlock Sholmes entered at last.
The smile upon his face assured me that, astounding as it was, he had been successful.
Mr. Pinch rose impatiently to his feet.
"Really, Mr. Sholmes, we are wasting time," he exclaimed. "If you are prepared to take up the search for the missing heir——"
"The missing heir is found," answered Herlock Sholmes calmly.
"What?"
"Here is his address."
Sholmes tossed a card lightly upon the table.
I glanced at it as eagerly as Mr. Pinch. The card bore the inscription:

"Welshem, Overreach, and Boodle,
House Agents,
Swindleton Street, London."

"That is the address you seek, Mr. Pinch," drawled Herlock Sholmes. "A very simple case, as I told you. Good-morning!"

CHAPTER 2

"Sholmes!" I exclaimed breathlessly.
Herlock Sholmes laughed, as he reclined in the arm-chair, and rested his feet on the mantelpiece in his easy, familiar way.
"Have I surprised you again, Jotson?" he asked.
"You have astounded me, Sholmes! You have discovered the missing heir——"
"Exactly."
"In so short a space of time——"
"It was long enough for me, Jotson."
"But how, Sholmes? Without a clue——"
"My dear Jotson, you heard Mr. Pinch give me the clue—an unmistakable one."
"I do not see——"
"Ah, you have not yet sufficiently studied my methods, Jotson. However, I will explain. The missing heir left his father's house with the declared intention of becoming a pirate."
"No doubt! But——"
"But in these prosaic days, Jotson, pirates are a thing of the past. On entering into the world, the ambitious young man found that his ambition was, as a matter of fact, out of date. He could not become a pirate in the old-fashioned sense of the term. Imagine for a moment, Jotson, that Captain Kidd, and Morgan the buccaneer, and Blackbeard the pirate were living these days, what would be their natural resource, since piracy is no longer practicable on the high seas?"
I reflected for a moment.
"I suppose they would become candidates for the House of Commons," I suggested.
"True. But you must remember that this disinherited young man was not in a position to do so. With the keenest desire to become a freebooter, yet lacking the necessary capital to set up as a politician, there was only one resource for him—to become a house-agent."
"Sholmes!"
"My task was, therefore, simple. I called in at the nearest free library, and obtained a directory of house-agents," yawned Sholmes. "As I expected, I found his name there. That is all, Jotson—a very simple case. Pass the cocaine!"

THE MYSTERY OF THE STUDIO

No. 47

The name of Mr. Smeary Smudgett was, of course, well-known to us; and both Sholmes and I were considerably interested when the famous impressionist painter was shown into our rooms at Shaker Street.
Sholmes had been busy that day. His services had been called upon by a demobbed Tommy who had lost his pension, and Sholmes had been engaged in the search with a powerful microscope. But with his usual polished courtesy, my amazing friend removed his feet from the mantelpiece, and pushed back the cocaine cask, as Mr. Smudgett entered.
The celebrated painter was in a state of agitation. Without even waiting for Sholmes to observe that he could speak quite freely before his friend, Dr. Jotson, Mr. Smudgett plunged into his story.
"Mr. Sholmes, I am surrounded by a ghastly mystery, or else I am the victim of a fearful hallucination. You have, doubtless, seen my pictures——"

Two huge, gaunt cats were chasing one another round the studio.

Sholmes nodded.

"I have seen your works, Mr. Smudgett. If you refer to them as pictures, I should say you are undoubtedly the victim of hallucination."

"You have seen them? Have you ever seen, Mr. Sholmes, in any of my paintings anything that resembles anything in the earth, or the sky, or the waters under the earth?"

"Never!"

"Exactly!" Mr. Smudgett wiped his heated brow. "It is to that, Mr. Sholmes, that I owe my reputation. You are aware, of course, that I stand at the very top of the tree—that I am universally acknowledged to be the chief of the Later-Super-Post-Impressionist School. Other artists have sought to rival me, in vain. Even those who have gone to the length of sitting on their canvas while still wet, have never succeeded in equalling my amazing effects. But——"

"But?" said Sholmes.

"Hear my secret, Mr. Sholmes. The extraordinary colour effects in my pictures, the deep and impenetrable mystery surrounding what they may possibly mean, have brought me fame and fortune. But—you will scarcely credit it—I was taught to paint——"

"Impossible!"

"It is only too true. In my early and thoughtless youth, I studied painting. Then I painted; but, daub and smear as I would, my pictures still resembled something—they were bad, they were out of drawing, but still they bore a remote resemblance of actual objects. I almost despaired of making a name. And then—the incredible happened. I will tell you what occurred."

Mr. Smudgett paused, and gasped for breath.

"My studio, Mr. Sholmes, is at the top of my house—it is approached by a narrow stair. No one can enter without my knowledge. There is only one door; the only other opening is the skylight. But the roof is inaccessible from without. Yet some mysterious being makes himself at home in my studio, and it is to him, or it, that I owe my success in my art. My first famous picture, it is called 'Girl Gathering Roses'——"

"I have seen it," said Sholmes.

"Well, Mr. Sholmes, I had spent weeks on that picture, seeking to produce a genuine impressionist effect. In spite of my efforts, the girl in the painting bore a remote resemblance to a human being; I threw my brushes at the canvas, I thumped it, still wet, with a hassock, but still the genuine impressionist effect was not produced. In despair I left it, and locked the studio door after me. But when I came back in the morning, Mr. Sholmes, can you believe me——"

"Go on!" said Herlock Sholmes, quietly. I could see that Sholmes was deeply interested by this time.

"I brought a famous art critic with me," said Mr. Smudgett. "Immediately he saw the picture, he fell into raptures. It was changed—utterly. Nothing in it bore the slightest resemblance to anything I had ever seen or heard of. Some mysterious hand had been at work. My fortune was made. Commissions rained in upon me—but——"

"Well?"

"But I could not reproduce the marvellous effects. I tried every means, from lying at full length on the wet colour, to dabbing it with a kitchen mop; but it was in vain. I was baffled; and, in despair, I left the picture alone in the studio, the skylight open, in a vague hope that the miraculous would happen again."

"And did it?"

"It did, Mr. Sholmes," said the painter hoarsely. "But the mystery is too great for me to bear. I must have it explained. That is why I have come to you."

Sholmes rose to his feet.

"To-night I will watch," he said, "with my faithful Jotson. Come!"

CHAPTER 2

I confess that my heart was beating rapidly, as I crouched in the darkness of the studio with my friend, Herlock Sholmes.

Mr. Smudgett had taken us there, and left us to watch; his own nerve was not equal to the strain.

It was the hour of midnight, and the great city was sleeping round us. Only from the dusk of night came, occasionally, the mournful wail of a cat on the tiles.

Herlock Sholmes grasped my arm, suddenly.

"Listen!" he breathed.

There was a faint sound at the open skylight.

I trembled.

Was the strange phantom about to appear—the mysterious being that, in the dark hours, touched with its magic hand the unfinished paintings, and turned them into Impressionist masterpieces?

Miau-au-iaou!

Zizzzzzzzzz!

There was a sound of hissing, and spitting, and howling in the studio. Herlock Sholmes sprang to his feet, flashing on the light of his electric torch.

I stared dazedly at the scene before me.

Two huge, gaunt cats were chasing one another round the studio, and clambering over Mr. Smudgett's wet canvas, daubing their fur with the colours.

Sholmes sprang forward.

In a moment, a fiercely-spitting tom-cat was struggling in his grasp.

"Sholmes!" I gasped. "What——"

"The mystery is explained, my dear Jotson," drawled Herlock Sholmes. "From what I have seen of Mr. Smudgett's work, I guessed it from the first."

CHAPTER 3

Sholmes had solved the mystery.

Needless to say, Mr. Smeary Smudgett was delighted at being relieved of his supernatural fears, and he thanked my amazing friend with heartfelt gratitude. Now that he knew the truth, he was able to avail himself more fully of feline aid in pursuing his art. He made it a rule to shut several cats in the studio of a night, and, on Sholmes' advice, added a dog. From that time Mr. Smudgett's fame as master of the Later-Super-Post-Impressionist School has known no bounds.

THE CASE OF THE MUSICIAN

No. 48

"A mysterious case, Jotson," remarked Herlock Sholmes.

"Put on your hat, my dear fellow, and I will tell you about it as we go along. I have promised to call at Mrs. Mopley's flat immediately."

I purred with pleasure as I walked down Shaker Street with Sholmes. It was always a delight to me to share in the investigations of my amazing friend.

"Some mysterious murder?" I inquired.

"Not so bad as that. It appears to be a case of theft—a very mysterious case. On half a dozen separate occasions a bottle of medicine has mysteriously disappeared from the Mopley flat. A few weeks ago, Mrs. Mopley began to take Toxin's Tonic regularly. Her husband is a musician, at present engaged in composing a symphony, and Mrs. Mopley has found it necessary to keep up her strength by this means. Now, on almost every occasion when Mrs. Mopley has been absent from the flat, her tonic had disappeared during her absence."

"Extraordinary!" I exclaimed.

"She is accustomed to leaving the bottle of tonic on the mantelpiece in the sitting-room of the flat. On almost every occasion on her return from any absence she has found the bottle empty. The contents have most mysteriously disappeared."

"The servants——"

"There are none. No one has access to the flat excepting Mr. and Mrs. Mopley."

"There are, perhaps, some suspicious characters in the same block of buildings?"

"Two," said Sholmes. "the flat above is tenanted by a member of Parliament, and the flat below by a house-agent. But these could hardly be suspected of annexing the contents of a bottle of tonic mixture; they fly at higher game. So far, it is inexplicable. But we shall doubtless learn something from our investigations on the spot!"

We arrived at Mrs. Mopley's flat, and were admitted by the lady herself.

Mrs. Mopley was very agitated.

"It is gone again, Mr. Sholmes," she exclaimed, as we entered. "While I was calling upon you, my tonic mixture was abstracted once more."

"You locked the door when you went out?" inquired Sholmes.

"Yes, it is a spring lock!"

"The flat was left empty———"

"Excepting for Mr. Mopley. He was at work in the next room as usual. He is there now!"

Sholmes nodded.

A sound resembling an air-raid mingled with a railway accident was proceeding from the adjoining room, and Sholmes had already divined that Mr. Mopley was there at work upon his symphony.

He stepped to the mantelpiece, and examined the medicine bottle. It was a large bottle, holding about a pint. It was quite empty.

"I left it nearly full," said Mrs. Mopley tearfully.

"Did Mr. Mopley hear anything during your absence?"

"Impossible. While he is composing, nothing else can be heard."

"True!"

"I have not mentioned the matter to Mr. Mopley at all, Mr. Sholmes, his mind is wholly occupied by music, and impenetrable to all other considerations. Will you—can you—solve this amazing mystery?"

I gazed silently at Herlock Sholmes. Well, as I knew his extraordinary powers, it appeared to me that this problem was beyond elucidation.

Sholmes was very thoughtful.

"It will be necessary for me to remain here for some time," he said, at last. "Place a new bottle of tonic on the mantelpiece, madam, and leave the flat as usual. I will remain in concealment with my friend, Dr. Jotson, and I have no doubt whatever that the mystery will be revealed."

A few minutes later we were alone.

On the mantelpiece stood a fresh bottle of Toxin's Tonic full of the mixture. Sholmes and I took cover behind a music-stand, to watch.

From the adjoining room came the crash of sound, showing that Mr. Mopley was very busy with the piano.

The sounds ceased suddenly.

Then there were footsteps, approaching the communicating door.

Sholmes pressed my arm.

It was a warning to be silent; and I scarcely breathed as I crouched behind the music-stand, and watched.

The door of Mr. Mopley's room opened.

A gentleman with rather wild eyes, and a remarkable head of hair, came into the sitting-room.

He did not observe us.

He moved restlessly about the room, muttering feverishly, and I caught the words "K sharp minor."

He seemed to be in search for something, and we watched him breathlessly.

He paused at a table where there stood a carafe, and seemed about to refresh himself with a glass of water. But he paused, and moved across to the mantelpiece.

I could scarcely repress an exclamation when I beheld him lift the bottle of tonic, draw the cork, and place the bottle to his lips.

Without stopping to take breath, he drank the contents of the bottle.

Herlock Sholmes sprang to his feet.

"Hold!" he exclaimed.

In a moment more, his grasp was upon Mr. Mopley's arms.

The musician spun round, with a startled exclamation, and the bottle crashed to the floor.

CHAPTER 2

"Sholmes!" I exclaimed, when ten minutes later, we were walking back to Shaker Street together.

Sholmes smiled genially.

"The denouement surprised you, Jotson!" he said.

"I was astounded. It was, then, Mr. Mopley who abstracted the contents of the bottles of tonic——"

"Undoubtedly. Mr. Mopley is a musician, it was therefore easy for me to deduce that he was of a thirsty nature!"

"True. But why should he drink a tonic mixture—a very disagreeable concoction?"

Sholmes smiled.

"Yes it is simple. Mr. Mopley, afflicted with the thirst natural to a member of his profession, came into the sitting-room for something to drink. You saw him pause at the carafe, as if he had resolved to take a glass of water. Then he crossed to the mantelpiece where the bottle stood. Had Mr. Mopley been an architect or a painter, or a poet, undoubtedly he would have quenched his thirst with the water instead of the tonic mixture. But he was a musician, and that made all the difference."

"I am still in the dark, Sholmes. Why——"

"Yet you have studied my methods, Jotson," said Sholmes, with some severity. "Mr. Mopley was undecided with what to quench his thirst. But he is a musician. It was natural—in fact inevitable—for a musician to resolve upon the tonic. Simplicity itself, my dear Jotson!"

THE MYSTERY OF THE TAXI-CAB

No. 49

The sudden and startling death of Mr. Swizzle caused a considerable sensation, and I was not surprised when my amazing friend Mr. Herlock Sholmes was called in to aid in elucidating the mystery.

The facts, so far as they were known, were simple.

Mr. Swizzle had alighted at his gate from a taxi-cab, and was seen to exchange a few words with the driver, who then drove off immediately.

Mr. Swizzle staggered up his garden-path, and sank down on his door-step in a state of collapse.

He never recovered.

The medical evidence was that Mr. Swizzle, who suffered from a weak heart, had perished from the effect of a sudden and terrible shock.

How that shock had been administered was a deep mystery.

Suspicion attached to the taxi-driver and Inspector Pinkeye, of Scotland Yard, was immediately set upon his track.

It was a week or so later that the inspector called upon us, in our rooms at Shaker Street, and requested the aid of Herlock Sholmes.

Sholmes smiled genially.

"Then your clue has led to nothing?" he remarked.

"We have no clue at present, Mr. Sholmes," confessed the inspector. "The matter is a deep and impenetrable mystery. If you can see a clue, you can see further than Scotland Yard."

"Which would not be a novelty," remarked Sholmes.

"Well, I shall be glad of your assistance, Mr. Sholmes," said the inspector, somewhat nettled. "You agree that the taxi-driver is the man we want?"

"No doubt."
"By some means as yet unknown he administered a fearful shock to the unfortunate victim, which practically killed him on the spot," said the inspector. "His motive we shall discover when we discover the man. If you can do that for us——"
"I will try," said Sholmes, with a smile. "No doubt the man has heard that he is under suspicion, and is afraid to come forward. But a taxi-driver of so unusual a character should be easily found."
"How do you deduce that he is a taxi-driver of unusual character, Mr. Sholmes?"
"From the nature of the shock which he administered to Mr. Swizzle."
"But that is precisely the mystery!" exclaimed the inspector.
"Not to me."
"Really, Mr. Sholmes——"
"Leave the case in my hands," drawled Herlock Sholmes. "Unless I am mistaken, which Jotson here will tell you is impossible, the taxi-driver will soon be found. I shall require a sum of ready money for expenses——"
"Of what nature?"
"Cab fares," said Sholmes tersely.
When the inspector was gone, Herlock Sholmes turned to me.
"If you are prepared to join me in this case, Jotson——"
"Certainly Sholmes."
"But your patients, my dear doctor?"
"I have given so much time to your affairs of late, Sholmes, that I have failed to pay my usual visits to my patients, and as a consequence most of them recovered. I am quite at your service."
"Bong! Allong dong!" said Sholmes, dropping into French, as he sometimes did. "Noose verrong!"
And, taking me gently by the ear, he led me into Shaker Street.

CHAPTER 2

For a week we were busy.
Accustomed as I was to the remarkable mental aberrations of my amazing friend, I could not help wondering at the methods he employed in this mysterious case.
The days past in a succession of taxi trips.
From early morn to dewy eve, Herlock Sholmes hailed taxi after taxi, and paid without question the extraordinary sums demanded by the drivers which never bore any approximation to the amounts indicated on the taximeters.
One journey over, another began, till it appeared to me that we must have driven in half the taxi-cabs that plied for hire within the limits of the county of London.
I was astonished, but I did not venture to question my amazing friend. I knew that he must be following out some deep-laid scheme, hatched in the recesses of his remarkable brain.
The denouement came suddenly.
One evening, as Sholmes asked the amount of the fare on alighting, the driver replied:
"Seven-and-six!"
I jumped.
Seven-and-six was the amount indicated by the taximeter!
I felt faint for a moment.
Then I gazed at the extraordinary man who had driven us.
Outwardly his appearance was normal.
Yet the astounding fact remained that he had only asked us to pay the exact fare, as indicated on the "clock"!
Sholmes's eyes glittered.
He handed over the seven-and-six-pence, and the next moment his grip fell upon the shoulder of the taxi-driver.
"I think you are the man I want!" he said calmly. "Jotson, call a policeman. I have found the man who drove Mr. Swizzle on the night of his death!"

CHAPTER 3

"Sholmes!" I gasped, as Herlock Sholmes, an hour later, came into our rooms at Shaker Street, and mixed himself a stiff glass of cocaine.
He smiled.
"Surprised again, Jotson?" he asked.
"Amazed! How——"
Herlock Sholmes laughed.
"A perfectly simple case, my dear fellow," he said. "The death of Mr. Swizzle was accidental, as I believed from the first. The taxi-driver was unaware of the fact that the hapless man had a weak heart when he administered the shock that caused his death.
"And that shock?"
"It was clear to me from the beginning," yawned Sholmes. "That was my clue, which I followed up

Jotson started violently at the words of the taxi-driver.

by taking a succession of taxi drives, until I came upon a taxi-driver who asked the exact fare. True, he was the only one of his kind in London, but I was certain to find him, sooner or later—and I found him. He is simply detained now for enquiries. The death of Mr. Swizzle was a pure accident. Had your heart been weak, Jotson, I should never have exposed you to the perils of this search. Yet, strong man as you are, I saw you stagger when the man asked us to pay the amount indicated on the meter, and no more."

"True. But Mr. Swizzle——"

"The poor gentleman alighted from his cab. He saw the amount on the meter. He expected to be asked twice or three times as much—and then came the shock." Herlock Sholmes brushed away a tear. "The taxi-driver asked him to pay the just fare. His heart was weak. The shock was too much. It overcame him—and he perished, Jotson. Voila tout! A simple though sad case!"

THE CASE OF THE STOLEN CAR

No. 50

Herlock Sholmes and I were dissecting the morning kipper when the telephone-bell rang.

I took up the receiver, my amazing friend being too busily occupied to attend to it.

"Is that Mr. Sholmes?"

"It is his friend, Dr. Jotson, before whom you may speak quite freely," I replied.

"This is the Spread-Eagle Garage. A motor-car has been stolen—one of our brand-new one hundred pounds Spread-Eagle cars! Will you ask Mr. Sholmes to step round as soon as possible?"

"Certainly."

I returned to the table, and to my breakfast.

No breakfast, however, remained. Herlock Sholmes, with the absent-mindedness characteristic of men of genius, was finishing my kipper.

"My dear Sholmes——" I murmured.

"What is it, Jotson?" he yawned. "Another case? You may speak quite freely before—— I mean, fire away!"

I explained.

"The Spread-Eagle Garage!" said Sholmes thoughtfully. "H'm! They import the very latest thing in up-to-date American cheap cars. And one of them has been stolen! Extraordinary!"

"I do not quite see how it is extraordinary, Sholmes," I ventured to remark. "Motor-thieves are very common nowadays."

"Have you seen a Spread-Eagle car, my dear Jotson?"

"No."

"When you have seen one you will realise that it is extraordinary for one to be stolen. An inexperienced motor-thief, I should say—or a very bold one. He has taken his life in his hands. However, let us go."

Sholmes hooked his umbrella on my ear, and led me out into Shaker Street.

In a few minutes we reached the Spread-Eagle Garage.

The manager met us at the door.

He explained the matter in a few words. The motor-thief had called under pretence of wishing to buy a car. He had been allowed to test it. Once in possession of the car, he had driven round the corner and disappeared at top speed.

"What steps have you taken?" inquired Herlock Sholmes.

"I guess we've telephoned to every police-station within a radius of twenty miles," was the reply.

"Twenty miles!" said Sholmes thoughtfully.

"Then the thief will be stopped on the road," I remarked.

Sholmes smiled his inscrutable smile.

"Kindly point out the direction taken by the motor-thief" he said.

The American manager did so.

"Thank you. We will do our best for you" said Sholmes. "Come Jotson!"

"I guess we can lend you a car to follow that pesky hoodlum, if you like, Mr. Sholmes."

Sholmes shook his head.

"Thank you," he answered. "My friend Jotson will tell you that I am not a man to shrink from peril. But there is no need to run unnecessary risks. We will walk."

We walked.

"My dear Sholmes," I observed, "far be it from me to doubt your judgment, which I know to be infallible. But is it really any use to follow a motor-thief on foot, especially when he has a long start?"

"If the thief had stolen a Rolls-Royce, or a Mercedes, Jotson, your question would be a natural one. But you must remember that he has stolen a Spread-Eagle American car."

"What difference does that make, Sholmes?"

"You will see," smiled Herlock Sholmes. "I do not think that the police at a distance of twenty miles will be required to exert themselves. I have no doubt that we shall make a discovery nearer at hand. However, you may now go and see your patients, my dear doctor. You must not neglect your practice,

Sholmes' barrow was piled with fragments of machinery.

which is helping to solve the problem of over-population."
And Sholmes left me.
Happening to glance back over my shoulder, I saw my amazing friend turn from the road and enter the yard of a local building-contractor. Consumed by curiosity, I remained standing close to the hedge, to await his reappearance.
I had not long to wait, for within five minutes Sholmes reappeared, trundling a large wheelbarrow in the opposite direction from me.
Fearing that the mighty brain of my extraordinary friend had at last given way beneath the strain, continually imposed upon it, I turned sadly away.
That morning was a very busy one for me, for I had more than the usual number of death certificates to sign for my patients, so temporarily I forgot the case of the missing car.

CHAPTER 3

When I returned to Shaker Street, Sholmes had not yet come in for lunch.
I decided to look in at the Spread-Eagle Company's garage, hoping to find him there.
I had hardly reached the garage when a large barrow came in sight, and to my astonishment I recognised my amazing friend between the handles.
The barrow was piled with what appeared to be fragments of wood and machinery, with a lingering smell of petrol clinging to the pile.
"Sholmes!" I exclaimed.
He smiled.
"Success once more, my dear Jotson," he said.
"And that?" I pointed to the barrow-load.
"Exactly. The stolen car."
Sholmes wheeled his load into the garage.
When he reappeared, he was smiling genially.
"And now for lunch, Jotson," he said.
"My dear Sholmes," I exclaimed, "you astonish me more than ever. You have found the stolen car——"
"As you have seen."
"At what distance."
"Half a mile. I hardly expected so long a walk," replied Sholmes.
"And the thief?"
"The police can lay their hands on him at any moment. I have ascertained which hospital he was taken to."
"My dear Sholmes! But how——"
"A perfectly simple case, Jotson," yawned Sholmes. "Having some acquaintance with the construction of the Spread-Eagle American car, I deduced at once what must have happened. The thief had driven it off at a high speed. The result was inevitable. Half a mile from the scene of the robbery I came across the wreck. The hapless motor-thief had already been taken away on a stretcher. As I was engaged to recover the car, I hired a barrow, upon which I wheeled home what remained of it. That is all, my dear Jotson. A very simple case."

THE CASE OF THE BALL DRESS

No. 51

"Where are we going, Sholmes?" I inquired, as my amazing friend, with a gentle application of his boot to my coat-tails, helped me out into Shaker Street, one afternoon.
"To Boodlesohn House!" replied Sholmes.
I was duly impressed.
Lord Boodlesohn was a great figure in London society, and his figure at the bank was even greater.
He had first come into prominence during the war. Repressing, with great difficulty, his ardent desire to join the fighting forces in Flanders, he had devoted himself to turning out munitions on a great scale, and had reluctantly seen his fortune increase by leaps and bounds. He dwelt now in one of the largest mansions in Park Lane, the family connection with Petticoat Lane being entirely severed.
His daughter, Lady Gloxiana Boodlesohn, was famous for her attractions, which ran into seven or eight figures.
"A robbery, Sholmes?" I enquired.
Sholmes shook his head.
"Possibly," he answered. "I cannot say as yet. Lady Gloxiana's new jazz-dress is missing. Its value is immense, though its size, I understand, is not at all commensurate with its value. It appears that Lady Gloxiana is to attend a dance this evening at Fitzoof Lodge. The dress was delivered this morning. When Lady Gloxiana went to her room to try it on, it had disappeared."

"Lady Gloxiana," said Sholmes, "I have found the ball-dress!"

"And nothing else is missing?"

"Nothing, apparently," said Sholmes. "Lady Gloxiana's jewels, to the value of two million pounds, were not touched."

"Then it can scarcely be a robbery, Sholmes. A thief would not leave two million pounds worth of jewels, and decamp with so very tiny a prize as a jazz-dress!"

"So it seems, my dear Jotson. Yet the dress has disappeared!"

We arrived at Boodlesohn House.

A gilt-edged footman admitted us into a large hall studded with diamonds.

We were shown at once into Lady Gloxiana's boudoir.

Her ladyship was in a great state of agitation.

Evidently she took the loss of her latest costume very much to heart.

It was not, as she explained to Sholmes, the value of it that mattered, a thousand pounds more or less made no difference in that wealthy mansion. But it was impossible to obtain another dress in time for the ball at Fitzoof House.

Unless the missing article was found, Lady Gloxiana would be reduced to the painful necessity of wearing a dress she had worn before.

Needless to say, my amazing friend was touched by this picture of distress.

"Find the dress, and name your own reward, Mr. Sholmes!" said her ladyship. "I have heard how you solved the mystery of the disappearance of Lord Stony de Broke's watch, after a visit to his uncle. I have every confidence in you."

Sholmes bowed.

"Let me be shown to the scene of the crime—I mean the place where the jazz-dress was last seen alive," he said.

"Immediately!"

Another gilt-edged footman conducted my amazing friend away, leaving me with her ladyship.

Sholmes, apparently did not need my assistance in looking for a clue.

We waited.

He was not long absent.

Lady Gloxiana looked up eagerly as he entered, with a smile upon his face. I knew that smile! Sholmes had succeeded! It was such a smile as he generally wore in moments of triumph, as on the unforgotten occasion when he had the cash ready for the gentleman who called in Shaker Street for the instalments on the furniture.

"Mr. Sholmes! You have found a clue?"

"Better still, Lady Gloxiana. 'I have found the dress!"

Lady Gloxiana started so violently, that every jewel upon her superb person jingled. It was like a peal of bells.

"You have found it?"

"I have!"

"But—but the house has been searched—not a nook or recess has been left unransacked——"

"No doubt——"

"Yet you, in a few minutes, have found the missing jazz-dress?"

"Look!"

Sholmes slipped his hand into his waistcoat pocket, and drew forth the folded costume.

Her ladyship uttered a cry of joy.

"My dress!"

Her beauteous face was irradiated with smiles.

"Mr. Sholmes," she cried, "how can I ever thank you?"

Fortunately at that moment, Lord Boodlesohn came in, and when he learned of the astounding success of my amazing friend, he was so overcome, that he presented us with two of his tenpenny cigars before he had time to recollect himself.

When we left the mansion in Park Lane, we left happiness behind us.

CHAPTER 2

"I feel unusually bucked, my dear Jotson," Herlock Sholmes remarked, as we walked back to Shaker Street. "It is always a pleasure to relieve beauty in distress."

"True!" I remarked. "But how——"

"Your usual inquiry, Jotson," said Sholmes, with a smile. "My dear fellow, it was not difficult—for me! The theory of robbery I did not entertain for a moment—it was evident that the jazz-dress had been simply lost to sight, though to memory, dear."

"But the mansion was searched, from the gilt-edged roof to the diamond-studded hall!"

"No doubt, but it needed a Herlock Sholmes to look in the right place, my dear Jotson. The first thing I observed, on entering the room, was a thimble standing on the table, evidently left there by ladyship's dressmaker."

"A thimble?"

"Exactly!"

"But what——"

"My dear fellow, I lifted the thimble, and looked under it," explained Sholmes. "That had not occurred to the Scotland Yard detective, who was first called in. It occurred to me. Under the thimble was the parcel containing the jazz-costume. The case was perfectly simple; the dressmaker, on leaving the apartment, had carelessly laid down the thimble, and inadvertently covered the jazz-costume with it. That is all!"

But it needed Herlock Sholmes to discover it!" I exclaimed.

Sholmes smiled.

"True! And now, Jotson, we will change the lady's cheque without delay. She has been very generous, and it will run to fish and chips for dinner. A very satisfactory case indeed!"

THE DISAPPEARANCE OF LORD ADOLPHUS

No. 52

Herlock Sholmes was reading the morning paper when an agitated official of the Red Tape and Sealing-Wax Department was shown into our rooms at Shaker Street.

"Mr. Sholmes!" he exclaimed breathlessly.

Sholmes politely laid down the journal, and removed his feet from the mantelpiece.

It was evident that something of a startling nature must have occurred to cause an official of the Red Tape department to be abroad, and wide awake, so early as half-past eleven in the morning!

"What has happened?" drawled Sholmes. "You may speak quite freely before my friend Dr. Jotson."

"Lord Adolphus Fitzfoozle, the head of our department, has disappeared!"

"Disappeared!" repeated Sholmes. "Kindly give me a few details."

"Little is known, Mr. Sholmes. Yesterday morning, as usual, Lord Adolphus arrived at the department, at a quarter past eleven. He seemed in his usual health and spirits, and slept peacefully in his bureau until twelve o'clock, when he left for lunch. It is his custom to walk across St. James's Park for lunch at his club; Lord Adolphus has always been a man of great energy. But—he did not arrive at his club!"

"Ah!" said Sholmes inscrutably.

"Inquiry was not made till evening, for sometimes his lordship sleeps at his club in the afternoon, instead of at the department. But when the inquiry was made, it was discovered that he had never arrived at the club. Search was made in the park. He was not there. He had not been heard of at his home. He had vanished completely! Find Lord Adolphus, Mr. Sholmes, and save the country!"

And the agitated official retired.

CHAPTER 2

Herlock Sholmes took up his morning paper again, glancing at me with a smile.

"Sholmes!" I exclaimed. "You are not going to read your paper now?

"Why not, Jotson?"

"My dear fellow," I said warmly, "the fate of the country may be at stake! The most important measure of modern times—that of dressing the Army in the style of Punchinello—may be hung up if the Red Tape department is paralysed by the loss of its chief! And what might happen to the country, if a fresh war should break out, and find our soldiers still dressed in khaki?"

"True. But I hope to find a clue in this journal, Jotson. Listen to this, my dear fellow:

"'Some excitement was caused at Colney Hatch yesterday by the escape of a lunatic. This man, after eluding the keepers, succeeded in getting as far as London, but he was recaptured in St. James's Park, and taken away immediately in a taxi.'"

I stared at Herlock Sholmes.

This item of news was, perhaps, interesting in itself, but I could see no connection between it and the affair of the missing Minister.

Sholmes smiled at my perplexed expression, and rose from his chair.

"Come!" he said; and, taking me playfully by the nose, he led me away.

In Shaker Street we stepped into a taxi. Sholmes gave the direction to the driver, and as I heard it, I blinked in amazement.

"Colney Hatch!"

"Sholmes," I exclaimed, "you are going to call upon your relatives at this crucial moment!"

"Not at all, my dear Jotson."

"Then why are we going to Colney Hatch?"

His answer astounded me.

"To find the missing Minister, Jotson!"

We arrived at Colney Hatch, where the name of Herlock Sholmes opened all doors. His request to see the lunatic who had been recaptured in St. James's Park the previous day was immediately granted, and we were conducted to his room.

A slim gentleman, with a vacant, aristocratic face, was dozing upon a couch when we entered. Sholmes touched him lightly on the shoulder.

"Wake up, Lord Adolphus!" he said.

The sleeper started up.

"Dear me!" he murmured. "Is it lunch-time already?"

"Come!" said Sholmes.

CHAPTER 3

The taxi bore us to Whitehall, where Lord Adolphus was returned, safe and sound, to his anxious friends in the Red Tape and Sealing-Wax department. His return brought joy to the seventy-five

thousand officials of that department. As we walked back to Shaker Street, I could contain my impatience no longer.
"Sholmes——" I exclaimed.
"A very interesting case, Jotson," said Herlock Sholmes. "One that might have baffled Scotland Yard for years, but which was, fortunately, simple enough to me. The clue was in the newspaper report."
"But how——"
"Consider, my dear fellow. A prominent Government official disappeared in the park. At the same time, an escaped lunatic was captured there, and taken away in a taxi. The conclusion was obvious. The Colney Hatch attendants had made a mistake—natural, under the circumstances. To the trained eye of a detective, Jotson, there are distinctions between a Cabinet Minister and lunatic. But asylum officials, of course, are not trained detectives. They made a natural mistake; they supposed that Lord Adolphus was their man, and took him away in a taxi."
"I see it all now, Sholmes! But what a dreadful shock to Lord Adolphus, to find himself in a lunatic asylum!"
Sholmes smiled.
"A painful shock, no doubt, if Lord Adolphus had given the matter any thought," he replied. "Fortunately, he is a member of the Corps Diplomatique, and not accustomed to think. Moreover, the difference between a lunatic asylum and a Government department is not very great, and Lord Adolphus had not yet observed it when we fortunately found him."
"True. And the escaped lunatic, then, is still at large?"
"Evidently! But doubtless he will be recaptured in time, unless——" Herlock Sholmes paused.
"Unless what, Sholmes?"
"Unless he should take refuge in a Government department, Jotson. In that case it will be a matter of exceeding difficulty to pick him out from the others."

THE MYSTERY OF THE GARDEN SUBURB

No. 53

It was during this period of our residence in Shaker Street that the musical world was shocked by the strange and inexplicable death of Signor Tremuloso, the famous Italian tenor.
The affair was wrapped in mystery.
The assistance of my amazing friend, Mr. Herlock Sholmes, was not at first sought by the police, and all we knew of the matter was gathered from the daily papers.
It appeared that Signor Tremuloso, who lived at Chumpstead, in the N.W. district, had gone out for a walk in the evening, and his footsteps had led him in the direction of the Garden Suburb adjoining Chumpstead.
All accounts agreed that he had left home alive.
At ten o'clock, Police-Constable XYZ123 was startled by the sound of deep groaning as he was passing through one of the streets of the Garden Suburb.
On the pavement, outside the garden gate of Mr. Voxbuster, a well-known resident and musical amateur of the Garden Suburb, he found the unfortunate Italian gentleman, writhing in anguish.
To add to the tragedy of the scene, Mr. Voxbuster's house was brilliantly lighted up, a musical party being in progress there. In the darkness outside, the Italian gentleman breathed his last in the constable's arms.
The only words he was able to utter, before he expired were:
"Crudele—troppo crudele!"
This was the constable's evidence at the inquest.
No cause could be assigned for the sudden and tragic death of Signor Tremuloso, but the police suspected foul play.
The papers referred to the affair as the "The Mysterious Murder in the Garden Suburb."
For a week the Scotland Yard authorities investigated the mystery in vain.
They could not discover how the Italian gentleman had come by his death, or by what felon hand he been felled.
Herlock Sholmes made no sign. He was prepared to place his vast abilities at the service of the authorities when asked to do so; but he waited for the request which he was sure would come.
It came at last.
One afternoon our old acquaintance, Inspector Pinkeye, was shown into our rooms at Shaker Street by Mrs. Spudson.
Sholmes greeted him with a smile.
"I have been expecting you, Pinkeye," he remarked. "Help yourself to the cocaine, my dear fellow; the cask is at your elbow. The Garden Suburb affair, what?"
"Exactly, Mr. Sholmes," said the inspector. "We find ourselves at a loss again, and if you care——"

Inspector Pinkeye was shown in by Mrs. Spudson.

"Certainly!"

"Thank you, Mr. Sholmes. An extraordinary affair—the most mysterious murder in my experience," said Inspector Pinkeye. "No sign of violence was found on the deceased—only an expression of terrible suffering was firmly fixed upon his face. The post-mortem was conducted by Dr. Turnemout, and proved that death could not have been due to natural causes. Yet what weapon was used baffles us——"

"Some deadly poison, that leaves no trace behind," I suggest.

The inspector nodded.

"It is possible," he said. "What do you think, Mr. Sholmes?"

Herlock Sholmes smiled.

"I am afraid I am going to give you a shock, inspector," he answered.

"In my opinion, which is, as Jotson will tell you, infallible, it is not a case of murder."

"Then what?"

"Accidental death!" said Sholmes, quietly.

"But what accident could have happened to Signor Tremuloso, which has left no trace upon him?" exclaimed the inspector warmly.

"My dear inspector, there are more things in artistic and musical garden suburbs than are dreamt of in your philosophy, as Shakespeare has remarked. Yet the clue is plain."

"It is not plain enough for me to see," said the inspector, somewhat gruffly.

"Possibly," assented Sholmes. "Yet you must be aware of the facts of the case. The Chumpstead Garden Suburb is well-known as a centre of artistic and musical amateurs!"

"But what——"

"Mr. Voxbuster is one of the best known of these, and he was giving a musical evening when the unhappy Italian tenor, led by a fatal chance, passed by his house——"

"I do not see the connection!"

"Naturally; if you could, you would not require my assistance," replied Sholmes. "However, let us go to the Garden Suburb and make enquiries at Mr. Voxbuster's house."

"Every enquiry has already been made there."

"From your point of view, doubtless; but I wish to make a few more." said Sholmes drily. "I shall see you later, Jotson, when I will furnish the usual explanation at the end of the story."

And Herlock Sholmes departed with Inspector Pinkeye, leaving me to await his return.

CHAPTER 2

Herlock Sholmes returned in time for dinner. The kippers were ready, and Sholmes dined before he condescended to gratify my eager curiosity as to what had happened in the Garden Suburb. The kippers and winkles having been disposed of, however, Sholmes drew his usual jug of cocaine from the cask, and his chin resumed its customary activity.

"As I said, a case of accidental death, Jotson," he remarked. "A few questions addressed to Mr. Voxbuster elucidated the whole mystery."

"You mystify me, Sholmes. What connection had Mr. Voxbuster with the sudden death of the Italian musician?"

"He was the unfortunate and unintentional cause of it, Jotson."

"Sholmes!"

"A pure accident, Jotson. Mr. Voxbuster was giving a musical evening at his home in the Garden Suburb, when the unhappy Italian, taking his evening stroll, passed along the street."

"But——"

"The windows were open, on account of the warmth of the evening. Mr. Voxbuster and his guests were having what they described as a 'little music.' It was ten o'clock that the constable found Signor Tremuloso expiring in anguish. I have ascertained that it was a few minutes earlier, that Mr. Voxbuster, who is well-known in the Garden Suburb as an amateur tenor, began to sing 'I'll sing thee songs of Araby!' The wide-open window allowed the dreadful result to pass into the street, and it smote, with full force, upon the unprepared and sensitive ears of the unhappy musician. His physical organisation was not equal to the strain. He fell!"

Sholmes took a deep draught of cocaine, to conceal his emotion.

"Mr. Voxbuster kept on grimly to the end, Jotson. No other casualties are recorded; the inhabitants of the Garden Suburb are a hardy race. But the hapless musician, whose fatal footsteps had led him within range of Mr. Voxbuster's tenor solo, fell, and expired in anguish before the solo was concluded. A sad case, Jotson—very!"

THE CASE OF THE SINN FEINERS

No. 54

"Pack your bag, my dear Jotson," said Herlock Sholmes, when I came down to breakfast one morning in our rooms at Shaker Street.

"We are going——" I began.

"To Ireland," said Sholmes. "You have just time to make your will and pay up on your insurance, Jotson. These little precautions are necessary—it is not as if we were merely going to Tartary or Timbuctoo."

"And our business in Ireland, Sholmes!" I inquired.

"You have heard of Sinn Fein, my dear fellow?"

"I have certainly heard the word, Sholmes. Is it a new breakfast food?"

"Nothing of the kind."

"A new parlour game? I hazarded.

Sholmes shook his head.

"If you were a regular reader of the 'Daily Snooze,' Jotson, you would know that Sinn Fein is the free and independent patriot party in the sister isle. If, on the other hand, you regularly read the 'Morning Ghost,' you would be aware that Sinn Fein is the unpatriotic and traitorous party in Ireland. Like the little boy in the story, you pays your money and you takes your choice."

"And the truth, Sholmes?"

Sholmes smiled compassionately.

"My dear fellow, all the news from Ireland comes in the shape of official reports or newspaper telegrams. There is no question of truth."

"True!"

"My services have been called in by Dublin Castle," explained Herlock Sholmes. "Sinn Fein outrages have now reached the culminating point, or the patriot movement has now become formidable, whichever you like. Police-stations have been burned; policemen have been potted; banks have been robbed; life and property rendered generally unsafe—but that is nothing out of the common—the climax has now been reached."

"Good heavens, Sholmes! What has happened?"

"A distinguished official has been kidnapped by the Sinn Feiners!" said Sholmes.

My hand trembled as I dissected my kipper.

This was, indeed, startling news!"

"He was taken from his car, on the road near Ballybooze," said Sholmes. "He has disappeared completely, with his kidnappers. What their intentions are is not known. They cannot blow his brains out——"

"Why not, Sholmes?"

"I have mentioned that he is a distinguished official, Jotson. The feat would therefore be impossible."

"Most true!"

"But he is deprived of his liberty, and in all probability restricted to a meagre diet of whisky and potatoes——"

"Horrible!"

"However I shall be there," said Sholmes carelessly. Once arrived at Ballybooze I do not anticipate great difficulties."

"You have a clue"

"None!"

"Then how——"

"I am going to call on my friend and colleague, Bexton Slake, and borrow his celebrate bloodhound, Squeedro," explained Sholmes.

"Ah!" I exclaimed. "You will show Squeedro something belonging to the prisoner, and he will follow the track——"

"Not at all."

"Then I do not see——"

"I do not expect you to, Jotson. Pack your bag, my dear fellow, and let us walk our chalks," said Sholmes.

On our way to the station we called in at the office of Bexton Slake, who was almost as famous as a detective as Herlock Sholmes himself.

Slake was lying back in an arm-chair, examining an ordinary glass tumbler filled with some dark-coloured liquid, which he tilted to his mouth. Strange gurgling noises emanated from the great detective's throat.

On his knee reclined the graceful form of the one and only Squeedro. Sitting on the floor, playing "noughts and crosses," was Slinker, Slake's handsome young assistant.

Without beating about the bush Sholmes stated his mission, and, having presented his friend and colleague with a fivepenny cigar given him by a noted criminal on the previous evening, Slake readily agreed to allow him the services of his bloodhound.

An hour later we were on route for Dublin.

CHAPTER 2

The shades of night were falling fast—as I believe some poet has already remarked—when we arrived at Ballybooze.

It was a lonely village in the midst of the Tippleary mountains.

We put up at the village inn, which, for some reason unknown to us, had not been burned to the ground.

We retired to rest early. The night was an unusually quiet and peaceful one. Not more than five or six dead bodies were visible from the windows when we rose in the morning.

After breakfast Sholmes led Squeedro, the bloodhound, to the spot where the kidnapped official had been taken from his car.

I watched my amazing friend with keen interest.

I had expected that he would show the bloodhound some article of clothing belonging to the missing gentleman, but this was not Sholmes's method.

"As the kidnapped gentleman was taken away in a cart, he cannot have left a scent behind him, Jotson," he explained.

"True," I remarked. "But, in that case, I fail to see how Bexton Slake's bloodhound will assist you."

Sholmes smiled.

"Squeedro will follow the scent of the Sinn Feiners," he answered.

"But they are unknown——"

"Quite so."

"You have nothing belonging to them!"

"True!"

"Then how——" I exclaimed.

"Patience, my dear fellow."

Sholmes drew a whisky flask from his pocket. It contained Irish whisky.

Uncorking it, he held it to the bloodhound's nose.

Squeedro gave one sniff, and started off at a loping trot across the mountain.

"Come on, Jotson!"

Sholmes followed the bloodhound, and I followed Sholmes, lost in wonder at the amazing sagacity of my astonishing friend.

The way was long, the wind was cold, but we pushed on rapidly, led by the unfailing Squeedro.

Over mountain and bog he led us, guided unerringly by the scent of Irish whisky.

Two hours later we arrived at the mouth of a solitary cavern. One glance at Sholmes's face was enough for the Sinn Feiners; they fled.

In the cavern lay a prisoner, who, by his expression of vacant imbecility, we knew at once must be a Government official.

"The kidnapped man, Jotson!" drawled Herlock Sholmes.

Once more my amazing friend had succeeded!

THE CASE OF THE MYSTERIOUS SOPRANO

No. 55

We sat down to lunch, when Madame Voceferoce was shown into our rooms at Shaker Street. Herlock Sholmes rose at once, and bowed over the sardine-tin with his accustomed grace.

The celebrated prima donna was, of course, well known to us.

The greatest of living sopranos, her top E flat had more than once made an anxious impresario tremble for the roof of his opera-house.

Crowded audiences had loudly testified their joy and thankfulness when Madame Voceferoce had completed a performance.

"Signor Sholmes!" she exclaimed, sinking into a chair, which groaned beneath her ample form.

Sholmes, who was a master of all languages ancient and modern, replied in easy Italian.

"Whatto! Soho squaro, ice-creamo, saffronillo!" he said, with a smile.

I could see that the prima donna was struck by my amazing friend's command of the Italian language.

"Per bacco!" continued Sholmes. "Vermicelli! maccaroni! Cosi fan tutti! Chatteriamo! But let us speak in English, for the sake of my friend, Dr. Jotson, before whom you may speak quite freely. How can I serve you, signora?"

"If you have lost your voice, madame," I suggested, "you have come to the right shop. My friend Sholmes will undertake to find it——"

"It is not that," said Madame Voceferoce, clasping her hands. "Signor Sholmes, I have a rival! You have, perhaps heard me sing——"

"True."

"You have heard my E flat?"

"I have," said Sholmes. "I shall never forget it. I never hear a railway-engine whistle without being reminded of it."

"You flatter me, Mr. Sholmes. But"—the prima donna made a tragic gesture—"I have a rival, an unknown rival, whose voice, remarkably like my own in tone and quality, exceeds it in compass. Imagine my feelings, Mr. Sholmes, when first I heard this rival's voice! Who it may be, I know not; but if once this singer comes before the public I shall no longer be the greatest soprano on the operatic stage. I shall be out-shone, out-done, out-screamed, out-E-flatted."

"Pray give me a few details," said Sholmes, who, I could see, was already interested in this extraordinary case. "You have not seen this marvellous singer?"

"Never."

"But you have heard her voice?"

"Every night for a week past," said the signora. "You must know, Mr. Sholmes, that every evening I give my voice a quarter of an hour's practice before an open window. My window overlooks an extensive view of leads. From somewhere in the darkness a voice comes in answer to mine."

"Extraordinary!"

"The voice of my unknown rival," continued the prima donna, in an agitated tone, "repeats my E flat in tones exactly resembling my own, and follows it with E, and even F."

"Amazing!" I could not help ejaculating.

"Find this mysterious singer for me, Mr. Sholmes," said Madame Voceferoce imploringly. "I will give her a thousand—ten thousand pounds to leave the country before she is snapped up by some ambitious impresario, and put on the operatic stage. My fame—my fortune—depend upon it! Name your own fee, but find her!"

"Expect me this evening!" said Sholmes.

CHAPTER 2

After dinner that evening I walked with my amazing friend to the fashionable flat occupied by Madame Voceferoce.

Blessed with a soprano voice to which a steamer's syren was a mere bagatelle, Madame Voceferoce had achieved fame and fortune; and now all was imperilled by the threatened advent of a successful rival.

We were shown into the signora's studio at the usual time for her evening practice.

The window was open. A gentleman who, to judge by appearances, was on very distant terms with his barber, was seated at the piano; and all was ready.

"Proceed!" said Sholmes.

Madame Voceferoce proceeded.

Her voice floated forth into the night, rising and culminating upon the celebrated E flat which had so often endangered an operatic roof.

Silence followed. I wiped the perspiration from my brow. Then, from the gloom without, came an answering note.

High and clear, like a repetition of Madame Voceferoce's own voice, rang the note from the shadows.

It was followed by others, rising higher.

I listened in amazement. Madame Voceferoce clasped her hands in anguish.

"Ha!" exclaimed Herlock Sholmes.

He sprang from the window upon the leads of the adjoining building.

"Sholmes!" I exclaimed.

The mysterious soprano ceased.

There was a sound of panting, howling, and spitting, and Sholmes suddenly reappeared in the window.

He did not come alone.

In his grasp was a large, savage-looking tom-cat, struggling and mewing. Sholmes held it up as he stepped into the room, with his inscrutable smile upon his face.

He bowed to Madame Voceferoce.

"Be at ease, signora—the mystery is solved," said Herlock Sholmes. "Behold your rival!"

"Un gatto!" gasped the prima donna.

"Exactly—the rival soprano—whom the most enterprising impresario would never dream of presenting on the operatic stage," said Sholmes reassuringly.

CHAPTER 3

"Rather a curious case, Jotson," Herlock Sholmes remarked, as we strolled home to Shaker Street. "Interesting, though simple."

"My dear Sholmes!" I exclaimed.

"Quite simple, my dear fellow, though Madame Voceferoce was far from suspecting the truth. As she stood at her window, and her top note floated forth, it fell upon the ears of the tom-cat, who naturally mistook it for the call of a lady-friend, and made answer. It was the tom-cat's penetrating voice, in answer to the signora's top E flat, that Madame Voceferoce took for the voice of a rival

" Proceed ! " said Sholmes. He placed himself at the window, and Madame Voceferoce proceeded !

soprano. I am very glad that I have been able to set her mind at rest. I am also rather glad," Sholmes added thoughtfully, "that we do not live next door to Madame Voceferoce. Shaker Street, after all, has its advantages."

THE MYSTERIOUS BOTTLE

No. 56

Herlock Sholmes had already been engaged upon a case of spiritualism—the well-known case of the Cottonshire vicar, who, seated in his vestry, was accustomed to hear mysterious voices from the worlds to which we pass at death. It was Sholmes who demonstrated that it was simply a case of bats in the belfry.

The case of Mr. Soker, however, presented greater difficulties.

Mr. Soker, it appeared, from a very early age had been subject to the influence of spirits.

This occult influence was at times so strong as to cause him actually to lose all sense of his own identity. On one occasion, arriving on his doorstep simultaneously with the morning milkman, he had announced in a loud voice that Champagne Charlie was his name. His name was, however, Joseph.

In his younger days he had been accustomed to attend spirited meetings at a resort known as the Peal of Bells, where there was a great deal of table-rapping, followed by the apparition of a waiter with a tray.

After these sittings Mr. Soker would return home completely overcome.

These seances, however, he no longer attended—Mrs. Soker having, with the aid of the family rolling-pin, persuaded him to give them up.

In spite of his wife's affectionate care and watchfulness, however, the poor gentleman was still subject to spiritualistic influences.

It was for this reason that the services of my amazing friend, Mr. Herlock Sholmes, were called upon.

"A peculiar case, my dear Jotson," remarked Sholmes, after Mrs. Soker had left our rooms in Shaker Street. "I am not sorry to have it brought to my notice. Spiritualism, is the latest fashionable imbecility, and this case——"

"Rum!" I remarked.

"Very rum, my dear fellow," assented Sholmes. "That is, I think, the right word. Pass me the looking-glass."

"What are you going to do with the looking-glass, Sholmes?" I asked, in surprise.

"Reflection is necessary before we act in this case, Jotson."

"True!"

A little later we started for Mr. Soker's residence.

My amazing friend was in a thoughtful mood, but he did not explain to me the result of his mental aberrations.

Mrs. Soker received us in the drawing-room, and as we entered the sound of falling furniture was heard above.

"It is Mr. Soker!" explained the lady. "He is now under the influence of——"

"Spirits!" exclaimed Sholmes.

Crash!

"My dear Jotson," said Sholmes, "we must do our best to rescue the unfortunate man from this malign and occult influence. Does it always make him like this, madam?"

"Frequently," said Mrs. Soker tearfully. "It is inexplicable. He no longer attends the seances at which he use to be so overcome. I have dissuaded him—effectually. After that he used to fall under the mysterious influence through the medium of a friend who visited him, who was also a spiritualist. These visits are no longer allowed. How this occult influence reaches him is, therefore, a mystery."

"Which I will solve!" said Sholmes.

Outside Mr. Soker's door we paused to listen.

A voice within was singing a snatch of a song, and this was followed by the sound of wild and erratic jazzing.

Sholmes smiled, his inscrutable smile.

"You have a theory, Sholmes?" I remarked.

He shrugged his shoulders.

"I do not deal in theories, Jotson, but in facts. You have, no doubt, in earlier days, read the 'Arabian Nights'?"

"Certainly."

"No doubt you remember the story of the fisherman who discovered the spirit in a bottle——"

"True."

"'Tis but an Eastern tale, Jotson, but it has, I think, a bearing upon this case."

He opened the door.

A wild-looking figure in a dressing-gown was jazzing about the room—no other than the unhappy

A wild-looking figure was jazzing about the room.

Mr. Soker, evidently deeply under the occult influence.

He caught his foot in the gown, and sat on the floor, as we entered.

"Hic!" he remarked.

That was his only observation, and I confess that I did not understand what it implied. The word, if word it was, was strange to me. Doubtless it had some connection with his spiritualistic practices.

Sholmes glanced round the room.

Upon a table stood a bottle, half-full of a mysterious-looking pale liquid.

Sholmes picked it up. He placed the bottle to his nose, sniffed, and shook his head thoughtfully.

"Sholmes," I exclaimed breathlessly, "is it—is it——"

Sholmes corked the bottle without replying, and placed it in his pocket.

Then we descended the stairs.

"Madam," said Sholmes, "I regret to say that Mr. Soker is still under spiritualistic influence, but he will recover shortly. The mysterious Presence that haunts him is conveyed into the house confined in a bottle, like the genie in the 'Arabian Nights.' I had guessed as much before I came here. Take care that no bottle of any kind is conveyed to Mr. Soker, and you will find that he will become quite free of these distressing occult influences."

And we took our leave.

CHAPTER 2

At Shaker Street Sholmes shut himself up in the laboratory with the bottle he had taken from Mr. Soker's room. I was very anxious to be present when he investigated the contents, but this Sholmes would not permit. Outside the door, I heard a sound of gurgling, and a little later, to my surprise, Sholmes's voice raised in song. My anxiety for my amazing friend was very keen. Was it possible that, in rescuing Mr. Soker from the occult spiritualistic influence, he had fallen under that terrible influence himself?"

"Sholmes!" I called through the keyhole.

"Hic!" was the reply from within.

I trembled.

It was the same mysterious monosyllable that I had heard upon the lips of Mr. Soker!

I hesitated no longer.

Pushing open the door, I strode in. Herlock Sholmes was sitting on the floor, the bottle empty at his feet, and a smile of imbecility upon his inscrutable features.

"Goo'-nigh', Jotty!" he murmured; and, to my consternation, he rolled over, and fell into a deep sleep.

The following day Herlock Sholmes made no reference to what strange experiences had passed in the laboratory, neither did I learn anything further of the mysterious contents of the bottle. Sholmes had a headache that morning, and his temper was slightly irritable. I did not venture to question my amazing friend, and so some of the details of this very strange affair still remain a mystery to me.

THE CASE OF THE MISSING PATIENT

No. 57

"Sholmes!" I exclaimed.

Herlock Sholmes lifted his nose from the tankard of cocaine, and looked at me inquiringly.

"Well, Jotson?"

"Sholmes! I need your help——"

"'My dear fellow, I am always at your service," replied Herlock Sholmes genially. "Do you, who have chronicled my astounding successes so long and so faithfully, require my aid in an affair of your own?"

"Exactly," I replied.

"Command me, Jotson! In this case there shall be no mention of fees," said Herlock Sholmes. "My dear doctor, what has happened? Have you lost your last 'bus?"

"No, no!"

"The contents of your brain-box are missing?"

"No!"

"I had supposed so," said Sholmes musingly. "However, come to the point, and tell me what is the matter. You may speak quite freely before my friend Dr. Jotson—I mean fire away!"

"One of my patients is missing, Sholmes!"

"Ah!" said Sholmes, with his inscrutable smile. "Give me a few details, Jotson. His name?"

"Mr. Goldbag."

"He had called you in?"

"Not at all; it was his nephew who called me in," I explained. "Mr. Goldbag suffers from dyspepsia——"

"A complaint of the wealthy," said Sholmes. "How thankful we should be, Jotson, that we have no likelihood of contracting any of the diseases caused by over-indulgence in the pleasures of the table! But continue."

"Mr. Goldbag's nephew was very anxious to secure my services," I said, with perhaps a little pardonable pride. "My reputation, he was good enough to say, was well known to him. As he is his uncle's heir, and stands to inherit a million pounds at Mr. Goldbag's demise, he is naturally anxious to do everything in his power for the old gentleman. Determined to leave no stone unturned, he sought out the very best medical aid——"

"Yours, Jotson!"

"Mine," I assented modestly. "He was kind enough to say that he knew he could rely upon me to do

The ruffian struck Jotson upon the nose in the most brutal manner.

exactly what he wished done. I was somewhat flattered, naturally. I found old Mr. Goldbag extremely dyspeptic, and very cross. He was not at all pleased at his nephew having called in medical aid. He even declared that when his time came he could make his transit to the next world without assistance. However, as I was there, I examined him. I found that an operation was necessary,"

"Ah!"

"To reassure him, I told him of my successful operation on Sir Snoozer Snooker—a very successful operation, Sholmes, which made some noise in the medical world at the time. But Mr. Goldbag seemed rather disconcerted by the circumstances that Sir Snoozer had not survived. He could not even understand that the operation was a complete success in itself, and that the death of the patient afterwards was a matter of small amount—a trifle light as air to a medical man. He looked at the matter from the point of view of an ignorant layman."

"Such prejudices exist, even in this enlightened age, Jotson," said Sholmes sympathetically. "There are even persons who object to vaccination, on the totally irrelevant ground that it does not protect from disease. How did you deal with this foolish and obstinate old man?"

"Kindly, but with firmness," I replied. "The operation was arranged for; the nephew was heartily in favour of it. As the foolish old fellow was staying in his nephew's house, and was too ill to move—as we supposed—there seemed no difficulty in the way. All was settled, and I returned home for my anaesthetics, and a saw and an axe——"

"And then?"

"When I arrived with my weapons he was gone. His nephew had foolishly left him alone for a few minutes, having been called down to see a member of the firm of Shylock, Shentpershent and Co., who came to see him on business. He accompanied me to his uncle's room. The window was open; Mr. Goldbag had disappeared! How the sick man had found the strength to escape—I mean to depart—we could not guess."

"The approach of danger had bucked him, no doubt," remarked Sholmes.

"Danger? I do not understand you, Sholmes!"

"You never do, my dear Jotson. But you wish me to find the missing patient?"

"Undoubtedly."

"So that you may operate on him?"

"Exactly."

Sholmes paused for a moment.

"Friendship before everything!" he exclaimed. "For your sake, Jotson, I will become an accessory before the fact. Let us mizzle!"

Puzzled as I was by my amazing friend's expressions, I was ready to mizzle, and we mizzled accordingly.

CHAPTER 2

Herlock Sholmes strode rapidly along Shaker Street, and to my astonishment proceeded direct to Mr. Goldbag's mansion.

Sholmes' summons at the door was answered by a remarkable personage. Instead of a footman, as he expected, a bulldog-looking man, with a broken nose and a spotted handkerchief, opened the door. The man looked like a retired prize-fighter, and such, we afterwards discovered, he actually was.

He glared at us suspiciously.

"Is Mr. Goldbag at home?" asked Herlock Sholmes genially.

"He are!"

"I told you so, Jotson," smiled Sholmes. "My good man, here is Dr. Jotson to see Mr. Goldbag——"

To our surprise and alarm, the broken-nosed man pushed back his shirt-cuffs and spat on his hands.

"Which Mr. Goldbag's told me to keep a heye open for you!" said the broken-nosed man, addressing me.

"Where will you have it?"

I started back.

"My good man——" I ejaculated.

I had no time to say more.

The ruffian rushed at me, and struck me upon the nose in the most brutal manner. He followed this up with his left, on my chin. I rolled down the steps.

The door slammed.

I sat up. From an upper window the face of Mr. Goldbag himself grinned down at us. Evidently the millionaire was a party to this extraordinary assault and battery.

Herlock Sholmes grasped my ear, and gently helped me to my feet.

"Come, Jotson," he said kindly. "You have found your missing patient—but I fear that an operation is out of the question. Evidently Mr. Goldbag has hired this prize-fighter to protect him from the best medical aid called in by his devoted nephew——"

"The man must be mad!" I gasped.

And we departed.

Naturally, I threw up the case at once. After such an occurrence, I would not have operated upon Mr. Goldbag if he sent me the most pressing entreaties to do so. But, as a matter of fact, he never did.

THE PURLOINED PORK

No. 58

"You have had a visitor, Sholmes?" I remarked, as I came in after visiting my patients one morning.

Sholmes smiled.

"How did you deduce that, my dear Jotson?" he asked.

"I have studied you methods, Sholmes," I answered. "As I came in a taxi drove away from the door. As I came upstairs Mrs. Spudson mentioned the fact that a gentleman had called upon you."

"And from that——"

"From those two facts, taken in conjunction, Sholmes, I deduce that you have had a visitor," I said modestly.

"Bravo, Jotson!" exclaimed Herlock Sholmes heartily. "I see that you have not, after all, studied my methods in vain. You are right; I had a visitor—a new case, Jotson. It was the Pork Controller who called upon me. I have agreed to help him. The police are, as usual, helpless in the matter."

"What has happened, Sholmes?"

"A cargo of pork has been surreptitiously removed from the docks at a certain port," explained Sholmes. "It will be necessary to proceed to the port to investigate the mystery. According to the Pork Controller, it is a theft upon an unusually large scale, a whole cargo having been taken, and a motor-lorry, at least, must have been used to convey it away. How the lorry passed out of the docks without detection is a mystery."

"An interesting case," I remarked. "It was newly-landed cargo, I presume?"

"Not at all. The history of the pork is interesting in itself," said Sholmes. "It was landed from an American ship some years ago. It was then, naturally, forgotten. Like the southern sun in Coleridge's celebrated poem, it grew higher and higher every day. A cargo of fertiliser was landed next to it the other day, and the dock authorities decided that unless one or the other was removed it would be necessary to close the port. An official was therefore sent to the Port Controller's office, to wake him up. Having wakened, the Controller gave orders for the pork to be removed at once. It was too late, Jotson! By the time the order reached the port the pork was gone!"

"Extraordinary!" I exclaimed.

"Quite so, Jotson—a case worthy of my powers," said Herlock Sholmes. "If you are ready, my dear fellow, we will proceed to the port at once. The pork must be found; goodness knows what may happen if it gets loose in the country. A cargo of American pork is no joke at the best of times, and after a couple of years in the open air, Jotson, it is probably in a very truculent state. The Pork Controller is very concerned about it. He fears that this incident may lead to public criticism of the Department—even to its abolition. Seventy thousand officials will be thrown out of employment if that should happen."'

"Good heavens, Sholmes!"

"Think of the distress that would be caused, Jotson!" said Sholmes, wiping away a tear. "Moreover, it is time—high time, in fact—that the pork was placed on the market. If it is left much longer it will be unfit for even the British public to eat. At least, the Pork Controller fears so. Let us go."

We went.

CHAPTER 2

We arrived at the port early in the afternoon, and proceeded at once to the docks.

We were conducted to the spot where the pork once had been, but where it was no longer. A scent very unlike that of attar of roses greeted us, and Sholmes turned to the official who was guiding our steps.

"It is certain that the pork is gone?" he asked.

"Undoubtedly."

"Then what is this aroma?"

"Merely the newly landed cargo of fertiliser," explained the official, with a smile. "It should have been removed yesterday, but the contractor has not yet sent for it."

"It was yesterday that the pork was purloined?"

"Yes."

"Ah!" said Sholmes mysteriously.

I looked quickly at my amazing friend.

His tone was sufficient to tell me that he had a clue.

He met my glance, and smiled in his inscrutable way. Then he turned to the dock official.

"Kindly give me the name and address of the contractor who should have removed the fertiliser," he said.

The official looked astounded.

"But it is the pork you are concerned about, not the fertiliser, Mr. Sholmes."

"I have my methods, sir," said Herlock Sholmes sternly. "The name and address of the contractor, sharp!"

The astounded official gave the name and address. Sholmes signed to me, and we walked away, leaving the official staring.

"My dear Sholmes——" I murmured.

"You may wait for me at the hotel, Jotson," drawled Sholmes. "I have to make a call. I am going——"

"To track down the pork?"

"The pork purloiner, at least," said Sholmes. "Au reservoir!" he added, dropping into French, as he often did. "Allong! Bunkez-vous! Scat!"

And we parted.

"It's the newly-landed cargo of fertiliser," explained the official.

CHAPTER 3

I waited with considerable curiosity for the arrival of my amazing friend at our hotel.
Herlock Sholmes arrived at last.
From the graceful and airy way in which he jazzed into the room, and from the gratified smile lurking round his extensive mouth, I saw at once that he had triumphed once more.
"Sholmes!" I exclaimed. "You have solved the mystery?"
"The mystery is a mystery no longer, Jotson," said Sholmes.
"It is, as I divined as soon as I was on the spot, a case of mistaken identity."
"Mistaken identity?" I repeated.
"Exactly. You are aware that the contractor was to have removed the fertiliser yesterday?"
"True."
"It was not removed, but the pork disappeared."
"No doubt. But——"
"The truth flashed into my mind at once," said Herlock Sholmes calmly. "The contractor arrived yesterday, according to arrangement, to remove the fertiliser. He made a natural mistake. The pork was stacked next to the fertiliser, and the wrong cargo was loaded upon the lorry and taken away!"
"Sholmes!"
"You must remember, Jotson, that it was American pork, under Government control. There was nothing, therefore, to distinguish it from the fertiliser, and the mistake was a natural one. The contractor is not to blame; he had not even suspected the truth, although he certainly thought that the chemical components of the fertiliser were of unusual pungency. The pork is now on its way back to the docks." Sholmes looked thoughtful for a moment. "By the way, Jotson, on our return to Shaker Street I think we may as well mention to Mrs. Spudson that pork chops had better be excluded from our menu for some time to come."

THE CASE OF THE BOLSHEVIK!

No. 59

I had noticed that Herlock Sholmes was preoccupied at breakfast. He was unusually absent-minded. At a time when his mighty intellect was concentrated upon some knotty problem he was generally a little absent-minded; it had sometimes happened that he had eaten my kipper as well as his own, unconscious of the rather serious inconvenience to myself. On this occasion he made a clean sweep of the margarine as well, and finished the shrimps to the last one. I did not venture to interrupt him. It was not for his humble friend, Dr. Jotson, to give a jolt to that powerful intellectual mechanism, when it was going at full speed ahead on its highest gear.
He broke the silence at last.
"You know what happens to-day, Jotson?" he asked.
"I have some death certificates to sign," I replied. "My practice keeps me rather busy."
"The Peace Conference meets again," said Sholmes, unheeding. "It is the seven-hundred-and-eighty-ninth meeting of the Peace Conference, Jotson—and unless I intervene there may never be a seven-hundred-and-ninetieth meeting."
"Good heavens, Sholmes!"
I was interested at once. Evidently it was an affair of international importance that was occupying my amazing friend's faculties.
"You may have heard of Smellowiski, the Russian Bolshevik," continued Sholmes gloomily. "I have had an eye on him for some time. I am perfectly well aware that he has nefarious designs upon the eminent statesmen who meet in conference to-day. If the conference should be blown up——"
"Sholmes!"
"You can guess what an irreparable disaster that would be, Jotson. At present all the eminent statesmen of Europe are occupied with the meetings of the Conference. Their attention is centred on it. Now that is has become a permanent institution, likely to endure as long as human life lasts on this planet, it fills the minds and the time of all these eminent statesmen, and keeps them out of mischief. The Peace Conference once abolished, they would seek some other outlet for their activities, and goodness knows what might happen! You are well aware, Jotson, of what an eminent statesman is like when he takes the bit between his teeth."
I turned pale.
Sholmes' gloomy words conjured up a terrible vision before my startled mind.
"The Peace Conference must be saved!" I exclaimed hastily. "For the sake of humanity at large, Sholmes——"
He nodded.
"You must help me save it, Jotson."
"Anything, my dear fellow, that I can do——"
"As it happens, Jotson, you are the very man."

"Command me!" I said.
"It is very fortunate that you are a medical man, Jotson. Otherwise with the best will in the world, you would not be able to help me. But I know your reputation—I know your skill——"
"Far be it from me to boast," I said modestly; "but it is fairly well known that when I gave up my last practice the Undertakers' Society presented me with a testimonial."
"You deserved it, Jotson."
"And if you are ever ill, Sholmes," I exclaimed, "place yourself in my hands, and rely upon me."
"I think my courage is well known, Jotson," said Sholmes, "but I should never carry it to the extent of dare-devil recklessness. But come, my dear fellow; it is time we were off."
He took me by the back hair, in his playful way, and propelled me from the room.

CHAPTER 2

We arrived at————, where the seven-hundred-and-eighty-ninth meeting of the Peace Conference was being held. We had followed on the track of Smellowiski, the Bolshevik. The town was crowded. There were thirty important Ministers at the Conference, and each had brought with him three hundred officials and thirty thousand typists. Herlock Sholmes and I mingled in the vast swarms of humanity, never losing sight of the grim, Tartaric visage of Smellowiski, the Bolshevik.
But I confess that I did not understand how I was to assist my amazing friend in my capacity as a medical man.
Sholmes suddenly left my side.
He rushed past the Bolshevik, and neatly tripped him up in passing.
Smellowiski fell heavily to the ground.
Herlock Sholmes waved back the crowd.
"Stand back! A man has fainted!" he exclaimed. "Is there a doctor here? Jotson!"
I pushed forward.
In a moment I was kneeling at the Bolshevik's side.
My professional instincts were aroused at once. I forgot that the man was a Bolshevik; I banished his felonious designs from my mind, and remembered only that he needed medical aid.
The crowd stood back to give us room.
Smellowiski showed signs of recovering. I soothed him in my well-known bedside manner.
"Calm yourself!" I said. "You have sustained a contorted contusion of the spinal column of the seventeenth rib, and collywobbleitis may supervene. An operation will be necessary. Bring a stretcher."
The Bolshevik would have objected. He would even have refused the aid of modern medical science. But he was placed on the stretcher. I followed, opening my case of instruments.

CHAPTER 3

The operation was a complete success.
I am no boaster, but I cannot think of that operation, conducted according to the latest scientific principles, without a flush of pride.
Had Smellowiski survived I am certain he would have overwhelmed me with gratitude, Bolshevik as he was.
When it was over I rejoined Sholmes. I was feeling a little elated, as was natural in the circumstances, and my amazing friend smiled as he met my glance.
"A success?" he asked.
"Complete!" I answered.
"I congratulate you, Jotson. And the patient? He succumbed to the operation?"
I gave Sholmes a severe glance.
"Really, Sholmes, he was not likely to succumb to an operation performed by me. It was, as I have told you, a complete success. The patient merely succumbed afterwards."
"Quite so," said Sholmes; and his inscrutable smile appeared upon his face. "My dear Jotson, you deserve another testimonial. Allons!"
There are some details in this strange case still mysterious to me. I give the facts as I know them. The decease of the Bolshevik averted the threatened danger from the seven-hundred-and-eighty-ninth meeting of the Peace Conference. That, of course, even Herlock Sholmes could not have foreseen. But whenever I have mentioned this circumstance to Sholmes he has only smiled his inscrutable smile.

THE CASE OF THE ORATOR

No. 60

Inspector Pinkeye was puzzled. It was for that reason of course, that he dropped into our rooms at Shaker Street to consult my amazing friend, Mr. Herlock Sholmes.

Sholmes smiled as the Scotland Yard man was shown in by Mrs. Spudson.

"Floored again, Pinkeye," he said genially.

"Not exactly, Mr. Sholmes," answered the inspector, with some slight stiffness of manner. "We should however, be glad of your assistance once more."

"My dear fellow, I am quite at your service. Pile in! You may, of course speak quite freely before my friend, Dr. Jotson."

The inspector sat down.

"No doubt you have read in the papers of the bomb outrage in Hyde Park, Mr. Sholmes?" he began.

Sholmes nodded.

"A well-known anarchist orator was blown to pieces," continued the inspector. In anarchist circles, this Mr. Nonstop Chinn was quite a celebrated character. His sudden and tragic fate has caused great excitement. His revolutionary comrades are, of course, extremely indignant at the idea of bombs being used by anyone outside their own ranks——"

"Quite so. But is it certain that a bomb was used?" drawled Herlock Sholmes.

Inspector Pinkeye stared.

"There appears to be no doubt on that point," he answered. "We have the evidence of eye-witnesses. Mr. Chinn was mounted upon a platform in the Park, addressing a large meeting. He had been talking for three hours when the outrage occurred. His secretary was near him on the platform. This gentleman, Mr. Sponge, testifies that he was standing only a few feet from the deceased, and was in the act of lighting a cigarette, when there was a sudden and terrific explosion. Afterwards he was collected up in a semi-detached state. Only a bomb, suddenly hurled, could have caused the explosion."

Herlock Sholmes smiled his inscrutable smile.

"Only that?" he asked.

"Really, Mr. Sholmes, I do not see what else could have caused the explosion," said the inspector, in a nettled tone. "We cannot, however, find a trace of the man who hurled the bomb. He must have been in the crowd; but his action seems to have passed unnoticed."

"You have been searching for him?" asked Sholmes.

"High and low; but without success, so far. It is necessary that the bomb-thrower should be discovered. Justice must be done, and the excitement in anarchist circles must be allayed. Mr. Chinn was very popular with the extremist party. He was booked for six hundred speaking engagements during the coming winter. These engagement have now, of course, had to be cancelled. But even Scotland Yard, Mr. Sholmes, cannot work without a clue——"

"There is no clue of the cigarette!" suggested Shomes.

"Eh!"

"Did you not mention that Mr. Sponge was lighting a cigarette within a few feet of the unfortunate man when the explosion occurred?"

"That is true; but I see no clue in this very ordinary circumstance," said Mr. Pinkeye.

Herlock Sholmes shrugged his shoulders.

"Yet it is fairly obvious!" he remarked.

"I fail to see——"

"My dear Sholmes," I murmured, "what necessary connection is there between Mr. Sponge having lighted a cigarette, and the explosion that blew up Mr. Chinn?"

"Yet you have studied my methods, Jotson."

"True; but——"

Sholmes yawned.

"I will look into the case, inspector," he said. "It is a very simple one, and I shall finish in time for lunch."

"Mr. Sholmes!"

"I will come with you now, inspector, and question your witnesses," said Herlock Sholmes, rising, "Jotson, see that Mrs. Spudson has the kippers ready at twelve-thirty precisely. I shall not be late for lunch, and this afternoon I have to go down to Bisley to investigate the case of the missing marksman. Come, Pinkeye!"

And my amazing friend took the inspector gently by the whiskers and escorted him from the room.

CHAPTER 2

The kippers were on the table when Sholmes returned.

He came promptly to time.

Punctuality was part of Sholmes' system, especially at meal-times. I have seldom, or never, known

Sholmes escorted the inspector from the room.

him to be late for a meal; though on some occasions meals have been late for him, at times when our finances were at a low ebb.

He smiled as he came in.

Nothing, however, would induce Sholmes to satisfy my curiosity until the kippers had been carved and disposed of, and he had drawn his usual pint of cocaine from the flask, and lighted his three-halfpenny cigar.

"And now, Sholmes——" I hinted.

"There is little to explain," yawned Sholmes. "The case was perfectly simple. There was, of course, no bomb in the affair at all."

"No bomb?" I ejaculated.

"None."

"But there was an explosion, Sholmes?"

"No doubt."

"The Anarchist orator was blown to pieces?"

"True."

"Then how——"

"As I remarked to the inspector, Jotson, the clue was in the cigarette."

I gazed blankly at my amazing friend.

"I confess I do not see," I murmured.

"To be more precise, the clue was in Mr. Sponge's act of lighting the cigarette, just when Mr. Chinn was in full blast of anarchist oratory," explained Sholmes. "You do not see the connection?"

"I do not!"

"My poor Jotson, you really ought to be at Scotland Yard," said Sholmes, with a smile. "Your intellect is eminently suitable for such a quarter."

"Really, Sholmes——"

"Have you ever listened to an anarchist orator in the Park?" asked Sholmes.

"Often."

"You have often heard their discourses?"

"I have!"

"Of what were they composed, Jotson?"

"Chiefly gas," I replied.

I reflected.

"Exactly! Mr. Chinn was an anarchist of the first water. He was accustomed to pouring out undiluted gas for hours together. He had been gassing for three hours when his misguided secretary, who ought really to have known better, struck a match within a few feet of him. The result was inevitable; the explosion followed, and Mr. Chinn was blown to pieces by the explosion of his own gas. A perfectly simple case!" Sholmes rose, "And now for Bisley, and the case of the missing marksman!"

THE TRUNK MYSTERY

No. 61

"My dear Jotson, we must start at once," said Herlock Sholmes, as I came down one morning into our sitting-room at Shaker Street.

I glanced towards the breakfast-table

"My dear Sholmes, I have not yet——"

"We have to call upon Colonel Collywobble without the delay of a moment," explained Sholmes. "But you know my efficient methods, Jotson. In order to save time I have eaten your breakfast, as well as my own. There is, therefore, nothing to delay us. Come!"

With a gentle pressure of his boot to my coat-tails, my amazing friend assisted me from the room.

As we walked down Shaker Street, Herlock Sholmes gave me some details of the strange case that was now claiming his attention.

"A trunk has been purloined from the colonel's house, Jotson. So much he has told me over the telephone. He has, of course, been to the police. They have several trunk mysteries on hand, and have kindly added this one to the list. That is very obliging of them, of course; but does not materially assist the colonel, who is anxious to recover his property. He has, naturally, returned from India, and the trunk had not yet been unpacked. It was taken away yesterday in broad daylight. Yet no one seems to have witnessed the theft."

"A curious case, Sholmes," I remarked.

"Very curious," assented Herlock Sholmes; and my friend remained plunged in deep thought until we arrived at the residence of Colonel Collywobble.

We were shown at once into the colonel's presence.

We found him in a great state of agitation.

"Herlock Sholmes?" he exclaimed, as my amazing friend entered.

"The same," answered Sholmes. "This is my friend, Dr. Jotson, before whom you may speak quite freely. Kindly give me a few details. A trunk has been purloined——"

Sholmes snapped the handcuffs on the wrists of the astonished Hindu.

"Exactly!"
"It contained valuables?"
"All my most precious possessions," gasped the colonel. "My medals—my ribbons—my Orders—the sword of honour presented to me at the relief of Jazzpore—the great diamond I received from the Nabob of Spoofembad—my collection of Hindu antiquities, among the finest ever manufactured at Birmingham—and a considerable sum in cash——"
"Where was the trunk at the time?"
"In the hall, sir, it had not yet been unpacked!"
"And when?"
"Yesterday afternoon in broad daylight."
"You suspected no one?"
The colonel shook his head.
"A very interesting case," said Herlock Sholmes, rubbing his hands. "No one observed the trunk being taken away?"
"That is the most surprising circumstance, Mr. Sholmes. The truck was removed in the daylight, yet though there were dozens of people in the street, it was not noticed. It was too heavy for any man to carry—some vehicle must have been used. Yet no one saw the removal."
Sholmes wrinkled his brows.
"It must have been seen, if there were dozens of people in the street," he suggested gently. "It was not, however, observed. The thief must have used some very cunning method of transport, to throw dust in the eyes of the spectators."
"No doubt, if you can discover——"
"I will do my best," said Herlock Sholmes modestly. "Allow me to ask you a question or two. Is there, to your knowledge, any native of India residing in the vicinity?"
The colonel stared.
"I do not understand."
"My dear colonel, a gentleman who has held a high military command in India is not expected to understand. But answer the question."
"There is an Indian merchant who keeps a bric-a-brac shop in the next street," snapped the colonel. "He has been here on business. But this man, Mr. Bhump Khlump Whallop, could not have taken the trunk."
"Good-morning, colonel!"
We left the house.
"My dear Sholmes," I murmured, as we turned into the next street. "Where are we going?"
"To call upon Bhump Khlump Whallop, my dear Jotson."
"For what purpose?"
"To ascertain whether, when he came to this country, he brought any animal from his native land with him as a pet."
"Sholmes!"
"Such an animal, for example, as an elephant," said Sholmes.
"An elephant?" I gasped.
"But here we are!" added Sholmes, as we entered a dusky little shop, filled with Oriental antiquities some of which had probably come from the Orient. "Ah! Good-morning, Mr. Whallop!"
A dusky Hindu came to serve us.
"I am not a customer," said Sholmes, with a smile. "I have simply called to inform you that your elephant has strayed, Mr. Whallop!"
The Hindu uttered an exclamation of alarm.
He rushed out of the shop, greatly agitated. Herlock Sholmes slightly moved his eyelid.
In a few minutes Bhump Khlump Whallop rushed in again, angry and excited.
"It is false," he exclaimed, "My elephant has not strayed!"
Sholmes nodded.
"Precisely," he said "I merely desired, my dear fellow, to ascertain in the simplest possible way whether you possessed an elephant. Simply one of my well-known master-strokes of diplomacy, Mr. Whallop. Now I will trouble you for your wrists. I have a pair of handcuffs here which, I think, will fit you nicely."
"Sholmes!" I exclaimed.
But my amazing friend only smiled his inscrutable smile, as he snapped the handcuffs on the wrists of the astonished Hindu.

CHAPTER 2

"How——" I gasped when we were back at Shaker Street, after the police had taken charge of Bhump Khlump Whallop, and the stolen trunk had been recovered from the Hindoo's premises.
"To an intellect like my mine, my dear Jotson," said Sholmes, "the case was clear from the start. The trunk had been taken away, in a crowded street, without anyone being the wiser. Had it been taken away on a motor-car, a handbarrow, or a lorry, somebody would certainly have observed the removal."

"True, but——"

"Therefore, I deduced an elephant," explained Sholmes, with his slightly bored smile. "A trunk upon a car, a cab, or a lorry would have been observed, but no one noticed anything unusual in seeing a trunk upon an elephant. It was a cunning device, Jotson, but our dusky friend has learned, by this time, that there is at least one man in London sharper than himself."

"Only one, Sholmes!" I exclaimed, with conviction.

And Herlock Sholmes smiled assent.

THE DISAPPEARANCE OF DR. JOTSON

No. 62

My amazing friend, Mr. Herlock Sholmes, generally enjoyed the best of health. Even after his most strenuous mental aberrations, he would come up smiling. During the period of our residence at Shaker Street, I never knew him to be ill, untiol the occasion of which I am about to speak.

I was, of course, glad that my friend enjoyed robust health. But my satisfaction was mingled with a little friendly disappointment. Nothing would have pleased me better than to have cared for him in sickness—my medical skill was entirely at his service, and I would have operated upon him at any time with pleasure.

Indeed, at one time I suspected appendicitis, and offered to remove his appendix; of course, without charging him any fee. Sholmes declined the offer, rather hastily I thought. Perhaps seeing my disappointment, he offered to allow me to removed the appendix from any volume in his bookcase. I explained that this was quite a different matter; but as my wonderful friend's intellectual powers were, for once he did not quite seem to comprehend, and the subject was dropped.

It was after his solution of the "Trunk Mystery" that my amazing friend was laid up; and sad as it was to see him stretched upon the bed of sickness, I will not deny that I felt a certain gratification in at last being able to attend him as a doctor instead of merely as a faithful and admiring follower. I assumed my well-known bedside manner at once, and soothed him gently; for Sholmes, brave as a lion in health, seemed now under the influence of some strange fear.

"At last, Sholmes," I said, "my dear fellow, rely entirely on me. You know my skill."

"I do!" said Sholmes, with a gasp.

"An operation will, I fear, be necessary." I said, as I felt his pulse. "You know how successful my operations are. I have never had a failure. Not one of the patients upon whom I have operated has ever complained afterwards——"

"Perhaps he couldn't!" remarked Sholmes, with what seemed to me a rather ghastly smile.

I did not quite follow the drift of this remark.

"Lie quite still, my dear fellow," I said. "I shall, of course, use anaesthetics. You will never know what has happened to you——"

"One moment!" gasped Sholmes. "Before you begin, take a message for me, my dear Jotson, in case of accidents!"

"There are no accidents when I operate, Sholmes," I said, with some severity. "I will send it by Mrs. Spudson."

"As a last favour Jotson, I beg you to take the message personally," said Herlock Sholmes, writhing upon his bed in a really alarming way.

I consented.

It was perhaps, weakness on my part, but my friend was growing so excited, that I felt it better to humour him.

I brought him a paper and pencil, and he scribbled a few lines, which he sealed in an envelope.

"Take it immediately, Jotson—and personally!" he said feverishly. "Mind, personally—no other messenger will do. Mrs. Spudson can remain with me while you are gone, Hurry—hurry!"

"I will fly!" I said.

I lost no time; I could see that Sholmes was anxious for me to return and operate.

A taxi bore me to the address on Herlock Sholmes's letter.

The house was situated in a somewhat unsavoury quarter of Limehouse.

I knocked at the door.

It was opened by a bull-necked man with one eye, who glared at me in what I thought a rather ferocious manner.

"A letter from Herlock Sholmes!" I said.

The bull-necked man took the letter opened it, and read it, while I stood in the doorway.

Then he gave me a very peculiar glance.

"Please step in, sir!" he said.

I stepped in, and the bull-necked man closed the door.

Then, to my utter amazement, he suddenly seized me in a pair of very powerful hands and rolled me down a flight of steps into the cellar.

By the time I gained my feet, a door had closed on me, and I heard a key turn in a lock.

I was a prisoner!

CHAPTER 2

I cannot describe my anguish of mind during the days that I remained a helpless prisoner in the cellar in Limehouse.

My best friend—the amazing Herlock Sholmes—lay upon a bed of sickness, and I was not there to attend him. His faithful Dr. Jotson was far from his side in the hour of need.

I may say with truth that I thought more of Sholmes than of myself during those terrible days of anxiety. What would happen to him if the operation was not performed at once! Without my pressing solicitude, it was doubtful whether Sholmes would submit to an operation at all. I knew that he was prejudiced on the subject—for some reason I could not grasp, he attached more importance to the recovery of the patient than to the success of an operation.

In vain I told my rascally kidnapper that Sholmes's life was at stake. He replied that he was aware of it, and that that was why I was kept a prisoner—an extraordinary statement, which I can only account for by the fact that the ruffian had been drinking.

My release came at last.

One morning the door flew open, and instead of the bull-necked ruffian, it was my amazing friend, Herlock Sholmes, who stood before me.

"Sholmes!" I gasped.

"Here we are again, Jotson!" he said genially.

"You have found me?"

"So it appears."

"And your health?"

"Quite restored."

"But the operation?"

"Prepare yourself for a shock, Jotson! I recovered without an operation!" said Sholmes.

"And in spite of that you are in health!" I exclaimed in amazement.

"Because of that, my dear fellow," he said, with his inscrutable smile. "But come, you must be tired of these uncomfortable quarters."

And hooking his umbrella gently in my ear, Herlock Sholmes led me out to freedom.

CHAPTER 3

"Sholmes!" I exclaimed, when we arrived at Shaker Street.

"How——"

Sholmes shook his head.

"For once, my dear Jotson, I cannot give you the full details of the case," he answered. "Enough to say, that immediately I recovered my health, I sought for you, and found you. There is an old proverb that he who hides can find. Once more we are re-united, my dear fellow, never to part again unless I should be ill—I mean—ahem!" Sholmes seemed a little confused for a moment. Then he smiled. "My dear Jotson, you shall operate on your kidnapper when I find him."

But this proved to be the only occasion upon which I ever knew Herlock Sholmes to fail. He did not find the kidnapper.

THE CASE OF THE BOAT CLUB

No. 63

A client was just leaving my amazing friend, Mr. Herlock Sholmes, when I returned from visiting my patients one morning. I bowed to him with deep respect as he passed me, for I could see at a glance that he was a member of the British peerage. His dark complexion, aquiline nose, black eyebrows, and the accent with which he bade Sholmes "Goot-morning" told me as much.

"Come in, Jotson," said Sholmes. "I dare say you know the nobleman who has just gone out?"

"I noticed that he was a nobleman, Sholmes."

"It is Lord Guggengugger," explained Sholmes. "One of the greatest noblemen in the land—connected with the families of Neinschmidt and Porkstein—in fact, with nearly all the nobility. He is the head of the most exclusive boat club in the United Kingdom—the Hellespont. He has called to invoke my assistance. But I have been set a rather difficult task."

"Not too difficult for you, Sholmes," I said, with conviction.

My amazing friend smiled complacently.

"At least, my faithful Jotty will never lose faith in me," he remarked.

"Never, Sholmes! Did you not rescue me when I was kidnapped—at the time you lay on a sick bed, and I was anxious to fly to your side?" I exclaimed. "You saved me, though too late to operate upon you, as I intended. But that was not your fault—it was your misfortune."

"Say rather my good fortune, Jotson. However, to return to the Hellespont Boat Club," said Sholmes hastily. "You may be aware of the extreme strictness of the club rules, Jotson. No one who is or has been in trade is allowed to become a member—a most aristocratic club."

"Only persons whose papas have made fortunes in trade, I understand?"

Jotson bowed to Sholmes's client with deep respect.

"Exactly."
"But what——"
"It is a question of a new member," said Sholmes. "A young man of the name of Beauclerc—Sir Paget Beauclerc."
"That sounds quite respectable, Sholmes."
"Possibly; but it is not a name that speaks for itself, like Porkstein or Guggengugger."
"True."
"The committee appear to have been a little negligent. The young man has been admitted a member, and now doubts have arisen. Is the young man connected with trade in any way? Lord Guggengugger is acutely distressed. As a polished nobleman of the old school, he is, of course, anxious to avoid wounding the young man's feelings, if possible. But he has his duty to do. The club looks to him as its head. Far be it from me, Jotson, to uphold anything in the way of snobbery. But social distinctions do exist. They must be regarded. A Beauclerc cannot be allowed to shove his way into the company of Guggenguggers and Porksteins unrebuked."
"True."
"The matter is to be handled as delicately as possible. Lord Guggengugger has engaged me to make inquiries in a quiet way. I am to ascertain whether this young man is tainted by any connections with trade. The rules of the Hellespont Club are rigid on that point, and must be observed. If it should prove to be so, he will be excluded as tactfully as possible—but he will be excluded."
"Quite so, Sholmes. And you——"
Sholmes rose, and knocked out his pipe, in his playful way, on the back of my neck.
I am about to begin my investigations, Jotson. I hope I shall be able to clear the young man of the unpleasant suspicions that have fallen upon him, and to save the Hellespont members from the horrid realisation that they have rubbed shoulders with a person connected with trade—a dreadful thing to happen to anybody, Jotson. Well, I must buzz."
And my amazing friend buzzed.

CHAPTER 2

It was more than a week before I saw my friend again.
He was busy upon the case of Sir Paget Beauclerc, which took him to a distance from London.
I understood that he was pursuing his investigations in the vicinity of the young man's residence in the country.
I was very keen to hear the result, and whether Lord Guggengugger and his aristocratic friends were to be saved from the humiliation with which they were threatened.
Well I knew what would be the internal sufferings of that haughty old nobelman, if it proved that he had inadvertently sat in the same room and breathed the same atmosphere as a person upon whom lay the taint of trade.
I was glad, therefore, when Sholmes came into our rooms at Shaker Street one evening and announced that the case was finished.
"My dear Sholmes," I said, "you will, of course, furnish me with the usual explanation, which comes at the end of the story."
"Undoubtedly, Jotson. Roll the cask of cocaine this way, my dear fellow, and terminate the activities of your chin, and I will explicate."
"You have been successful?"
Herlock Sholmes raised his eyebrows.
"Jotson!"
"Your pardon, Sholmes," I said hurriedly. "I should not have asked that question. You have, of course, succeeded? Is the young man whose case you have been investigating innocent of any connection with trade? Can the members of the Hellespont Club breathe again freely, with the happy knowledge that they have not, after all, been contaminated?"
Sholmes shook his head sadly.
"No!"
"Sholmes! Then Lord Guggengugger——"
"We have all much to endure in this life, Jotson, and Lord Guggengugger must learn to bear this terrible shock. He may, in time, forget. He may find distraction in counting over his millions at the bank, or in poring over the historic pedigree of his family which was compiled for him at such great expense when he entered the peerage. I hope for the best. But I was bound to tell him the truth, Jotson. The new member of the Hellespont Club has not only been engaged in trade, but is still carrying it on, openly, shamelessly, as though it were not a crime."
"Sholmes!"
"'Tis true, Jotson, and pity 'tis, 'tis true!" said Sholmes. "Shakespeare, I believe, has made a remark to that effect."
"But in what trade, then, is the unhappy young man engaged?" I asked.
"He inherited a large landed estate from his father," explained Sholmes. "Ever since he came of age he has been engaged in letting unfurnished land to farmers."
"Shocking!"

"But true. He will, of course, be instantly excluded from the aristocratic circle of the Hellespont Club, and we can only hope, Jotson, that Lord Guggengugger and his noble friends will in time recover from the terrible shock they have sustained. Their noble blood, the ancient traditions of their race, will, I hope, enable them to recover. We can only hope for the best."

THE CASE OF THE GUNPOWDER PLOT

No. 64

"Probably, my dear Jotson, you have heard of Guy Fawkes?" Herlock Sholmes remarked to me, as I returned one day from a post-mortem on one of my patients.

I reflected.

"The name seems familiar, Sholmes——"

"Pleased to remember the Fifth of November," suggested Sholmes. "The gunpowder treason and plot."

"True!" I assented. "I see no reason why gunpowder treason should ever be forgot."

"Exactly. It is many a year now, Jotson, since Guy Fawkes attempted to blow up the House of Commons by storing barrels of gunpowder in the cellars under the chin-wag department. But he has found an imitator in these latter days——"

"Sholmes!"

"It is true, Jotson," said Herlock Sholmes gravely. "The ancient gunpowder plot was a failure, owing to a warning conveyed, I understand, to a lady upon whom Fawkes was spoons. The present plot will owe its defeat to——"

"To Herlock Sholmes!" I exclaimed.

"Just so."

"But the plot—it is known?"

"The suspicions of the police have been aroused, Jotson, by the sight of a number of masked men stacking barrels of dynamite under the windows of the House of Commons. I must compliment them upon their unusual sagacity—for once Inspector Pinkeye has been wide awake. My services have been called in to discover the arch-conspirator, the author of this fearful plot, which, if successful, would have deprived the country of six hundred of its most active and untiring chins."

"Terrible!"

"Terrible, indeed, Jotson. The explosion was apparently timed to take place when our greatest non-stop orator was addressing the House—that great and justly celebrated statesman, Jotson, who won the war, slaying, like Samson, his thousands and tens of thousands, and with the same weapon, the jawbone of an ass!"

I trembled. The thought of those six hundred tongues being stilled—of half the chinwag in the kingdom being silenced at one fell swoop—was terrible.

"Sholmes!" I gasped. "You must save them!"

"I will!" exclaimed Herlock Sholmes. "They shall be shaved—I mean saved! Come!

He took me quickly by the nose and led me away.

CHAPTER 2

Herlock Sholmes paused as he led me into Shaker Street, still with that powerful and friendly grasp on my nose.

"Have you a ten-pound note, Jotson?"

"I have."

"Then we will take a taxi—we have a mile to go."

"Mr. Sholmes!"

"Ah! It is our friend Pinkeye!" said Herlock Sholmes, with a smile. "What luck so far, Pinkeye?"

The Scotland Yard inspector shook his head.

"None, Mr. Sholmes. We are relying on your aid——"

"But you are searching——"

"All the criminals known to be in London have been tracked out and examined," said Inspector Pinkeye.

"Is that all?"

"All the anarchists——"

Sholmes shrugged his shoulders.

"And you expect to find the gunpowder plotter among criminals and anarchists, Pinkeye?" he asked sarcastically.

The inspector stared.

"Inspector, I am about to look for the gunpowder plotter," went on Herlock Sholmes. "Not, however, in the purlieus of crime—not in the haunts of anarchists. Come, Jotson!"

"You need my assistance, Sholmes?" I asked.

"Undoubtedly. The taxi must be paid for."

We took the taxi, and—doubtless on the principle that one good turn deserves another—the taxi took us.

We arrived at our destination—a building which bore a brass plate, with the inscription "Society for the Prevention of Cruelty to Bipeds."

"Wait here, Jotson."

Herlock Sholmes disappeared into the office of the Society for the Prevention of Cruelty to Bipeds.

I waited.

In a few minutes my amazing friend emerged.

He did not come along. He was leading a benevolent-looking old gentleman by the arm, and upon his prisoner's wrists the handcuffs clinked.

"Make room for the gunpowder plotter, Jotson," said Sholmes with a smile.

"Sholmes! How——"

"We will hand over our prisoner to the good Pinkeye," said Herlock Sholmes. "Let us mizzle."

We mizzled.

Sholmes emerged leading a benevolent old gentleman.

"Sholmes!"

My amazing friend smiled as he stretched himself on the sofa in our rooms at Shaker Street, and rested his feet on the mantelpiece in his easy, graceful manner.

"A few words will explain, Jotson," yawned Herlock Sholmes. "The plot was laid to blow up the House of Commons on the Fifth of November—and our friend Pinkeye sought for the gunpowder plotter among the anarchists and criminals."

"But surely——"

"Not at all. Had the plot been laid to blow up any other building, Jotson, Pinkeye's methods might have been right. But you must remember that it was the House of Commons—the Mummy of Parliaments—that was to be blown. That famous building, Jotson, where the flow of chinwag, the tide of jawfulness, ceases not, and only ebbs in the small hours. With my usual perspicacity, Jotson, I grasped the truth at once. It was the work, not of an anarchist, but of a philanthropist."

"A philanthropist, Sholmes!'

Sholmes nodded.

"Exactly. Some tender-hearted man had asked himself the question, why should not the wicked cease from troubling, and the weary be at rest? For centuries, Jotson, that tide of talk has swelled, and swelled, and never ceased; generation after generation that unending prattle has dinned in the ears of humanity, till it has become a weariness of the flesh. Eloquent orator after orator has spouted and spouted. War, famine and pestilence may come and go, but the spouting goes on for ever. To stop it might seem, to the philanthropic mind, the greatest possible boon and blessing to men. I left Inspector Pinkeye, therefore, to look amongst the anarchists, while I looked among the philanthropists."

I gazed at my amazing friend in speechless admiration.

"I had a painful duty to perform," said Sholmes rather moodily. "For once my sympathies were with my prisoner. Perhaps he was carrying a philanthropic kindness to his fellow men too far. But his intentions were good. But be that as it may, Jotson, I have done my duty, and the House of Palaver will not be blown up on the Fifth of November."

Herlock Sholmes was right.

It wasn't!

THE CASE OF THE LOST CHORD

No. 65

Among the most perplexing cases upon which my amazing friend Mr. Herlock Sholmes was engaged during the period of our residence at Shaker Street was the one which I am about to relate—the mysterious case of the Lost Chord.

It is safe to say that in all his astounding career Mr. Herlock Sholmes had never been set so difficult a task.

As a detective who knew the ropes, he was, of course, the very man to find a chord, if it could be found.

But for the impatience of the hapless composer, I have no doubt that my amazing friend would have discovered the lost article, and restored it to its owner little worse for wear. But we must not anticipate.

A wild-eyed, long-haired young man rushed from the room as I entered one morning. As he flew downstairs I heard him mutter in distracted tones:

"Was it the dominant nineteenth in K major? Was it an unresolved diminished discord in Z flat——"

I heard no more.

I turned inquiringly to Sholmes.

"A musician?" I asked.

Herlock Sholmes nodded.

"You have guessed it first time, Jotson," he replied. "Doubtless you observed that he appears to be on distant terms with his barber. A very curious case, Jotson."

"But what——"

"It is Mr. Twidley Bitz—one of our most promising young composers," explained Sholmes. "His work is the very latest sample of the newest of the new school of modern composers. Richard Strauss is an ass to him, Wagner a stale joke, a sawmill in full action is scarcely his equal. Earthquakes and volcanic eruptions are trifles light as air compared with an orchestra engaged upon one of his latest productions. He has had a terrible loss!"

"And that?"

"A lost chord!" said Sholmes impressively.

I started.

"I appear to have heard, somewhere, of a Lost Chord before," I remarked thoughtfully.

"It seems," continued Sholmes, "that, seated one day at the organ, he was weary and ill at ease——"

"And his fingers wandered idly——" I suggested.

"Over the noisy keys," said Sholmes.

"He knew not what he was playing?" I inquired.

Sholmes shook his head.

"Nor what he was dreaming then?"

"No. But he struck one chord of music like the sounds from a cattle-pen," said Sholmes.

Herlock Sholmes knitted his brows thoughtfully, and laid down the knitting-needles.

"That chord is lost, and it is up to us to find it. It may be, of course, like your umbrella, Jotson—past recovering."

"Not to you," I said with conviction. "If you switch your powerful brain upon the subject, Sholmes, I am assured that you will succeed in finding even the Lost Chord."

Herlock Sholmes smiled.

"I shall do my best, Jotson, to save the unhappy young man from despair."

My amazing friend lost no time in getting to work.

I was very busy with my medical practice at this time, and was unable to render Herlock Sholmes

Sholmes and Jotson peered round the glass-doors.

the aid he was sometimes kind enough to accept from me. In my interest in my amazing friend's work, I had, indeed, somewhat neglected my practice of late, and several of my patients showed signs of recovering.

By steady application to my work, however, I soon produced a change for the better. In this remark I refer to the practice, not to the patients.

Being so busy with these duties, however, I unfortunately missed the first details of one of Sholmes's most interesting cases.

Later, however, I went in search of my famous friend, and came upon him closely examining the ground with a reversed telescope, near to the building from which presumably the chord had escaped.

Not wishing to disturb Sholmes, who was obviously on the scent, I calmly waited until the great detective should notice my presence.

Instead, Sholmes looked aloft towards the wires strung between two telegraph-poles. There, entangled in the wires, was a long strand of some black material!

With a cry of triumph Sholmes leapt to his feet and swarmed up the nearer telegraph-pole. But even as his hand stretched out to clutch the substance entangled in the wires a groan escaped from his thin lips. In stead of the lost chord it was but the string of a kite!

It was a bitter blow to my famous friend, but he did not lose heart. For six weeks he was on the trail of the Lost Chord. Once a clue led him into Bloggins's Circus, which arrived in the neighbourhood, but, alas! he only discovered the missing link on view to an open-mouthed audience.

The disappointment played havoc with the nerves of my amazing friend.

Sholmes returned to Shaker Street, gave Mrs. Spudson a bad half-crown, and sent her out for a quart of the best cocaine.

"My dear Sholmes," I remarked, "doubtless the strain of recent work has affected even the superlative grey matter stored in your cranium. Softening of the brain should be dealt with in its incipient state. I will treat you myself, and——"

"Grrrr!" growled Sholmes.

Never had I known my remarkable friend to be in such a bad humour.

That, given time, Sholmes would have succeeded in his quest I have not the slightest shadow of doubt.

And Mr. Twidley Bitz, as a musician, should surely have known the value of time. His own happiest time, I believe, was two in a bar:

"The case is ended, Jotson," said Herlock Sholmes one evening. "I have received a check."

"Then let us cash it at once," I suggested. "Will it run to fish-and-chips?"

"I have not received that kind of cheque, Jotson. It will not run to fish-and-chips," said Sholmes. "Mr. Twidley Bitz lost his patience——"

"I can feel for him, as a medical man," I remarked. "I frequently lose mine."

"In a short time," continued Sholmes, "I have not the slightest doubt that I should have found the Lost Chord. But it is too late! Despairing of finding it, the unhappy Twidley Bitz retired to his room, locked the door with the key of C major——"

"Good heavens, Sholmes!"

"And hanged himself with the chord of the dominant seventh," said Herlock Sholmes sadly.

He wiped away a tear, and hid his emotion in the cocaine cask.

THE CASE OF THE CHARLADY

No. 66

With his usual politeness Herlock Sholmes removed his feet from the table as the ringing of our bell in Shaker Street announced a caller.

"A client," remarked Sholmes.

As a creaking on the stairs sounded, Sholmes rose to tidy the room for the reception of our visitor. having covered the cocaine cask with the hearthrug, he went to the window and gazed out on the rain-swept expanse of Shaker Street.

A moment later Mrs. Spudson entered with a buxom member of her own sex in tow.

"Mrs. Clutterbuck," announced our landlady.

"Pray be seated," murmured Sholmes without turning. Then as Mrs. Spudson withdrew and closed the door, he added: "It's a bad morning for shopping, isn't it madam?"

The lady sank into an armchair with a gasp.

"How——"

"But it is better than the hot weather for a lady of your proportions, eh, Mrs. Buttercluck?"

"Clutterbuck! Clutterbuck is my name," said the visitor, with a touch of annoyance in her voice. "But how on earth, Mr. Sholmes, did you know I had been shopping, and——"

"In need of a course of weight-reducing exercise?" Sholmes turned from the window with a smile. "It was simple. My supersensitive nasal organ detected the presence of a haddock in the string-bag you are carrying, madam. From the creaking of the springs of the armchair as you sat down, I deduced you were a woman of—er—comfortable proportions.

This display of my amazing friend's acute perspicacity had its due effect on our client. She fanned herself with the bag containing the haddock for some seconds without speaking.

"And now madam," said Sholmes settling himself in an armchair opposite the lady and placing the tips of his fingers together, "you have come here for the purpose of consulting me."

With an effort Mrs. Clutterbuck roused herself.

"You are right, as you invariably appear to be, Mr. Sholmes," she said. "I want your help in unravelling an extraordinary mystery that has baffled my husband and me for the past month."

"The past month!" echoed Sholmes. "What steps did you take prior to calling here towards solving it?"

"We called in the aid of the police."

Sholmes eyed Mrs. Clutterbuck severely.

"I said what steps did you take towards solving it?" he said. "However, first explain the nature of this baffling mystery."

"It concerns the family linen, Mr. Sholmes," said Mrs. Clutterbuck.

"Each Tuesday morning this is washed and hung in the back garden to dry by Mrs. Scrounger, a charlady who visits me daily. On the last four occasions when the washing has been brought in from the garden the pillow-cases, shirts, handkerchiefs, and other articles have been in threads. They looked as though some fiend armed with a sharp rake had been at work on them. With linen at its present price, Mr. Sholmes, my husband and I have been nearly distracted.

Mrs. Clutterbuck wrung her hands in her agitation.

"And neither you nor Mrs. Scrounger have any suspicions as to how or by whom this destruction has been caused?" said Herlock Sholmes.

"I haven't, but Mrs. Scrounger believes that some neighbour with a grudge against me destroys the clothes."

"How long has Mrs. Scrounger been in your employ?"

"A matter of six weeks, Mr. Sholmes," said Mrs. Clutterbuck.

"Surely it's very unusual for a charlady to stoop to the washing tub?" said Herlock Sholmes.

"It is," replied our client, "but Mrs. Scrounger is a paragon among charladies. Of course, she uses the best drawing-room for her washing operations, and neither my husband and myself are allowed in there during the process. Mr. Clutterbuck and I consider ourselves extremely lucky to have the use of her services."

"So I presume," said Sholmes, "that on the first two occasions that Mrs. Scrounger did the washing, the laundry was quite O.K."

"Quite—beyond the fact that the linen looked as though it had been dragged through a duck-pond. Anyway, it was not torn at all."

"Have you any enemies among the neighbours as far as you are aware?"

"Absolutely none."

"You have not a baby in the house?"

Mrs. Clutterbuck and I looked at Sholmes in amazement.

"A baby! What has——"

"Answer my question, Mrs. Clutterbuck," said Sholmes severely.

"There is no baby in the house."

"Have you a cheap American piano?'

"We have no piano of any sort."

"A gramophone, perhaps?"

"We have a phonograph," admitted Mrs. Clutterbuck. "But we never play it until after eleven o'clock at night—and then only the most popular jazz music. We have received several offers for that phonograph, Mr. Sholmes, the neighbours on both sides have expressed a desire to possess it."

"So I should imagine," remarked Sholmes drily. He rose to his feet. "By the way, where was Mrs. Scrounger employed before she came to you?"

"The Disham Steam Laundry at Disham."

"Ah!" said Sholmes. "Well, I must bid you good-morning, Mrs. Clutterbuck. I am busy at present on the case of the missing link, and my dear friend Jotson must attend to a few of his patients, who show alarming symptoms of recovery. Leave your card with me. You may expect a visit from me next Tuesday."

CHAPTER 2

Sholmes preserved a complete silence concerning the case of the charlady. He did not even seem to occupy his mind with the matter. My eager inquiries merely elicited from him the remark that the case was really too simple for his metal.

On Tuesday morning he was particularly cheerful.

"Come, Jotson," he said cheerily, "we have an engagement at Mrs. Clutterbuck's residence to-day."

Linking his stick back in my ear, he led me into the street.

Instead of going to the front door of the Clutterbuck's suburban house, Sholmes led the way over a garden wall at the back of the house. Steam was issuing from between the open glass-doors of the drawing-room.

"Prepare for the denouement, Jotson," said Sholmes cheerfully.

Together we made our way to the glass-door and peered in. There, before a large wash-tub, with her sleeves rolled up, was a large woman, without doubt, Mrs. Scrounger, the charlady. In her hand she held a heavy studded roller with which she was pounding a wet tablecloth laid out on a washboard full of brass nails. By her side was a curious collection of gear, including a curry-comb, a bottle of sulphuric acid for removing fruit stains, and a sledge hammer for the demolition of buttons on shirts.

"Now, my dear Jotson," said Sholmes. "We will communicate our discovery to Mrs. Clutterbuck, who, through retaining Mrs. Scrounger for ordinary charring purposes, will doubtless deem it advisable to relieve her of her laundry duties."

An hour later, in our rooms at Shaker Street, I sought an explanation from my amazing friend.

"My dear Sholmes," I exclaimed. "What gave you the clue that Mrs. Scrounger was the culprit who destroyed the linen?"

Sholmes rolled the cocaine cask towards him, and smiled serenely.

"The mystery was no mystery to me, Jotson," he said, "when I learned that Mrs. Scrounger had been employed in a steam laundry. By inquiring at the Disham Laundry, I discovered that some of the instruments used in their washing process had been missing for several weeks. I immediately deduced that Mrs. Scrounger had taken them home with her. For two weeks she did the Clutterbucks' washing without mechanical aid, but, missing the help these afforded, she afterwards brought some of the instruments she had previously used in the steam laundry to the home of the Clutterbucks. The result, my dear Jotson, was as our client described."

Sholmes drowned a sigh in the cocaine cask.

THE CASE OF THE CORN-PLASTER

No. 67

Herlock Sholmes was deep in thought in the arm-chair, when I came into our rooms at Shaker Street one evening.

I glanced at him inquiringly.

"A new case, Sholmes?" I asked.

"I am undecided whether to act in a certain case, Jotson," answered Sholmes. "I am going to ask your advice. Being in perfect health, my dear doctor, and not in need of medical attentions, I feel that I can ask your advice with perfect safety."

This was one of Sholmes' rather inscrutable remarks, which I did not quite follow.

"Come here, my dear fellow," added Sholmes.

I approached him.

Sholmes laid his hand on my shoulder, and I grinned the grin of affectionate friendship, taking this for one of his rare signs of attachment. He sat down again.

"Where is your handkerchief, my dear Jotson?" he asked.

I felt in my pocket.

"Upon my word! I must have left it inside my latest patient," I ejaculated in alarm. "I have been performing an operation, Sholmes. I remembered, too late, that I had sewn up some of my instruments in him by error; but I was not aware that my handkerchief was also missing. This is rather serious!"

"For the patient?"

"I was not, for the moment, thinking of the patient, Sholmes. Handkerchiefs are very expensive now. I cannot afford——" I broke off. "Excuse me, Sholmes; I had better return at once to my patient and re-open the matter!"

"Calm yourself, Jotson," drawled Sholmes. "Here is your nosebag."

To my great amazement, Herlock Sholmes held up my handkerchief.

"My dear Sholmes! How——"

"I am glad to see that I have not lost my old skill, Jotson," said Sholmes. "I simply picked your pocket, my dear fellow, to test my deftness. I find it is unimpaired."

"I never knew you exercised any other profession before you became a detective, Sholmes?"

"Tut, tut!" said Sholmes. "Now, Jotson, Inspector Pinkeye is very keen on my lending my aid in the case he has now in hand. I am dubious.

"Any advice I can give——"

"Exactly! No doubt you remember a war that occurred some time ago, Jotson, with Hunland. This case deals with one Smith, who lost a leg, as is alleged, in the war. The Pittance Department has to shell out the enormous sum of I forget how many halfpennies to Smith. That is to say, it will have to shell out the halfpennies, unless it can be demonstrated that the loss of the leg was not due to the war. As you know, these tiresome claimants for halfpennies have to appear before a Medical Board—so called because it is composed of bored medicos—and if it cannot be proven that the loss of the limb is merely a figment of the man's imagination, the hafpennies have to be handed over. Naturally, care must be exercised. Economy must be considered."

"But——"

"You see, Jotson, money is urgently required for more important objects. Four ex-Lord Chancellors are entitled to pensions of five thousand a year each, for instance. You would not see a retired lawyer run short of a few thousand pounds, merely for the sake of a man who has fought for his country!"

"But——"

Inspector Pinkeye held up a small, circular object.

"The case of Smith seems to be fairly genuine. The leg is undoubtedly gone. But it may turn out that this loss was not due to the war. Smith may have suffered from shin trouble or housemaid's knee, before the war, and if the pittance can be saved, Jotson, it helps the national economy, the man then simply comes on the rates. Now, with my vast abilities, there is no doubt that I could discover enough to deprive Smith of his allowance of halfpennies, but——" Sholmes paused. "I know it is absurd, Jotson, but I have a feeling that if a retired lawyer is worth five thousand a year a disabled soldier ought really to be allowed some coppers. It is a weakness, I know; but——"

The telephone-bell rang, and Sholmes took up the receiver. The voice of Inspector Pinkeye came through.

"No!" said Sholmes. "I have decided not to take the case, Pinkeye——"

"I think we shall manage, Sholmes," answered the inspector, with a trace of irony in his tones. "In fact we have managed!"

"Indeed!"

"In order to prove to you, Sholmes, that we can get on sometimes without your aid, I will call, and show you what I have discovered."

Sholmes rang off.

CHAPTER 2

Inspector Pinkeye was smiling with satisfaction when he came in. Evidently he was pleased to be able to demonstrate that the official police could get on—occasionally—without the aid of my amazing friend.

"Well!" said Sholmes, rather grimly.

"I have succeeded Sholmes." The inspector purred with pleasure. "Smith loses his twopence-halfpenny."

"The loss of the limb was not due to the war?" I inquired. I felt interested from the point of view of a medical man.

"Evidently not," answered Inspector Pinkeye. "I have searched the man's house, and made a discovery."

"Of what nature?" asked Sholmes.

Inspector Pinkeye held up a small, circular object.

"A corn-plaster?" I exclaimed.

"Exactly! And Smith could not deny that it was his property, and bought before the war," smiled the inspector. "He had corns—the plaster proves it—and the official theory of the Pittance Department therefore is, that the loss of the leg was doubtless due to this complaint, and not to the bomb which struck him on the knee." Pinkeye replaced the corn-plaster in his pocket. "Good-evening, Sholmes, we have done without you for once, my boy."

Sholmes crossed the room and shook hands with the inspector as he turned to go. Inspector Pinkeye left us, still smiling.

"So poor Smith loses his halfpennies, after all, Sholmes, just as if you had taken up the case," I remarked.

Sholmes smiled.

"Perhaps not, Jotson."

"But the inspector——"

"You observed that I shook hands with him before he left?"

"True, but what difference does that make?"

"Lots, my dear Jotson. Remember the incident of your handkerchief."

"Sholmes!"

Herlock Sholmes laughed, as he unclosed his hand, and revealed a circular object in his palm.

"Dear old Pinkeye will miss his precious discovery, when he arrives at Scotland Yard," yawned Sholmes. "I am sorry to deprive him of the only triumph in his career. But I really think Smith ought to go on drawing his halfpennies, even if retired lawyers have to be cut short a bottle or two of port."

And Herlock Sholmes, with a smile, tossed the corn-plaster into the fire.

THE CASE OF THE PODGERS M.P.

No. 68

There was a distinct odour of kippers about Herlock Sholmes as he came into our rooms at Shaker Street, late one afternoon. He laid a parcel on the table wrapped in several sheets of manuscript. I glanced at it inquiringly.

"Our frugal dinner, my dear Jotson," said Sholmes, with a smile, as he unwrapped the kippers. "It will not run to chips this evening. I almost wish, sometimes, that one of your wealthier patients would make a will in your favour, my dear fellow, and then allow you to operate upon him."

"My dear Sholmes——"

"The paper wrappings are of some interest," continued Sholmes. "As you see, they are written manuscript."

Mr. Podgers stuffed the tell-tale manuscript into the fire!

"Doubtless the work of some aspiring author, which has found its way to the waste-paper basket," I remarked.

"Not at all, Jotson. The handwriting is that of a well-known member of Parliament—a slashing opponent of the Government."

"The written copy of a speech delivered in the House?" I asked, with some interest, glancing at the sheet Sholmes had spread out on the table. It began, "The monumental stupidity and evasive disingenuousness exhibited by the honourable gentlemen opposite——

I had read no further, when there came a tap as the door.

I had just time to whisk the kippers into the coal-scuttle, and Sholmes to slip the somewhat kippery manuscripts into his pocket, when the door opened, and a visitor rushed in.

He was evidently in a great hurry, for he did not wait for Mrs. Spudson to announce him.

The coast was, however, clear. Save for a lingering aroma of kippers, there was nothing to betray our dinner reposing in the coal-scuttle.

"Herlock Sholmes!" gasped the portly gentleman who had rushed in, sinking into a chair.

"Calm yourself, Mr. Podgers," said Herlock Sholmes quietly.

"You know me, Sholmes—Podgers, M.P.!" gasped our visitor. "You must help me—save me—or I am lost. I have had a terrible misfortune, which bids fair to ruin my whole Parliamentary career!"

"Pray give me a few details, said Herlock Sholmes. "You may speak quite freely before my friend Dr. Jotson."

Mr. Podgers gasped for breath. He was in a state of great agitation, and it was some moments before he could proceed.

"Mr. Sholmes!" he spluttered, at last. "My speech is missing! The speech I wrote out this morning for delivery in the House this evening. It is a slashing attack on the Government. It commences 'The monumental stupidity and evasive disingenuousness exhibited by the honourable gentlemen opposite——' "

I started.

Sholmes made me a sign to be silent.

"You need not recite the speech, Mr. Podgers,' he remarked. "Life is short, and Parliamentary eloquence is long. The speech is missing?"

"Yes."

"But doubtless you can remember sufficient to deliver the speech in the House?"

"I can remember every word," groaned Mr. Podgers. "But you do not understand yet, the fearful seriousness of the situation. My speech was written out, a slashing attack on the Government, raking them off, fore and aft, so to speak, and leaving them simply without a leg to stand on. I had finished writing it, when I was called away to answer the telephone."

Mr. Podgers paused to mop his perspiring brown.

"I was called," he gasped, at last, "to receive the offer of an official job, at a handsome salary."

"Ah!" said Sholmes.

"I accept the offer, and returned to my library to write out a new speech, upholding the policy of the Government, and pouring scorn upon its opponents and critics. Before doing so, however, I intended to destroy the first speech—it was no longer of any use, owing to the change of circumstances. But it was gone."

"Gone!" repeated Sholmes.

"Gone!" exclaimed Mr. Podgers, with a gesture of despair. "During my absence from the library, a maid had tidied up the room, and the manuscript had been removed. Ignorant of its value, the foolish girl had taken it simply for waste-paper. And it unfortunately happened that a waste-paper merchant had called at the house a few minutes later, and all the waste-paper had been sold to him, including my manuscript. Imagine my feelings, Mr. Sholmes!"

I gazed sympathetically at the unfortunate Member.

"I sought out the waste-paper merchant immediately, but in the interval, before I could trace him, he had disposed of some of his stock to various tradesmen, for use as wrapping-paper for their goods—and my manuscript was among the quantity he had disposed of. It had disappeared—gone, vanished, he not know whither." Mr. Podgers gasped. "The manuscript may, of course be used in the ordinary way of trade, and vanish; but if it should by some awful chance come to light, Mr. Sholmes—if it should fall into the hands of some enterprising journalist, it would ruin me! Once published, or even shown, it would deprive me of the post of Under-Sub-Controller of the Tin Tacks Department. Mr. Sholmes, I have heard of your wonderful powers. You must find the missing speech—find it for me, so that I can see it destroyed with my own eyes; and name your own reward."

Herlock Sholmes was absent only a few minutes.

When he re-entered the room, he held in his hand several sheets of written manuscript, which had a greasy look, and an ancient and fish-like smell.

Mr. Podgers sprang to his feet. Never have I seen a man so amazed as Podgers, M.P. at that thrilling moment.

"Mr. Sholmes!" he stuttered.

"The missing speech, Mr. Podgers!" said Herlock Sholmes, negligently.

"You—you have found it?"

"As you see!"

Mr. Podgers grabbed the manuscript. He glared at it, and a grin of satisfaction overspread his beefy features. Without wasting a moment, he rushed to the grate, and stuffed the tell-tale sheets into the fire, driving them well home with the poker. Owing to the kippery stains the paper blazed up quickly, and was at once consumed.

The happy member wrung my friend's hand.

"Mr. Sholmes, you have saved me! Send in your bill—any sum you like!"

"Sholmes!" I exclaimed.

"Well, my dear Jotson?" said Herlock Sholmes.

"The manuscript it was the wrapping round the kippers," I ejaculated. "You have been singularly favoured by chance in this case, Sholmes."

"Chance, my dear Jotson, is not a word in my vocabulary," he said coldly. "My success is, of course, owing to my astonishing insight and marvellous powers. Could it be otherwise?"

"But——"

"You bore me, Jotson. Take the kippers down to Mrs. Spudson, and dry up."

THE CASE OF THE CUBIST

No. 69

Mr. Smoodge, the celebrated Cubist painter, was in a state of great agitation when he was shown into our rooms at Shaker Street.

He forgot even to remove his "Daily Mail" hat as he sank into the armchair my amazing friend pulled out for him.

"Mr. Sholmes," he exclaimed, "I have come to you, as a last resource. My picture—my portrait, painted by myself—must be traced——"

"Ah! It is missing?" asked Herlock Sholmes.

"Not at all."

"Stolen?"

"No, no!"

Sholmes raised his eyebrows.

"I must explain," said the celebrated Cubist. "The picture is at the present moment in my studio, but I cannot trace it——"

"Eh?"

"Because there are a dozen other pictures in the studio——"

"Ah!"

"And there are no means of distinguishing the portrait from the others——"

"Oh!"

"I will be more explicit," gasped the agitated painter. "Doubtless you have heard of my fame, Mr. Sholmes, and your friend, Dr. Jotson, cannot be ignorant of the fact that I have carried Cubism in painting to a length previously undreamt of outside the walls of Hanwell and Colney Hatch. The Picture-Puzzle Society gave me an order for my own portrait, painted by myself in my celebrated style—and I painted it," said Mr. Smoodge, almost tearfully, "and left it in my studio while I went down to Winkleton-on-Sea to inhale for a few days the balmy ocean breezes. When I returned——"

He clutched his hair.

"When you returned?" asked Sholmes.

"Some friend who had called into the studio—a scoundrel of a practical joking turn—had removed the tickets from all the pictures—the labels bearing their titles, Mr. Sholmes. You can guess the result? Without the attached label, there is no means of distinguishing my "Vesuvius in a State of Eruption" from my "Nelson on the Quarter-Deck of the Victory," or either of them from my "Nero Fiddling while Rome Burnt!" Among the rest is my portrait—painted by myself—and to-morrow it should be delivered to the Pciture-Puzzle Society. I have roamed up and down that studio, Mr. Sholmes, liked a caged tiger, seeking which cannot be found. The picture is there. I know it is there, because I know the total number of pictures that should be there. But——"

The artist paused and wiped the perspiration from his brow.

I gazed at him sympathetically.

Sholmes drummed thoughtfully on his knee. I could see by the glitter in his eyes that this was a problem that appealed strongly to his wonderful powers of elucidation.

To distinguish one Cubist picture from another might be a task beyond the powers of an ordinary man. But Herlock Sholmes was no ordinary man. Bristling with difficulties as the matter undoubtedly was, I had every faith in my amazing friend.

"You are my last resource, Mr. Sholmes," said the painter. "The portrait must be traced, and undoubtedly it is there. But to pick it out from the rest——" He made a gesture of despair.

"My dear fellow, calm yourself," said Sholmes. "Let us proceed to your studio, and rely upon me. Come my dear Jotson."

"But my patients, Sholmes——" I murmured.

"Let them live, my dear Jotson."

I followed Herlock Sholmes and the celebrated Cubist from the room, and a quarter of an hour later we were in Mr. Smoodge's famous studio.

The dog began to lick the picture with great affection.

CHAPTER 2

Herlock Sholmes was quite at home in the studios of the artistic fraternity. He visited them often. On such occasions he would leave his ready cash in my charge, and so was able to mingle with any artistic circle with impunity.

He glanced round Mr. Smoodge's studio with his keen, penetrating eye. Penetrating as his eye was, however, I doubt if even Herlock Sholmes could have guessed what Mr. Smoodge's picture represented, in the absence of the necessary labels.

There were a dozen pictures, on easels or against the walls, all of them painted in Mr. Smoodge's celebrated style, which was certainly well ahead of that of any other Cubist. How to pick out the one that was Mr. Smoodge's own portrait, was the task that now confronted my amazing friend. He did not seem dismayed by the magnitude of the problem.

"You have a dog, Mr. Smoodge?" he asked. "I think I remember seeing him when I visited you once."

"Yes, my little Fido. But what——"

"Bring him here."

"But why——"

"The sagacity of the dog," said Sholmes, in his rather didactic way, "is well known. Fido is accustomed to feed from your hand, Mr. Smoodge——"

"Yes, but——"

"He will pick out your portrait," said Sholmes.

"I fear not. Even a dog's sagacity——"

"Mr. Smoodge, you have called me in for advice and assistance. Kindly fetch Fido here."

"Oh, very well!" said Mr. Smoodge.

He quitted the study, with an impatient expression on his face. It was clear that he placed no faith whatever in the method of my amazing friend for tracing the Cubist portrait.

As soon as the door had closed upon him, Sholmes stooped over one of the pictures that stood leaning against the wall. He took something from his pocket and rubbed the picture, and then returned the article—whatever it was—to his pocket again.

"Sholmes!" I exclaimed.

He placed his finger on his lips.

A minute later and Mr. Smoodge entered, leading Fido.

"There is the dog, Mr. Sholmes," he said gruffly. "I may say that I have no faith whatever in the method you have selected——"

"Patience!" said Sholmes. "Let the dog loose."

Fido was released.

"Good dog, Fido!" said Sholmes encouragingly. "Find your master, Fido!"

Fido sniffed round.

Without a pause he ran towards the picture over which I had seen Herlock Sholmes stoop.

He began to lick the picture with great affection.

"Upon my word!" ejaculated Mr. Smoodge, in great astonishment.

Herlock Sholmes smiled.

"The affection and instinct of a dog may always be trusted, my dear Smoodge," he said. "Good-afternoon! Come, Jotson!"

"Thanks, thanks!" exclaimed Mr. Smoodge. "You have extricated me from my fearful difficulty. It is undoubtedly the portrait. What amazing sagacity—what really wonderful sagacity——"

Herlock Sholmes drew me from the studio, leaving Mr. Smoodge in ecstacies over the discovered portrait. We departed so quickly that the artist had no time to borrow any money of us.

CHAPTER 3

"A simple case, Jotson!" Herlock Sholmes drawled, as he walked back to Shaker Street.

"Wonderful!" I ejaculated.

"Wonderful!" agreed Sholmes. "And it would have been still more wonderful, my dear Jotson, if I had not rubbed a piece of sausage upon the picture!"

"Sholmes!"

"I wonder," added my amazing friend reflectively, "which of those works of art was really the portrait? There are some problems, Jotson, beyond human power to solve; but it is always a pleasure to give satisfaction to a client!"

THE CASE OF THE DENTIST

No. 70

"Extraordinary!"

Herlock Sholmes gave his breakfast egg a playful tap with the poker and looked across the table. "What is extraordinary, my dear Jotson?"

"That the Fellows of the Royal Zoological Society have not yet sought your assistance, Sholmes." I indicated a paragraph in the "Daily Outrage" which I had been perusing. "Binko, the blue-faced baboon, one of the most venerable residents of the Zoo has gone."

"Escaped?"

"Yes. It appeared that while Binko was toying with his usual breakfast kipper yesterday morning, the keeper inadvertently left the cage door unlocked. In consequence, the aged ape sauntered forth into the cold, hard world—or, that portion of it known as Regent's Park—and has not been heard of since. I repeat, Sholmes, that it is extraordinary that the responsible authorities have not yet sought the assistance of your trained intellect and acute perspicacity."

Sholmes pushed the remains of his breakfast egg aside and stirred a liberal teaspoon of cocaine into his coffee.

"H'm," he remarked. "I suppose they have taken the usual inexplicable course of reporting the loss to the police."

"My dear Sholmes," I exclaimed, "but surely men of intellect as we may presume the Fellows of the Royal Zoological Society to be, would do nothing quite so foolish?"

"There is no limit to human folly, my dear Jotson."

"True, Sholmes. But in this case, even if the authorities are unconcerned themselves about the loss of the aged baboon, they should consider the feelings of the public. Binko was more than a mere monkey—he was an ancient institution as firmly established as some of the Fellows themselves."

I sighed reminiscently.

"No longer will his shiny bald head, snub nose, toothless gums, and blue chin decorate the iron bars in the precincts of the Monkey-house. No longer will small boys prepare apples full of mustard for his consumption. No longer will old ladies have the simple pleasure of seeing the trimmings of their hats removed by the dexterous fingers of the grand old blue baboon. The cage is empty. And the authorities are blind to the fact that you alone, my dear Sholmes, can fill it!"

"Eh?"

To my astonishment, Herlock Sholmes took a firm grip on the poker, and advanced on me threateningly.

"My dear Sholmes, I——"

"Were you suggesting that the substitution of my person for that of the blue-faced baboon would be calculated to deceive the public?"

"No—no, not at all," I hastened to assure my extraordinary friend as I retreated round the table. "As you are clean-shaven, and the baboon in question has a fine crop of whiskers, there can be no——"

Herlock Sholmes gave a howl of rage.

Why my amazing friend should be so annoyed, I had no idea.

That I should have suffered a severe contusion of the cranium is certain, had not a knock at the door sounded.

Sholmes hastily slipped the poker up the sleeve of his dressing-gown as Mrs. Spudson ushered in a short, sallow man wearing spectacles.

"Mr. Diggan-Wrench," announced our landlady.

"Mr. Sholmes——" began our visitor excitedly.

"Be seated, my dear sir, and help yourself to the cocaine," said Sholmes soothingly.

The visitor dropped into a seat. Sholmes subsided into an armchair opposite and placed the tips of his bony fingers together.

"Now, Mr. Wrench," he murmured. "You may speak quite freely before my—er—friend, Dr. Jotson. You are a dental surgeon are you not?"

The visitor gave a violent start.

Sholmes smiled easily.

"The excessive development of the ligaments in your right wrist, Mr. Wrench," he explained, "and your unconscious habit of moving your hand as though invisible corks from imaginary bottles, proclaim the fact that you are either a dentist or a wine steward. The fierce, peculiar joy which flits ever and anon across your face, however, led me to deduce that the former was your profession."

"You are right, Mr. Sholmes," said Mr. Diggan-Wrench, "and I am not unknown in my profession, being a member of the Royal Institute of Qualified Molar-Extractors, and Secretary of the Dentists and Butchers Union. My success I attribute to the fact that I am an artist, I take positive pleasure in my work. Never do I manhandle a molar or undermine a wisdom tooth, but a thrill of joy and satisfaction passes through me.

"But, Mr, Sholmes," continued our client, "to-day I have suffered a loss which has upset me more than I can say. Among my instruments, I possessed a pair of forceps which I had retained ever since my student days. At the end of the them, I have had the pleasure of seeing hundreds of my patients writhe. This pair of forceps has been stolen!"

The voice of Diggan-Wrench trembled with emotion.

"When and where did you last use this pair of pincers?" asked Sholmes.

"The forceps?" said the Dentist. "This morning in my surgery in Soho, I left them on a small table while I was attending to the removal of my last patient on an ambulance. There were carpenters working outside the building, and I strongly suspect one of those unscrupulous fellows took the forceps with the notion that they would come in handy for the extraction of tin-tacks."

"The case interests me, Mr. Wrench," said Herlock Sholmes rising. "For the pleasure of elucidating the mystery, I will assist you. Come!"

In less than fifteen minutes we reached the dentist's surgery in Soho. It was situated on the first floor, and, entering the building, Sholmes became galvanised into intense activity. With a lens borrowed from one of my microscopes, he carefully examined the floor, the furniture, and even the window-sill.

Suddenly he straightened himself.

"My work here is finished. Mr. Wrench," he said. "You shall hear from me later."

In the street Sholmes hailed a newsboy and purchased an evening edition. Knowing that he had scientifically deduced that Flying Duck would win the three-thirty, the circumstances did not strike me as peculiar.

"Come, my dear Jotson," he said, suddenly casting aside the newspaper, "let us spend the afternoon visiting our relations in the Zoo."

"But, my dear Sholmes! The case of the dentist——"

Hooking his stick round my neck, my amazing friend assisted me on to a passing 'bus.

Arriving at the Zoological Gardens, Sholmes led the way straight to the Monkey-house. He halted before the cage of the truant Binko.

"Look, Jotty!" he cried.

I gave a gasp of amazement. There, sitting in the cage was the toothless old blue baboon cracking nuts with a shimmering pair of dentist's forceps.

Sholmes threw a monkey-nut at the ape, and, in response, Binko threw the forceps at Sholmes.

"And now, my dear Jotson," said my amazing friend, as he fondled his damaged eye, "we will return Mr. Wrench his priceless pincers."

Not until we had returned to Shaker Street after a visit to the delighted Mr. Diggan-Wrench, did Sholmes satisfy my curiosity.

"The case was simple, my dear Jotson," he said. "On the window-sill of the dentist's surgery, I discovered the footprints of a creature I rightly deduced to be a monkey. In the newspaper this afternoon I read that Binko had been recaptured from an Italian organ-grinder in Soho. As Binko was toothless, what was more natural than that he should have climbed into the dentist's surgery and stolen a pair of pincers which which to crack the nuts his ancient jaws could not effectively deal with? Simple, as you see. Pass the cocaine, Jotson."

THE MYSTERY OF THE MINCE-PIE

No. 71

It was Christmas-eve. There was an air of seasonable good cheer about our apartments in Shaker Street, Herlock Sholmes, wrapped in a quiet comfortable dressing-gown of mauve, pink and green checks, was reclining in his armchair. Between his thin lips was a large meershaum pipe, at his elbow stood a foaming tankard of cocaine, and under his long, handsome blue chin rested his unique Vadistrarius violin. The violin under the lean, capable hands of my famous friend, was emitting the strains of that well-known Christmas carol, "Rest you merry gentlemen." Unfortunately the lodgers in the flat above refused to be rested. They stamped on the floor with their hob-nailed boots, they dropped enamel plates and started an atrocious gramophone in opposition. But then they weren't gentlemen.

Imbued with the spirit of goodwill on earth, inseparable from the season, I laid aside the Treatise on Rat Poison I had been studying and perused with kindly interest the obituary notices of some of my late patients.

In the midst of our Christmas-eve festivities, a sharp knock sounded on the door. Suspecting it was Mrs. Spudson in search of her annual Christmas-box, I reached for the vase on the mantelpiece where we kept our savings and emptied the sevenpence-ha'penny it contained into the palm of my hand. Then our landlady entered followed by a tall young man wearing a heavy fur overcoat and a look of intense worry on his face.

"Mr. Turnham Greene," announced our landlady.

I placed Mrs. Spudson's Christmas-box in my pocket as Sholmes raised his lean form to greet his client.

"Just roll the cask of cocaine under the table, Jotty, and draw a chair to the fire for Mr. Greene."

As Mrs. Spudson withdrew, the client dropped into the chair and interlaced his fingers nervously.

"Mr. Sholmes, I need your help," he said. "Six months ago I got married and——"

Herlock Sholmes nodded sympathetically.

"The more dire a man's need the more ready I am to afford my aid," he said. "You can speak quite freely before my friend, Dr. Jotson."

"Thank you, Mr. Sholmes," returned Mr. Greene. "But it is on account of the mysterious disappearance of a diamond ring belonging to my wife that I want your capable assistance. You see, Mrs. Turnham Greene and I intend having some guests to dinner to-morrow night, and to add a spice of fun to the proceedings. I bought an imitation diamond ring to place in one of the mince-pies. This afternoon while Mrs. Slackbake, our cook, was chopping the mince, my wife assisted by making the pastry. It was her first attempt, Mr. Sholmes, and she did it especially to please me."

Mr. Turnham Greene shuddered slightly.

He served the guests with pudding about the size of a piece of loaf sugar, the remainder he put on his own plate.

"Well," he went on, "after a time my wife went out to purchase a few pounds of monkey-nuts and other Christmas luxuries, and Mrs. Slackbake cooked the mince-pies. Then the cook, who is employed by us by the day, went home. Early this evening, my wife remembered that she had taken off her diamond ring prior to making the pastry and had left it on the kitchen table. The imitation ring was there—the real one was gone!

"Thinking Mrs. Slackbake had dropped the diamond ring into one of the mince-pies by mistake, we obtained a hammer and chisel and opened them; but could find no ring. I rushed off to the home of our cook to question her, but I suppose I was tactless in my anxiety. Mrs. Slackbake thought I was accusing her of stealing the wife's ring, and she seemed to get a trifle annoyed. Anyway, she threw a scraper and a flower-pot at me and threatened to spoil my face completely if I showed in her neighbourhood again. Really, I do now suspect that woman of having stolen my wife's ring, and I want you to investigate the matter. Only find the ring, and I will write you a cheque for any amount you care to name up to fifteen bob."

"Such generosity always produces my best efforts on behalf of a client," murmured Herlock Sholmes. "To-morrow your wife shall be in possession of her ring again, Mr. Greene. Meanwhile, leave your address and that of your cook's."

When Mr. Turnham Greene had departed, Sholmes entered the capacious dressing-room, where hung his numerous disguises. throwing aside costumes designed for an Admiral of the Fleet, Boy Scout, gas-fitter, jockey and hall porter, he produced a battered old uniform which had been presented to him by P-c. 49, when that notorious officer had left the Force and gone into the comic song profession.

"It's the policeman's blue that attracts the cooks," chirped Sholmes as he emerged dressed as a Bobby. "Stay here, my faithful Jotty."

He made a hasty exit. From his remark I judged he was about to pay a visit to Mrs. Slackbake.

A couple of hours later he returned, but to my numerous questions he only returned the cryptic remark, "Hic!" Not until the following evening did he again refer to anything in connection with the Turnham Greenes.

"Come Jotty," he said. "Get on your best bib and tucker; to-night we dine with the Turnham Greenes. I wangled an invitation this morning to their Christmas dinner."

Having ordered Mrs. Spudson to hold over the fish and chips until Boxing Day, we set out in high spirits. Our reception, I thought, was a trifle chilly, due undoubtedly to the fact that my friend had not the diamond ring to produce. However, Sholmes soon made himself at home. He insisted on sawing the turkey, cracking the nuts for everybody, pouring the ginger-beer and helping the Christmas pudding.

With some dismay I noticed that my amazing friend was suffering from a severe lack of proportion. He served the Turnham Greenes, their guests and me, with a cube of pudding about the size of a piece of loaf sugar. The remainder he placed on his own plate. Even though the dinner was a change from the kippers and pancakes of Mrs. Spudson, Sholmes might have controlled his voracity. Once he nearly choked with a large mouthful of pudding and had to bury his head in the large red pocket-handkerchief.

After dinner a distinct chilliness was to be noticed in the attitude of our hosts and their guests towards us. I longed for the festive activity of the operating theatre, but Sholmes was a host in himself. He helped to build up the fire, but even when he playfully dug Mr. Greene in the ribs, that young man never even smiled. Instead he referred brusquely to Sholmes' promise of the previous day.

"Oh, the diamond ring?" said Sholmes. "Of course—how forgetful of me! Here it is!"

He placed his fingers in his waistcoat pocket and withdrew the object in question.

After that the atmosphere cleared. Everybody shook Holmes by the hand and Mr. Greene presented him with some cigars and nuts. Then we played "Begger-your-neighbour," and afterwards Sholmes produced the violin he had brought and rendered that pathetic little ballad "Everybody calls me Tarzan."

Not until Mrs. Spudson had helped us up to our apartments and we were trying to hold the mantelpiece still, would Sholmes reveal the manner in which he had discovered the diamond ring.

"It was simple, Jotty," he said. "In my policeman's disguise I paid attentions to Greene's cook. Misshis Slackbake, and in return the good woman informed me that instead of putting a ring into a mince-pie, she had placed it in the Christmas pudding as her dear old man used to do. I took good care to serve the pudding to-night myself, so there was a hundred to one chance I should find the trinket. When my molars encountered the ring, I placed it in my pocket to produce at a more dramatic moment. As you know, Jotty, I do not give my method away to clients—save of course in exceptional cases at the end of the story.

"Goo'-night, my dear fellow—Merry New Year—Hic!"

1921

PINKEYE'S NEW YEAR RESOLUTION

No. 72

The date was December 31st. In a few short minutes the Old Year would go out and the New Year come in.

Herlock Sholmes, resplendent in a dressing-gown of pale green with purple dots, reclined deep in his armchair, smoking like a furnace. Opposite him, his bulbous nose shining like a railway danger signal in the glare of the fire, sat Inspector Pinkeye, of Scotland Yard. I squatted on the edge of the cocaine cask between the two.

After the clock had struck thirteen—ever since Sholmes gave it a wash and brush up it had worked overtime—the conversation turned on New Year's resolutions.

"My resolve for nineteen twenty-one, Mr. Sholmes," said Inspector Pinkeye, "is that never again will I seek your assistance in any of my cases. In future I shall only take in hand those cases I can solve myself."

"Splendid, Pinkeye!" ejaculated Sholmes. "You always looked forward to the time, when you would be a man of leisure."

"I don't know about that, Mr. Sholmes," said the inspector. "I've a case in hand at present. A Burmese forger, who came to this country as a ship's cook, is at large in London. His name is Tuo Yaw, and he is a dangerous character. But I have an excellent description of the fellow, and to-morrow he will be safely under lock and key.

"Information at my disposal leads me to the conclusion that he has rented an office in the wing of a large building, owned by the Limehouse Trust, Limited. Moreover, he has had the temerity to put his real name on the door."

"A foreign forger, who is wanted by the police, has put his real name on door of his office!" I ejaculated. "The man must be mad!"

"On the contrary," said Inspector Pinkeye, "the fellow is extremely cute! That is the last thing a criminal would be expected to do, and that is just why the astute Tuo Yaw has done it. The ruse would have deceived a Scotland Yard detective of less experience, but fortunately the case was placed in my hands, and I saw through the trick. To-morrow morning at ten o'clock a cordon of police will surround the place, and I shall lay my hands on my Burmese quarry."

"Ten o'clock," murmured Sholmes. "I should like to see the arrest."

"Delighted, Mr. Sholmes!" said Inspector Pinkeye affably. "And by all means bring along Dr. Jotson as well."

Promptly at ten o'clock on the following morning, Herlock Sholmes led me by the ear to Limehouse, the Asiatic quarter of London. Round about the building owned by the Limehouse Trust, by the riverside, were grouped a few burly men in plain clothes, Pinkeye's subordinates. A number of lascars and other seafaring Asiatics slouched along the streets from the docks.

We turned into a narrow street that skirted, the side of the building, and Inspector Pinkeye stepped from behind a lamp-post and greeted us.

"Ha, good-morning, gentlemen!" he said briskly. "My man hasn't arrived at his office yet, so I intend entering the building and waiting for him. That's the place where the Burmese hangs out."

He pointed to a narrow door with a glass top. Across the glass in bold black letters was painted the name of the inspector's quarry—TUO YAW.

A broad smile wreathed the face of Sholmes as Inspector Pinkeye led us through the door into the building. In the semi-darkness of the passage he halted and jangled the handcuffs in his pocket.

"We will wait here," he said, "and you can watch me nobble our Burmese friend, Tou Yaw, as he comes in."

"Tou Yaw!" chuckled Sholmes. "Look my dear Pinkeye!"

He pointed to the glass door through which we had entered the building. My eyes started from my head; Inspector Pinkeye appeared smitten with ague. The black letters on the door read: WAY OUT!

"Seen from the outside the words are reversed, and read 'Tuo Yaw,'" murmured Sholmes, "that is the name of your Burmese forger."

Inspector Pinkeye stared blankly from the door to the face of my amazing friend. Then his New Year's resolution went West!

"Mr. Sholmes," he cried, "I shall be the laughing stock of the Force when this is known! What shall I do? Give me your advice."

"My dear Pinkeye," said Herlock Sholmes, "my powers, as ever, are at your service. Feeling confident that you would require my aid, I came prepared to give it."

He drew from his capacious overcoat pocket a long, grey-coloured roll of what at first glance appeared to my short sight to be asbestos.

"This is what Kipling would call a 'whacking big cheroot,'" he explained. "It is in fact, a real Burma cheroot. It was presented to me by an Anglo-Indian gentleman, for whom I had secured a term of imprisonment."

Sholmes lighted the cheroot and puffed out a dense cloud of acrid, blue smoke. Gasping and

"Tuo Yaw, I arrest you on the charge of forgery!" said Inspector Pinkeye.

spluttering, Inspector Pinkeye and I groped our way to the street. Shomes, followed, puffing away merrily.

"Come with me, my dear Jotson," he said. "You, inspector, remain here, and have your handcuffs ready!"

Leaving the inspector staring open-mouthed I walked up the street with my amazing friend, taking care to keep to leeward of his forty horse-power Burma cheroot. Curious though I was as to my companion's intention, I asked no questions. Well did I know that Sholmes would not explain until the end of the story.

Sholmes strode on, through one narrow street after another. He seemed to be making an aimless tour of Limehouse. The curling whisps of blue cheroot smoke he left in his wake caused the pedestrians to cough and stagger. White men, Chinese, Hindus, and Japs, threw nervous glances in his direction. Then as we turned back towards the building by which Pinkeye and his men were waiting, I noticed we were being shadowed by a short, stocky man of dusky complexion.

The coloured man pranced behind us, eagerly sniffing the fumes of Sholmes' cheroot. A beatific expression wrapped his features and his eyes rolled in his keen enjoyment.

Suddenly Inspector Pinkeye hove into view. He made a dash for the little brown man. There was the snap of steel on the man's wrists.

"Tou Yaw, I arrest you on the charge of forgery, according to advice received from Burma!" Inspector Pinkeye held out his hand to my companion. "Thank you, Mr. Sholmes!" he said humbly.

Ensconced in our rooms in Shaker Street, half an hour later, Sholmes made light to me of the extraordinary foresight and sagacity which had led to the capture of the notorious Burmese criminal.

"The Burma cheroot was a real inspiration, my dear Jotson," he said. "I had one in my smoking cabinet of that extraordinary type smoked by the natives. Limehouse is full of certain kinds of Asiatics, but a real Burmese is a rarity. The cheroot, therefore, was the bait. Its fumes penetrated to every nook and corner of Limehouse. They nearly asphyxiated some of the inhabitants, and I must confess that even my iron constitution now feels the need of something milder to offset its effects—a pipe of black shag, for instance. But to one man the fumes of that cheroot were like zephyrs from his native land. Tou Yaw, the Burmese forger, came beneath the influence. To him the cheroot exuded a homelike atmosphere. He followed us—into the arms of the worthy Pinkeye."

"You astound me, my dear Sholmes!" I exclaimed. "The whole police force should take correspondence lessons in your methods. Inspector Pinkeye did well to ask your aid when his professional reputation was at stake. His New Year's resolution didn't last long."

Sholmes took a pinch of cocaine and smiled.

"Pinkeye's resolution lasted as long as most people's," he murmured.

THE CASE OF THE PINK RAT

No. 73

The magnificent yellow motor-car swung down Shaker Street and drew up smartly before the house in which Mr. Herlock Sholmes and I had our apartments. Three minutes later Mrs. Spudson ushered in a burly gentleman in a blue reefer suit.

"Mr. Sholmes! Thank 'eavins you're hin!"

At the exclamation Herlock Sholmes raised his lean form from the depths of his armchair.

"Be seated my dear sir," he said; "my services are at your disposal. If you are a Labour M.P. in difficulties——"

"I ham not, Mr. Sholmes," said the man, dropping heavily into a chair. "I'm Bill Slack o' Poplar, well-known in local dockin' circles. I've come to ask your 'elp. I've seen 'em again!"

His voice rose to a wild howl of fear.

"See what again?" asked Sholmes.

"The pink rats!"

Herlock Sholmes and I regarded the burly visitor severely.

"Pardon me, sir," I said, "I am the qualified medical practitioner of this establishment. You wish to consult me I presume?"

Mr. Slack brought down a fist the size of a ham on to the padded arm of his chair with a thump which sent the dust flying.

"No!" he roared. "I'll 'ave you know I'm a member of the Pussyfoot Anti-Wet League! That's jest it; no sooner do I tawk about them there pink rats than people think my favourite exercise is liftin' glasses."

"Perhaps, Mr. Slack," murmured Herlock Sholmes soothingly, "you will favour me with more details about yourself and the matter which is troubling you."

Herlock Sholmes lifted the rat by its tail for the purpose of examining it.

Mr. Slack wiped the beads of perspiration from his brow with an enormous red handkerchief, and made a great effort to compose himself.

"Well, it's like this 'ere, Mr. Sholmes," he said. "some months ago I was approached by a deppytation o' riverside employers and foremen wot offered me a job as a dockhand, unloadin' ships and sich like. After smokin' a doped cigar given me by one o' the bosses. I agreed to work from eleven to four for ten pun a week, providin', o' course, that a motor-car was sent to take me from my 'ome to the docks an' back."

Mr. Slack moistened his lips. Mention of work out of hours was naturally distressing to the cultivated sense of this hardy old Briton.

"Anyway, I started in at the Poplar docks," he continued. "and as me and my mates didn't strike no more'n six times durin' the year, we made plenty of money. Then one night, a fortnight ago, I saw the pink rats, and, like a hidiot, told my mates about 'em. Since then I've been the laughin' stock o' the whole waterside."

"And you hadn't touched a drop, Mr. Slack?" murmured Herlock Sholmes sympathetically.

"Not a drop!" said Bill Slack vehemently. "Yet no less than three times I've seen them there pink rats on the wharf. Each time they appeared in the same place in Number Four Shed, South India Dock, while I was alone, restin' alongside o' my work. My reppytation is bein' ruined, Mr. Sholmes. Even the Pussyfoot Anti-Wet Society has asked me to resign. Only by trackin' down an' capturin' one o' them there pink rats in the flesh will save the family name o' Slack from the slur o' bein' coupled with nasty remarks about D.T.'s and 'bats in the belfry.'"

"But surely, Mr. Slack," I suggested, "you would do better to consult a ratcatcher, not the greatest living detective?"

"Ratcatcher!" snorted our client. "At the docks they've tried ratcatchers, traps, cats, dogs, and poison; but dock rats are too cute for sichlike things. Besides, it ain't ordinary brown rats I want caught; it's one o' them there speshul pink 'uns."

"The case is rather out of my special line." said Herlock Sholmes, rising. "Nevertheless, I will undertake to elucidate the mystery, not merely on account of the fact that you can afford an exceptionally heavy fee, but because the novelty of the case interests me. Come, let us proceed in your car to the South India Docks."

Although it was nearly four o'clock when we reached popular Poplar, the docks represented their usual animated appearance. A large steamship was unloading malt opposite Shed No. 4, and a number of dockhands were busy holding up the bulky sacks and discussing the chances of Woolwich Arsenal beating the Wapping Wanderers on the morrow.

Bill Slack led the way into a far corner of the shed.

"That's the spot I saw them there pink rats," he said, "near the pile o' malt sacks."

Herlock Sholmes wasted no time. He drew us into hiding behind the sacks. What his plan was I could only surmise, but I guessed it would entail a long vigil.

But nothing of the kind. The famous detective made a noise like a piece of cheese, and immediately a large rat darted into the open. I gave a gasp of amazement, and Mr. Slack clutched his throat, for that rodent was as pink as the pills for pale people!

The next moment Sholmes brought his walking-stick down with a thud, and the four-footed intruder gave a loud squeal and rolled over.

As my amazing friend lifted the rat by its tail for the purpose of examining it, Mr. Slack darted forward and gripped his hand. There were tears of relief in the fellow's eyes. The vindication of the name of Slack had been accomplished!

"Listen!" said Sholmes. "Take this creature and show it to your pals of the Pussyfoot Anti-Wet Society, and then send it along by parcel post to me. But don't keep it too long. There is more in this than meets the eye."

Leaving the overjoyed Mr. Slack, we made our way by 'bus back to Shaker Street.

"My dear Sholmes," I exclaimed, "you should report this discovery to the Royal Zoological Society! A pink rat——"

"To the President of the Society for the Investigation of the Migratory Habits of Rodents, you mean, Jotty," said Sholmes. "Were you as keen a student of the daily newspapers as I am myself, you would know that a number of rats were captured by Professor N. O. C. Parker of Woolwich, who painted them pink and set them free again. The idea was to learn how far, and to which parts of the country, the rodents migrated. Purple, yellow, and blue rats have also been loosened in various other places, to the consternation of local topers. I have no doubt the President of the S.I.M.H.R. will be duly grateful to us for informing him that some of his pink rats have found their way across the river from Woolwich to Poplar. But we must send also the defunct specimen as proof.

THE CASE OF THE LAME SNAIL

No. 74

Herlock Sholmes opened his morning mail with his fish-knife while consuming his breakfast kipper. From one envelope he drew forth a small green slip of paper, and his face split into one of his rare dazzling smiles.

"Here's luck, my dear Jotson!" he said genially. "The other day I entered a shilling football sweepstake, organised in aid of the Home for Mentally Defective Detectives. All the teams that play in the Lambeth League, including such well-known exponents of the game as the Vine Street Vampires, the Kilburn Kickanruns, and the Blind School Reserves, were put in a hat and drawn for——"

"And the team you drew, my dear Sholmes was——"

"The Wobbly Wanderers!" exclaimed Sholmes excitedly. "One of the best in the league! If they don't score the most goals to-day, I'll stop taking cocaine with my coffee!"

He rose from the table and placed his hand affectionately on my shoulder.

"This afternoon we will make merry, my dear Jotson," he said. "You shall accompany me to see the Wanderers whack the Vampires."

"But, my dear Sholmes," I protested, "what about the patients?"

"You must risk a few of 'em getting better." said Sholmes. "A day in the fresh air on the Gaswork Marshes will do you all the good in the world."

A little after two o'clock that afternoon my amazing friend hooked his stick in my ear and led me to the football ground.

Sholmes, who had insisted on coming in his favourite mauve-and-green check dressing-gown, seemed to be recognised instantly by everyone.

Promptly to time the rival teams made their appearance on the ground, the Wobbly Wanderers in green jerseys with pink trimmings, and the Vampires in strawberry shirts with lemon stripes.

No referee was available, for refereeing for the Vampires and Wanderers was considered unlucky. At the last meeting of these old rivals, the referee had lost things—first his temper, then his whistle (which he swallowed), and, lastly, an ear and six teeth.

The game started briskly by the Vampire's centre-forward kicking the ball into the eye of the opposing inside-right. It was soon evident that it was going to be a big goal-scoring game, for the Wanderers netted three times in the first half, while their opponents found the net twice and the goalkeeper's eye once. The smile on the face of Herlock Sholmes revealed his inward satisfaction at the progress of events.

After half-time, the teams returned to the attack with redoubled violence, and two or three players from both sides were carried to the local hospital by obliging spectators.

With but five minutes to go, the score stood seven goals to six in favour of the Wobbly Wanderers. That any other team in the Lambeth League would top the score of seven goals in the matches being played elsewhere that afternoon was extremely improbable. Like Sholmes, I felt the sweepstake was as good as won. The vision of a bumper fish-and-chips supper was before my eyes, when a startling thing happened. In attempting to clear from a rush by the Vampire forwards, the left full-back of the Wanderers miskicked. The ball went spinning from his toe and over his head. The Wanderers goalie, who had gone to borrow a pipe of tobacco from one of the spectators, arrived back between the posts a second too late. Twisting and squirming like a thing possessed, the ball dropped on the ground in the goal-mouth, bounced up against the crossbar, and rebounded into play.

"Goal!"

The cry of triumph which went up from the Vampires was drowned in wild shouts of protest. Then a violent argument started, in which the teams and near-by onlookers joined in a pandemonium of sound. The Vampires claimed the ball had dropped into the goal and spun back against the crossbar; the Wanderers maintained it had fallen outside the goal-line. For some minutes the argument raged, with no solution of the incident in sight. The crowd in our immediate vicinity, which, like ourselves, had not been in a position to judge the flight of the ball, began to wax impatient. Then an ex-policeman, who was standing on my toes, was struck with a brilliant idea.

"Settle it by harbitration," he shouted. "Let Mr. Herlock Sholmes decide!"

This way of settling the dispute was taken up with great enthusiasm by others round us.

"We—want—Mister—Sholmes!"

Willing boots assisted my friend and me on to the football pitch. As Herlock Sholmes picked himself up and strode towards the excited group of players, a sudden hush fell over the scene. The rival captains, who had been trying to make themselves heard for over ten minutes, rapidly exchanged views. Then one of them stepped forward and led the famous detective to the goal-mouth. Herlock Sholmes was the cynosure of all eyes as he picked up the football and drew from his pocket a large magnifying glass. Having examined the ball carefully, he stooped and surveyed the ground in the region of the goal-mouth. Standing near to him, I drew patterns in the mud with my walking-stick in interested silence. Around the goal in a wide circle grouped the players and spectators.

For some moments Herlock Sholmes worked quietly and systematically, and then he gave a little murmur of satisfaction. There was an expectant craning forward of heads.

"You've discovered where the ball fell, Mr. Sholmes?" asked the Vampire captain eagerly.

Herlock Sholmes nodded and pointed to a small object in the goal-mouth.

"I have," he said. "It dropped on this snail, and cracked the shell of the unfortunate creature, as these marks on the ball, testify."

"Wonderful, Mr. Sholmes!" exclaimed the captain. "Then, as the snail is over the goal-line, that proves the Vampires equalised?"

"On the contrary," said Herlock Sholmes, "the fact that the ball bounced from the snail's back proves that no goal was scored.."

An excited murmur ran through the onlookers.

"The fact is," went on my amazing friend imperturbably, "that the snail was not in the place it is now when the ball fell on it. It was here."

He pointed out a track in the mud which led to a spot a few inches on the other side of the goal-line.

"No snail in the possession of all its faculties would leave a lop-sided trail like this," said Sholmes. "The fact is, this track was made by the snail after it was lamed by the descent of the football. The poor little creature dragged itself through the mud in obvious pain."

"The fact is," went on the amazing detective, "the snail was not in the place it is now when the ball fell on it."

Herlock Sholmes brushed away a tear and restored the magnifying glass to his pocket. I remained in mute astonishment. The track in the mud pointed out by Sholmes had been made by my walking-stick as I had idly traced patterns on the ground! The game was resumed, but there was no further socre, and it ended seven goals to six in favour of the Wobbly Wanderers.

Not until we were back in Shaker Street did I dare broach the subject, which had been on my mind since the afternoon.

"My dear Sholmes," I remarked, "never have I known you to make a mistake. Yet the track you pointed out as having been made by the lame snail was, in reality, the mark drawn in the mud by the ferrule of my stick. Your mistake cost the Vampires a goal."

"Well, it's an ill wind that blows nobody any good," mused Sholmes, as he lifted a dainty morsel of fried plaice between his finger and thumb. "It was a mistake on the right side of the goal-line. Have you forgotten already, my dear Jotty, that I drew the Wobbly Wanderers in the sweepstake?"

And my amazing friend hid a prodigious wink in the cocaine tankard.

THE CASE OF THE POTATO JACKET

No. 75

Exclamations of protest and the tramp of hobnailed boots on the stairs caused Herlock Shomes and I to exchange meaning glances. Then there burst into our room a foreign-looking gentleman, followed by the gesticulating Mrs. Spudson.

"Ah, Signor Sholmio!"

To my astonishment Sholmes leapt out of his chair, and put his hands above his head.

"So you have come for your revenge at last, Waldo Sapolio," he said. "Strike! I am not afraid! I but hope your stiletto is sharper than the safety razor you used this morning."

The Italian—as his name and appearance convinced me he was—shook his dusky head with a vigour that caused his brass earrings to rattle like a chain drawn over cobblestones.

"Revenge?" he said in perplexity. "What for should I take revenge on my good friend Signor Sholmio? Did you not save my life?"

Herlock Sholmes drew a sigh of relief and lowered his hands.

"I—I suppose I did, if you say so," he remarked. "But I have removed the bucket from the path of so many people likely to kick it that the particular way in which I acted as your saviour escapes my mind for the moment. If you will permit me to turn up the records kept by my faithful friend, Dr. Jotson, I—"

"But surely you have not letta my case slippa da memory already?" broke in the stranger. "Did you not getta me three years for selling strawberry ice-creamio-coloured with brickdust?"

"Of course I did, my dear fellow!" said Sholmes heartily. "But how was that the means of saving your sunburnt skin?"

"Like so. A badda man called Slipperi Spaggetti had threatened to sticka me in da weskit. On da day you senda me to da lock-up he waita at my front door in Soho with a hatpin. Had I maka the return home instead of having da nice ride in da black motor-car to Wormwood Scrubs, I should no more have lived to mixa da ice-creams in summer or to baka da potato in winter. You sava my life, and thus I calla to see you and thanka you."

"Well, sit down, Waldo," said Herlock Sholmes genially, "and help yourself to the cocaine. I see you have taken up the baked-potato business again already."

"Signor Sholomia," gasped the Italian "you can reada da mind like a wizard!"

"Not at all!" smiled Sholmes. "It was a simple case of observation by a trained eye. Those blisters at your finger-tips give you away, my friend."

"Well, you speaka da truth," said Waldo Sapolio. "I baka da potato again for a living; but soon I sella da business. While I taka da rest in Wormwood Scrubs I maka da invention, which when I have patented him, will bring me mucha da money."

"An invention?" said Herlock Sholmes, "This is very interesting. A new way of preparing straw for making into ice-cream wafters, maybe?"

"No; the invention I maka is quite outside of my business," said Sapolio. "It is something that alla da new rich in da British Isles will maka da rush for when it goes on da market."

His white teeth gleamed in a smile as he drew a table-knife from his pocket, Sholmes leapt to his feet, while I, with great presence of mind, ducked swiftly behind the cocaine-cask.

"What were you afaraid of, gentlemen?" murmured Signor Sapolio. "This knife is da invention I told you about. It strika me a long time ago that most people can't eat peas off deir knives properly. I have solved da problem by this."

He tapped the table-knife in his hand with a grimy finger. For the first time we noticed it had a narrow groove running parallel with the blade.

"My dear Sapolio," cried Sholmes mopping his brow in his relief, "this is a most excellent idea! You are a public benefactor! When this goes on the market you will gain friends galore among all the newly-created members of the British peerage."

Waldo Sapolio replaced the knife lovingly in his pocket.

"I thinka so," he said modestly. "But this is by da way. Really, I have come to invite you and your friend, da noble Dr. Jotson, to the annual dinner of the Worshipful Company of Baka Potato-Jacks, which is being held at Sarsparilla Villa, Soho, to-night. It will be a very good affair. After da feed I am going to maka da sing-song with da little ballad, 'Row me on da river, Romeo'. It is at eight o'clock. Here are da tickets."

Promptly on the stroke of eight, Herlock Sholmes led me by the nose to the door of the Soho address that had been given to us. As we were ushered into a long room, where a number of green felt hats and purple, red, and yellow chokers were hanging on pegs, Waldo Sapolio rushed forward to greet us. Next moment we were being introduced to various friends of our host, all members of the Worshipful Company of Baka Potato-Jacks. The breath of garlic which permeated the room reminded me of sun-kissed onion-fields in far-away Italy.

At last dinner was announced, and we trooped into a large adjoining room. This apartment was tastefully furnished with a long table and some chairs and about a dozen movable baked potato ovens ranged near the walls.

Just as we were moving towards our seats, our host halted suddenly and felt in his pockets. Then his classical Roman face paled beneath its protective layer of grime, and he clutched Herlock Sholmes roughly by his arm.

With a lightning movement, Sholmes whipped the knife from the breast-pocket of Spaggetti.

"Da knife—da patent knife!" he whispered hoarsely. "It is gone! While we were maka da talk in da cloak-room I saw Spaggetti put something in his breast-pocket. To-morrow I was to go patent da knife. Now villain Spaggetti has stolen him!"

"Keep calm, my friend," said Herlock Sholmes hastily. "There is a chance that you may be mistaken. Leave the case in my hands, and before the evening is out I hope to restore your ingenious invention without creating a disturbance."

I noticed, as we took our seats at the long trestle-table down the centre of the room, that Sholmes manoeuvered himself into a seat between Sapolio and Spaggetti. With his usual adaptability my amazing friend immediately placed himself en rapport with the assembled diners. He juggled with a hot potato as to the manner born, while his request to the waiter, "Plenty of salt, Jack!" was greeted with great approval by all the professional "Jacks" present.

After dinner, speeches were the order of the day—or, rather, night. I rose to emit a few bright words on "The Digestive Organs in Relation to Baked Potato Skins," which were received in gratifying silence. Suddenly Herlock Sholmes reached over and hurled me back into my seat.

"Attendio, gentlemans!" he cried, in fluent Italian. "I can no maka da speech, but I can do conjuring trick!"

At once everyone woke up and were all attention.

"Watch me," said Sholmes, reverting to English. "I pick this table-knife up from behind the plate of my good friend Sapolio, and place it in my pocket. Then I wave my hands in the direction of my right-hand neighbour, so—and, hey-presto!—the knife is transferred to the pocket of Spaggetti!"

With a lightning movement he whipped a table-knife from the astonished Italian's breast-pocket, and handed it to Waldo Sapolio.

Roars of applause greeted this astounding feat of my amazing friend. Spaggetti, with confusion written all over his dusky features, slunk out of the room. Unnoticed by all, Sapolio replaced his beloved patent pea-retaining knife back in his pocket.

THE SARAH JANE MYSTERY

No. 76

As I emerged from the coal-cellar, I bumped my cranium against the angular frame of Herlock Sholmes.

"Ah, experimenting again, I perceive, my dear Jotson," said the great detective. "Have you yet succeeded in tracking the elixir of life to its lair?"

I gazed at my old friend in amazement. By what means he had deduced that I had been using the cellar for my scientific experiments, I could not imagine. Never had a word fallen from my lips about the important reasearch work I had been conducting.

Herlock Sholmes, by his marvellous psychical power, detected the question which was framing itself in my mind.

"So you are astonished to find me so cognisant of your affairs, my dear Jotson?" he said. "When, however, a reputable medical practitioner descends into the solitude of the coal-hole night after night, carrying a lantern, note-books, bottles of chemicals, Bunsen-burners, dead guinea-pigs, rabbit corpses, and the skeletons of sundry haddocks. I am forced to the conclusion he is engaged upon some scientific experiment. The fact that your face has failed to turn the milk sour for the last few days tells me that you have achieved a measure of success."

"Wonderful, my dear Sholmes!" I exclaimed. "The success I have achieved is beyond my wildest dreams. By grafting the wish-bone of a rabbit on to the apex of the left collar-bone, and taking three drams daily of a potion dispensed with equal portions of bromide, hypo, and oil of haddock, a tremendous increase in vitality can be effected. A grafted monkey gland is not in it!"

"And you have tried this interesting experiment on yourself, my dear Jotson?" asked Sholmes curiously.

"I have," I replied excitedly, "and I feel that I could push a bus over!"

Herlock Sholmes was silent and pre-occupied as he led the way up from the basement to our apartments. Once in his armchair with his ornate cocaine cask at his elbow, however, he evinced the greatest interest in my scientific discovery.

"You really feel that your youth and strength has been renewed, my dear Jotson?"

"In the most remarkable manner, Sholmes," I replied. "I feel that I could lift one of Mrs. Spudson's plum-cakes with one hand—that I could knock Joe Beckett through the roof of the Albert Hall!"

"Ah, cried Sholmes, "then I am going to crave your valued assistance in a case I have on hand! In your college days you were the champion boxer at Sawbones Acadamy. Now you have renewed your youth and strength, you could put up a good scrap with anyone of your own weight?"

"Undoubtedly," I replied, wondering what request my amazing friend was about to make of me.

"Excellent!" exclaimed Sholmes. "To-day, while you were out signing the death certificates of some of your patients, a deputation, consisting of members of the Metropolitan Hospital Boards, called on me.

These gentlemen wish me to investigate the cause of the inconvenient overcrowding of the hospitals in the East End at present with fly-weight pugilists suffering from fractured jaws. They know the immediate cause—a little pug, known as Tornado Tishbite, who has rapidly come to the fore. He has put it across each of these unfortunates with what he playfully calls his 'Sarah Jane'—a swinging right upper-cut to the point. But the amazing circumstance is that this little fellow of about half your own weight, my dear Jotson, can so put over knock-outs with the padded mitt as to suggest that a sledge-hammer has been used. At present no more boxers can be found to enter the ring with this miniature human hurricane, whom I am very anxious to see in action. Now I propose that you should fill the gap made by the Tornado's Sarah Jane.

"The Tornado has a private ring at his training quarters in the Mile End Road, where he entertains his friends. Anyone going there may have the privilege of a round or two with him. Remember, he is only half your weight, and that you will only indulge in love-pats. Never let it be said that Jotson deserted his old friend in the hour of his need."

He regarded me sorrowfully for a moment – then his fist swung slowly back.

After that pathetic appeal, I reluctantly agreed to Sholmes' proposal. In high glee, my amazing friend set off to arrange the friendly bout with Tornado Tishbite, the proprieter of Sarah Jane.

Two evenings later Herlock Sholmes hooked his stick in my ear and led me to the Tornado's training quarters, which were situated conveniently near the Mile End Accident Hospital. To my surprise, quite a large gathering of well-dressed gentlemen with prominent white shirt fronts and red nasal organs, were seated round a roped-in arena, over which arc-lights were suspended. On my appearing there was some whispering among the audience, and a round of cheering broke out.

With a dressing-gown thrown over my vest and shorts, I entered the ring. Cheers greeted me, and these were renewed when a diminutive man, wearing white bandages on his hands, leapt lightly through the ropes. It was the Tishbite of Sarah Jane fame!

Another qualm of apprehension possessed me. I did not like the look of those business-like bandages, neither did I like the attitude of my second, Herlock Sholmes. He was standing by in my corner with revivers, in the shape of a bucket and a hose-pipe. A referee entered the ring and introduced me and Tishbite. Sholmes then watched Tishbite drawn on his gloves, while the Tornado's second viewed the same operation in my corner.

"Time."

Bearing well in mind that it was but to be a friendly bout, with love-pats the order of the night, I stepped nobly forward to the centre of the ring. As first I proceeded cautiously, and although I landed some straight lefts and crooked rights, he seemed to bear me no ill-will. He took my face effectionately between his gloved hands and regarded it more in sorrow than in anger for a moment or two. Then his right hand swung slowly back. I followed it with fascinated eye. Next moment an earthquake hit me under the chin, and I described a graceful somersault backwards through the air. As I groped my way through a million dazzling stars and comets to blissful oblivion, a roar of voices burst forth into a delighted exclamation:

"Sarah Jane!"

No sooner was I reclining on my back than Herlock Sholmes leaped through the ropes, hose-pipe in hand. He turned the nozzle in the direction of my face and made a signal for the water to be switched on. But, even as the water spurted out in a stream, to the astonishment of all Sholmes switched the hose full on to the Tishbite's boxing-gloves. Immediately the water splashing from the gloves became discoloured with some greyish substance. Sholmes dropped the hose-pipe, which played merrily over the select audience, and snapped a pair of handcuffs over the Tishbite's wrists.

"Tornato Tishbite," he said, "I shall give you in charge for intent to do grievous bodily harm to my unfortunate colleague!"

A moment later Inspector Pickeye, disguised as a gentleman, stepped into the ring and arrested the cowed pugilist.

. . . . . .

All this I learnt whilst reclining in the Mile End Accident Hospital with my jaw in splints. Herlock Sholmes narrated the story with great gusto.

"All along I suspected Tishbite had something up his sleeve—or, rather, in his glove!" he said. "Formerly one of his seconds was a conjurer by profession, and after the Tornado's gloves had been examined before a bout, this man contrived to introduce some plaster of Paris into his mitts. Then, on the pretext of having a drink, the boxer would pour a little water into the gloves, thus causing the plaster of Paris to set into a solid lump. An old trick of the third-class ring, my dear Jotson, but a stream of water from my hose-pipe speedily revealed the presence of the substance in the gloves. But to you, Jotty, belongs the main credit for bringing the unscrupulous Tishbite to book. You performed your part admirably!"

With a loud groan I turned my battered physiognomy to the wall.

THE MYSTERY OF THE VACANT HOUSE

No. 77

With the approach of the holiday season I noticed alarming symptoms in my amazing friend, Mr. Herlock Sholmes. At frequent intervals his eyes would turn inwards and concentrate on the end of his aquiline nose. Then he would make a vicious sweep with his hand as though to remove an imaginary fly from the tip of his highly-developed proboscis. He would awake at night yelling that spotted starfish were jumping at him. These symptoms led me to the reluctant conclusion that Sholmes was suffering from a condition known to the medical profession as temporarius non compos mentis, or, in other words, a temporary attack of bats in the belfry.

For a few days a natural delicacy forbade me to broach the subject that was worrying me even more than the demise of a brace of my wealthiest patients. But as Herlock Sholmes became more restless and absent-minded I determined to exert the prerogative of an old friend and colleague. For my task I selected breakfast-time one morning.

"My dear fellow," I said, as Sholmes absent-mindedly helped himself to my kipper, after devouring his own, "it is imperative that you should take a holiday. You have been working far too hard. Now, I know a little country place called Wigglesmire, in Wapshire, nine miles from the railway, where I propose you shall accompany me for a complete rest and change."

"An excellent suggestion, my dear Jotson!" exclaimed Sholmes. "But where do you propose to obtain the wherewithal with which to pay for our fares and lodgings?"

I smiled serenely.

"I have quite sufficient for the purpose." I replied. "A fortnight ago I helped an old gentleman—one of my patients—to make his will. A week later he submitted to an operation at my hands. Needless to say, the operation was a complete success. Fortunately—er—i mean, unfortunately—the patient kicked the bucket before he had time to reap the full benefit of my skill."

"Quite so," said Sholmes. "And you have now received the legacy? Good! I will pack my dressing-gown, my violin, and the cocaine cask immediately after breakfast, and accompany you to Wigglesmire this very day."

With a cry of joy, Jerry Jobbs leaped from the debris.

Needless to say, I was delighted in having so easily persuaded Sholmes to take a well-deserved holiday. That afternoon we set off on our journey. We travelled all night on the Mudbury, Metropole, and Mausoleum Railway to Mudbury Junction. Thence we proceeded on foot towards the rustic village of Wigglesmire. Daft Jimmie, a well-known local character, preceded us with our luggage.

Midway between Mudbury and Wigglesmire, three miles from anywhere, Daft Jimmie suddenly stopped short. A crash of broken glass sounded as he dropped our luggage on the road. Then he stared ahead, his mouth wide open, heedless of the flies which took refuge therein.

"Well, Oi be fair blessed!" he ejaculated. "Old Jerry Jobbs' house! Look at it!"

Sholmes and I gazed in the direction indicated by the yokel's grubby forefinger. All we could see was a scattered pile of bricks, plaster, tiles, broken glass, and splintered wood.

"A house!" I exclaimed. "That heap of rubbish!"

"It were a house when Oi come by here first thing this mornin'," mumbled Jimmie. "That be a fair knock-down, that be! Oi be blessed if 'tain't!"

Sholmes hooked his stick affectionately round my neck!

"Come, let us proceed on our way, my dear Jotson," he said.

Together we walked down the lane, leaving Daft Jimmie to pick up the luggage. As we approached the wreckage we discerned a stout figure, wearing side-whiskers, sitting huddled in despondent attitude on the main heap of rubbish.

"That be poor ole Jerry Jobbs, the builder," said the voice of Daft Jimmie from behind us.

We halted by the side of the lane, and the dejected figure raised his head. His eyes lighted upon the lank form of my companion. Then, with a cry of joy, Jerry Jobbs leaped from the debris.

"Mr. Sholmes!" he exclaimed. "I recognise you at once from your portraits in the 'Popular'! 'Tis a wonderful coincidence! You have stumbled across a great mystery."

I groaned aloud.

"My dear sir," I protested, "my colleage, Mr. Herlock Sholmes, has come to the country for complete repose. As his friend and medical adviser, I could not dream of letting him exercise his already overtaxed brain on any intricate problem."

"Bow-wow, Jotty!" ejaculated Sholmes, removing an imaginary fly from his nose. "There is no mystery here. The solution of Mr. Jobbs' trouble is as clear as the nose on your face on bath night."

Like the builder, I gazed at my amazing friend in utter astonishment.

"Why, my dear Sholmes," I exclaimed, "Mr. Jobbs has not even told us his trouble yet, so how the dickens——"

"Simplicity itself, my dear Jotson," said Sholmes. "This pile of debris is obviously the remains of a new vacant house built by Mr. Jerry Jobbs. The wallpaper was quite thick enough to keep the walls up. Yet the place collapsed. The house did not just fall down, as the manner in which the doors are splintered amply testifies.

"Wonderful!" ejaculated the wide-eyed Mr. Jobbs. "My men finished erecting the house yesterday. This morning I walked out to look at it. It was a total wreck. I was so surprised you could have knocked me down with a brick!"

"Maybe you have an enemy, Mr. Jobbs?" I suggested.

"Ah, I fear you are right, sir," said the builder sadly. "Several people have bought similar four-roomed dwellings from me, though why they should have their knives in me I can't make out. I only charged them two thousand pounds apiece."

Feeling I had unearthed an important clue. I looked towards Herlock Sholmes for approval. My famous friend merely smiled.

"A good attempt, my dear Jotson," he said; "but you are quite off the track. Cast your eyes about you."

I looked at the wreckage carefully.

"H'm!" I remarked. "It seems rather as though an anarchist has set off a bomb here."

Sholmes regarded me with his peculiar smile.

"Have you every heard of a four-legged anachist, my dear Joston!" he asked quietly.

I shook my head sadly. In that moment I feared that my friend's overworked brain had given way completely. Just then an angry shout came to our ears from across some meadows. We swung round. Then, with a dramatic gesture, Sholmes pointed towards a small wood.

"There is your anachist unless I am greatly mistaken, Jotson" he said.

Mr. Jerry Jobbs and I gazed in amazement. From the wood trotted an old dilapidated grey mule, followed by a perspiring rustic.

"Well, I'll be jiggered!" gasped the builder. "Old Podger's Army mule!"

"I think you will be able to claim substantial damages against friend Podgers, Mr. Jobbs," said Sholmes. "But leave the matter to me for the present. Let us accost the fellow."

Leaving Daft Jimmie to sleep by our luggage, we set off across the meadows.

By this time the mule was about played out. So was Podgers, but he managed to clutch the halter that was fastened round the animal's neck. The mule halted, and started cropping grass. Sholmes strode up to the man, with Jerry Jobbs and me close at his heels.

"Good-morning, Mr. Podgers!" said Sholmes amiably. "A nice mess your mule has made of my friend's house."

Mr. Podgers' jaw dropped with a resounding click.

"Herlock Sholmes!" he breathed hoarsely. "You—you've found out? I felt in my bones when I bought this Army moke that one day I should land into trouble through the beast!"

"You should not have allowed the fierce animal to break loose, Mr. Podgers," said the great detective severely.

"Allowed him!" snorted Mr. Podgers indignantly. I was just hitching him into my baker's cart this mornin' when he took a bit out o' my left leg with his teeth. Then he made off like a streak. I chased him three miles down the road, I did. Then I caught him by Mr. Jobbs' new house. The beast backed, and lashed out with his heels. Good-bye house! I followed him over ten fields, across six streams, and through three woods; but I got him at last. Kim up, you brute!"

"Stop!" cried Jerry Jobbs. "This morning's work will cost you a pretty penny. I'll—I'll sue you, and——"

"Send my commission to the Cow and Cartwheel Inn," said Herlock Sholmes. "Good-morning, Mr. Jobbs! We'll leave you to it."

And, with the toe of his boot, Sholmes helped me back to where we had left Daft Jimmie.

As we resumed our walk to Wigglesmire my admiration for my amazing friend found expression in words.

"You are superb, Sholmes!" I said. "How you knew that a four-legged creature had been responsible for the damage before ever Podgers' mule came into sight beats me hollow! Did you note some specific clue that escaped our eyes?"

"No," replied Sholmes. "I deducted the fact by a process of elimination. Directly I saw the wreck of Jerry Jobbs' newly erected house, I knew that such damage could only have been done by a South Sea hurricane, a Zeppelin bomb, or a British Army mule. We have no South Sea hurricanes in this country, thank goodness, and the war is over. Therefore, it was obvious to even an average intelligence that an Army mule must have been responsible for the complete annihilation of the building. By searching for clues, I easily could have tracked the animal to its lair, as you well know, my dear Jotson. However, I was saved that trouble, thanks to the timely appearance of the brute. I trust Jobbs' remittance to us will be a substantial one."

THE CASE OF THE LOST SAPPHIRE

No. 78

Mrs. Spudson placed the fish knives and forks and two cracked wineglasses on the supper-table, and then brought in the "bubble-and-squeak" and a large jug of cold water. While with practised dexterity, my friend, Mr. Herlock Sholmes, apportioned this former delicacy, our amiable landlady launched into the story of all the offers of marriage she had during the last twenty years of her exciting life.

"By the way, Mrs. Spudson," interrupted Herlock Sholmes, as he liberally sprinkled the cocaine over his bubble-and-squeak, "how are the chickens?"

Mrs. Spudon's jaw dropped with a click like the trapdoor in a pantomime. I must confess, too, that I started back in surprise. While I was extracting the forkful of bubble-and-squeak which had slipped between my collar and neck, Mrs. Spudson recovered herself somewhat.

"Your're a fair coughdrop, Mr. Sholmes!" she said admiringly. "How you knew I was keeping fowlbI really don't know! Why, I only bought 'em yesterday!"

A slow smile spread over my amazing friend's hatchet face.

"It is not often I am led on a fowl scent, Mrs. Spudson," he murmured, sniffing the air significantly, "but as I was passing out of the house this morning I was drawn irresistably in the direction of your backyard. There I saw your recent purchases, including the sitting hen."

"Ay, and a fine one that broody hen is, Mr. Sholmes," said Mrs Spudon. "Nine eggs fresh from the grover's she has under her, so there'll be plenty o' young pullets for Sunday dinners soon. I hopes that you and Dr. Jotson here will——"

She stopped short as a violent peal sounded on the front-door bell.

"An impatient patient, I expect," I murmured jocularly.

"I'm afraid not, my dear Jotsdon," replied Sholmes. "The visitor arrived in a taxi, which drew up outside a few moments ago. As none of your patients is able to stir abroad save in an ambulance. I deduce that the caller is a prospective client of mine. But kindly answer the door, Mrs. Spudson.

A minute later Mrs Spudson returned, and ushered in a stout florid gentleman fashiuonably attired in a green-and-yellow check sports suit and purple socks with spots. The visitor was evidently labouring under some intense emotion. Both Sholmes and I recognised him instantly. He was none other than Sir Diggory Dugg, the man who had made a fortune supplying upholstered nosebags to Army mules during the war.

"Mr. Sholmes!" gasped the newcomer. "Thank 'evans you're hin!"

Herlock Sholmes disposed of the remains of the bubble-and-squeak with a gulp, and indicated the armchair.

"Pray be seated, Sir Diggory," he said. "You may speak quite freely before my friend and colleague, Dr. Jotson."

"Thank you, Mr. Sholmes," said our visitor, as he burst the last two springs in the armchair. "You can't 'ave no idea of the relief it'll be to get my troubles off my chest. This afternoon I had a round of golf with my friend, Lord Shovel, at the Post Hall Club, and I lost——"

"And Lord Shovel won?" I put in.
Sir Diggory Dugg glared furiously in my direction.
"That's nothin' to do with it, drat you, sir!" he snapped. "I was about to say I lost my famous Jollipore sapphire—a wonderful white stone as big as a pigeon's egg!"
Herlock Sholmes leaned back in his chair with his finger-tips together.
"You interest me, Sir Diggory," he mused. "I remember reading in the 'Morning Moan' about your purchase of that unique Indian gem. Take a pinch of cocaine, and tell me the circumstances of the loss."
Sir Digby helped himself liberally from the cask by the fireplace, and continued in a calmer tone.
"Well, it was like this 'ere," he said. "When Lord Shovel called for me this afternoon in his Rolls-Royce I slipped the sapphire into my vest-pocket, intending to take it to a gentleman named Solomon Shentpershent after the game. You see, Mr. Sholmes, I spent a holiday and about ten thousand pounds round the 'Crown-and-Anchor' boards at Monte Carlo last season. I wanted to raise a bit on the stone. To my 'orror, 'owever, after the golf match I found the sapphire was no longer in my pocket. It is serious; the loss o' the stone renders me stony."
Sir Diggory Dugg buried his purple face in his red handkerchief, and gave a sob like an expiring buffalo.
"And did you institute a search for the sapphire!" asked Sholmes.
"No. Natchurally, I became very excited an' told Shovel o' my loss. He strongly advised me not to say a word to anyone, pointin' out that if the caddies get wind of the affair I might never get the stone back again. Anyway, it would 'ave been like lookin' for a needle in a 'aystack. So I 'ired a taxi and came straight 'ere for your advice an' 'elp."
Herlock Sholmes nodded approvingly. Then he rose and crossed to a cabinet on the far side of the room. From a drawer he fetched out a plan of the Posh Hall Golf Course.
"You see, Sir Diggory," he remarked, with a smile. "I keep the plans of all the golf courses in the country close to hand. Owing to the regularity with which I have had to investigate cases of slaughtered caddies, I have found it saves time to do so. Now, can you point out the course you took round the course?"
Sir Diggory Dugg took a pencil from his pocket and drew curious zigzag lines all over the plan. Apparently his memory was as good as his golf had been bad.
"Thank you," said Sholmes. "It is too late to undertake any investigations to-night, but I shall begin firtst thing to-morrow."

CHAPTER 2

At five o'clock on the following morning Herlock Sholmes playfully took hold of my ear with the fire-tongues and dragged me out of bed.
"Come, Jotty," he piped merrily; "let us away to the Posh Hall Club! When you have dressed, go into Shaker Street and find a taxi."
Half an hour later Sholmes joined me in the vehicle, clasping a bulky bundle under his greatcoat. As the cab bowled on its way to the golf club curious clunkings proceeded from under my companion's coat, and once the head of an indignant fowl protuded. Astonished as I was, I asked no questions.
In less than an hour we arrived at the golf course, which was situated some miles out of town. So intent was Sholmes on the problem of the lost sapphire that he absent-mindedly left me to pay the ten guineas demanded by the taxi-driver.
When I rejoined my amazing friend I found him standing on the end of a sea of gorse on the deserted golf course. In his right hand he held the plan which delineated the excursions Sir Diggory Dugg had made "among the wee bonnie heather" during the previous afternoon. Then Sholmes began the most astonishing performance I had seen him give since he lassooed the missing link with a strand of the last chord. From under his greatcoat he drew a plump and motherly-looking hen with a long piece of string tied to its leg, and set her running in the gorse. Suddenly the fowl stopped, cackled exuberantly, shook her feathers, and sat down. Sholmes glided up to the bird, drew a small white object from under her, and placed it in his pocket.
Again the hen ran off, and repeated her former antics. Again my amazing friend collected a white object. Altogether, this astonishing performance was repeated two or three dozen times, until we had zigzagged our way a quarter of the distance round the course. Then, as Herlock Sholmes stooped to retirve the thirty-seventh object, a little cry of satisfaction left his lips. He grasped the hen, thrust her under his coat, and, hooking his stick in my ear, made for the exit-gates as the first golfers arrived.
We returned to town by train. At the door of our lodgings in Shaker Street we met Mrs. Spudson, who was evidently in a state of great agitation.
"Mr. Sholmes," she said, "you're the werry one I've bin lookin' for! I want your 'elp sir. My broody hen—it's gone, and——"
With a dramatic gesture Sholmes brought the somewhat shop-soiled creature from beneath his greatcoat.
"Here is your broody hen, Mrs. Spudson," he murmured soothingly. "No, don't thank me for finding it for you. An extra kipper for breakfast to-morrow will amply repay me for my time and trouble.
Sholmes led me to the parlour on the first floor. Then from his pockets he drew out three dozen golf-balls!
"Now, my dear Jotson," he said, "you see how useful a broody hen can be as a detective's assistant. The poor soul was anxious to do her bit hatching out eggs. Naturally, when I let her run on the golf course, she thought each white object she scraped into view was an egg. Thus I have become the possessor not

only of these golf-balls, for which we can obtain a least four-pence each, but also of Sir Diggory Dugg's lost sapphire! I shall return the gem to him before noon to-day as I promised."

As Herlock Sholmes drew from an inside pocket the beautiful white Jollipore sapphire I could only gasp my admiration of his genius!

THE CASE OF THE HAUNTED COAL SHED

No. 79

"It is positively ludicrous, Sholmes!"

"What is, my dear Jotson? Your face?"

I looked up with a frown from the newspaper which I have been perusing.

"No!" I snapped. "This account in the 'Evening Muse,' about the haunted coal-shed."

"Ah, the Peckham house mystery!" exclaimed Herlock Sholmes. "I read a short account of it in the 'Morning Moan.' What has the 'Muse' to say about the affair?"

My famous friend, Mr. Herlock Sholmes, and I were spending an evening together in our rooms in Shaker Street. Having exploited to the full the uproarious joys of Tiddly-Winks and Beggar-Your-Neighbour with him, I had picked up the evening paper Mrs. Spudson, our landlady, had brought in. At once my eyes had been attracted by a column report headed: "Uncanny Coal-shed!—Dark Mystery of Moving Lights at Peckham!"

"The whole affair is most riduculous on the face of it, Sholmes," I said. "A man named Nathaniel Nobson and his wife, living at a small villa in Runner's Walk, Peckham, claim to have witnessed the most astonishing occult phenomena while engaged in the task of getting coals in from their shed. According to them, pieces of coal, stick, and old vegetables have moved in the most uncanny manner. Once a lighted candle moved unaided from one side of the shed to the other. The Ghost Research Society are investigating the affair. Personally, I consider that a competent physician like myself should be called in to examine the people who claim to see such things. It is positively ludicrous that great scientists like Sir Gulliver Dodge should be taken in by the hallucinations of ill-balanced folk such as the Nobsons."

Sholmes rose from his seat, drew aside the blinds, and peered out of the window.

"Unless I am greatly mistaken, my dear Jotson," he said quietly, "here is Nathaniel Nobson himself!"

Almost incredulous, I joined Sholmes at the window. On the pavement staring about him, was a small man, whose highly-coloured nose and mutton-chop whiskers would have made him a distinguished personage in any assembly.

"Really, Sholmes," I exclaimed, "how do you know that is the man whose exploits with the ghosts have caused so much comment in the Press?"

Sholmes smiled in that superior fashion of his.

"By simple deduction, my dear Jotson," he said. "From the way the gentleman staggered in the direction of our front door, it was obvious that he had been associating with spirits. But we shall be able to inspect him at closer quarters in a few moments. Ah, he has found the bell!"

A loud peal resounded through the house, and ten minutes later the shuffling feet of Mrs. Spudson were en route for the door. Another few minutes elapsed, during which time sounds of animated conversation proceeded from the hall. Then our landlady ushered in our visitor. It was obvious that Mrs. Spudson had given way against her better judgment. She folded her arms, and gave a loud sniff.

"A pusson to see you about some goats, Mr. Sholmes," she said.

"Ghosts!" corrected Sholmes. He waved Mrs. Spudson aside, and beckoned to the little man in the mutton-chop whiskers. "Come in and take a seat Mr. Nobson."

Mr. Nobson staggered into the armchair, and drained Sholmes' tankard of cocaine before the latter could put it out of his reach.

"I—I don't know how you knew my name, Mr.—hic—Sholmes," he said, wiping his mouth. "And how did you guess I'd come to see you about the g-g-g-ghosts? It's 'astrordinary, 'pon my word!"

"It may seem extraordinary to you, Mr. Nobson," said Herlock Sholmes easily, "but it is my business to get to know things. You have come here to solicit my help?"

"That's it," said Mr. Nobson; "I want you to find out the names of these spooks who get up to their monkey-tricks in my coal-shed. Sir Gulliver Dodge and the Great Research Society have been nosing about the place for days with cameras, taking flashlight photographs. They say there must be the shades of former tenants hanging round. But they haven't had a shade of success yet. The photographs have given only negative results."

"What other means have been taken to lay these spooks by the heel—if spooks they be?" asked Sholmes.

"I've been to the fire-brigade and the p'lice station," replied Mr. Nobson huskily, "but all I got out of 'em was the address of a veterinary surgeon."

"They thought you were a little 'hoarse,' perhaps!" suggested Sholmes, with a twinkle in his deep-set, green eyes. Suddenly he brought his hatchet jaws together with a smart click. I sat up expectantly, for I knew that this little mannerism on the part of my amazing friend meant business.

"But joking apart, Mr. Nobson," Sholmes continued, "this mystery greatly interests me. I should like to examine your coal-shed.

"Then come with me now, Mr. Sholmes," pleaded our visitor. "Only this very evening, when I went there to get a scuttleful of Derby Brights, a most 'strordinary thing happened. I put a lighted candle down on a chunk of coal, and turned to find the hammer for breaking up some pieces. Imagine my surprise when I turned round again to see that candle slowly walking across the shed! That's the second time I've seen that done! It gave me the cold shivers. I dropped the hammer, put on a cap, and came to you at top speed, only stopping five minutes for refreshment on the way."

A few minutes later, Sholmes and I, together with Mr. Nobson, were seated in a taxi, bowling along in the direction of Peckham.

Alighting from the cab, Herlock Sholmes slipped his hand into Mr. Nobson's pocket, and generously gave the taxi-driver double the correct fare.

"Now," he said genially, turning to our client again, "lead us to this dark mystery of the coal-shed."

After some difficulty, Mr. Nobson unlocked the front door and led us through the house. He explained that his spouse was away attending a whist-drive in aid of the Fund for Supplying Tatcho to Baldheaded Bashibazooks. The coal-shed was situated in the small garden at the back of the Nobson residence. From the shed a faint, ghostly light flickered. A cold shiver ran down my spine.

"I—I must have left the c-candle burning," stammered Mr. Nobson. "It might have set the place on fire."

He took a step forward, and peered into the coal-shed. A moment later he staggered back with a gurgling cry. His face was the colour of the best cream cheese, and only a vestige of pink remained in his bulbous proboscis.

"Look!" he gasped hoarsely. "The c-c-candle! It's moving again!"

With commendable presence of mind, Herlock Sholmes pushed me forward and peered over my shoulder. Incredulous as it may sound, a small stub of lighted candle set among the coal was swaying slowly as though imbued with life.

"What do you think of that now?" demanded Mr. Nobson, in a hoarse whisper. "There you are—a candle, stuck on a chunk of coal, moved by invisible hands!"

Suddenly, Sholmes pushed me aside and dropped to his knees at the entrance to the coal-shed. Then, to our astonishment, he grabbed an old cabbage-top that was lying on the ground near by, and began to drag it along the coal a short distance before the candle. My hair stood upright as the lump on which the candle was set, detached itself from the rest of the pieces in the coal-shed and slowly moved forward, the candle flickering unsteadily the while. A moment later Sholmes reached out both his hands. He whipped off the candle, and picked up the object on which it had stood.

"Here is your ghost, Mr. Nobson!" he cried triumphantly.

And he held up before our astonished eyes a common or gardon tortoise!

Before Mr. Nobson was able to recover from his surprise, Sholmes had extracted the fiver fee from him.

"This poor creature is so covered with coal-dust and grime," murmured my amazing friend, returning to the tortoise, "that he was quite undistinguishable from the lumps of coal in the shed. He was responsible for all the ghostly phenomena you witnessed. Place him in a box in a safe place. To-morrow, make inquiries among your neighbours as to which of them has lost a valuable garden tortoise. You may get a reward for returning it—though perhaps not as much as a fiver. Come, Jotson, let us seek the gaiety of a fish-and-chips emporium!"

THE CASE OF THE CREEPING KROOBOY!

No. 80

As Herlock Sholmes buried his nose in the tankard of cocaine I leaned across the table and glanced at the half-sheet of notepaper on which he had been scribbling. To my astonishment, the following enigmatic inscription met my eyes.

"Creeping Krooboy a bob e. w."

"Er—excuse me, Sholmes," I said, "you didn't tell me that you had another case on hand."

Sholmes set the tankard, and politely wiped his mouth on the tablecloth before speaking.

"No, my dear Jotson," he replied, "for the very simple reason that I am not engaged on any case at present. What put the idea into your head?"

I indicated the note on the table.

"Merely that the line you have just penned appears to be a copy of one of those Agony Column advertisements. So many of your cases are founded on them that I thought——"

Sholmes broke in with an amused chuckle.

"Well, you thought wrong for once, Jotty," he said. "Had you read the newspapers recently you would have known that Creeping Krooboy is the favourite for the Derby, which is to be run at Epsom to-day. Once a year I have a little flutter. That note is to convey to a certain gentleman known as Welsher Wiley that I want to put a bob each way on the favourite. The Welsher is Mrs. Spudon's stepson, so our esteemed landlady will see that the note is delivered into the right hands."

"H'm!" I remarked. "I'm afraid hose-racing doesn't interest me."

"Possibly as a sport it does not afford the exhilarating joys of the operating-theatre," admitted Sholmes. "However, you shall have the opportunity of judging for yourself. Get you hat and stick, while I borrow Mrs. Spudson's opera-glasses. To-day we journey out to Epsom Downs."

"But, my dear Sholmes," I protested, "I can't possibly——"

Herlock Sholmes interrupted my remarks with the upholstered toe of his carpet slipper. Realising the futility of argument with such a masterful character, I went forth to prepare for my unexpected outing.

Less than an hour later, Herlock Sholmes and I, garbed in our most sporty attire, were ensconed in a first-class carriage on the "race special." Unfortunately, before the train left the station the ticket-inspector appeared, and we speedily found ourselves among some undesirable, dishonest-looking characters in a third-class compartment lower down.

One of these racegoers, an individual in a very noisy check suit, brought out playing-cards, and cordially invited us to "find the lady." I smiled confidently, well knowing that my famous friend could find anything from a lost memory to a missing link. Sholmes spotted the right card with uncanny precision until he had cleaned out the pockets of the sporty gentleman. The astonishment and chagrin of the man and his shady companion knew no bounds. As, however, we alighted at Epson Downs Station, Sholmes handed the sportsman his card. The fellow glanced at the famous name engraved upon it, gave a gasp like an expiring codfish, and collapsed under the seat.

"Now my dear Jotson," murmured Sholmes, as we wended our way to the racecourse, "we can afford seats in the grand-stand. Also, I shall sport a fiver on the chances of Creeping Krooboy."

Swinging Mrs. Spudson's opera-glasses carelessly in his hand, Herlock Sholmes led the way to the most select enclosure on the Epsom racecourse. All the nobility and gentry of the land were present, including such illustrious lights as Sir Sam Isaacs, the Marquis of Schweppes, and Lady Cherry Blossom. Many recognised my famous friend at once, and greeted him with easy familarity. Sholmes, however, averred his inability to loan anything above a bob save on the most favourable security. Among the number who thus fraternised with Sholmes was none other than Lord Spavin of Spearmint, the owner of the Derby favourite.

"I hope, my dear Sholmes," he said, flicking his cigar-ash into my eye, "that you have put your last bean on Creeping Krooboy. Believe me, the other knock-kneed nags won't see the tail of my colt for dust in the big event."

"Rest assured of that, your worship," said Sholmes easily. "I am looking forward to returning to Shaker Street laden with boodle after the race."

Lord Spavin turned to greet a well-dressed, horsy person who strolled up to us.

"Ah, here is my trainer, Mr. Hoofitt!" he exclaimed—"the man who brought the Krooboy to his present state of perfection!"

We shook hands with the well-known trainer, who chatted confidently about the colt's chances.

Suddenly a great cheer rent the air. The magnificent Derby thoroughbreds filed from the paddock on to the course. For my benefit Spavin pointed out the Krooboy. He was a splendid animal, as black as the ace of spades, with four tapering legs and a like number of hoofs which would have done credit to a Shire horse. A great feeling of confidence possessed me. I felt sure that Sholmes would not drop his fiver on account of the favourite falling down.

As the horses sped away to the starting-point the excitement grew apace. Then a great shout arose:

"They're off!"

It seemed but a few minutes later when the leading horses swung round Tattenham Corner. A jet-black colt was leading the field by a length.

The silken jacket worn by the jockey was of pink and yellow stripes with green noughts and crosses—Lord Spavin's colours!

"Creeping Krooboy leads!"

A thunder of cheers echoed across the Downs as the favourite pounded down the straight. The Krooboy was gaining. Now he was four lengths ahead of his nearest rival. I smacked my lips in anticipation of a bumper fish supper at Sholmes' expense.

"Creeping Krooboy wins!"

The favourite rapidly approached the red-and-white winning-post opposite to the judges' stand. All seemed over bar the shouting. But then occurred one of the most astonishing incidents witnessed on a racecourse since the Derby favourite, Black Treacle, stooped to munch the artificial flowers from a lady's hat in the great race of 1783.

Creeping Krooboy, as has been stated already, was four lengths ahead of the nearest horse. With but fifty yards to go he slowed down. Twenty yards from the winning-post he reared up on his hind legs and pawed the air. His jockey plied the whip vigorously, but the Derby favourite backed from side to side like a broncho in a Wild West show. His mouth flecked with foam, his ears dropped back, and his eyes dilated in sheer terror. Horse after horse shot by him until the whole field of Derby runners had passed the post ahead of him.

Lord Spavin gasped in stupefield amazement. Mr. Hoofitt, the trainer, gave vent to a series of choking noises. Even Sholmes' jaw dropped on to his dicky with a click at the sight of the astounding spectacle. As for me, I groaned inwardly. Visions of a sumptuous fish supper on my companion's winnings faded like a beautiful dream.

Meanwhile, the crowd on the racecourse set up a fierce booing. Most of them had had "a bit on" the favourite. The air was filled with raucous cries intermingled with the chuckles of the delighted bookies.

"Can it be that Spadger, the jockey, pulled the horse?" muttered Lord Spavin, in a dazed sort of voice.

"Surely not! I'd have trusted that lad with my last pawnticket!"

Herlock Sholmes took a large pinch of cocaine, and drew the disappointed owner to one side.

"There is some deeper mystery about this," he said, in a voice trembling with emotion. "Let us inspect the horse at closer quarters."

Together we made our way to the paddock, The horses filed in, Creeping Krooboy creeping in the rear. While Lord Spavin sought explanations of the jockey, Sholmes examined the distressed thoroughbred with a powerful magnifying-glass. Suddenly he spun round on his heel.

"Quick! There is no time to be lost, Spavin. Hand me a tenner for expenses, and let me have the loan of your Rolls-Ford, and I will unearth the mystery for you."

With eyes filled with gratitude, his lordship gave Sholmes both the money and permission to use his magnificent twenty mule-power hybrid.

Sholmes hesitated.

"Perhaps you had better come with us, your worship," he said, stowing the banknote in his breast-pocket. "Tell your chauffeur to walk home, and you drive us yourself with all speed for your training stables."

Lord Spavin was reluctant to leave the course, but Sholmes was insistant. Soon the Rolls-Ford was rattling and banging on its way to the Spavin stables, steered by its aristocratic owner. Arriving at the stables, Sholmes began flying about like a bee in a bottle. He peered into every cranny and corner, under the mangers, and into the loft.

"Now lead us to the residence of Hoofitt, your worship," he said at last.

Lord Spavin screwed up his face in surprise, thereby shattering his rimless monocle into a thousand pieces.

"Great pip, Mr. Sholmes!" he exclaimed. "You don't think——"

"I never think!" snapped Sholmes. "I merely deduce from facts as I find them."

And this cryptic utterance was all the great detective would make.

Hoofitt's house was only a couple of hundred yards from the stables. At the back of it was situated a wood-shed, and into this Sholmes dived like a hound on the scent. Lord Spavin and I remained outside. What my amazing friend hoped to find I could not guess. Moreover, I did not ask him, for well I knew that he would not deign to explain until the end of the story.

Suddenly a triumphant cry sounded from the interior of the wood-shed. Next moment Sholmes emerged bearing a red-and-white circular board attached to a long pole.

"The mystery of Creeping Krooboy is solved, your worship!" he said to Lord Spavin. "Your trainer, Hoofitt, is an unscrupulous scoundrel of the deepest dye. He it was who caused you to lose the race and me to lose my fiver—not to mention that bob I put on with Welsher Willey."

"Egad!" ejaculated the astonished racehorse owner, "I don't see——"

"Then listen!" said Sholmes. "This affair I am holding is an exact replica of a racecourse winning-post. With it Hoofitt has beaten your horse, Creeping Krooboy, on the sly until the poor creature has become terrified at the mere sight of a red-and-white post. Therefore, when the gee saw the winning-post at Espom to-day he stopped dead in sheer fright!"

"The traitor!" thundered Lord Spavin. "I'll have him turfed off the Turf! But what put you on to Hoofitt's track?"

"Two clues which I discovered at Epson," replied Herlock Sholmes. "The first consisted of some suspicious bald patches on Creeping Krooboy's back. The second was the curious chuckle Hoofitt gave as the nag reared up before the winning-post."

"Why, I thought he was chocking with chagrin!" I cried, in amazement.

"Choking with laughter!" corrected Sholmes. "But now we must leave the matter of your trainer in your hands, Lord Spavin. Jotson and I must be getting back to Shaker Street. Any cheques sent to to that address, care of Mrs. Spudson, will always find me."

THE CASE OF THE LOST NUGGET

No. 81

Herlock Sholmes was having a busy morning. Among the usual crowd of tax-collectors, bill-collectors, brokers and autograph hunters that thronged our waiting-room at Shaker Street, were two clients.

As all my patients, save one, had died during the previous week, I was reclining in a chair in Sholmes' consulting-room, in the anticipation of hearing something interesting. My anticipations were fully gratified.

The first client proved to be none other than Mr. Leo Hammergugger, of Regent's Park, the fmaous importer of wild animals. He was greatly distressed. It appeared that his valuable chimpanzee, Cuthbert, had disappeared. It was not often that Mr. Hammergugger had made a pet of any of his imports, but he had made an exception of the ape in question. Cuthbert had been brought up in his household. He had been taught manners, and could eat peas from a knife with the best of the Hammergugger family. Now Cuthbert had disappeared. No wonder Mr. Hammergugger sought the aid of my famous friend, Mr. Herlock Sholmes!

Having received two studio portraits of the missing chimpanzee, Herlock Sholmes saw the animal importer safely down the back stair-case. Then he rang the bell for Mrs. Spudson to show in the second client. This proved to be another fine old lusty Briton, named Yobbo Mosenstein.

Mr. Mosenstein was even more excited than Mr. Hammergugger had been. In his mental distress he spluttered like a Ford car with cramp in the carburettor.

"Come, calm yourself!" said Herlock Sholmes soothingly. "You can speak quite freely before my colleague, Dr. Jotson."

Making a supreme effort, Mr. Mosenstein pulled himself together.

"I have been the victim of a most astounding theft, Mr. Sholmes!" he blurted out. "In my library at home I had a great gold nugget, which I brought back from California with me some months ago. It was on a writing-table by the window, acting as a paper-weight. This morning at ten o'clock I saw it there with my own eyes. I was called out of the room. Five minutes later when I returned it was gone–vanished into thin air."

"Who was in the house beside yourself?" asked Herlock Sholmes.

"Only my sister, who acts as my house-keeper. Nobody could have possibly entered the library by the door. The window, by which the table was situated, was slightly open, but the room is up on the second floor of the house. There is a bit of ivy on the wall outside, but it is quite impossible that anyone could have climbed up by that. The whole thing is inexplicable."

"To you, maybe," said Sholmes, smiling, "but not to me. You live in the neighbourhood of Regent's Park, possibly?"

Mr. Monsenstein raised his curly black eye-brows in amazement.

"I do," he said. "But how the mischief you guessed——"

"I never guess," put in Sholmes. "I deduced the fact in question with the massive brain with which kind Nature has endowed me. Come, let us proceed to your home! Jotson, my trusty friend, I shall need your assistance."

Together we took our departure by the back exit to avoid the bill-collectors. In Shaker Street we obtained a taxi, and alighted ten minutes later at Mosenstein's house in Regent's Park. As we stepped on to the pavement, who should we run against but Inspector Pinkeye, of Scotland Yard.

"Why, hallo, Pinkeye!" was Sholmes' cheery greeting. "Any cases on hand at present?"

Pinkeye smiled complacently, and politely ejected the quid of tobacco from his mouth before replying.

"I'm on my way to make a capture now, Mr. Sholmes," he said. 'It has come to the knowledge of the Yard that a boy chimney-sweep is being employed at a place called the Cedars, in Tipdown Road, near here. You probably don't know that under section forty-three, folio B, paragraph two o' the Sweepers' Act of 1881, that 'no minor is allowed to climb up inside o' any chimbley, smoke-stack, funnel-flue, or vent-pipe for the removal of any soot or other extraneous or combustible substance whatsoever hereinafter mentioned or not mentioned within the scope of this here Act.'"

"And somebody has been committing this heinous offence, eh?" said Sholmes.

"He has," said Inspector Pinkeye. "A young urchin was distinctly seen to appear out of a certain chimbley-pot at the Cedars. I'm on my way to nab the malefactor now."

"Highly sootable employment for you, Pinkeye," said Sholmes jocularly, as the burly Yard official rolled on his way.

As we entered the garden of Mr. Mosenstein's house, Sholmes at once asked to be shown the window of the library. Mr. Mosenstein led us round to the side of the house. An idea which had been simmering in my head suddenly came to a boil, causing me to give a cry of satisfaction.

"My dear Sholmes," I whispered excitedly. "I have been putting two and two together, and my deduction is that Mosenstein's gold nugget was removed by Mr. Hammergugger's ape!"

"Of course, that theory occurred to me as soon as it became apparent that the two addresses were in the Regent's Park district," said Sholmes. "However, my dear Jotson, it does you the greatest credit that you should have been able to deduce the possibility in less than half an hour."

I glowed with pleasure at this high praise from the great detective. Just then Mr. Mosenstein stopped, and, pointing up to a window, indicated that that was the position of the library.

"Perhaps you would like to go inside the house now," he suggested.
"No, there will be no need for that," said Sholmes.
He drew from his pocket the magnifying-glass that had disappeared from my consulting-room on the previous day. With it he carefully examined the ground beneath the ivy-clad wall. Then he replaced my magnifying-glass in his pocket, and turned to the expectant client.
"I need make no further investigations here, Mr. Mosenstein," he said. "You shall hear from me later. Good-day!" And with that curt remark Herlock Sholmes hooked his stick in my ear, and led me from the garden.
With me in tow, Sholmes strode rapidly through the street, as though anxious to reach some particular destination as soon as possible.
"Really, this case is too simple, my dear Joston!" he chuckled softly, at length. "The footprints of a member of the ape species were plainly visible on the soft ground in Mr. Mosenstein's garden. Therefore, by following the trail of Hammergugger's monkey we may confidently hope to recover Mosenstein's nugget."
"Quite so, Sholmes," I agreed. "But where is the chimpanzee? That is the question."
"Really, I despair of you at times, my dear Jotson. Good fortune has put a clue as plain as a pikestaff into our hands. With all the opportunities you have had of witnessing my methods, I am surprised that you have not grasped it."

I gazed aloft, and saw a thin line of blue smoke ascend from the chimney. Then a shower of soot shot out, followed by a screeching black figure who clutched frantically at Pinkeye's whiskers.

Feeling duly humbled in the presence of my famous friend's amazing intellect. I followed faithfully at his heels without further comment. Presently I noticed the name, "Tipdown Road," up on the side of a house, and the burly form of Inspector Pinkeye came into view. Pinkeye was solemnly regarding a rambling old house, notebook in hand. Suddenly a shower of soot flew out of a chimney on the house, and there appeared an ugly head as black as night.

"Come down out o' there, you young rip!" roared Pinkeye. "I'll have you if I have to wait here all day!"

"My dear Pinkeye," said Sholmes, approaching the irate detective, "you haven't arrested your young chimney sweep yet, then?"

Pinkeye swung round with a growl.

"No!" he snapped. "But I'll have him as sure as there's only one eye in my name! I'd have had him long ago, but I can't make anyone hear up at the house. I believe that's the selfsame boy who's been purloining door-handles in this neighbourhood. See! He's got one in his hand now!"

Sholmes and I gazed in the direction of the chimney. Certainly the bobbing black figure held something that gleamed yellow in its hand. I turned and looked at Sholmes in triumph, but the great detective avoided my gaze, and addressed himself to Pinkeye.

"Perhaps the people of the house have all gone out while the chimneys are being swept," he murmured, with a suspicion of a smile. "They may be a long time in coming back. Now, I presume you are anxious to make your capture and return to your favourite corner of the Bobbies' Rest as soon as possible? Ah, I thought so! Well, at the side of the house there is a ladder. Mount on to the roof, have your handcuffs ready, and leave the rest to me."

Inspector Pinkeye gripped Sholmes by the hand. In spite of his disparagement of my friend's amazing powers at times, he was not above accepting assistance in the hour of need. As the officer went round the house, Sholmes stopped and picked up a brickbat.

"I shall need your valuable help in this case, my trusty Jotson," he said. "Directly you see me reach the porch of the house, throw this brickbat at the figure in the chimney-pot."

Greatly wondering, I took the brick and watched Sholmes depart. When he had reached the porch I followed his instructions. With a mighty heave, I sent the brick flying in the direction of the chimney. The black figure ducked its head into the chimney-pot in the nick of time. Then it came up, gazed at me reproachfully for a second, and sent the yellow substance it held in its hand hurtling in my direction! I made a frantic effort to jump aside, but I was too late. The solid chunk hit me full on the top of my bowler-hat, sending my headgear over my eyes, and knocking me head over heels into a flower-bed!

While I sat there watching the North Star chasing the Milky Way round the firmament, I heard a familiar voice.

"Well done, Jotty, my dear fellow! You performed your part splendidly! Thanks to you, the Mosenstein gold nugget is in our hands."

"I–I thought it was on my head!" I groaned.

"Well, the weight's off you mind now," said Sholmes soothingly. He helped me to emerge from my battered bowler, and raised me from my seat on the geraniums. Then he led me, dazed, but happy with the praises ringing in my ears, to an open window at the side of the house. Together we climbed into the place. With unerring instinct, Sholmes made for the deserted library, and touched a match to the fire that was laid in the grate. Then we clambered through the window again.

"Look, Jotson!"

I gazed aloft. On the roof was Inspector Pinkeye, his handcuffs ready for action. A wisp of blue smoke curled up from the chimney-pot. Next moment a shower of soot shot out, followed by a screeching black figure with a long tail. Pinkeye started back in astonishment, and nearly fell from the roof. Then as the thing descended upon him, he remembered his duty, and snapped the darbies over the creature's wrists!

Terrified almost out of its wits, Cuthbert, the human chimpanzee, fastened its sharp teeth into one of Pinkeye's plump arms. Next instant the man and monkey rolled from the roof to the ground twenty feet below!

Fortunately, Inspector Pinkeye fell on something soft. He rose at once, rubbing his head. The ape landed on the bed of geraniums. Like lightning, Sholmes snatched my battered bowler from my head, and pulled it down over the eyes of the unfortunate Cuthbert.

By this time quite a crowd had collected in the street outside. A portion of it made its way round to the side of the house, headed by none other then Mr. Hammergugger.

"Mr. Sholmes!" cried the animal importer. "You have found him–my little Cuthbert!'

The reunion between Hammergugger and his favourite chimpanzee was touching in the extreme. Pinkeye took one look at the monkey, and faded away in the direction of the Bobbies' Rest!

That evening, with two handsome cheques in his pocket–one from Hammergugger, and the other from Mosenstein for the return of his nugget–Sholmes stood me a fish supper in the Criterion.

"A very successful day, my dear Jotson," he said, with his mouth full of chips. "That meeting with Pinkeye outside Mr. Mosenstein's house was most fortunate. It gave me the clue that led to the recovery of both the monkey and the nugget. Your health, Jotson!

No. 82

It was Christmas Eve, I had been summoned by telephone to the side of my one remaining patient. A glance informed me that he had developed oblique curvature of the off-side vertebrae, and that an immediate operation was necessary. Setting down my little black tool-bag, I extracted the various saws, files, and chisels needed for my humane task.

That operation I regard with pleasure as one of the most successful of my career. I removed the obstraneous cuticle and the veriform valvulae in a manner which would have been a credit to the surgeon royal himself. After I had signed the death certificate, I set out in high fettle for home. Never before had I been so conscious of that Yule-tide spirit of "Peace on Earth and Good Will to Men!"

As I turned into Shaker Street, in which my famous detective friend, Herlock Sholmes, and I had our apartments, I saw a long, attenuated figure a little way ahead. A bulky parcel swung from his right hand. Hastening along, I clapped the pedestrian on the shoulder.

"Ah, my dear Sholmes! Taking home the Christmas goose, I perceive?"

Herlock Sholmes regarded me with a smile.

"You have deduced rightly, Jotson!" he said. "How did you know!"

"I noticed that your hand was gripping a pair of yellow webbed feet. There was an odour of well-hung poultry in your track, and——"

"Enough, my dear Jotson!" cried my famous friend. "I see you have proved an apt pupil of my methods! Directly you began speaking, I knew you were on the right scent."

I flushed with pride at this "high" praise.

"But let us not talk shop!" I said jocularly. "This is Christmastide. Knowing that my one remaining patient is out of his pain, I can enjoy the season in comfort. You yourself have no case on hand, I believe?"

Instead of replying to my remark, Herlock Sholmes gripped my arm.

Look, Jotson!"

I followed the direction indicated by my friend's bony finger. In the middle of the muddy road almost opposite our apartments, a tall gentleman, clad in a moth-eaten over-coat was performing the most extraordinary contortions on his neck. He had just descended from a swiftly-moving bus.

As Sholmes and I hurried to his assistance, he sat up in the soft mud, and, gazing sky-wards, began making spasmodic movements with an upturned forefinger, as though counting to himself. What he was counting I utterly failed to perceive. Around him lay scattered a number of bills and other documents that had fallen from his pockets.

"The man is evidently a member of our British aristocracy!" muttered Sholmes, as we crossed the road.

"My dear Sholmes!" I panted. "What on earth makes you——"

"Simple deduction, Jotson. His poverty stricken though genteel appearance, the enormous number of tax and rate forms in his possession, and that ring that glitters on his finger. And, unless I am greatly mistaken—which I never am—he was on his way to visit our rooms."

As I helped Sholmes to raise the man, I glanced at the gold ring which the eagle eye of my astounding friend had noticed from twenty yards' range. The ring bore the crest of a famous family—a dying duck dormant with crossed battle-axes on a background of split peas.

By this time an amused and curious crowd of wayfairers was collecting. Sholmes and I lifted the dazed unfortunate to his feet, and escorted him to the house wherein we had our apartments. Mrs. Spudson, our landlady, opened the door. The good woman was not surprised that we had brought something home with us. She was well used to Sholmes turning up with an assortment of things that he had run to earth.

Repairing to our consulting-room, Sholmes offered our guest a pinch of cocaine and my favourite armchair.

"Thank you, Mr. Sholmes!" said our visitor, who had recognised the great detective . I was on my way to consult you when I met with my unfortunate side-slip!"

"Your lordship may speak freely before my friend and colleague, Dr. Jotson," said Herlock Sholmes. Sholmes discarded his coat, and slipped into his dressing-gown—that famous checked article which he had presented to him by Messrs. Isenstein and Blommbaum, otherwise the All-British Clothing Corporation, for services Sholmes had rendered in solving the mystery of the Second Hand. Then he sank into his armchair, and placed the tips of his fingers together. I found a perch on the cocaine cask.

The visitor showed surprise at Sholmes' manner of address.

"Yes," he remarked. "I am indeed Baron Battledore, of Bodkin Castle, Swapshire. I seek your aid, Mr. Sholmes. A terrible mystery is gradually driving me insane. Castle Bodkin has become haunted, though by what, I shudder to think! Hollow groans, the rattling of chains, and the shuffling of feet have reached my ears in the dead of night. It is horrible—uncanny—I cannot stand it longer! Come back with me to Bodkin

Castle, Mr. Sholmes! Although I am a member of an ancient titled family, I can still afford to offer you Christmas hospitality!"

I glanced at Sholmes anxiously. It seemed most unfortunate that this distressed client should arrive on Christmas Eve, of all times.

"I will accompany you to your ancestral home to-night, your lordship," returned Sholmes, "on one condition—that my colleague Dr. Jotson may come, too! I may need his valuable assistance in the case."

A happy smile lighted my face as the baron readily agreed.

Ten minutes later, after I had packed a valise, Herlock Sholmes picked up his violin-case, without which he seldon journeyed far afield. Then, hooking his walking-stick in my ear, the great detective followed our aristocratic client from the house.

During the short railway journey to Swapshire, Herlock Sholmes plied Baron Battledore with questions.

"Have you any enemies of whom you are aware, your lordship?"

The baron looked surprised.

"Scores," he replied; "the income-tax officials, the whole Labour Party in the House of Commons, a butler named Spivet, whom I dismissed recently for possessing a whistle——"

"A whistle!" I cried.

"A whistle!" repeated the baron. "He was always wetting it—with my rare old wines!"

Herlock Sholmes cast a pitying glance at me, and then resumed the cross-examination of our client.

"How many servants has your lordship at Bodkin Castle?" he inquired.

"Only two footmen and a cook. The others have been driven away by the recent mysterious occurrances. And these three have threatened to leave."

"Do no relatives reside with you at the castle?"

"None! I have only one relative, and he lives at Poshe Hall, over a mile away. He is my nephew, Sir Eggbert Makesplash, the heir to the Battlemore title."

"You are on good terms with your nephew, your lordship?"

"Excellent terms, my dear Mr. Sholmes. You will have the pleasure of meeting him over the Christmas table tomorrow."

"Does anyone know that you intended making the journey to London to seek my assistance?" then asked Herlock Sholmes.

"Not a soul!" replied the baron. "I told one of my footmen I might bring guests back for Christmas, and that I should probably return before midnight."

After this Herlock Sholmes relapsed into a thoughful silence.

It was past eleven o'clock when the train drew up at a little country station, and we alighted. The Baron stated that it was but a short distance to the castle. As he had hired out his remaining Ford-Royce over the holidays to a gentleman who had supplied the infantry with corn-plasters during the Great War, we hoofed it along the darkened country lanes to the baron's ancestral home.

Bodkin Castle was a fine old pile of masonry that looked as though the rats had got at it.

Passing the lodge, we arrived before the massive portal, which was opened by a sleepy-eyed footman.

"Thank 'eavans you've come 'ome, me lord!" murmured the servant. "The queer noises and shapes floatin' about has fair given me the collywobbles!"

Baron Battledore turned the colour of a ripe Gorgonzola cheese.

"N-n-nonsense, P-P-Parrott!" he stuttered. "You've been asleep, and dreaming in the servants' hall. You may now go to roost."

It was the one witticism the baron ever permitted himself, fortunately, and the footman smiled respectfully. While the man was locking up, Sholmes and I followed Baron Battledore through the spacious, holly-bedecked hall. On either side stood suits of mediaeval armour like a number of knightly sentinals. The Battledore ancestors glared down at us from between the frames of huge pictures on the walls.

Having shown us our rooms, the baron led us into the library, where he provided us with a night-cap each. Having drunk mine, I felt bolder than I had done since setting foot in this eerie old castle.

Baron Battledore, I could see, was strangely affected by the place. His eyes rolled, and his face had become pale and scared-looking. The frights he had received had brought him to the verge of a complete breakdown. He told us a gruesome story of his ancestor, the first Baron Battledore, who had had a penchant for playing "post-man's knock" on the heads of his unsuspected guests with his mailed fist. The victims were buried beneath the castle keep. It was obvious that our agitated client suspected the ghostly visitors to be none other than this playful gentleman of the eleventh century.

"Once," said Baron Battledore, "when I heard the clanking of armour, I went down to the hall. Nothing was to be seen. But as I made my way back to my room something hit me a hefty clout behind the back of the skull. When I came to my impression was it must have been a mailed fist."

"Or a piece of plaster from the ceiling," I suggested brightly.

Baron Battledore glared. For some reason or other he had taken a violent dislike to me.

"Ah, well," murmured Herlock Sholmes, stretching himself, "let us retire! You may sleep peacefully to-night, your lordship. If your ghostly knight comes I will lay him for you."

After this we went to our separate rooms. Personally, I undressed and got into bed, but a sense of strange things pending kept me awake. Slipping on a dressing-gown, I crept into Sholmes' room for a chat. The room was in darkness. No response came to my knock. Opening the door, I entered. A shaft of moonlight rested upon a pile of white sheets. The bed was empty.

"Sholmes is on the track of the ghost!" I muttered to myself.

Going back to my room, I waited anxiously for the return of my amazing friend. But no Sholmes appeared.
Suddenly my blood froze, my hair rose like a parrot's crest, and my knees became of the consistency of Jivvers' jelly. From down the hall the faint clanking of armour came to my ears!
Then I pulled myself together. Sorry I was that Sholmes had not sought my assistance in his midnight quest. But my old friend might be in deadly peril. Never should it be said that he was deserted by his faithful Jotson!
Holding a candlestick in my hand, I made my way down the stairs. The lighted candle caused the suits of armour in the hall to cast weird shadows on the walls. The silence was positively chilly.
"Sholmes! Sholmes!" I muttered anxiously.
There was no response. It was uncanny. I began to wish I'd stayed between the blankets. But as I was about to retreat from this eerie part of the old castle I saw something small and yellow on the oaken floor. It was a real golden English sovereign—one of the pre-war variety!
In my excitement, I forgot Sholmes and the ghost. Instead, I saw a vision of unlimited fish-suppers. I stopped to pick it up, when——
"Ooch!"
That agonised remark left my lips as I sprang bolt upright, clasping the back of my dressing-gown. What had felt like a pick-axe had caught me bending!
Trembling with fear and pain at this uncanny experience, I turned about to see who or what had done the cowardly deed. All I saw was a motionless suit of armour. It struck me as queer that it wore long, pointed boots of tempered steel. Then, to my horror, the suit of armour placed a mailed finger to its visor.
"'Sh-sh!" it said.
I stood rooted to the spot.
"'Sh—'sh! 'Sh—'sh, my dear Jotson!" went on the suit of armour. "Put out that candle. If you must see this adventure through, hide in that alcove!"
"Sholmes!" I gasped, in heartfelt relief. "I thought you were the ghost!"
Sholmes chuckled.
"Did my goodly boot of pointed steel feel so ethereal, then, my noble Jotty! I came down and got into this tin Mallaby-Deeley the better to watch for the spook."
"Of course it will prove to be that butler fellow, Spivet," I said lightly. "He's hanging around the castle and playing tricks for vengeance on the old baron. But what's that you've got in your hand?"
Sholmes held a large round weight at the end of a short piece or rope.
"I found this in the kitchen," he said. "It is a Christmas-pudding. With this rope tied round it, it makes an excellent mediaeval-looking weapon. But get into hiding, Jotty!"
A sound from the direction of the library reached us. Quickly I got into an alcove in the hall and blew out the candle. Sholmes remained motionless. What terrible sight were we to see?
We had not long to wait. There was a clanking of chains and deep groans. Then out of the library stepped an old-time knight, a short length of chain trailing behind one foot. His hands were encased in chain gloves, with gauntlets attached. His face was pale and luminous.
The moonlight that streamed into the hall via the open door of the dining-room lighted up the golden coin I had failed to retrieve. The knight passed my alcove so close that I might have touched him. But apparently he was hard up himself, for he bent down to pick up the soverign, even as I had done.
Sholmes' pointed boot of steel shot out as though operated by a string. It caught the ghostly knight on the same tender spot as it had caught me.
"Yoop! Yow-wow!"
The ghostly knight grasped the back of his leathern hand-me-downs and shot upright. As he did so Herlock Sholmes brought the Christmas-pudding down on his steel helmet with a dull thud. The knight fell prone. Sholmes' ruse of placing the golden sovereign on the floor had given him the grand opportunity he had sought.
"Quick, Jotson—fetch a tin-opener! The kitchen is just through the end of the hall."
I lighted my candle and started on my errand. The scared faced of baron Battledore and the servants peered over the broad banisters.
"It's all right, your lordship!" called out Sholmes cheerily. "I've laid your ghost. You have nothing more to fear!"
On my return with the tin-opener I found Sholmes, Baron Battledore, and the servants grouped round the prone figure of the knight. As I held my candle above the victim of the Christmas-pudding, our client gave a cry of amazement.
"Sir Eggbert Makesplash!" he gulped.
"None other," siad Sholmes, with a smile. "He has dressed up and put luminous paint on his face for the sole purpose of scaring you out of your skin—and the title. It was a fiendish scheme. Too cunning to give you a dose of Rough-on-Rats, he hoped, none the less to speed your departure from this sphere and assume the Battledore title himself!"
When Sir Eggbert Makesplash came round and saw Sholmes calmly swinging the fatal Christmas-pudding in his hand, he broke down utterly and confessed all. He had discovered a secret underground passage between Poshe Hall and the library of Bodkin Castle, and it had given him the idea of playing upon the nerves of his august relative.
The scoundrel was assisted from the castle by the carpet-slippers of Baron Battledore and the footmen. But just as he thought he was getting off easily, Sholmes added his pointed steel boot to help speed the parting guest.

1922

THE LOST PERSIAN

No. 83

Overwork had brought about a temporary breakdown in the health of my amazing friend, Mr. Herlock Sholmes. Although the season was mid-winter, he developed the alarming habit of making vigorous swipes with his hand in frantic endeavours to catch imaginary flies from the end of his acquiline nose. At times he complained of feeling old and decrepit. These alarming symptoms of a brain creaking beneath the strain imposed upon it caused me considerable anxiety.

Of course, I would have operated on my friend free of charge, with the greatest of pleasure, but to my astonishment, when I suggested grafting a monkey gland to his left ear, he was positively rude about the matter. But this I attributed to his overwrought condition.

Then Mrs. Spudson, our landlady, told me about her sister, Mrs. Spivitt, who made a genteel living by letting apartments in a small country town, Slushby-cum-Slush in Slopshire. To this place, after much persuasions, I induced Sholmes to accompany me for a long week-end.

As I expected, the change proved of the greatest benefit for Sholmes. No longer was he bothered by flies on his intellectual face, no longer did he see purple lizards floating in the air before his eyes.

"This is peace, my dear Jotson," he said contentedly, while we waited for breakfast one morning. "It may not be so exciting as the last holiday I spent in Killarney, but it is none the worse for that."

He selected a book from the ancient volumes in the small bookcase in Mrs. Spivitt's parlour and dropped into a chair. Our furnished apartment was on the ground floor facing the street, and I crossed to the window and gazed out to where a few early pedestrians were doing gymnastics on the frost-covered pavements.

Suddenly a stout and obviously excited lady slid past, and brought up all sitting outside of our front door. A few moments later there was a loud peal on the bell. Above the sizzling of frying kippers, excited female voices were discernible in conversation. Footsteps sounded on the stairs, and there entered the room, Mrs. Spivitt, followed by the stout lady.

"I hopes you'll pardon me, Mr. Sholmes," said our landlady, "but I was telling my friend, Mrs. Nobbson, the other day as you were staying here, and——"

"I'm in such distress, Mr. Sholmes, sir!" burst in Mrs. Nobbson excitedly. "Fatima has gone! She went out, and I've seen nothing of her since."

"Madam," I said severely. "Mr. Sholmes is staying in Slushby for the benefit of his health. He is not open to accept a case of any kind. You would be well advised to go to an employment agency and apply for another cook."

"Another cook?" shrieked Mrs. Nobbson. "Fatmia is worth all the cooks in Slushby! Fatima is a Persian—a beautiful Persian, sir!"

I preened myself and stroked my moustache meditatively. I imaged myself in the role of confidential friend and assistant to Sholmes, rescuing the fair Fatmia from the hands of scoundrels who had kidnapped her from her kind English guardian.

"Of course, that alters the case, somewhat, madam." I began, when Sholmes interrupted me.,

"Mrs. Nobbson," he said. "I am staying in Slushby for the benefit of my health, as my friend Dr. Jotson, has so truthfully remarked. But I am always ready to assist beauty in distress." He bowed low. "When did you last see the cat!"

"C-c-cat!" I stammered.

Mrs. Nobboson gave me a look that would have withered an oak tree.

"Of course," she snorted. "What did you think it was—a Persian camel! It was the finest blue Persian cat that ever——"

"Quite so, quite so," mused Sholmes. "But answer my question, madam."

"Fatima jumped through the parlour window just after ten o'clock last night and hasn't been seen since."

"Have you inquired of the neighbours? None of them has heard of her, I suppose?'

"Oh, yes, they heard her on the tiles up till four o'clock this morning, but she hasn't been seen since last night."

"Well, you can safely leave the matter to me. Mrs. Nobbson," said Herlock Sholmes. "Return here at eleven o'clock, and then, I hope to be able to restore the wayward Fatima to your arms."

When the gratified Mrs. Nobbson had departed and Mrs. Spivitt had gone to dish up the luscious kippers for our breakfast, Sholmes picked up his book again.

"I have been reading 'the Pied Piper of Hamelin,' my dear Jotson," he said. "A most amusing poem. The idea of 'long rats, short rats, thin rats, fat rats, grey rats, black rats,' all dancing along behind a man in response to his piping, appeals to me immensely. I think I shall borrow Master Spivitt's tin whistle and go round the town bringing all the Slushby cats to heel. Then Mrs. Nobbson can pick out her property from among the dancing feline horder. A romantic idea, eh, Jotty?"

I shook my head sadly. In spite of the mental renovation afforded my amazing friend by our holiday, it was evident there still remained a few bats in his belfry.

At breakfast, Sholmes' appetite was enormous! Even the bones, skins and tails of the nutrious kippers disappeared like magic from his plate. He actually handed Mrs. Spivitt half-a-crown to buy another half-dozen to fry for his consumption.

The scent of these kippered herrings filled the house, and glad as I was to see my friend in such good form, I had to take a walk round the local gasworks for a breath of fresh air.

When I returned to our apartments, I found Master Spivitt, our landlady's nine year old son, in tears. Sholmes, it appeared, had borrowed his penny tin whistle without asking, and had sailed forth into the streets of Slushby to the shrill but martial air, "The March of Tarzan." At this startling news I became seriously concerned for the welfare of my old friend and companion.

At eleven o'clock, when Mrs. Nobbson arrived at the house, there was no sign of Herlock Sholmes. But just after the hour we heard a shrill piping. We rushed to the window to gaze upon the truly astounding sight!

Herlock Sholmes was marching down the centre of the street piping unmusically on Master Spivitt's tin whistle. On the pavements a crowd of school children jostled one another. Behind Sholmes trooped a horde of cats such as I have never seen in my life – long cats, short cats, thin cats, fat cats, black cats, tabby cats, tom cats and she cats, all miaowing and cavorting.

Mrs. Nobbson gave a loud cry. Next moment she dashed out of the house, burst through the crowd of laughing children and snatched up a large blue Persian cat from the midst of the feline host.

"Fatima!" she cried in accents of relief. "How am I to thank you Mr. Sholmes!"

"By saying no more about it, my dear Mrs. Nobbson," said Herlock Sholmes gallantly.

Gazing from the window, my admiration for my amazing friend knew no bounds.

"Wonderful, my dear Sholmes!" I called out. "That you should be able to emulate the 'Pied Piper of Hamelin,' and attract all the cats in the town by the magic of your piping, would have been incredible to me but for the evidence of my own eyes."

Herlock Sholmes smiled inscrutably. Then he darted into the house and slammed the door against the feline horde. I ran to receive my amazing friend. Then I stopped short, staggered back, and drew my pocket handkerchief.

"Phew! W-w-what the——"

Sholmes tossed the tin whistle to the delighted Master Spivitt, and made his way to the backyard. I followed at a respectable distance.

"The tin whistle lent a necessary touch of romance to what would otherwise have been a prosaic case, my dear Jotson," he said light-heartedly. "Mrs. Nobbson and the other worthy residents of Slushby-cum-Slush, will have something to talk about at the local bunfights for the rest of their lives. Probably some local poet will perpetrate a peom about me. But now to reveal the secret of the magic piping!"

And from each of his bulging pockets, Sholmes drew forth the remains of a dozen large, powerful kippers and deposited them in the dustbin.

1924

THE SCHWOTTEM RAY

No. 84

"Great pip!"

It was seldom indeed that I allowed myself the luxury of any such juvenile expression. Nevertheless, that exclamation escaped my lips as I reached across the breakfast-table and drew that 'Daily Buzz" towards me.

Herlock Sholmes, his slim fingers delicately dissecting a kipper, smiled patiently.

"You are surprised, my dear Jotson? And yet what more natural than that Mynheer Schwottem's great discovery should be stolen?"

"You have seen the newspapers, Sholmes?"

"No, I have seen nothing–except a couple of dozen bills from butchers, bakers, and rate-collectors. But it was perfectly obvious to the meanest intelligence that the notorious Ray apparatus would be stolen. Are not ninety per cent of modern inventions stolen by someone or another? Go down to the Thames Embankment any fine night, my dear Jotson, and inquire of the poor, homeless wanderers you will find there. Most of them were inventors, the remainder devotees of that obnoxious game known as auction bridge–gentlemen who failed to lead trumps and suffered the inevitable penalty."

With a dainty gesture he flicked a kipper-bone from the lapel of his becoming mauve dressing-gown.

Heaving a sigh, I turned to the front page of the 'Buzz" and perused the print beneath the bold headlines which first had attracted my eye.

"THE SCHWOTTEM RAY STOLEN!"

That was what the newspaper shrieked across its front page. And below there followed an account of how Mynheer Schwottem, the discoverer of the patent ray, of which all England had been talking for the past week, had had the ray apparatus filched from him.

In the midst of my perusal of the meagre newspaper account of the affair, Mrs. Spudson, our landlady, appeared.

"Inspector Pinkeye to see you, sir!"
"Hah! Let him enter!" said Sholmes.
He rose gracefully from the breakfast-table, rolled the cocaine cask within easy reach of his arm-chair, and reseated himself near the empty fire-grate.
A minute later our old friend, Inspector Pinkeye, entered the room. The nervous way in which he tore tufts of hair from his bushy moustache did not escape the eagle eye of the famous sleuth.
"You are upset, my dear Pinkeye," drawled Sholmes, taking a liberal pinch of cocaine. "The Schwottem Ray case, I suppose?"
"You're right, Mr. Sholmes," said the Inspector, "though how you guessed I cannot make out. At one-thirty this morning I received a telephone message from Mynheer Schwottem informing us that his secret ray apparatus had been stolen. It was in my office at the Yard at the time, and I told him he could rest assured that heaven and earth would be moved to recover the invention. When I woke up seven hours later I discovered that Mynheer Schwottem himself was also missing."

Schwottem pressed a button on the ray and a taxicab, that had been rattling along, came to a stop and the wheels fell off.

"Missing!" I gasped.

"Vanished! Vamooshed! Skiddooed! Anything you like!" Inspector Pinkeye tore another tuft from his ample moustache and savagely scattered it upon the carpet.

"I called at the Hotel Rookham, Pimlico, where he has been staying. He had left there the previous evening."

"No mystery in that," murmured Sholmes, placing the tips of the elongated fingers together. "I know the Rookham."

"The worst of it is, I've never seen Mynheer Schwottem," groaned Pinkeye. "He's a bit of a mystery man, as you know. Beyond the fact that he was fat, wore a heavy flaxen moustache and beard and blue spectacles. I can get no good description of him. Help me to find him and his ray apparatus, Mr. Sholmes, and if ever you are arrested for not paying your income tax, I'll visit you in prison."

A minute later our old friend, Inspector Pinkeye, entered the room, tearing nervously at his hair.

"You may rely upon me, Pinkeye," said Sholmes quietly. He reached into the coal-scuttle for his valuable Vhadistrubius violin. "Don't hurry away, Pinkeye. But it is ten o'clock, and I must run through Yugelstein's thumb-and-finger exercise in B sharp."

"Er-er–I have an appointment at the dentist's," muttered Pinkeye, rising hurriedly. "My corns have troubled me fearfully lately. Au revoir–and if you have news for me I shall be in the Yard."

"Back or Scotland?" drawled Sholmes, with that humorous twinkle that always accompanied a display of his scintillating wit.

After the burly inspector had fallen down the flight of stairs leading from our apartments, and had been shown out by Mrs. Spudson, Sholmes began to play his violin. Sitting opposite him, I employed myself sharpening a few handsaws and chisels, for I had an appointment to remove a brace of inflated tonsils from one of my patients that afternoon.

But we were not to be left in peace. Mrs. Spudson put her head into the room and shrieked that there was a "furrin gent" on the premises.

"A foreigner!" exclaimed Sholmes, desisting from his musical efforts. "Did he give his name?"

"Mynheer Schwottem, he called himself, sir!" replied our landlady. "He repeated it ten times."

Both Sholmes and I were on our feet.

"Mynheer Schwottem!" cried Sholmes. "Show him up."

Hardly had Sholmes replaced his violin in the scuttle and I had put my surgical instruments in my little black bag, than Mrs. Spudson appeared again. With characteristic politeness she ushered our visitor into the room.

"The furrin gent!" she announced.

Stepping outside, she closed the door as Sholmes greeted the guest. The latter was a man of distinguished appearance. He was about five feet four in height, ninety inches in circumference, splay-footed, wore blue glasses, and had the most amazing jungle of face-fungus that I had ever set eyes upon. So luxurious was the yellow beard, that it was imposible for me to see whether he wore a collar or not. Under his arm he carried a large brown-paper parcel. When he spoke his voice sounded as though it were coming from his fashionable, elastic-sided boots.

"Mynheer Herlock Sholmes, aind't it? Vos dot not so? Yes? No?"

"Exactly." replied my famous friend. "Pray be seated, Mynheer Schwottem. Jotson, produce the pickled gherkins."

As I took the bottle from the sideboard and placed it hospitably within reach of our visitor, I noticed that Shomes was regarding him intently.

"Ach!" exclaimed our client, helping himself from the jar. "I vos in sad troubles, Mynheer Sholmes."

"Trouble?" drawled Shomes. "You're found, aind't it–er–I mean, aren't you?"

"Found! I half never been lost–nein! It vos der ray!"

"But you have it in that parcel," said Sholmes.

Plainly our client was perturbed at Sholmes' perspicacity. Personally, I had imagined that the brown-paper contined a new wireless set or a dozen haddocks. But the look on the face of Mynheer Schwottem–or, rather, on that part not concealed by his massive whskers–showed that Sholmes was nearer the mark.

With fat hands that trembled, he unwrapped the parcel, to reveal a metal cylinder, a couple of electric batteries, and a Dutch cheese.

"Look vot I vill do," grunted our client.

He rose and held the cylinder near the window. Sholmes and I gazed down upon the traffic of Shaker Street. Schwottem pressed a button. A taxi-cab that had been rattling along at three miles per hour came to a dead stop, and three wheels fell off.

"Plaster pills!" gasped I. "Amazing!"

A boy with a pea-shooter was standing on the kerb. Evidently the flabbergasted taxi-driver imagined he had something to do with his misfortunes. The driver stumbled off his vehicle, collared the lad, and cuffed him soundly. Policemen arrived on the scene. There was a whirling of arm and legs; a free-for-all fight developed on the spot.

"Der ray vos der greatest invention for der cause of peace in der world," remarked Mynheer Schwottem, blowing a Tube train near Shaker Street Station off the rails. "I vill now blow der head off der captain of one of der British battleships in Blackpool Harbour."

"One moment!" said Sholmes. "You'll be hurting someone in a minute. Have another gherkin, and——"

At that moment I saw a man coming down Shaker Street in a Ford car. He was a most detestable person, and I owed him one-and-sixpence.

"Quick, Mynheer!" I cried, "Turn the ray on that Tin Lizzie!"

With a smile, Mynheer Schwottem pressed the button. There was a clatter of tin. The Ford had disappeared, and the street was scattered with what looked like fragments of old tomato-cans. I gave a grim chuckle as I saw my enemy seated in the middle of the road, gazing round in blank bewilderment and rubbing his coat-tails.

"Magnificent!" I cried."The ray is the invention of the century. When it is on sale at the shops, I'll buy a couple."

"Ach, you do not understand!" roared Mynheer Schwottem. He pressed the button and blew a bus over. "It is no goot. Dat bus, for instance, it should have been nodings but matchwood."

For a moment I thought our client was suffering from batisimus belfritis–in other words, bats in the belfry. Overwork and worry in connection with his great discovery may have affected his bokoranium.

"No good?" I echoed. "The Schwottem Ray no good?"

"Dis ray vas no goot," said the visitor gloomily. "It is not der Schwottem Ray at all! Nein!"

Even my illustrious friend, Herlock Sholmes, evinced a modicum of surprise. I distinctly saw his ears give a slight flap as he paused in the act of conveying a pinch of the best cocaine to his aquiline proboscis.

"This is interesting," he said. "Pray explain yourself, Mynheer."

"I vill explain meinself mit der exceeding clearness. I vas a Dutchman dot vos come to dis country for to try and sell der ray I haf invented. Last nights somebodies come to mein hotel and vot you call snaffle him, aind't it? Dot's clear, Yes? No?"

"As clear as pea-soup," I remarked jocularly.

Sholmes frowned.

"Proceed, Mynheer."

Schwottem proceeded.

"Ven der thief snaffle mein lofely invention I was snoring asleep. Ven I vake up der ray was gone and dis vun left in der blace of it."

"Ah, I see," drawled Sholmes. "A thief stole the ray apparatus from the room in your hotel, and left another invention in its place. The apparatus in your hand is not so powerful as your own invention."

"Nein! Dot is so. Dis vas a fraud – vat you call 'all fiddlesticks,' aind't it?"

"Extraordinary!" muttered Sholmes. "On the evening prior to returning you had also had a shock. You had seen the hotel bill."

Mynheer Schwottem gasped.

"Vot makes you tink so, hein?"

"You yourself left the hotel, quietly during the night," said my brilliant friend. "Now, whom do you suspect of having robbed you?"

"Vun rascally German named Von Schneider," replied our client. "And I haf reasons to believe der fellow haf gone to Scotland. Follow him there. Mynheer Sholmes, and find mein lofely ray, and I will pay you a hundred marks. Puseness calls me back to der Hook of Holland, but you can write to me at de Post Office, Ammercheeseron. Goot-mornings!"

"One moment!" said Sholmes. "Dr. Joston and I are taking a taxi. We will drop you on your way."

A gale of wind was blowing in the street. The three of us waited outside the house until Sholmes summoned a taxi. He ushered our client and myself into the vehicle, and whispered to the driver.

Rapidly the taxi bowled through the London traffic. Suddenly it came to an abrupt halt.

"Vere we vas?" demanded our client, startled.

"Scotland Yard!" replied Sholmes.

The fat foreigner leaped to his feet with a snarl like an enraged bull-frog. There was a click like a penny dropping in the gas-meter; then to my utter amazement, I saw that our caller was wearing a pair of darbies on his wrists.

Calmly filling his pipe with a couple of ounces of black shag, Sholmes ordered me to open the door of the cab. On the pavement was Inspector Pinkeye.

"A prisoner for you, Pinkeye," said Sholmes, picking a card from the foreigner's waistcoat-pocket. "Let me introduce you to Herr Schneider, who stole the famous Schwottem Ray last night. This apparatus is the true Schwottem Ray. Knowing that I am the only man in England likely to get on his track, he tried to send me on a false scent to Scotland. Then he intended catching the boat to Harwich to sell his booty to a foreign Government. I will now trace the real Mynheer Schwottem for you. By the way, you might look under the dyed beard of your prisoner. He has a bomb concealed there."

When the fuming Schneider had been taken to the cooler by Pinkeye, Sholmes leaped back into the taxi. He gave the driver the address written on the card he had extracted from Schneider's pocket.

"It is likely that we shall find Schwottem there," said Sholmes, as we bowled along. "I deduce that he suspected Schneider of being on his track, and went to his address to accuse him of the theft."

Sholmes' theory was proved to the hilt. In a cellar, gagged and bound, we found the missing Dutch inventor. He had gone to Schneider's address, and had been captured and gagged by the scoundrel who was making preparations for his getaway.

The gratitude of Mynheer Schwottem knew no bounds. He presented Sholmes with a fiver, three Dutch cigars, a couple of hyacinth bulbs, and invited both of us to call and see his uncle, the Burgomaster of Schwenkschiffen, next time we were in Holland.

Leaving us, Schwottem proceeded to Scotland Yard to identify his ray and Scheider.

As Sholmes and I drove back to Shaker Street, my curiosity could be restrained no longer.

"My dear Sholmes!" I cried. "How did you know? I never dreamt our client was other than an honest man."

Sholmes smiled patiently.

"From the first I suspected he was not all he professed to be. When waiting in Shaker Street for the taxi, a gale of wind was blowing. Yet his beard never swayed to the icy summer blast. Therefore, I deduced he had a bomb or some other heavy missle attached to it out of sight. In the taxi I distinctly caught a glimpse of the infernal machine, with 'Made in Germany' stamped on the percussion-cap. The case was ridiculously simple. But let us stop at the corner and regale ourselves with a couple of fried dabs and parsley."

THE MYSTERY OF THE GREEN CRAB

No. 85

"A letter for you, sir!"

My famous friend. Mr. Herlock Sholmes, took the envelope from the grubby paw of our landlady and scanned the crest on the flap. It consisted of three cannon-balls, rampant on a canister of grape-shot.

Sholmes' hatchet-like face lighted perceptibly.

"From my old friend, Colonel Curry-Cummerbund, of Cocklemouth-cum-Cookham," he volunteered.

He tore open the envelope, and read the contents.

"The colonel wants us to spend the week-end at his seaside bungalow, Jotson. An opportune invitation, methinks. Can you manage to get away?"

"Yes, to-morrow," I replied. "My patient will not survive the next visit to him, I fear."

I flicked a tear from my cheek with a piece of blotting-paper with which I happened to be toying. The thought affected me deeply. I had to keep my patient alive—if not too robust—for many years. That by my professional skill I could have accomplished it, I am certain, but for inadvertently giving him a dose of rough on rats in mistake for syrup of figs.

The prospect of a holiday appealed to Sholmes keenly. Although no detective myself, even I could discern how his spirits had risen. He stood on his head on the lid of the cocaine cask, and kicked his check slippers to the ceiling. Resuming a more normal position, he gave me a playful dig in the waistcoat that sent me backwards into the coal-scuttle.

On the following day, after I had left a wreath at the house of my late patient Sholmes and I took train for the old-world fishing village of Cocklemouth-cum-Cookham. Colonel Curry-Cummerbund himself was at the station to meet us, and gallantly insisted on carrying Sholmes' tin of shag to the waiting bus.

A delightful penny ride along the promenade, where the invigorating odour of seaweed and whelks wafted to our nostrils, brought us to Howitzer House, the colonel's residence. Here the colonel's sole retainer, a spry old Army servant of ninety-seven, took our luggage upstairs. Sholmes followed, carrying the cocaine cask and his violin, while I brought up the rear with the tin of shag.

As we dressed for dinner the veteran entertained us with a thrilling account of how he saved the British tanks at the Battle of Inkerman. But for him the troops would have had the supplies of water cut-off, and have been forced to consume their lime-juice rations neat. For this magnificent feat the fine old soldier had been rewarded by having a sentence of ninety days C.B. reduced to only sixty.

After dinner Colonel Curry-Cummerbund, Sholmes, and I took our ease on deck-chairs on a balcony overlooking the sea. The sun, a blaze of glory like a poached egg, setting behind the cockle-sheds to the west, gave a mellow touch to the peaceful scene.

"This is bliss!" I murmured, as I quietly dropped over the balcony the Flor de Stingaree cigar given to me by the colonel.

Sholmes asphyxiated a cloud of midges as he lighted his pipeful of shag, and sent a cloud of acrid smoke swirling in the air.

"You are right, my dear Jotson," he said contentedly. "A peaceful holiday, far from the atmosphere of crime and criminals, is what I have sighed for during the last thirty-five years!"

We listened to the colonel's thrilling story of how he rode the winner on the Grand National switchback at Wembley. Then, just as our host was starting an account of a shooting exploit, by which he won a furry Felix the cat mascot at the same Exhibition, the old soldier-servant announced a visitor.

To our amazement, the caller was none other than Inspector Pinkeye, of Scotland Yard.

"Bless me, Pinkeye!" exclaimed Sholmes, after he had introduced him to the colonel. "What strange case has brought you to Cocklemouth-cum-Cookham, of all places, at this merry holiday season?"

"The mystery of the green crab," answered Pinkeye darkly.

He drew the back of his hand across his mouth. The colonel, noticing the unconscious action, called for his servant to bring a jug of iced cocoa.

"The green crab!" I exclaimed. "What's that?"

"Ah!" said Pinkeye, even more darkly. "That is what I have to find out. But I have a shrewd suspicion."

"What?" I asked eagerly. "That it's a lobster?"

Pinkeye gave me a nasty look, and turned to Herlock Sholmes.

"This would have been a case after your own heart, Mr. Sholmes," he said. "Fortunately, I have practically solved the mystery now. Yesterday the local police telephoned to Scotland Yard to seek my expert aid in solving the curious case of Benjamin Bagwash!"

"Benjamin Bagwash!" exclaimed the colonel, gripping his chair. "Not old Benjamin Bagwash?"

"None other," answered Pinkeye. "It seems, Mr. Sholmes, that Bagwash is a well-known local character who lives alone in a cottage called the Hippsyhoys. He has been regarded for years as being a wealthy old miser. The day before yesterday he was found unconscious sitting in a gooseberry-bush in his own back garden. He was removed in a wheelbarrow to the Cocklemouth Cottage Hospital, and found to have the acute collywobbles."

"Collywobbles!" I remarked. "Doubtless you mean the patient was suffering from intermittent hypollocisis of the thaumaturgical duodenum?"

"Ahem—y-yes! What you said, doctor!"

Pinkeye took a draught from his goblet of iced cocoa, and resumed:

"Well, after Bagwash had been put to bed in hospital, a startling discovery was made. A lady called Mrs. Noggins, who went to the Hippsyhoys three times a week to do charring, found that a purse of golden sovereigns, which the old miser kept in the soup-tureen, had disappeared."

"Stolen?" cried the colonel.

"Clearly," remarked Pinkeye. "Since coming to Cocklemouth-cum-Cookham I have been putting two and two together. When I saw old Benjamin Bagwash in the hospital ward he was slightly dilirious. But he kept repeating these remarkable words: 'At the back of the green crab under the shell.' My theory is that someone who knew of the existence of the gold sent Bagwash a present of a crab. The old man, all unsuspecting, opened it, and consumed the portion from under the shell at the back of the crab.

"As later he was peacefully plucking gooseberries in his garden he was attacked by the—er—what Dr. Jotson said, and fell unconscious. Meantime, the sender of the crab, who doubtless had watched the sufferings of his victim, entered the house and snaffled the doings from the soup-tureen."

Pinkeye shot four feet into the air, and an agonised howl left his lips. There was the green crab clinging to his coat tails.

A queer smile hovered over the lean face of my famous friend as Pinkeye finished.

"Then you won't need my assistance, my dear Pinkeye?" he remarked. "I may enjoy my holiday in peace?"

You may, Mr. Sholmes," said the bluff inspector, with a laugh. "The case is as good as ended. Although, unfortunately, the last remains of the particularly green crab of which poor Bagwash partook were not to be found in the dustbin at the Hippsyhoys, I have no doubt they can be traced. And so can the thief."

"But supposing Benjamin Bagwash did not partake of a crab of any descripton?" murmured Sholmes quietly.

"He must have done!" replied Pinkeye emphatically. "It fits in excactly with my theory. Besides, how otherwise would he have got the—the—er—collywobbles?"

Yawning gently, Sholmes raised his long, lean frame from the chair.

"Let us retire to our beds," said he. "May you bring the mystery of the green crab to a satisfactory end as speedily as you imagine, my dear Pinkeye!"

To my surprise, instead of seeking his bed, Herlock Sholmes spent a few minutes in the colonel's library. The book that attracted his attention was the "Cocklemouth-cum-Cookham and District Directory."

When he had carefully perused it, I inquired what he had been seeking. In response he merely gave a gruff chuckle, and poked his long forefinger playfully in the ribs.

On the following morning Colonel Curry-Cummerbund announced that he had an important appointment at a meeting held in connection with a sports tournament. Being President of the Cocklemouth-cum-Cookham Shove-ha'penny Club, he could not very well fail to turn up at the meetings when the date of the local autumn tournament was to be decided.

When the colonel had set off, appropriately dressed in a gay silk hat, immaculate wash-leather gloves, red and green blazer, white flannel trousers, yellow spats, and brown sand-shoes, and wearing a gilt ha'penny, souvenir of the last shove-ha'penny tournament, on his gunmetal watchchain, Sholmes and I discussed our plans for spending the morning.

"That fine sportsman, our host, has fired me with the desire to disport myself to-day, my dear Jotson," said Sholmes. "Let us purchase nets and go a-shrimping."

Hunting for elusive shrimp in the thunderous surf along the seashore appealed to my mood, too. Leaving Howitzer House, Sholmes and I brought a brace of shrimping-nets, and sauntered on to the beach. There we discarded our boots and stockings, and disported ourselves.

I was in the act of chasing a vigerous young cockle across some rocks when I heard a gruff voice. It was Inspector Pinkeye, who had come down to the pebbly beach.

Sholmes and I placed our nets down, and donning our footwear, went to greet him.

"Well, what luck with the green crab mystery?" inquired Sholmes.

"Good progress, Mr. Sholmes," answered the inspector, smiling. "Anxious to trace the origin of the green crab that poor Benjamin Bagwash must had eaten, I have questioned some of the honest fishermen of Cocklemouth. They informed me that a special variety of crab, bright green of colour, is sometimes caught in these waters. They hadn't any by them first thing this morning. When, however, I called again on them at ten o'clock, they were able to supply me with one."

He opened a wicker basket he had with him, and showed us a large live crab. It was grass green in hue, and had powerful claws which it waved threateningly.

With characteristic boldness, Sholmes took the crustacean by the back, and held it up for inspection with a powerful magnifying-glass.

I see, my dear Pinkeye," he drawled. "This crab was given you by the honest fishermen?"

"I bought it," corrected Pinkeye.

"Quite so," agreed Sholmes. "You 'bought it,' my dear fellow—with a vengeance! This is but an ordinary crab that has been dipped in a dye-tub!"

With a gesture of contempt, Sholmes tossed the crab on to a deck-chair, and took the wicker basket from Pinkeye's hand.

"See, Pinkeye," he remarked, "You will notice that the sides of this basket are streaked with the green dye rubbed from the crab's shell. Those honest fishermen have sold you a pup, if I may so describe the transaction."

Giving a deep groan, Pinkeye sank back into the deck-chair, and grasped his forehead in his hand. Next instant he shot four feet into the air, and an agonised howl left his lips.

"Yow! Ooops! Garoogh! I'm stung!"

As he spun round we saw that the green crab was clinging affectionately to his coat-tail with its powerful claws.

"Yaroooogh! Wow! Call it off!" shrieked Pinkeye, doing a war-dance. "Slaughter it!"

"Keep calm—keep calm, my dear Pinkeye," he said. "I will then smite the ferocious crustacean with the deck-chair."

After accidentally awarding the unfortunate inspector half a dozen mighty thwacks with the chair, Sholmes eventally smote the crab, and caused it to let go its hold and scuttle hurriedly into the sea.

Heartrendering were the moans of the unlucky inspector as he nursed his injured anatomy.

"Pinkeye," said Sholmes, "you cannot do without me, after all. Your theory of Bagwash's missing gold and his mysterious illness is all wrong. Come with me, my dear fellow."

Walking from the beach, Sholmes led the inspector and myself to the railway station. Here, to our astonishment, he brought three tickets for Little Sniggersby, an almost unknown village four miles distant. So well had Sholmes arranged everything, that we caught the only train that day, and duly arrived at

Sniggersby two and a half hours after our departure from Cocklemouth.

In the straggling little village Sholmes stopped opposite an attractive hostelry almost hidden behind a large chestnut-tree and the outhouse of a fried-fish establishment.

"Note the signboard of the inn," commanded Sholmes quietly.

Pinkeye and I looked up, and an exclamation left our lips simultaneously.

"The Green Crab!"

"Yes," said Sholmes, smiling, "it is the Green Crab Inn, though the crab on the sign board looks more like a spider. We will now go round the building. Remember the oft-repeated words of poor Benjamin Bagwash—'at the back of the Green Crab, under the shell.'"

"The shell!" echoed Pinkeye, utterly bewildered.

"This may prove to be a large fancy seashell, such as some people use on their garden rockeries," said Sholmes, "or it may be a brass shell-case, a souvenir of the Great War. The matter is quickly settled."

Sure enough, at the back of the Green Crab was a large fancy sea-shell, decorating the corner of a bed of sweet-smelling beetroots. Without troubling to seek permission from the proprietor of the inn, Sholmes obtained a spade from a tool-shed. With it he dug under the shell.

Suddenly he stopped. When he rose upright again, he held in his hand a purse of golden sovereigns!

"The mystery is solved," he said. "When you mentioned the strange remark of Bagwash in hospital, Pinkeye, I shrewdly suspected he had an inn in mind. So I confirmed this by looking up a district directory, which showed the Green Crab licensed house was situated at Little Sniggersby. Doubtless the collywobbles with which Bagwash suffered were due to a prolonged visit to the Green Crab, followed by exposure to the fierce rays of the August sun. He succumbed into a gooseberry bush upon arriving home."

"But—but the gold!" stammered Pinkeye. "Why did he hide that behind the inn?"

"Clearly because he was afraid even that the charlady might rob him," replied Sholmes. "Evidently he is a very unpleasant old miser. He chose the ground under the shell to hide the money, because the shell formed a good mark to show its where-abouts."

"Amazing, Sholmes!" I gasped, overcome by admiration.

"A ridiculously simple case," answered Sholmes lightly. "We shall enjoy our holiday the better for knowing we have done a good turn to our old friend, the inspector."

THE GOLDEN COW

No. 86

Herlock Sholmes stood by his armchair, his slippered foot resting gracefully on the cocaine cask, as a stout, well-dressed lady of fifty summers and goodness knows how many winters, was ushered into the rooms by Mrs. Spudson, our landlady.

"Mr. Sholmes!" cried the visitor. "I am in such distress!"

With graceful courtesy, Sholmes flicked the lid of the cocaine cask with my handkerchief. The lady seated herself, and Sholmes dropped back into his cushioned armchair.

"I am Mrs. Harbottle," began our client. "I and my husband live in the little old-world town of Sourby-cum-Tarpool in Rockinghamshire. Recently we have met with a great misfortune, Mr. Sholmes—at least, my husband has. The Golden Cow that used to sit on his writing-desk was stolen mysteriously. Since the theft my poor husband has been prostrate. It is most distressing."

"The Golden Cow, madam?" murmured Sholmes, lifting his eyelids. "That is a lucky charm, is it not?"

"It was supposed to bring good luck," piped Mrs. Harbottle. "The cow was about four inches high. It was of solid gold and as heavy as lead. Its eyes were a pair of small green emeralds. From its head extended some long, curly horns."

"You're sure it was a cow, madam?"

"Certainly, Mr. Sholmes."

"And not an octopus?"

"No. I'm positive it was an image of a cow—the Sacred Cow of Burmah. It was presented to my husband by the Emperor Bmung Bhang of Burmah for a great service indeed. That was long ago, In 1879, to be precise."

"Ah, I remember," drawled Herlock Sholmes. "I remember reading about it at the time in the 'Undertakers' Weekly Record.' Your husband, whizzling through Cocoanut Street, Rangoon, on a Thunder Mark II, motor-cycle, ran over three of the emperor's wives. The treble funeral was one of the greatest social events in Burmah in the 'seventies."

"Marvellous!" exclaimed Mrs. Harbottle. "Your memory for detail astounds me, Mr. Sholmes."

My amazing friend inclined his head, and said sharply:

"Tell me, when did you and Mr. Harbottle notice the loss of the Golden Cow?"

"Last Thursday. I remember it well. The cook was ill, and my poor husband was in one of his tantrums."

"Ahem: I see, You had prepared the dinner?"

"Yes. I made my husband an apple turnover."

"Which he did not appreciate?"

The distressed lady shook her head and wiped a tear from her eye with her glove. Evidently the memory was a bitter one.

"Who was in the house at the time of the theft?"

"Only Sarah Miggs, our cook. She had been out in the afternoon. That is why I made the turnover. When she returned, Mr. Harbottle and I went to the pictures to see Tishoo Hawakawawa in 'The Fatal Jujube.'"

"You have had Sarah Miggs in your employ a long time?"

"Yes, as cooks go–about three weeks."

"You do not suspect her?"

"No, Mr. Sholmes. But I looked through her boxes. The Golden Cow was not among her posessions, or in the house at all, for that matter. The glass of the study window was broken. Someone entered the room from the garden."

Sholmes rose and reached for his pipe.

"Why did you wait four days before notifying me?" he asked.

"I told the local police," confessed Mrs. Harbottle, with a catch in her voice.

"The mistake people invariably make," murmured Sholmes soothingly. "And, of course, you telephoned to Scotland Yard?'

Sholmes rapidly broke the stale crust and revealed the missing image of the Golden Cow.

"Y-yes," quavered the woman. "I–I telephoned there just before I came to you. An inspector called Blinkeye took the message."

"Pinkeye, you mean," said Sholmes. "He's an old friend of mine. Tut, tut! How you have mishandled matters, madam. However, Jotson and I will accompany you to Sourby-cum-Tarpool immediately. Let us be going."

A journey of a few hours on the Slowcombe branch of the Southern Railway brought us to picturesque Sourby-cum-Tarpool. The villa to which Mrs. Harbottle led us proved to be a pretty, detached residence overlooking the cemetery. Entering the front parlour, we discovered Inspector Pinkeye of Scotland Yard standing near a small man with old-fashioned side-whiskers, who was groaning upon a couch.

"Well, Pinkeye," said Sholmes cheerfully, "Have you found the thief?"

Pinkeye bowed to Mrs. Harbottle and me, and then took Sholmes on one side.

"To be frank, Mr. Sholmes, I don't know what I'm here for. I had hoped to see the lady who telephoned. All I can gather from Mr. Harbottle here is that he has a sneaking affection for the Golden Cow. Pity he doesn't try a temperance club for a change, I'm thinking."

"Sh-sh!" whispered Sholmes. "This unfortunate gentleman is steeped in gloom, not liquor, He has suffered a grievous loss. A brass talisman called the Golden Cow, presented to him by the Emperor Bmung Bhang of Burmah, has been stolen from him."

At the request of Sholmes, Mrs. Harbottle led us into the study, the room from which the image had been removed. Mr. Harbottle stayed on the couch, still groaning feebly.

"H'mm! A broken window, I see," remarked Pinkeye astutely. "The burglar broke in here. And note the particles of glass on the study floor."

Sholmes took a magnifying-glass from his pocket, and bending low, carefully examined the fragments. When he had concluded this examination, he looked at the window again, and silently left the room. We next saw him below the study windows, peering at the ground. Presently he came indoors.

"Let us seek out Sarah Miggs," he remarked.

The cook was at the kitchen window, starring down the tradesmen's entrance with a rapt expression on her face. From her parted lips and glazed eyes, I imaged at first that she was suffering from that rare disease known in medical parlance as aquascutum bokumphobia. But even as I stepped forward, with a cry of delight, Sholmes pushed by face back with his hand and touched the cook on the shoulder.

"Sarah Miggs," said he lightly, "you are in love! Do you expect your Romeo to appear thus early in the day?"

The cook came to earth with a thud.

"Herlock Sholmes," she gasped, "how–how did you know?"

Sholmes smiled inscrutably.

"What is his name?" he demanded.

"D'Arcy," breathed the buxom cook.

"A brave name!" said Sholmes. "What is he like?"

Plainly Pinkeye was bored to tears at this apparent waste of time. But Sarah Miggs was enraptured.

"Ooh! 'E's wonderful, Mr. Sholmes!" she sighed. "So brave, so 'andsome, so noble is D'Arcy! You should see some of 'is drorings! Ought to be an artist, 'e did!"

"'E's on the staff o' the Sourby-cum-Tarpool Municipal Authority."

"In other words, a dustman" sniffed Mrs. Harbottle, in an aside.

If Sholmes heard, he took no notice.

"I understand, Sarah Miggs," he remarked, with oily politeness, "that you were in this house on the evening when the Golden Cow was purlioned from Mr. Harstudy's bottle–er–I mean, Mr. Harbottle's study. Did you hear no sound–not a crash like the shattering of glass, for instance?"

"No, sir!" replied the cook. "I had been reading the last chapters of 'Her Boy was a Catsmeat Man' in the 'Purple Paper,' and had fallen asleep. When I woke up, I ses to meself: 'There's a draught, Sarah! Someone's left the garden gate open!' Then I discovered that the study had been broken into, and the yellow crocodile had been pinched."

"Golden Cow, Sarah!" corrected Mrs. Harbottle severely. "It was presented to my husband by the Emperor of Bmung Bhang of——"

"Quite so, madam!" interrupted Sholmes sternly. "There is one other question I wish to put to this intelligent cook. The theft occurred two days ago. Has Mr. D'Arcy called since then to take you out or to remove any other rubbish from the premises?"

"No, sir. 'E ain't been 'ere a-courtin' nor in 'is hofficial capacity on behalf o' that Sourby-cum-Tarpool Municipal Authority."

The metallic ring of a dustin-bin lid sounded from without.

"Ah, he is here at last!" cried Sholmes.

He bounded out of the kitchen and through the scullery door out of the house. We followed at his heels, and I could not fail to notice the scared expression upon the face of Sarah Miggs.

D'Arcy, the dustman, was standing by the dustbin, examining something he had taken from it.

"The apple-turnover!" cried Sholmes.

He snatched it from the astonished dustman's hands, and rapidly broke the stale crust, scattering the pieces upon the ground. And, as though he had performed a conjuring trick, we saw in his hands the image of the Golden Cow!

It is difficult to say who was the most flabbergasted–Mrs. Harbottle, Pinkeye, Sarah Miggs, D'Arcy, or myself.

"Here is the thief!" said Sholmes, pointing dramatically at Sarah Miggs. "Your cook stole the Golden Cow, Mrs. Harbottle, and left it for her fiancee to remove with the refuse! Do you wish to charge her with theft, and D'Arcy with being a receiver of stolen goods? If so, Pinkeye is ready with the darbies!"

But Mrs. Harbottle, for her husband's sake, was so pleased at getting the image back that she was satisfied with giving Sarah Miggs the sack on the spot. Weeping bitterly, the misguided cook left the house with the chastened dustman, who later gave up his fine position on the staff of the Sourby Municipal Authority, and took to scratching a precarious livelihood as a comic artist in what he called the "great metrollopus." That the pair had hoped to sell the Golden Cow for a good round sum to pay their marriage expenses was clear. Thanks to Sholmes, the guilty plan was frustrated, and the valued curio restored to the gratified Mr. Harbottle.

As Sholmes, Pinkeye, and I returned by train to London, each smoking a Flor de Staggarino given us by Mr. Harbottle, my curiosity overmastered me.

"How did you even guess the Golden Cow was in the turnover, Sholmes?" I asked.

"I never guess, my dear Jotson," said Sholmes dreamfully. "It was simple deduction. In the first place, I satisfied myself that the robbery had been committed by someone in the house. The splinters in the window-sash and a piece of glass I discovered on the lawn below the study window prove that the window had been smashed from the inside."

"B-but there was glasss on the study floor," interposed Pinkeye.

"Quite so," said Sholmes. "It had been cunningly placed there by Sarah Miggs to mislead. That glass, Pinkeye, was a sixteenth part of an inch thinner than the window-pane glass."

"Amazing!" I muttered.

"Simple observation," obsered Sholmes modestly. "Well, having smashed the window and stole the Golden Cow, Sarah Miggs wasa faced with the problem of concealing the image until she could get it into the hands of D'Arcy. The apple-turnover made by Mrs. Harbottle suggested a solution. She cut out the interior of the turnover, and inserted the Golden Cow, carefully plastering the sodden crust about it. There was no likelihood of anyone wanting to eat the dumpling, and if Mrs. Harbottle happened to pick it up, it would reveal no appreciable difference in weight.

"As she guessed, Sarah Miggs had to throw away the apple-turnover after it had been put on the table two or three times. She deposited it in the dustbin, having first notified D'Arcy of the precious image within the pastry. Luckily, I was summoned in time to be present when the dustman called."

THE WHITE RABBIT

No. 87

Directly I had signed the death certificate at the house of my late patient, I packed the saws and chisels in my little black bag and headed for Shaker Street.

Herlock Sholmes stylishly attired in a yellow-mauve dressing-gown, and wearing a check cap on his head, was reclining in his armchair. The cocaine cask was at his elbow, and his violin under his chin.

"Good-evening, Sholmes!" said I, placing my bag on the table. "You have not forgotten that we have an appointment to-night?"

Sholmes looked up with a languid smile upon his face.

"I never forget a dinner appointment, my dear Jotson," he said. "And it would be impossible for me to forget that our late friend, Inspector Pinkeye of Scotland Yard, had invited us to a little celebration in honour of his birthday,"

He tossed the violin on to a bookcase and raised his languid form from the divan chair.

Directly I had washed and changed into a brand-new celluloid collar, my famous friend and I left our apartments in Shaker Street and took the bus to the Thames Embankment. Calling at Scotland Yard, we were immediately shown to the beautifully furnished office of Inspector Pinkeye.

The burly inspector rose from his desk and grasped our hands fervently.

"Delighted to see you, Mr. Sholmes! Glad you have come, Dr. Jotson! I shall be ready to take you to Spaggetini's in five minutes. I have only one more schedule to dictate. I have been looking forward to this little birthday treat. Spaggetini's chef is the best in England. His potage pom-pom, followed by a little tripe a la delicatessen, with a few pickled prawns and some filleted prunes for desert, is a feast for the gods."

We seated ourselves on a settee as Pinkeye began to dictate to one of his lady secretaries. Then the door of the office was suddenly opened, and a lean man, garbed in blue uniform with brass buttons, and wearing a peaked hat, burst past the policeman who tried to bar his entrance, and addressed himself to the inspector.

"Come at once, sir! Come at once! Uncle Joseph has escaped, and——"

"I cannot help your Uncle Joseph!" snapped Pinkeye. "Report the matter to the constable downstairs."

"I did so, sir, and he told me to come to you. It is a case where brains is needed——"

"Ahem! Then perhaps I had better attend to it," murmured Pinkeye.

He sent his lady secretary away. Then, turning to Sholmes and me he said:

"Would you mind waiting in the ante-room for a few minutes? I will just hear the details of this case. Perhaps it is a matter I can solve without leaving the office."

We were in no hurry, and took seats in the ante-room. Pinkeye left the door ajar, and I shrewdly expected it was with the idea of impressing us with his importance as a sleuth.

"Now, my man," we heard Pinkeye say, as he returned to the uniform client in his private office, "who are you?"

"I am Keeper Paul Pognoddy, sir. I have come on a matter of life and death. Uncle Joseph was in my charge. This evening he escaped, and there will be killing done if he is not caught mighty quick."

"Oh-ho!" said Pinkeye. "Dangerous, is he?"

"I should think so," said the uniformed man. "We never had one quite like him. He has been in my charge now come Christmas twelvemonth, and I never saw one more dangerous in my life."

Inspector Pinkeye picked up a pen.

"His full name?" he demanded.

"Uncle Joseph," he said. "That's all we ever called him."

"His age?"

"Dunno, exactly—about fifty I should say. But what on earth——"

"Colour of eyes?"

"Pale blue. But——"

"Colour of hair?"

"Hair! Uncle Joseph hasn't got a hair on his head! He's——"

"Bald,"said Pinkeye, making a note on the form in front of him. "What size was he?"

"Oh, go and chop chips! There's no time to——"

"Answer the question put to you, Keeper Pogtoddy," said Pinkeye sternly.

"Pognoddy," said the visitor.

"Have it your own way," said Pinkeye. "Now, where was Uncle Jospeh seen last?"

"In Regent's Park. He chased a nurse, and frightened two policemen out of their wits."

"Impossible!" said Pinkeye. (None knew the police better than he.) "You may stay your fears, Keeper Dogbody——"

"Pognoddy!" shrieked the visitor.

"Keep your hair on," said Pinkeye. "You will make yourself as Uncle Joseph if you get into those tantrums. I have assured you that I will take the case up, and therefore you must rest assured that Uncle Joseph will be captured and restored to safe custody in a minimum amount of time. Oh, by the way, is there any special trait in his character about which I ought to know?"

"Only that he is dangerous and that he has a great craving for rabbits—white rabbits, for preference. He would wake out of his sleep or come a mile if you put a white rabbit near him."

"That might be useful to know," was Pinkeye's comment. "Where shall I find you to let you know when I have recaptured Uncle Joseph?"

"Phone Hampstead 6014," answered keeper Pognoddy.

Without waiting for further questioning, he rushed out of the office, saying something about returning to Regent's Park to join in the hunt.

Directly he had gone Inspector Pinkeye beckoned Sholmes and myself from the ante-room.

"What bad luck, gentlemen!" he said. "I am afraid that little dinner will be a washout, after all. A dangerous lunatic has escaped, and is at this very moment roaming about Regent's Park. Where danger calls, it is the duty of Inspector Pinkeye to be on the scene."

I do not know who was the more disappointed, Sholmes or me. That beautiful description by Pinkeye of the tripe a la delicatessen, followed by preserved prunes, had sharpened our appetites. However, we recognised, as Pinkeye said, that it was a case of duty first.

Pinkeye picked up a beautiful white-Polar bearskin which was lying across his office floor and flung it across his shoulder like a coat. Then, taking a pair of scissors from his desk, he snipped off the white bobble from the hat of his lady secretary, hanging on the peg near the door.

"My dear Pinkeye," said Sholmes, "what is the idea?"

"Come with me," answered the inspector darkly, "and you shall see."

There was an inexplicable smile on Sholmes' face as he and I followed the burly inspector out of the Yard into the street. Here Pinkeye engaged a taxi and pushed us in. He was in fine form, and was obviously very determined to throroughly impress us with his abilities.

To my great surprise, Inspector Pinkeye instructed the driver to proceed direct to Drury Lane Theatre. Leaving Sholmes and me in the cab, our friend entered by the stage door, and returned in less than five minutes bearing a great white pantomime mask of a rabbit's head and ears.

"You see the scheme now?" chuckled Pinkeye, as he reseated himself in the cab. "By astute questioning, I elicited the fact from Keeper Dogbody that white rabbits have a strange fascination over the patient. My plan is very simple. I shall disguise myself as a white rabbit, and when the lunatic, attracted by my approach, sees me, I shall up and grab him."

"Simple, yet ingenious," remarked Sholmes, with a smile. "But mind that Uncle Joseph does not grab you first, my dear fellow."

As the taxi rattled through Soho, Sholmes suddenly requested that it might be stopped for a minute. Pinkeye was annoyed at the delay, particularly as my famous friend refused to impart any information as to the reason for the delay. Apparently, however, Sholmes desired to do a little shopping at one or two of the stalls that were still doing business at that hour of the night.

In less than five minutes he returned to the cab bearing a brown-paper parcel and looking considerably stouter than usual. Both Pinkeye and I knew that it was useless questioning him. When Sholmes desired to explain he would do so, but not before.

With a piece of string, Pinkeye tied the white bobble he had borrowed from his lady secretary's hat to the Polar bear-skin. The taxi was dismissed near the northern gate of Regent's Park, and Sholmes, Inspector Pinkeye, and I climbed over the tall railings. The inspector seemed greatly gratified at having an audience for his display of detective skill.

Getting near some bushes, Pinkeye donned his disguise. He adjusted the bear-skin over his back and the white rabbit mask over his head. Then, grabbing our hands, he went strolling through the darkness, while Sholmes and I watched him from behind the bushes. Like an overfed white rabbit, Pinkeye bounded along the ground as bait to entice Uncle Joseph back to captivity.

Suddenly Sholmes gave a whistle. Pinkeye came bounding back.

"What is it?" he mumbled.

"I thought," murmured Sholmes, "that as you might be out all night on this dangerous case, you might like a little refreshment."

"M'mm, I should!" murmured Pinkeye.

Herlock Sholmes threw the brown-paper parcel he had obtained in Soho into the hands of the inspector.

"Well, there is a nice fresh cabbage for you, Pinkeye."

Never in my life before did I hear a rabbit make such a remark as Pinkeye did. Leaving the cabbage, he bounded off.

"Come!" said Sholmes, grabbing my arm. Suddenly a yell of terror rent the air.

"Ooh! Yoops! Garoogh! Call it off!"

Then Pinkeye came rushing towards us, the rabbit's mask at the back of his head and the bear-skin flying after him. Close at his heels was a great snake!

"Behind the bushes, quick!" cried Sholmes to me. "It is Uncle Joseph!"

The way that Pinkeye went out of that park and over the park railings would turned a film comedian green with envy.

The secret of Sholmes' increased size was revealed as my famous friend unwound a rope from about his thin waist. From his pocket he took a toy dog and tied it on the end of the line. Then he began drawing it over the ground. Suddenly there was a scrape, and a great boa-constrictor, which had chased Pinkeye out of the park, slid by. There was a snap, and the toy-dog attached to the string disappeared into the monster. With incredible swiftness, Sholmes tied the other end of the rope round a tree.

"There," he said, "Snakey can remain there while you and I go and telephone Hampstead 6014, my dear Jotson. The staff of the Zoological Gardens will be greatly gratified to know that Uncle Joseph, the famous boa-constrictor, has been captured!"

No. 88

With that amazing intuitive perspicuity of his, Herlock Sholmes darted out his fork and helped himself to the last rissole. The secret flank attack, which I had developed from behind the potato dish, had come to naught. I sat back in my chair and tried to look dignified.

"Half the ills of the human flesh are due to over-eating," I remarked ponderously. "I strongly advise——"

There was a knock at the dining-room door and Mrs. Spudson put her head in the room.

"Two footballers and a gentleman to see you, sir."

"Shoyummup!"

"Show them up!" said Sholmes.

A minute later we heard ponderous footsteps on the rickety stairway, and rising from the table Sholmes led the way to the consulting-room. Here we found the "two footballers and the gentleman" announced by our landlady.

Herlock Sholmes greeted the visitors and found seats for them.

"Pray be seated on the cocaine cask, my dear Jotson," he said to me, as he sank into his armchair. "Gentlemen," he went on, addressing his clients, "this is my faithful friend, Dr. Jotson, a surgeon of no small ability. Anything you have to say may be safely said in front of me."

Seated on the hard wooden lid of the cocaine cask, I was able to take stock of our queer callers. Two of them were dressed in football garb with overcoats. Their jerseys were green and sky-pink—such as one sees at sunset—and their navy knickers were caked in mud. The third man was a stout, ponderous individual of about fifty years who wore a heavy gold watch-chain across his ample yellow waistcoat.

At first I thought he was a pawnbroker or a bookmaker. But he introduced himself as Erasmus Pondersby, the Mayor of Dudmore, proprietor of the Cow and Cartwheel Inn and patron of the Dudmore Hyenas Football team.

After providing us with this information, the plump visitor in the stylish civilian attire furnished us with the names of his companions—George Gumble and Fred Bunyan, the Captain and Vice-Captain respectively of the Dudmore Eleven.

When the introductions had been completed, Herlock Sholmes placed the tips of his elongated fingers together and lay back in his chair in the characteristic pose I knew so well.

"Now, gentlemen," said Sholmes, "if you will state the case which has impelled you to visit me here in Shaker Street, I will do my best to render you such service as I can."

"To begin at the beginning, sir, the Dudmore Hyenas are in the consomme," said Gumble. "just on the very day when we have the most important match of the season we have got it where the chicken got the chopper. In other words, we are flummuxed, flamboozled, fed-up, and far from home and off the map completely. If it were any other than Ginger Dick I should say let it rip, but seeing as it's Ginger——" He paused. "I hope I am making it clear, Mr. Sholmes?"

"As clear as pea soup," said Sholmes smiling. "From what I can make out, the team has suffered some reverse just before an important match, and that Ginger Dick is in someway mixed up with the catastrophe."

"Ginger Dick's our goalie," continued Gumble. "the finest goalie as ever bumped his head against a cross-bar. And here, just before the match, he has gone off!"

"Off his chump?" asked Sholmes.

"No; off the map. He has vamoosed, hopped it, done a bunk, hit the trail and gone to Jericho. Anyway, he is not at Dudmore, and in half an hour's time we have got to play the Punkton Blades for the Pondersby Bowl."

"You suspect foul play?" demanded Sholmes.

"We do," said George Gumble. "Some of those Punkton blokes have spirited him away, I am reckoning. We want you to find Ginger Dick. Godling's his real name. If we take the field at three o'clock without him, we are licked."

"Have you no other goalkeeper?"

"No, Mr. Sholmes. Not one that is a patch on Ginger Dick. He is the most tallest, elongated, spryest, nimblest specimen of a goal guardian as ever punched a forward's nose."

Sholmes glanced at the clock.

"There is little time to spare!" he remarked, rising. "the match begins at three o'clock, and you say it is a most important game?"

"It is for the Pondersby Bowl," cried Fred Bunyan. "It has been the custom of Mr. Pondersby here to fill the bowl for the victors at his hospitable hostel, the Cow and Cartwheel, every October. It ain't so much the Bowl that matters, though the boys like to win that—but what Mr. Pondersby fills it with. As sure as eggs ain't cheese, the bowl will go to the Punkton Blades if Ginger Dick ain't found."

"He shall be found," said Sholmes. "Where did you see him last?"

"We went out this morning for a limb-loosener. When the other chaps left the stand, Ginger Dick stopped to look out some of his old football togs for the wash. Old Daniel Dibbett, the club groundsman, never saw him leave at all. He never left that football stand. He has vamoosed completely. Fred Bunyan and me went back and could find no trace of him. It is a mystery—a dark mystery, Mr. Sholmes."

Sholmes filled his snuff-box with cocaine out of the cask and strode across the room.

"Come," he said, "we will take a taxi to Dudmore—ahem! at your expense."

We arrived at the football clubhouse at Dudmore at two-thirty p.m. Only half an hour before the match against the notorious Punkton Blades was due to begin.

Sholmes' first move in the investigations was to submit Old Dibbett the groundsman, to a thorough cross-examination. The old man swore that Ginger Dick had never left the stand. He had seen the other players depart and had remained at the place for over an hour.

"Did no one enter that stand during that period?" enquired Sholmes.

"No, sir—er—that is no one except the men who called for the laundry."

"What!" almost shouted Sholmes. "How many men entered this place?"

"Four, sir. They had a cart with them and they brought out the big bundle of washing."

Sholmes grabbed my arm and entered the players' club-house, almost falling into a plunge-bath fitted with green water. To the dismay of myself and the Dudmore men, a big, shameless patch lay under the water at the bottom of the bath.

"Good gracious!" breathed George Gumble, going pale. "It's Ginger Dick!"

"Ginger Dick! Fiddlesticks!" said Sholmes. "It is the bundle of washing! Ginger Dick must have had a knock on the head and was then carried away under the very eyes of Dibbett wrapped in a canvas bag."

The two Dudmore footballers and Mr. Pondersby, their patron, gave deep groans.

"Then Ginger Dick will not be here for the match this afternoon?"

The steely eyes of Sholmes glistened with determination.

"Your goalkeeper shall be found," he said. "Listen to me. Take the field at three o'clock with your ten men. The goalie of the team shall appear in his appointed place. Leave it to me, Gumboil—er—Gumble, I mean. Have you a photograph of Ginger Dick?"

The Dudmore captain took down a small print from the wall. I looked over Sholmes' shoulder as my famous friend took it. The photo showed a hatchet-faced individual with a mop of fair hair and a toothbrush moustache.

"Good! I will keep this for the time being," said Sholmes. "now, tell me, how far's Punkton from here?"

"It's the next town," said Gumble—"five miles distant."

"Is Ginger Dick known in the district?"

"No, I should say not," volunteered Mr. Pondersby.

As Sholmes strode away I bounded swiftly after him; but he laid his hand across my moustache and pushed me back.

"Remain in the grand-stand, my dear Jotson," he said. "I can travel fastest alone. Look out for me at three o'clock or there about."

Seldom did Herlock Sholmes treat me in this fashion, and I knew that there was some deep reason in his mighty brain.

In due course the Dudmore and Punkton players rolled up, and garbed themselves for the fray. Then the lads of the village surged to the grandstand, together with hundreds of Punkton supporters. At ten minutes to three a mass of spectators bordered the playing-pitch, and with every passing minute I grew more anxious.

Three o'clock struck in the local church tower, and the Punkton Blades, in their pale-green-and-yellow jerseys, filed on to the field, to be greeted by a thunderous cheer. Then George Gumble led his men out—ten of them.

"Gin-ger! Where's Ginger?"

That cry was being hurled from stand to stand throughout the vast assembly.

But Ginger Dick did not appear. The captains tossed and the referee blew his whistle for the kick-off, and as the teams lined up there was the Pondersby goal unguarded.

"Good gracious!" I murmured. "Has Sholmes failed?"
The cold perspiration broke out on my brow as again that cry arose from the anxious Dudmore supporters:
"Gin-ger! Gin-ger!"
And then I felt a foot placed heavily against the small of my back, and I was rudely hurled on one side.
Two lean, lank individuals had thrust their way through the crowd in the grandstand. One was wearing blue knickers, red jersey, football-boots, and huge leather gloves. By this attire, and the fact that he had ginger hair and a toothbrush moustache, I was able, thanks to the detective abilities I had developed with Sholmes, to identify him as Ginger Dick, the missing goalie. The other elongated figure, attired in a mauve dressing-gown and check cap with flaps, was none other than my old friend Herlock Sholmes!
Now the crowd saw the couple. They cared not a wrap for the famous sleuth in the dressing-gown, even if they recognised him. Their eyes were fixed on the ginger-headed individual scrambling through the throng to gain the field.
"Gin-ger! Gin-ger!"
Now there was no tinge of anxiety in the cry—naught but a note of ecstatic triumph. Bounding across the field, the tall goalie took his place between the posts. Directly the ball was kicked off the Blades started up the field, and Ginger Dick ran out to clear a fast grounder. He missed the ball entirely, but kicked the ground in front of it, sending a huge clod of earth against the forward's chin. luckily, the ball rolled behind, and the goalie went to retrieve it as the unfortunate centre-forward was being revived.
Clearly Ginger Dick was not in form, and I shrewdly suspected that his unfortunate kidnapping experience was responsible for it. But I said nothing to Sholmes, who stood morose and silent. Well I did know that Sholmes would speak when the time came for explanations at the end of the story.
Three times did Ginger Dick kick chunks out of the football-field instead of the ball, and only by good luck and bad throwing on the part of Punkton was the Dudmore citadel unfallen at the end of the fifteen minutes' play.
The first score was registered by the captain of Dudmore with a beautiful straight drive into the centre of the net.
At half-time the score was still at one—nil in favour of Dudmore. The return of the players to the field was greeted with enthusiastic cries of the Dudmore supporters, who were not inclined to overlook the curious displays given by their much-vaunted goalie.
"Hy-een-as! Hy-een-as!"
Now, however, the Punkton Blades were on their mettle. The captain, dribbling the ball through the Dudmore wing and directing the half-back, sped down to the Dudmore goal. Ginger Dick rushed out to meet him. His left fist caught the Punkton captain on the nose, his right struck the ball as it rose from the forward's foot. There was a sound like a burst motor-tyre, and the leather football hurtled through the air in a shapeless mass.
"Good old Gin-ger!"
While the Punkton captain was being taken to hospital a fresh ball was procured; but ten minutes later Ginger Dick disposed of that in the same manner. The third ball shared the same fate. Never had the audience seen such a terrific display of punching.
At last the final whistle sounded. The Hyenas were the victors by one goal to nil! Once more they had won the Pondersby Bowl!
My silent friend in the dressing-gown and I followed the Dudmore team to the Cow and Cartwheel directly the men had changed.
Ginger Dick was carried shoulder-high.
In the quiet secrecy of the hostel Pondersby produced a great silver goblet, and filled it with nut-brown brew.
And then the cry arose from the footballers:
"Herlock Sholmes!" And once more the metal bowl passed round. Then, to the surprise of everyone, the goalie in the red jersey slipped to the sanded floor from the shoulders of those who supported him.
"Thank you gentlemen, for drinking my health! I have been happy to render the Dudmore Hyenas a service!"
A great gasp of astonishment arose. The appearance of the man was that of Ginger Dick. The voice was the voice of Sholmes himself!
Then, to the further astonishment of everyone, the goalie proceeded to divest himself of a ginger wig and false toothbrush moustache.
"Tarn me!" gasped George Gumble, "Then it was you who played in goal, Mr. Sholmes?"
"None other," he said. "This gentleman who is wearing my dressing-gown is Ginger Dick. Unfortunately, he has had a nasty crack on the head, and would have been useless. Therefore, as we were both of a height, I disguised myself and took his place on the field."
"But how did you find him?"
"It was ridiculously simple," answered the great detective. "At first I could not make out how the men, who were four members of the Punkton team, would dispose of their bundle. But after I saw

that photo of Ginger Dick I knew that one method would surely present itself to them. Ginger Dick was not known in the neighbourhood of Punkton, so he could be safely taken in that direction. There were fields on the road. All the men had to do was to put a prop up his coat and another through his sleeves and stick him up to scare crows. They estimated that it would be some time before he returned to consciousness, and that, anyway, he would be too ill to take his part in the match. So, gentlemen, I proceeded along the Punkton road, and sure enough I discovered our friend frightening birds in a cornfield!"

"But how on earth did you manage to play the game you did, Mr. Sholmes?" asked George Gumble. "I was not aware you were a footballer. The way you laid out the Punkton captain and burst those balls would have done credit to an International!"

Giving another smile, Sholmes drew off his left glove. There was a metallic clatter as a horseshoe fell on the floor.

"I carried this for luck," he murmured.

Then he drew off the other glove. In his hand was a nail, firmly held between his first and second fingers.

"Always in this world, gentlemen," said Herlock Sholmes. "brains will beat brawn. And proof is that you have again won your biggest match of the season!"

No. 89

A ring at the front-door bell of our residence in Shaker Street caused Sholmes, and I to look at one another hopefully.

Clients had been few and far between of late, and a nice remunerative criminal case was just what we needed to restore our shattered finances.

Footsteps sounded on the stairs and Mrs. Spudson opened the door to announce a visitor.

"A Mrs. Pudsnick to see you, sir," said our landlady.

"Show her in!" said Sholmes.

Mrs. Spudson stood aside, and a fat, fair female of forty or fifty, flauntering frills and flounces, fluttered into the room.

"Oh, Mr. Sholmes!" she cried. "You remember me, of course? I am little Lena. Surely you remember little Lena, who went to the Tooting Common Board School when you were a boy?"

"H'm, yes!" said Sholmes. "Lena! Lena! But you are a little fatter now, madam. And you are in trouble. No worry concerning your husband, I suppose?"

"None, Mr. Sholmes," answered the lady. "He passed to his long rest eight months ago. It is about my unfortunate brother-in-law, Puddersby Pudsnick, that I have come to see you."

"Please state the case, Mrs. Pudsnick," said Sholmes. "You may speak quite freely before Dr. Jotson here. He is as close as an oyster, even if not so good-looking."

The lady laid a haddock, wrapped in a piece of newspaper on her lap, and, taking a magazine from the parlour table, fanned herself gently.

"It is too dreadful, Mr. Sholmes!" she began. "At present my poor brother-in-law Puddy is lying in the Moldy Cottage Hospital in a delirious condition. Two weeks ago he started a chicken farm.

"It wasn't the chickens that were responsible, Mr. Sholmes," she continued. "How he got into the trouble he is in at present, no one can say. And so I have come to you as an old friend to try and solve the mystery."

"The fee is five pounds in advance!" murmured Sholmes.

Absent-mindedly. Mrs Pudsnick fanned herself with the haddock.

"Money is no object, Mr. Sholmes," she said. "Fortunately my late husband left me well provided for. I will double your usual fee if you can solve the mystery of Moldy Manor."

"What's that?" asked Sholmes.

"The Manor is the place where my brother-in-law rented, near the little village of Moldy, in Sussex. He started a chicken farm there, having as an assistant a deaf old man named Garge Gobbles. I tried to persuade dear Puddy not to take it, for it had a reputation of being haunted by the ghost of a highwayman, who was hung in chains outside the place in the seventeenth century. But Puddy would have his own way, and now he is raving in the Moldy Cottage Hospital."

She paused, and flicked a big, wet tear from her eye with the haddock.

"Yes," she continued, "it happened a few days after he had taken possession of the Manor. Old Gobbles went in one morning to find my brother-in-law lying fully dressed and unconcious on the flags of the large cellar under the house. A revolver was by his side, and five cartridges were in the weapon."

"Was it a six-shooter?" demanded Sholmes alertly.

"It was," answered Mrs. Pudsnick. "The evidence would seem to show that my unfortunate brother-in-law had fired one shot from the revolver for a villager called Daft Jimmy, passing the house about midnight, distinctly heard a loud report."

"Your brother-in-law was not wounded?"

"No. Clearly he had not pointed the revolver at himself. The strange thing was that the cellar walls show no mark of the bullet. There was an expression of deadly fear on poor Puddy's face which reminded me of my dear late husband every time a summons was served on him. It is clear that his brother saw something dreadful in that cellar. What did he see?"

"Ah, what?" I demanded eagerly.

"That is what I wish Mr. Sholmes to discover," she said. "The doctors at the Cottage Hospital believe that poor Puddy saw some terrible apparition. Sometimes he cries, 'The ghost—the ghost! I can hear the chains a-rattling and banging.'"

Despite that the day was warm for the time of the year, I gave a shiver. I sincerely hoped that Herlock Sholmes would not undertake this eerie case. But I was doomed to disappointment.

"Mrs. Pudsnick," he said, "you can safely leave the matter in my hands. Dr. Jotson and I will proceed to Moldy Manor forthwith, if not sooner, and lay this phantom which has brought such misfortune to your brother-in-law!"

"Ah, thank you, Mr. Sholmes! Here is five pounds, and I will send you a cheque for five pounds more directly you have solved the mystery."

Directly after a meal, Sholmes took the railway time-table, and looked up the trains to Moldy. The distance, we discovered, was nineteen miles from London, and the three o'clock express on the Southern Railway did the journey from London Bridge in a little under three hours.

Luckily the train was only three-quarters of an hour late in reaching Moldy. In the village itself, Sholmes stopped to question the lad, Daft Jimmy, who had heard the report while passing the Manor. His story was a simple one. He was returning from a shove-ha'penny tournament just after mid-night, when he heard a bang "like a bust ballon." He ran all the way home.

Sholmes thanked the honest fellow, and gave him a pat on the back.

"Now to interview old Garge Gobbles," said my famous friend cheerfully.

We found the man Gobbles chasing snails off one of the chicken-houses near the imposing pile known as the Manor.

"Good-evening!" said Sholmes.

He handed Gobbles a card. The old man took it.

"I am Herlock Sholmes, the detective," said my friend, with dignity. "I have come to question you about the strange affair of Mr. Puddersby Pudsnick. It has been reported to me that the Manor is habited of ghosts."

"Heh?" said Garge Gobbles, cupping his hand to his ear. "Speak up, young fellow! I be a bit hard o' hearing!"

"I say," repeated Sholmes, in a louder tone, "that I understand you have ghosts about?"

"No, only chickens," said Gobbles. "Goats don't pay."

Sholmes took a silk handkerchief from the breast-pocket of his overcoat, and wiped his brow. Then, in a loud voice, he said, slowly and clearly:

"Kindly show us the place where Mr. Pudsnick had his adventure with the spirits."

Old Gobbles seemed to understand, and, taking a lantern, he led the way into the Manor, and down to the cellar. There he pointed out some black, dust-covered bottles labelled "Old Methuseleh***."

"There 'ee be, sir," said Gobbles. "Powerful fond o' they spirits he were an' all."

"The silly old mugwump's potty!" whispered Sholmes to me.
'Strangely enough Gobbles heard that.
"Who be a potty ole mugwump?" he demanded angrily. "Now 'ee can find out things without my help!" And he strode fiercely up the cellar steps and out of the house.
Considerately, he left the lantern.
"Thank goodness, he's gone!" breathed Sholmes. "Now we can pursue our investigations in peace, my dear Jotson!"
Taking his magnifying-glass from his pocket, Herlock Sholmes began his examination of the cellar where poor Pudsnick had been discovered.
A number of cider-bottles occupied one dusty shelf. One of these was empty; the contents were still damp on the cellar flags. Sholmes picked up the cork in a far corner and slipped it in his pocket.
Leading the way upstairs, he entered a bed-room. In a drawer was a revolver that answered to the description of the one found by Pudsnick.
"This revolver was never fired, my dear Jotson," said Sholmes, dropping it in his pocket. "Now let us take blankets and pillows to the cellar."
"Great Scott! What for?" I asked, in alarm.
"We will sleep there," answered Sholmes. "Who knows?" he added, in a sepulchral tone. "We may be privileged to see or hear the dreadful thing that put poor Pudsnick in the casualty ward."
"I—I think I'll put up at the Knave's Head in Moldy village," I murmured.
But Sholmes would have none of it. He made me help take the blankets and pillows below stairs and make up beds on the floor.
We turned in at ten o'clock in the darkened cellar. Sholmes, rather tactlessly I thought, passed the time by narrating a true (?) ghost story of a spook who jumped at people in the dark and bit their ears.
I must have gone to sleep, but I awakened suddenly with a most unpleasant sensation in the vicinity of my ear.
"Yoops! Help!" I gasped, shuddering in the blankets.
Then I saw it was a the lean form of Herlock Sholmes, clad in a dressing-gown, standing near my feet.
"It is the hour of midnight," said Sholmes solemnly. "Come Jotson!"
I had forgotten that Sholmes had aranged that we were to take watch and watch throughout the night.
'But hardly had I stepped from between the blankets than I heard a faint squeak as of the agony of a lady who has sat on a hot stove. It was followed by the dull metallic rattle of a chain being dragged along the floor overhead.
Sholmes told me afterwards that my face went the colour of ripe gorgonzola, and that I trembled like a leaf in the icy blast. Perhaps that was so. I know my feet refused to mount the cellar stairs until my famous friend assisted me with the toe of his carpet-slipper.
What dreadful spook should we behold?
Sholmes pushed his way into the kitchen, which was directly above the cellar, in front of me. Stooping, he snatched something from the flolor. I started back as I heard the dread jangle of a chain.
"No, do not be alarmed, my dear Jotson," said Sholmes, with a laugh. "The spook is scotched!" And he revealed a great rat caught in a steel trap to which was attached a heavy chain.
"A powerful brute," remarked my famous friend. "He dragged the trap fully three yards. The Manor is infested by rats. Old Gobbles is in the habit of setting this trap. Last night Pudsnick went to the cellar to pour himself a nightcap. A Nervous man, he took a revolver with him. While there he heard the death squeak of a trapped rat and the rattle of this chain. The circumstance proved too much for his weak nervous system, and he subsided in dire fear upon the floor, where old Gobbles found him."
"But the shot that Daft Jimmy heard?" I said. "How can you account for that?"
"He heard no shot," replied Sholmes. From his pocket he took the cork he had picked up in the cellar. "Daft Jimmy heard this cork fly out of the cider-bottle. The bursting of a cork is a common occurrence where cider-bottles are concerned Jotson.
"It now remains only to convince poor Pudsnick that his fear of a spook inhabiting the manor is groundless. Then he will speedily recover. And, by the way, my dear Jotson, kindly remind me to collect that other fiver from his sister, Lena!"

Another queer adventure of Herlock Sholmes, the World's Worst Detective, recorded by his faithful friend, Dr. Jotson.

No. 90

Mrs. Hatchett, gaunt as a signpost, stood on the landing and swept a be-ringed hand towards a couple of half-open doors.

"There's your apartments, sirs!" she said. "I'll serve the kippers in the parlour in two shakes of a shrimp's tail!"

My famous friend, Herlock Sholmes, had brought me to Codport for the fishing

As Mrs. Hatchett ambled down the rickety stairs again Sholmes entered the parlour. He laid a packet of fish-hooks he had bought on the table.

I staggered into the room at his heels with the rest of the baggage. Dropping two portmentaux and the handbag on the floor, I put the fishing-rods in a corner. Sholmes' violin, cocaine-cask, and jar of shag I placed on the table. Umbrellas, macintoshes, and a half-packet of ham-sandwiches I laid on the mantelpiece.

"Good!" said Sholmes, rubbing his hands. "Just as well we didn't spend money on a cab from the station. It was quite an easy walk."

"For you!" I puffed. "It's just about broken my spinal vertrebrae!'

Footsteps on the stairs brought hope to my heart.

"Ah!" I murmured. "Here comes Mrs. Hatchett with the grille!'

"No, my dear Jotson," said Sholmes. "The footsteps upon the stair are those of a man—and a man who wears number fourteen boots into the bargain."

"Sholmes," I exclaimed, "you astonish me!'

I turned at the thunderous rap on the door. Into the room strode a great, beefy-looking man with a mottled, red face.

"Mr. Sholmes," he said, "pardon this hintrusion, but Mrs. Hatchett tole me down at the shop some days ago as you were coming!"

"Drat her!" muttered Sholmes beneath his breath.

"Take a seat," I said, indicating the armchair. "It is springless, though, I'm afriad."

The plump visitor subsided into the chair.

Putting his finger-tips together, the famous sleuth regarded him narrowly.

"You are a pork butcher, sir," he said.

The visitor gaped like a deceased codfish.

"Jumping polonies! How did you know that. Mr, Sholmes?"

"Simple deduction," replied the master-sleuth. "You have lost three fingers of your left hand, and particles of fresh peas-pudding, veal-and-ham-pie, and black pudding are adhering to the blue apron which is protruding under your waistcoat!"

"Wonderful!" gasped the visitor. "And you will help me, Mr. Sholmes?"

"I will hear the case first," said my famous friend cautiously. "Dr. Jotson and I have come to Codport for a brief fishing holiday. I didn't intend to work."

"But I'll pay you handsomely, Mr. Sholmes. Ask anyone in Codport if Joe Gammon, pork butcher, hasn't got the dibs!"

"Proceed!" said Sholmes.

"Well, it's like this here," said Mr. Gammon. "I've been a hard worker all my life, for a long time I never did much good for myself. Two years after taking my present shop in Codport my luck changed. It may sound foolish, but I've allus thought it was partly due to a silver wishbone which my rich uncle left me. I started wearing it on my watch-chain, From that time money began to come easy."

"The wishbone was of no great intrinsic value?" said Sholmes.

"No, sir," replied Mr. Gammon. "It couldn't ha' been worth more than fifteen bob at the most. But, as I've said to all my customers and friends in Codport for the last seven year, it was worth a thousand times its weight in gold to me."

"And now you have lost it, Mr. Gammon?"

"That's just it, Mr. Sholmes," said the pork burcher, again startled by Sholmes' perspicacity. "Returning from a dance one night with the missus, I found it was gone."

"You felt no one take it?'

"No, Mr. Sholmes."

"You suspect none of your dancing partners?"

Mr. Gammon punched a lump of horsehair out of the armchair with his mottled fist.

"I suspect 'em all, Mr. Sholmes!" he said heatedly. "There was that Mrs. Todsniff, of the haberdashery; then there was Mrs. Nuggett, of the boot-shop near me; old Mother Giggleswick, and Miss Goldenstein."

Sholmes nodded sagely.

"You can remember no more?'

"Nothin'."

At that moment Mrs. Hatchett appeared with a brace of luscious, sizzling, golden brown kippers.

Herlock Sholmes rose from his chair.

"My good friend, Dr. Jotson, and I are about to dine," he said. "The details you have been able to give me are but meagre. However, in any spare time I may have, I will bear your case in mind."

A relieved smile wreathed Mr. Gammon's chubby face as he bowed himself out of the room backwards and fell down the stairs over the cat.

Together Sholmes and I partook of the meal prepared by our landlady.

Directly after dinner Sholmes, with his huge pipe in his mouth, led the way to the sea-front.

Unfortunately for Sholmes and fortunately for me, we discovered that the tide had gone out a mile or two. A fat and genial boatman informed us that it was not expected back until to-morrow.

"Hide the rods and tackle under that old bathing-hut, Jotson," said Sholmes to me. "Then go and eat worms – I mean, dig worms. They will come in useful for bait when we go out in the rowboat to-morrow."

I groaned and turned to obey. Puffing contentedly on his pipe, Sholmes wended his way up-town. We next met again in the apartments in Trafalgar Villas. The way that Sholmes was playing leap-frog over the cocaine cask told me that my famous friend was in the best of spirits.

"My dear Jotson," cried Sholmes, as I entered the room, "you will be pleased to know that I have solved the mystery of the missing wishbone."

I dropped the tin of worms with a clatter.

"What! Already? You astonish me!"

"The case was even more simple than I had supposed," replied Herlock Sholmes. "The thief undoubtedly was Mrs. Nuggett, the bootmaker's wife."

"Then you have actually found the wishbone?" said I.

"No. But it's as good as found. In the first place, by making inquiries in the town I discovered that Nuggett, the bootmaker, had been jealous of Gammon's success for years. By the simple expedient of throwing a horseshoe over my left shoulder in his shop, I discovered he was superstitious."

"Bless my heart!"

"Yes, He considered that the throwing of a horseshoe over the left shoulder was distinctly unlucky."

"Then you think——"

"Exactly," went on Sholmes. "I think that Nuggett really believes that the silver wishbone was the chief factor in Gammon's success in business. At the dance Mrs. Nuggett removed the charm from Gammon's watch-chain and handed it to her husband."

"And does Nuggett wear it in his watch-chain?"

Herlock Sholmes regarded me with an expression of deep pain.

"That is feeble, even for you, my dear Jotson," said he. "Needless to say, Nuggett would not wear the wishbone on his watch-chain. He would wear it under it. While I was in his shop I accidentally – for the purpose – fell up against him. I could distinctly feel the shape of a hard substance fashioned like a wishbone beneath his waistcoat. How to take it from him is the problem. He's a man six feet two in height and broad in proportion. And, as you know, my dear Jotson, I never seek the assistance of those dunderheads, the official police."

Suddenly he slapped his thigh with great enthusiasm.

"I've got it!" he cried.

I knew it was useless to ask my famous friend to explain his plan. As usual I should have to exercise patience.

On the following morning Herlock Sholmes sent me to hire a rowboat. I went with the deepest misgivings. Sholmes was an excellent sailor. I was not.

Obeying my orders, I engaged the rowboat, and stowed rods, fishing-tackle, baskets, and worms in the frail little craft.

Presently Sholmes came along. To my surprise, I saw that he was accompanied by a regular giant of a man.

"This is Mr. Nuggett," said Herlock Sholmes, introducing him. "I was in his shop to purchase a pair of shoelaces, and I persuaded him to accompoany us on this little fishing trip."

"Ay, and highly honoured I am to come," said Mr. Nuggett.

Sholmes and Mr. Nuggett took their seats in the stern-sheets of the boat. I pushed it off, and rowed them a couple of miles out to sea.

The sea was distinctly choppy. Sholmes put on this favourite pipe. I noticed that he sat to windward of Mr. Nuggett.

Soon, as in a nightmare, I became aware that Mr. Nuggett had joined me at the side of the boat. His face was as green as seaweed, and his hands flapped feebly on the water. By means of his pipe of s ag, Sholmes had overcome him with a bad attack of mal de meerschaum.

Herlock Sholmes very kindly loosened his short-front. Incidentally, he took a small silver wishbone from a thread which Mr. Nuggett wore round his neck.

It was Sholmes himself who rowed us to the shore. He delivered Mr. Nuggett to the police, and restored the silver wishbone to the gratified Mr. Gammon. But I only discoverd this afterwards. Very kindly Sholmes had delivered me to the hospital first.

When I returned to Trafalgar Villas later that day, I found Sholmes sitting down to a table piled with black pudding, veal-and-ham pies, polonies, cuts from the joint, and other delicacies—presents from the grateful Mr. Gammon.

"Better now, Jotson?" mumbled Sholmes, with his mouth full. "Not a bad plan of mine for recovering the wishbone, was it?"

THE SECRET IN THE PUDDING BAG

No. 91

Before revealing the amazing Secret of the Pudding Bag, I, Herlock Sholmes, detective of Shaker Street, London, desire to explain my action to the readers of the "Popular."

For years my faithful friend, Dr. Jotson, who assists me to pay Mrs. Spudson's exorbitant rent, had acted as the official recorder of my cases. Never was there a better man. Although a general practitioner, he is an expert on disordered brains. As I have told him many a time, he should be in a mental asylum—as a house-surgeon, of course. Yet his great talents have not been wasted altogether in Shaker Street.

But his very devotion to me has one drawback. He refuses to record any but my astounding successes. And the case of the Pudding Bag can hardly be classified as one. But because of its Christmas flavour the Editor of the "Popular" desired it greatly—the story, but not the pudding bag.

One day just after I had successfully solved the mystery of the Poisoned Doughnut, in Tooting Bec, I found the Great Man in our consulting-room at Shaker Street, begging Jotson to narrate the tale for the benefit of his million readers. Jotson refused. Therefore, I insisted on recording this amazing case myself."*

**And on pocketing the fee usually awarded to poor Jotson*—Editor.

For long Dr. Jotson had been run-down and depressed. Ever since that day when he left his best pair of silver-plated scissors inside the patient upon whom he had operated for liver trouble, he had not been himself.

For some time I must admit it did not occur to me that there was anything else wrong with poor Jotson save worry for the loss of his patient and the scissors. But shortly before Christmas it was borne on me that something else was amiss.

One night as I sat in my armchair playing Schnoffenstein's Five Finger exercise in B flat on my violin, curious rumbling noises assailed my ear. At first I thought the G string wanted tightening; then it occurred to me that the strange, deep sounds were proceeding from the next room.

I ceased playing. Creeping stealthily towards the bed-room door, my fiddle grasped in my right hand ready for any emergency, I stooped down with the skilled grace of long practice, and applied my ear to the door.

Now I could hear the rumbling clearly. Dr. Jotson was talking to himself. Throwing open the door, I stood a tall and, I hope, dignified figure in my purple dressing-gown with the little green birds on the holly branches round the hem.

"Jotson!" I cried. "You are distraught!"

My old friend Jotson, who had been pacing the bed-room, stopped, his hands behind him. There was a startled look on his face, his sandy, walrus moustache drooping guiltily.

"Sholmes," he said, "you have been listening! What have you heard?"

"Aah!" I said. "What! Well might I ask you a question. What are you concealing from me, Jotson? What have you behind your back?"

"He, he, he! Only a couple of patches," replied Jotson, faintly laughing at his own feeble joke. "Now pray go and resume your amateur vivisection on my guinea-pigs!"

Candidly, I felt offended, and I left the room. But I resolved to keep my eye on my old and faithful friend for any further symptoms before formally notifying Colney Hatch.

Gradually, as the days sped by, I became more convinced that Jotson was ailing mentally. Several times I heard him mumbling behind closed doors. Occasionally, too, he left the house in the evenings on some pretext or another. But I felt that when Jotson needed my help he would tell me. So I snuffed my cocaine, played my violin, and solved a couple of dozen poison mysteries which had baffled Scotland Yard and the Continental police, and temporarily left Jotson to look after himself.

On Christmas Eve, Dr. Jotson made one more of his mysterious disappearances. For long I sat before the fire in the consulting-room, casually perusing the evening paper as I smoked my pipe. Outsdide the snow snowed and the waits waited—I was hard up that Christmas.

Suddenly a paragraph on an inner news page riveted my attention. It was headed: "Proposed River Trip for Crown Prince," and read: "The Crown Prince of Schlacca-Splittzen, who arrived this afternoon in London from Paris, has expressed a desire to see the London County Council Hall from the river. He remarked to reporters that his view of the magnificent structure from the railway reminded him of the municipal Torture House in Tchmnomzyte, the capital of his own state of Schlacca-Splittzen, which lies to the south of Russia. The Crown Prince is being carefully guarded by Inspector Pinkeye and three other well-known detectives from Scotland Yard. These precautions are being taken because it is rumoured that the Schlacca-Splittzen Co-operative Society of Anarchists have threatened to drop a bomb into his porridge if he visited Britain's shores."

As I read this little paragraph a dark suspicion entered my mind, and there I determined that Jotson must be watched.

It was at eleven o'clock on Christmas Eve. Mrs. Spudson, her hair in curl-papers, had retired to rest. I damped down the fire, covered the canary's cage, turned the consulting-room lights out, chained up the dog, put out the cat, and left the key under the doormat for Jotson. Then I went to my room.

I was about to doff my dressing-gown when I heard Jotson enter the house. Slowly he came upstairs, and I heard him switch on the consulting-room light. Leaving my room, I crept along the passage and quickly opened the door of the consulting-roomn.

As I did so Jotson leaped from the hearth as though stung.

"Great porous plasters!" he gasped, "What a fright you gave me! For a moment I thought you were the ghost of Old Man Scrooge. You see I've been attending the recital of the 'Christmas Carol.' He, he, he!"

The halting words of my old friend and his unmusical cackle told me he was not speaking the truth.

"Jotson,' I said sternly, "you've no more been to any recital to-night than I've been to the tax-collector to pay next year's income-tax in advance. Now, tell me. Where have you been?"

As I spoke my trained eye swept the fire-grate. From the flames and ashes which I saw there I deduced that Jotson had been burning something. Quickly I averted my gaze so he should not know I knew.

My old friend tugged nervously at his moustache.

"It's nothing, really, my dear Sholmes," he said nervously. "If I told you, you would only laugh at me. And I hate being laughed at!"

"Nonsense, Jotson!" I said heartily. "Everyone laughs at you—er—except your patients, of course. And they usually don't last long enough to laugh long."

This I said in a gentle, bantering tone to cheer Jotson up. To my surprise, it seemed to have the opposite effect, and he stumped out of the room in a huff.

That was the opportunity I wanted. In a moment my nose was in the fender. Quickly I peered about. Before you could say "force-meat stuffing" I had found a narrow strip of torn paper bearing some typewritten words. Hearing Jotson's footsteps returning, I hastily crammed it in my pocket, and was innocently cracking Brazil nuts with my teeth when he entered the consulting-room to apologise for his former rudeness.

I said nothing about my discovery, but in my bedroom I examined the find carefully. To my stupefaction the typewritten words, which were in English, read as follows:

"...this honour. You have been chosen, comrade. See you fail not."

Ding, dong! Clatter! Bang! Ding, dong!

The merry Christmas bells were chiming as Jotson and I met at breakfast on the following morning, and exchanged greetings.

My eagle eye was quick to notice that Dr. Jotson was not himself at breakfast. Quite asbsent-mindedly he helped me to the larger half of the breakfast kipper, and then gave me the first cup from the coffee-pot, instead of the usual dregs. All my old fears for my poor friend's condition returned with renewed force.

Sitting in my chair, daintily flicking the kipper-bones from the lapel of my mauve dressing-gown, I watched Jotson as he went to the window and tried to entice the friendship of a robin redbreast by means of a fish-head.

"What do you say to a walk round Marylebone Station or the Waxworks, to get an appetite for our

Christmas dinner, Jotson?" I remarked casually.

Jotson's walrus moustache gave a perceptible quiver.

"Er—I'm afriad you will have to excuse me, my dear Sholmes!" he stammered. "A new patient of mine, a dear old lady, who is suffering from a temporary attack of suspended vibration of the right bozookum, wishes me to test her high tension battery, to enable her to get 2LO for the Christmas glee singers. I'm afraid——"

"Tut, tut!" I said. "I'll come with you, Jotson."

"No, my dear Sholmes," said Jotson, more firmly. "I shouldn't think of taking you to a case like this on Christmas Day. Why don't you take the bus up to the Zoological Gardens, or, if you prefer it, remain in front of the fire cracking a few-monkey nuts yourself?"

I said no more, but I thought a lot. For a time I sat myself in the armchair.

Speedily it became apparent that Jotson was up to some game. It seemed almost impossible to keep track of his movements. He was slippery as an eel in an oil vat. But at last I heard him stealthily take his hat and coat from the peg in the hall and leave the house.

Within a minute I was tracking my old friend down Shaker Street. Dr. Jotson had a large brown parcel under his right arm. The parcel looked innocent enough.

What did that parcel contain? That I was determined to find out.

Poor Jotson was worried. I deduced that from the absent-minded way that he pushed the face of a little boy who asked him for a cigarette-card. Stopping at the corner outside the Goat and Gooseberry Bush, he hesitated a moment, and then leaped on a passing bus. I waited until he gone inside with his parcel; then I swung myself on the step and darted aloft.

Peering from the bus stop, I saw Jotson alight at Charing Cross. I waited a few moments until the bus had started to move again, and then I ran nimbly down the steps. As I did so, with consummate cunning I knocked off the conductor's hat and leaped into the road. As he prepared to stop the bus I swiftly tossed him my own cap, and retrieved his fallen property. Then, replacing the peaked blue cap on my head and gumming a black moustache to my upper lip, I followed in the track of my old friend.

Once Jotson stopped and looked back. All he saw, apparently was an attenuated bus-conductor about to turn into a near by chop-house.

Waiting in the shelter of the doorway a minute, I emerged and followed him again. As I watched his stocky form stumping down Whitehall towards the Houses of Parliament, a gust of wind blew the paper from under his arm. A white, earthenware pudding-basin was revealed, with a cloth cover over the top of it.

After a vain attempt to retrieve the paper Jotson went on his way, looking uncommonly foolish walking down Whitehall holding that pudding-cloth, with the basin swinging at his side.

At first the sight of that pudding-basin brought a sense of relief to me. Then a horrible thought occurred to me. This was no pudding-basin. It was a bomb! Rapidly I reviewed in my mind the events leading up to this Christmas morning walk. I remembered Jotson's curious mumblings. I remembered the paragraph about the Crown Prince of Schlacca-Splittzen. I called to mind the mysterious message on the scrap of paper I had taken from the fire-grate. With a bomb in that innocent-looking bag, Jotson was on his way to the river to fulfil his dread mission.

My friend strode firmly to the Thames Embankment.

Quite a crowd was lining the parapet.

"What's the excitement?" I heard him ask a low-looking ruffian.

"It's that there Crown Prince of Slaccy-Splittem," replied the fellow. "He's just about to land at the jetty."

Jotson pushed his way through the crowd to the parapet. I kept close at his heels, my heart hammering against my ribs.

With a gasp of dismay I saw Jotson hoist the pudding-basin on to the parapet and give it a gentle shove.

"Stop!" I cried, and thrust my hand forward.

I must have diverted Jotson's aim, for the basin struck a jutting edge of the Embankment. There was no time to duck, for I feared the next moment there would be an explosion that would bring about the end of all things as far as we were concerned. To my surprise however, the basin broke, and out shot a great plum-pudding. It struck a boatman standing on the jetty waiting for the prince's launch right on the back of the neck and burst into fragments, while the onlookers gasped with astonishment. Then, when they realised what had happened, a great shout of laughter burst forth. The boatman was annoyed—very! He looked aloft, with a great piece of pudding crowning his head, and passed a few remarks totally unconnected with that "peace on earth and good will to men" which one associates with the Yuletide season. Then, as the fellow turned to help with the moorings of the prince's launch, I grasped Jotson by the hand and dragged him away.

"You thundering idiot!" I said. "What do you mean by it all?"

"Sholmes!" cried Jotson. There was both surprise and disappointment in his tone.

And then bit by bit I dragged the story out of Jotson, He knew Mrs. Spudson had made a Christmas pudding and that she would insist on him and me partaking of it at the Christmas dinner.

"Knowing your good nature, Sholmes," he said, "I knew that you would have eaten some of it to avoid offending our landlady. You did last year, and what was the consequence? For two days you groaned on the couch with the collywobbles. This year I determined at all costs I would get rid of the Christmas pudding. As a medical man I knew it was positively dangerous, but I didn't want to drag you into the matter, nor did I wish to offend Mrs. Spudson. And so I quietly lifted the basin containing the pudding, intending to dispose of it in the first possible way that presented itself. As you know, in desperation I finally toppled it over into the river."

Then I told him how his rumbling had roused my suspicions, and the finding of the torn piece of typewritten paper had corroborated them.

Now it was Jotson's turn to laugh.

"'Pon my word, Sholmes!" he chuckled. "I didn't know you were so worried about me! You see, a fortnight ago I joined the Marylebone Dramatic Society, and was offered the role of Koffituppe in the play 'Crown Jewels in Pawn' by Msmooji, the famous Russian dramatist. Afraid you would laugh at me, I would retire to my bed-room to study my role. Finally, in disgust at my inability to learn the part, I tore it up and threw it on the fire. The typewritten piece of paper you found was a portion of the play."

"But why one earth didn't you tell me all this before, my dear fellow?" I cried.

"Because," answered Jotson, "I should have had to acknowledge failure, and, as you know, no man likes to do that."

"Ah, well," I laughed, "the mystery is solved! And we can safely return to Shaker Street to pull the wish-bone of a turkey without the fear of having to partake of any of the amazing stodgy concoction which Mrs. Spudson calls Christmas pudding!"

1925

THE GREAT WAXWORKS MYSTERY

No. 92

"Person to see you, sir."

Mrs. Spudson, our landlady, put her head into the consulting-room and made that announcement with a pronounced sniff. From her remark and the tone of it, Herlock Sholmes, with his usual perspicacity, deduced that a lady had called.

"Show her up, Mrs. Spudson, please."

Our landlady withdrew, and two minutes later reappeared with a large, red-faced, perspiring, puffing woman in tow.

Mrs. Spudson gave another sniff, and closing the door behind her, left the visitor panting like a stranded grampus in the consulting-room.

"Good-afternoon, Mrs. Wudger!" said Herlock Sholmes, rising and doubling himself up like a penknife.

The lady gave an extre-loud snort which sounded like the effort of a hunted hippopotamus upon being punctured by an arrow.

"B-bless me, Mr. Sholmes!" she panted. "You know me?"

"I have never had the pleasure of your acquaintance before to-day, madam," said Sholmes politely. "But it was easy for me to recognise that you were the Mrs. Wilhelmina Wudger, who is proprietress of the waxworks in the Charing Cross Road. Odd bits of coloured wax adhering to your hands and the lobes of your ears made the recognition a matter of merely simple deduction."

"Wonderful!" I exclaimed.

"It is nothing to what I can do, as you know, my dear Jotson," said Sholmes modestly. "But pray be seated, Mrs. Wudger, and state the reason for your call here to-day."

Mrs. Wilhelmina Wudger broke the last spring our our armchair as she subsided into that article of furniture.

"Oh, it's dreadful, Mr. Sholmes!" she said, mopping her brow with the somewhat old-fashioned muff she carried. "Some of my best wax models have wilted away."

"Wilted away?" said Sholmes. "Pray be more explicit, madam."

"Well, it's like this, Mr. Sholmes," said our visitor. "I have a particularly fine lot of models in the Mixed Department. They are almost as good as the bunch down in the Chamber of Horrors. Among them I had some of the greatest politicians of the day."

"In the Chamber of Horrors?" said Sholmes keenly.

"No—in the Mixed Department. There was Lloyd George, Joe Beckett, and Jackie Coogan, Salmon and Gluckstein, Sam Slammer, Mr. Pickwick, Horatio Bottomley——"

"Quite so, madam," put in Herlock Sholmes; "but we are drifting away from the point. Kindly explain the reason for the wilting away of these—ahem!—effigies of the great."

"Ah, that's just it, Mr. Sholmes! If I knew that, as like as not I shouldn't have called here to-day. I woke one morning to find that the face of Mr. Lloyd George had wilted. His forehead was all flopping down and his nose was about six inches long. Looked more like Shylock than Lloyd George, he did!"

"I see," murmured Sholmes. "Something had happened to the face of his waxen image during the night."

"Yes, something had happened to it," affirmed Mrs. Wudger. "At first I suspected that that Lloyd George had been there himself and spoiled it. I wrote a letter to his secretary, I did, but I was assured that Mr. Lloyd George was in Wales at the time. Next Ramsay Macdonald went to rack and ruin."

"Ramsay Macdonald!"

"As sure as my name's Wilhelmina Wudger! His whiskers had turned black, and his face had grown long."

"What did you do?" queried Sholmes.

"Well, the first thing I did was to go round to his house. In my experiences as a waxworks proprietress I have learned that some of these bigwigs don't feel too pleased with their effigies in my waxworks. I thought maybe Mr. Ramsay Macdonald had been having a little game. But his chauffeur assured me that Mr. Macdonald had been in bed and asleep all the previous night. The next night Joe Beckett and four other lads near him in the Mixed Department went west. You'd have thought that Joe had been hit by the fist of Georges Carpentier to have seen his face. Looked like a piece of pounded dough, it did. Half a dozen of my best waxworks absolutely spoiled! And the thing a perfect mystery!"

As the lady concluded her strange story, Herlock Sholmes rose to his feet.

"Come, get your hat, Jotson," he said. "We will accompany Mrs. Wudger to her waxworks." And he added in a whisper: "It will be a free show—a sort of combination of pleasure with business."

A penny bus ride brought us to Charing Cross Road. Mrs. Wudger let us in by the front door of her small house, which adjoined the waxworks proper. In the kitchen we found Inspector Pinkeye sharing a rabbit-pie with Veronica, the maid.

Hastily the inspector concealed a large portion of crust under his tunic as we entered the room, followed by Mrs. Wudger.

"M'mmm, m'mm!" mumbled Pinkeye. "I just dropped in, hearing there was a mystery afoot," said he.

Sholmes laughed.

"The mystery of the missing rabbit-pie, eh, Pinkeye?" said Sholmes jocularly. "But come with us. You may be useful."

Mrs. Wudger said nothing. She merely favoured Pinkeye and the maid with a stony stare. The mystery of other missing things, such as sausage-rolls, apple charlotte, and so forth, had become solved in her mind.

"That door leads through into the waxworks," said Mrs. Wudger, pointing to one in the passage.

Sholmes entered the room indicated and glanced alertly about him.

"I see there's a window broken here," he remarked.

"It was done yesterday, sir," said the maid. "I think the fellow who has been spoiling the lovely waxworks must have got in by this way."

"Nonsense!" said Mrs. Wudger.

"We can soon test the matter," said Sholmes.

He took from his pocket a large magnifying-glass, and, bending low, examined the pieces of glass which lay scattered on the carpet. Rising, he gave his opinion.

"There is no mystery about this," said he. "One of the particles of glass clearly shows a mudstain. A muddy tennis-ball broke that window."

"Well, how the man gets in to spoil the lovely waxworks beats me," mumbled Vernoica, the maid.

"Be quiet!" snapped Mrs. Wudger. "Go back and prepare tea, my girl. Mr. Sholmes and Dr. Jotson will take tea with me. You may show your tram-conductor friend the back door, Veronica."

When Sholmes had explained that Pinkeye was really an officer from Scotland Yard, Mrs. Wudger became more reconciled to his presence. Together they all entered the waxworks, which had been closed to the public since the last outrage.

Sure enough, in the Mixed Department, as Mrs. Wudger called it, a number of the effigies had been completely spoiled. Some of the faces had been so melted that they looked almost as though they had icicles suspended from their noses and chins.

After a glance at these, Sholmes, somewhat to the astonishment of Mrs. Wudger, asked to be shown to the Chamber of Horrors, situated in the basement of the building.

For half an hour we wandered among the effigies of the criminals. Sholmes was like a child with a new toy. He admired the features of one notorious character after another. He tinkered with the guillotine. He fondled the relics of the rock-cake by which the notorious Schlitzhanger had choked her seventh husband.

"Now," said Sholmes at last, rubbing his hands, "let us get to the business of the afternoon."

Together we all returned to the "Mixed Department."

"It looks to me," said Pinkeye, tugging his moustache, "as though the criminal who has spoiled these beautiful effigies has come to the place during the day."

"Ah! And remained hidden?'" I said.

Inspector Pinkeye favoured me with a look of scorn.

"In a sense, yes, Dr. Jotson," he said. What would be more simple for a person to adopt the role of a waxwork figure model? You would only have to strike a position and stand in an odd corner to be missed completely at shutting-up time."

Herlock Sholmes laughed lightly.

"Ingenious, but hardly creditable, my dear Pinkeye," he remarked. "See that?"

He pointed aloft. Directly above that portion of the Mixed Department where the outrages had taken place was a small skylight. It was not more than a foot square. Then it was Pinkeye's turn to laugh.

"Ho, ho! You don't think that the miscreant got through there, Mr. Sholmes?" he guffawed.

"No, my dear Pinkeye," said Sholmes. "As the old proverb says, there are more ways of killing a cat than by choking it with butter. I don't believe for a moment that the culprit ever set foot in the waxworks. Let us now take tea with Mrs. Wudger. With her permission, we will keep watch here to-night, and I think that I can capture the misguided rascal who spoils her excellent effigies."

As we were walking back to Mrs. Wudger's living-rooms Sholmes who had been deep in thoughts, asked suddenly:

"By the way, Mrs. Wudger, have you an enemy?"

"An enemy?" said Mrs. Wudger. "Hundreds and hundreds of them! Every human being who is reproduced in that Mixed Department is an enemy of mine."

"Quite so," said Sholmes. "I meant a special enemy."

Mrs. Wudger shook her head.

After a good tea, to which we all did full justice, Sholmes, Inspector Pinkeye, and myself returned to Shaker Street together.

That night we went back to Charing Cross Road. By means of a key, which Mrs. Wudger had given Sholmes, we let ourselves into the waxworks, and made our way to the Mixed Department. It was an eerie sort of visit. I confess to a shiver as I made my way among the gaunt rows of politicians, prize-fighters, and other desperate characters.

From a corner Sholmes obtained a step-ladder which he had noticed during the previous visit. This he placed directly under the skylight. Mounting it, he took from his overcoat a length of strong cord with a loop in the end. The loop he arranged about the skylight lightly by means of some little wire staples, which he pressed in with his thumbs.

Dismounting, Sholmes, put the step-ladder back in its place, and, taking the long end of the cord, walked with it among the effigies.

"Listen!" said he. "If my theory is correct, the miscreant will crawl along the roof gutter to that skylight. I noticed to-day that is would be easy to reach the gutter from the next-door building. When we hear a sound, we three must remain perfectly motionless, so our quarry will not be scared away."

For nearly two hours we watched and waited. Then suddenly there was a scraping sound on the roof. Sholmes and Pinkeye who were together, stiffened like sentinels on the approach of the major-general. I, who had walked a few yards to stretch my cramped limbs, also stopped, motionless. I was directly under the skylight. But I think it speaks well for my presence of mind that I did not even glance up.

A few seconds later I became aware of a small, dark object before my head. Next instant I let out an agonised bowl.

"Yow-wow! Oe-er! Help! I'm scalded!"

A moment later there was another howl from the skylight, and something fell with a clatter at my feet.

"Got him!" cried the jubilant voice of Sholmes.

He had jerked the long cord, and the snapping of the little staples from the woodwork had caused the loop to close about the arm of a man that had been inserted in the skylight. While he himself held the cord, Pinkeye ran out of the waxworks, loudly blowing his whistle.

Ladders were procured, and a ladder brought down through the roof by two burly constables and placed before Sholmes.

"Sam Slammer!" cried Sholmes. "It was as I expected!"

"Yes, it's me!" growled the prisoner! "And I'd do it again! I'll learn that old Mother Wudger to put me in the waxworks!"

"Remove the prisoner!" said Sholmes. "Pinkeye, take that dark lantern attached to the string with you. It will form valuable evidence."

As Sholmes and I made our way out of the building to rouse Mrs. Wudger and report the capture of the miscreant, my famous friend explained the whole extraordinary affair.

"As I suspected in the first place, Jotson," he said, "the destruction of these wax models was done out of revenge. At one time Sam Slammer was a noted election agent, but later he became footpad and burglar. Naturally, having a sort of right to a place in the Chamber of Horrors, he considered it undignified, to say the least, to be included among the politicians. Very annoying to a gentleman of Slammer's ideals."

Out of revenge he started to destroy some of Mrs. Wudger's wax models. By lowering a lighted dark lantern through the skylight and dangling it near the face of an effigy, he was able to melt the wax by the heat of the lantern, and was the hot lantern that burnt poor Jotson's face.

Slammer avoided destroyng his own effigy probably with the hope in his mind that it might eventually be included in the Chamber of Horrors.

"Altogether, a sad case," concluded Sholmes, "and I'm not with a certain sympathy for Slammer. He'll get three months in gaol, and, probably in consideation of this fact, Mrs. Wudger will at last decide to put his effigy in the more respectable company in the basement, where an extra sixpence is charged for admission. And I think that you will agree with me, my dear Jotson, that Slammer has earned the honour!"

THE NABOB'S ELEPHANT

No. 93

Ting-a-ling-a-ling-a-ling!

Herlock Sholmes and I were seated in the consulting-rooms as the telephone-bell rang.

I laid aside the guinea-pig I was in the act of skinning and took off the receiver. The familiar voice of our butcher came floating over the wire.

"Our old friend, Briskett!" I remarked to Sholmes. "He wants to know about that back end of gammon and the——"

"Tell him I'll set my bloodhound at him if he doesn't ring off!"

Hardly had I set the receiver up and resumed my studies when the bell burst forth again.

Sholmes leaped out of his armchair and snatched up the receiver.

"Oh, go and chop coke and eat chips, you aggravating cow-carver! I'll——"

Sholmes stopped suddenly, and listened while his voice and face underwent a startling change.

"Oh, by all means, your supreme Highness! Needless to say, my few remarks were addressed to the lady telephonist. I'll be with you in a few minutes!"

Sholmes hung up the receiver, and then he tripped lightly from the telephone and danced me round the room.

"Put on your hat, my dear Jotson!" cried he. "We are going to an important appointment at the Splitz Hotel."

"The Splitz!" I spluttered.

"Even so—the most luxurious super-hotel in London, and our host will be his supreme Highness the Nabob of Bhungpor!"

"Great porous plasters!" I gasped. "The most wealthy prince who ever came out of India!"

We went dowstairs and out into Shaker Street. Taking a taxi, Sholmes and I drove up in style to the Splitz Hotel. The native retainers of the illustrious Indian prince were awaiting us, and escorted us to the nabob's sumptuous apartments.

The Nabob of Bhungpor, wearing wonderful jewelled robes and a green turban encrusted with sapphires, emeralds, rubies, topaz, diamonds, and moonstones, was seated, looking worn and worried, in a magnificent gold chair upholstered in purple plush.

Herlock Sholmes coughed.

"Ahem! Your supreme Highness sent for me?"

The nabob waved us to be seated.

"I did, Sholmes sahib," he said. "I have lost little Loola!"

"One of your wives?" I said. "But surely, your supreme Highness, the loss of but one little wife is hardly——"

"Bah! You are talking through your honourable hat, Dr. Sahib!" said the nabob. "Loola was my esteemed elephant!"

At great length the Nabob of Bhungpor explained matters. He had come from Bombay to Tilbury in the steamship Sea Beaver. On board were a number of animals, birds, and reptiles, conveyed from the East on the order of Otto Bagstein, the well-known animal dealer of the Wapping Road. On board also was the nabob's pet elephant, Loola.

As the nabob paused for breath, Sholmes put his first question.

"Tell me, your supreme Highness, when did you mislay this elephant of yours?"

"When I was leaving the honourable ship," replied the nabob, "Casandra Chau Ram Bojum Bottlewalla, my secretary, had been looking after Loola. But Casandra, he did not know where she was. Loola was mislaid."

"Tut, tut!" I said, thinking it time I made a remark.

"We hunted everywhere for the esteemed Loola on the honourable ship," said the nabob. "We looked on all the decks. We made inquiries everywhere. Some men said that the animal had been landed. Casandra himself said that he had arranged for this to be done. He had spoken to the honourable Bill Gudger, who was landing the esteemed animals for the illustrious Otto Bagstein. Then we discovered that among the animals sent from Tilbury were three elephants. These esteemed animals arrived at Fenchurch Street. Then poor Loola vanished into thin air, and neither we nor the honourable police can find her."

"Good gracious!" said Herlock Sholmes. "An elephant vanish into thin air! It scarcely seems possible, your supreme Highness! Were there any special points or marks about your elephant to distinguish it from others of the species?"

"Yes, Sholmes sahib. On one of its tusks was carved a crown, on the other an anchor. Find the esteemed Loola, and I will give you all the gems in my esteemed turban!"

"Half will do, your Excellency!" said Sholmes.

I rose as Sholmes went forward and kissed the dusky monarch's toe.

Suddenly remembering something, Sholmes borrowed a tenner off the nabob, and led me from the apartment.

Taking a taxi outside the hotel, Sholmes ordered the driver to proceed to Fenchurch Street Station. There he made a series of inquiries of ticket-collectors, porters, jumpers, bookstall clerks, newsboys, and refreshment-room waitresses. The result was that he discovered that three elephants had reached that station in a special train at seven o'clock on the previous evening. A fleet of lorries had been lined up in the station approach to receive the cages containing the creatures. Three elephants had been put into three separate lorries and driven away.

And then Sholmes made a startling discovery. A smart newsboy had noticed the names on these lorries. Two lorries had borne the well-known name of Tibbett & Sons, while on the other was painted "Woggs Bros."

Sholmes handed the bright lad a cigarette-card, and jumped in the taxi again.

"To Bagstein's," he said.

The cab rattled and banged its way to the Wapping Road. We dismounted outside the world-famous premises of Bagstein, the animal dealer. Going into the great yard at the back of the shop, we found Otto Bagstein himself, feeding a giraffe with macaroni. He paused in his task upon learning the name of his distinguished visitor.

"Herlock Sholmes," said he, "if I can be of any assistance to you, pray command me!"

"Firstly, sir," said Sholmes, "I should like to view the two elephants which were sent to you yesterday."

The animal dealer ordered the two lumbering animals to be brought forward, and Sholmes examined their tusks. neither of them was marked with a crown and anchor. Having satisfied himself upon this point, Sholmes made inquiries with regard to the man employed by Bagstein to superintend the unloading of animals at Tilbury.

"He was my assistant, William Gudger," said he. "Strangely enough, he has not been home since he was at Tilbury yesterday."

"Ah!" exclaimed Sholmes. "Now, tell me how many elephants have you had on order—that is, how many customers have you on your books for these quadrupeds?"

"Three," answered Mr. Bagstein. "Two for the London Zoo, and one for the Duke of Duckswede, of Dilwater, Hampshire. These two elephants here at present are for the Zoo. I was unable to obtain another specimen among the last lot imported for the duke's private collection."

Thanking Otto Bagstein for his help, Herlock Sholmes left the premises of the animal dealer. I followed at his heels. Once more we entered the taxicab.

"Drive to Wobbs Bros., the cartage contractors of Hoxton Road!" he ordered.

Sholmes stopped the cab some couple of hundred yards from the premises of the cartage contractors.

As it happened, a big lorry, marked "Woggs Bros.," was standing some little distance away from the cartage place. No one was in attendance, and Sholmes quickly scrambled inside. I followed him.

Taking out his magnifying-glass, he made a swift examination of the wooden sides of the lorry.

"Marks of elephant's tusks!" he muttered.

"And look!" I exclaimed excitedly. "Here is a piece of grey leather stuck in the crack of this door!"

Sholmes looked at the object.

"No, my dear Jotson," said he; "this is a bit of the elephant's ear. The poor mammal was unfortunate enough, apparently, to catch its ear in the crack of the door."

Leaping out of the lorry, he examined the wheels.

"See?" he said. "These blue-grey splashes above the mudguards are quite freshly made. Mud of exactly that colour is found in only one county in England—Hampshire. The Duke of Duckswede has Loola, or I never hope to touch one of those gems from the nabob's turban!"

Together we returned to Shaker Street, but not before Sholmes had sent a telegram to the duke inquiring if the elephant had been delivered to him. The prepaid reply reached us in a little less than three hours:

"Yes; elephant delivered here yesterday by lorry.—DUCKSWEDE."

Jubilant, Sholmes rushed me to the Hotel Splitz. We roused the nabob, who was taking his afternoon siesta.

"Loola is found!"

A few minutes later Sholmes, the nabob, and I were bowling down to Dilwater, in Hampshire, in the nabob's sixty-horse-power Rolls velocipede.

The duke's palatial country residence proved to be some three miles outside Dilwater village. The duke himself received us, and Sholmes explained the situation.

"You have been the victim of a gross fraud, sir," he said. "Some time ago you placed an order with Otto Bagstein for your private Zoo?"

"That's so," said the bewildered Duke.

"Recently you were informed by Bagstein's assistant, William Gudger, that an elephant had been obtained for you. Doubtless Gudger collected a handsome sum from you on account of that fact?"

"I gave him five hundred pounds," said the duke, "and he delivered the elephant to me yesterday."

"And he has himself disappeared." said Sholmes. "The elephant which Gudger sent to you did not belong to Otto Bagstein. It was the property of this gentleman, the Nabob of Bhungpor."

"Bless my heart!" said the duke.

"Show me Loola," cried the nabob, "and I will repay you the five hundred pounds willingly, honourable sir!"

Hastily the duke led the nabob to his very fine back garden, a part of which was laid out as a menagerie. There, staked in the garden, was a fine young elephant with its tusks carved with a crown and anchor.

"Loola!" cried the nabob.

"Br-r-rmph!'" trumpeted the elephant.

The meeting touched the hearts of all concerned. Then the duke touched the nabob for the five hundred pounds. Sholmes, in turn, touched the selfsame prince for a few of the jewels from his turban. It only remains to say that the swindler, William Gudger, was captured in Wigan on the following day, and eventually touched for twelve months in the lock-up.

1950

THE MISSING MILLIONAIRE

No. 94

I had sat down to breakfast with Herlock Sholmes, in our rooms at Shaker Street, when the telephone bell suddenly rang.

Sholmes glanced up from his kipper.

"Take the call, Jotson," he said.

I willingly complied. I was not without hope that it might prove to be a call for my professional services. My medical practice was not so lucrative as I could have wished, owing to the difficulty I often found in collecting my fees from executors.

I put the receiver to my ear, and a voice, which sounded as if it proceeded slowly through a long nose, came over the wires.

"Say, big boy, I guess we got the joint all hunky for Old Man Guggerhunk. You sure want to tote that guy along to Number Five Limehouse Alley. You get me?"

"I am afraid that I do not quite follow," I answered, somewhat perplexed. "Possibly you have been given the wrong number."

"Aw! Shucks! Carry me home to die!" came a startled ejaculation. "If that ain't the elephant's hind leg, and then some!"

"This is Dr. Jotson speaking," I said, "if you are requiring my services as a medical man—?"

There was no rejoinder. My unknown interlocutor had wrung off.

I returned to the breakfast-table, and sat down. To my astonishment, my kipper had vanished from my plate.

"Dear me!" I ejaculated.

"What is the matter, Jotson?" asked Herlock Sholmes.

"My kipper has disappeared!" I answered, in amazement. "During the few minutes I was at the telephone, it has completely vanished."

"Extraordinary!" said Sholmes.

"It is somewhat disconcerting, as well as extraordinary," I replied. "I have not breakfasted, Sholmes. In the present state of the money market, I cannot call upon Mrs. Spudson to produce another kipper. This is an opportunity for you, Sholmes, to exercise your amazing gifts. Oblige me by solving the mystery of the missing kipper.

Herlock Sholmes shook his head.

"I hardly think, Jotson, that even I could detect the present whereabouts of that kipper, without the aid of an X-ray outfit," he said.

"You do yourself injustice, Sholmes," I replied, warmly. "Such a problem would be child's play to you. Did you not solve the mystery of the disappearance of Lord Stony de Broke's watch after a visit to his uncle? I really beg of you, Sholmes, to set your vast intellect to work on this problem."

Again Herlock Sholmes shook his head.

"There are some problems, my dear Jotson, better left unsolved." he said, enigmatically, "but you have not yet told me what was said on the telephone."

I repeated to Herlock Sholmes the strange words that had been spoken over the wires. He listened attentively: seeming, for some reason, desirous of dropping the subject of the kipper.

"No doubt a wrong number was given at the exchange," he said. "The message was intended for someone else—doubtless an American, as it was spoken in that language. But—"

"But the kipper—!" I said.

"Never mind the kipper, Jotson," said Herlock Sholmes, with a touch of asperity. "I am fed up with that kipper."

He rose from the table.

"The American language," he remarked, "is an abstruse but interesting study. I have been thinking—"

"Of my kipper?" I asked. I found it somewhat difficult to dismiss the mystery of the missing kipper from my mind. Though lost to sight, it was to memory dear.

"Certainly not!" said Sholmes. "I have been thinking of taking up the study of American, Jotson. In many respects it bears a resemblance to our own tongue. Take for example the verbs "to have" and "to do." These are certainly English in origin: but in American they have a much deeper significance, and are carried, in practice, to much greater lengths. The conjugation is, I believe, something like this—'I have, thou art had!' and 'I do, thou art done!' With regard to nouns, such things as cash, dollars, dimes, spondulics, dough, and so on, are always in the possessive case. Americans speak always in the active voice, generally very active—a passive voice seems unknown among them. Further—"

Herlock Sholmes was interrupted by a knock at the door.

It was Inspector Pinkeye, our old acquaintance at Scotland Yard, who entered.

"Sholmes!" he exclaimed.

Herlock Sholmes smiled.

"Scotland Yard bunkered again?" he said. "You have come to me, as usual, for first aid. Proceed, my dear fellow. You may speak quite freely before my friend Dr. Jotson."

"The fact is, Mr. Sholmes, that we need your help," confessed the inspector. "The American millionaire Guggerhunk—the celebrated Phineas K. Guggerhunk—has been kidnapped."

I could not help giving a start. The name had a familiar ring.

"No doubt you have heard of Mr. Guggerhunk," continued Inspector Pinkeye. "He made an immense fortune as a pork packer in Chicago. Owing to the number of employees who became mixed up with the machinery, and were unavoidably packed with the pork, his products achieved an enormous popularity in the South Sea Islands, which laid the foundation of a fortune running into a dozen figures. Mr. Guggernunk then became the object of the special attention of the kidnapping industry in his native country. After many narrow escapes, he finally decided to live in Europe. But—"

"But—?" asked Herlock Sholmes.

"But that has not saved him, after all," said the inspector, shaking his head. "Only this morning, Mr. Sholmes, he was kidnapped."

"Kindly give me a few details," drawled Sholmes.

"Mr. Guggerhunk occupied a mansion in Park Lane. At an early hour this morning the constable on the beat was passing the mansion, when his suspicions were aroused by the sight of three masked men climbing into a bedroom window by means of a ladder—"

"An observant man!" remarked Sholmes, with a nod.

"The officer did not, at the time attach any particular importance to the incident," continued Inspector Pinkeye, "but he remembered it, and when Mr. Guggerhunk was stated to be missing, he reported it to his superiors. The matter was immediately placed in the hands of the most capable inspector at Scotland Yard, and I proceeded to the spot. But—" He shrugged his shoulders.

"No clue?" asked Herlock Sholmes.

"None: except that some words, spoken by one of the kidnappers in the hearing of the butler, seemed to indicate that the gang came from Mr. Guggerhunk's own country. I have taken down the words, as repeated to me: and with your well-known linguistic skill, Mr. Sholmes, you may be able to state definitely in what language they were spoken."

"No doubt," assented Sholmes.

Inspector Pinkeye opened his note-book, and Herlock Sholmes read aloud the curious phrase used by the kidnapper.

"Guess we done cinched dis guy."

"You can identify the language, Sholmes?" asked the inspector, eagerly.

"American," answered my amazing friend, without a moment's hesitation.

"Good!" exclaimed the inspector. "Then there can be no doubt that the Chicago gangsters have followed Mr. Guggerhunk over here, and are seeking to carry on a purely American profession in this country. You will help us track them down, Mr. Sholmes—on the usual terms—"

"Cash!" said Herlock Sholmes, tersely.

"But the credit to us," said the inspector.

Herlock Sholmes smiled.

"A poet, my dear Pinkeye, has said 'Ah! take the cash, and let the credit go!' I am of his opinion, and I am entirely at your service."

I thought it time to speak.

"Sholmes," I began. "That telephone call—"

"My dear Jotson, it is time you went to see your patients," said Herlock Sholmes, interrupting me somewhat sharply.

"You do not need my assistance in this case?" I asked, a little disappointed.

"On this occasion, no, Jotson. Scotland Yard may be baffled, as usual, by this problem: but I shall very soon be able to put our friend Pinkeye on the track of the missing millionaire."

"You think so, Sholmes?" exclaimed the inspector, eagerly.

"I do not think," answered Herlock Sholmes, coldly, "I know."

"You have a theory—?"

"I do not deal in theories, but in facts, Pinkeye. Jotson, my dear fellow, it is time you were off."

"I was about to mention the peculiar telephone call we received this morning, Sholmes—owing to a wrong number having been given to our interlocutor. It appears to me—"

"If you have one fault, my dear Jotson, it is that you talk too much," interrupted Herlock Sholmes. "Say no more."

"But I think, Sholmes—"

"Nonsense, Jotson. You over-estimate your mental process. Thinking is not in your line. Indeed, as a medical man, it would amount, in your case to unprofessional conduct," said Sholmes, severely. "Pray go."

"But—"

"Remember your patients, Jotson—waiting for you to put them out of their pain! Lose no more time."

I departed accordingly. I could not help thinking that the mysterious telephone call at breakfast might have some bearing on the case of the kidnapped millionaire. But in these matters, of course, I had to yield to the judgment of my amazing friend.

Deeply as I was interested in my colleague's work, and in the mystery Inspector Pinkeye had brought to him to solve, I dismissed these matters from my mind, while engaged upon a round of visits to my patients. I have never been one to take professional duties lightly, and all my medical work has been done in deadly earnest.

My round, however, did not occupy me very long. My patients were fewer in number than at the time I had bought the practice. It is well said that the work of a good and conscientious doctor tend to diminish his own practice, and this was undoubtedly the case with me. Indeed, the more assiduously I attended my patients, the more they diminished in number. This went to such a length at times, that I had little income, beyond the dividends on my investments in Fashionable Funerals, Ltd., and the Monumental Masons' Company. Luckily, by some happy coincidence, these dividends increased as fast as my patients diminished.

I was back at Shaker Street early: and, as I entered, my thoughts reverted to the case of the missing millionaire, and I wondered whether Inspector Pinkeye had yet succeeded in tracing Phineas K. Guggerhunk with the help of my amazing friend.

This matter was of some serious interest, for owing to the mysterious disappearance of my kipper, I had breakfasted very lightly: I was ready for lunch, and there was some doubt whether lunch would be ready for me.

Herlock Sholmes was seated in the armchair in our sitting-room, in his usual graceful attitude with his feet on the mantelpiece, when I came in. He glanced round at me with a smile.

"Success, Sholmes?" I asked.

"Need you ask, Jotson?" said Sholmes, reprovingly.

"True!" I exclaimed. "You have, then, solved the mystery, and put your finger—or at least Inspector Pinkeye's finger—on the kidnapped millionaire?"

"I have been of some little assistance to the official police in the matter," drawled Herlock Sholmes. "By a process of reasoning which is so far above your intellect, my dear fellow, that I will not attempt to explain it to you, I have been able to tell Pinkeye exactly where to look for Mr. Guggerhunk."

"Wonderful!" I exclaimed.

"Elementary, my dear Jotson," said Sholmes, with a yawn. "I am expecting a telephone call from the inspector every moment now, and I have no doubt that he will report that he has rescued Mr. Guggerhunk, and arrested the gangsters. All the credit, as usual, will go to Scotland Yard: but I shall draw my fee, Jotson, and I think I can guarantee that it will run to fish and chips for lunch."

"Splendid!" I exclaimed, heartily.

A few minutes later the telephone bell rang. I took off the receiver, and recognized the voice of Inspector Pinkeye. The exchange had apparently given him the right number: from what cause I cannot say.

"Is that you, Sholmes—?"

"Dr. Jotson speaking," I answered.

"We've got him," said Inspector Pinkeye. "We went to 'Number Five Limehouse Alley—"

I started.

"Number Five Limehouse Alley!" I repeated.

"Yes—and there we found Mr. Guggerhunk and the gangsters. Tell Mr. Sholmes that by putting us on the track so quickly, he has saved the kidnapped man from terrible usage. They were feeding him on his own pork, packed in Chicago."

"Horrible!" I exclaimed with a shudder.

"They're a tough gang," said the inspector. "I'm not sure whether this may not enable us to bring a charge of attempted manslaughter, as well as kidnapping. The usual fee is waiting for Mr. Sholmes to collect, and he need bring no change for the ten-shilling note. Mr. Guggerhunk is so overcome with gratitude that he has added a sixpenny cigar at his own expense. Good-bye."

I put up the receiver, and repeated the inspector's message to Herlock Sholmes. He nodded nonchalantly.

"Exactly as I expected—with the exception of the sixpenny cigar," he said. "That, I confess, I did not foresee." He disconnected his feet from the mantelpiece, and rose from the armchair. "Come, Jotson, my dear fellow. The sooner we collect the fee, and invest it in fish and chips the better—and I should like to get hold of that cigar before Mr. Guggerhunk changes his mind."

"But, Sholmes," I could not help saying. "It appears to me that that curious telephone call at breakfast had some bearing—"

"Indeed!" said Sholmes, coldly.

"It was a curious chance—"

"Chances, Jotson, have nothing to do with my methods! You should know me better than that."

"True! But—"

"My deductions," said Herlock Sholmes, "proceed with mathematical precision from one aberration to another. You should know that, Jotson."

"True! Nevertheless—"

"Come, come," said Sholmes, impatiently. "Although 'I had an unusually ample breakfast, I am ready for lunch. Come!"

And I said no more, as I followed my amazing friend from the room. With the reticence he sometimes displayed when I was most curious, he declined to explain the masterly process of reasoning by which he had deduced that Phineas K. Guggerhunk was imprisoned at Number Five Limehouse Alley, and I had to be content to wonder.

1952

THE CASE OF THE PERPLEXED PAINTER

No. 95

The Case of the Perplexed Painter was one in which were displayed most brilliantly the remarkable mental aberrations of my amazing friend, Mr. Herlock Sholmes. We were at lunch in our rooms at Shaker Street when the telephone bell rang, and Sholmes, slipping his fish sandwich into his pocket, removed his feet from the mantelpiece, and answered the call. His face was very grave when he turned from the instrument.

"A client, Sholmes?" I asked.

"A distinguished one, Jotson," he answered. "No less a person than Mr. Scrooluce, the celebrated painter. You have heard of him, of course. His rise to fame has been recent, but his system of painting his pictures with a blacking-brush, and the mystery surrounding their meaning, if any, have made him a great figure in Art circles. No doubt you have heard how he achieved sudden and dazzling success with his picture 'October Moon.'"

I shook my head.

"As a medical man, Sholmes, I have to give my attention to more practical matters than Art," I replied.

"True, my dear doctor. But the story is an interesting one," said Sholmes. "Scrooluce, as a young painter, had no success. He painted ships that looked like ships, cornfields that looked like cornfields, clouds that looked like clouds: and but for a happy accident, might have gone on doing so till this day. But it chanced that, having painted one of his usual landscapes, he inadvertently leaned against the canvas while the paint was still wet: after which it resembled nothing in earth or in the waters under the earth. A great Art critic came into the studio, while he was cleaning his coat: and, seeing the picture, was overcome with admiration. He hailed it as a work of undoubted genius: and Scrooluce, who had thought of cleaning the canvas for future use, wisely decided to leave it as it was. He was undecided whether to call it 'Venus Rising from the Waves' or 'The Battle of Lepanto,' but finally decided on 'October Moon.' From that time, he never looked back. However," added Sholmes, briskly, "we must not waste time. Mr. Scrooluce is in great trouble, and requires my professional assistance."

"What is the nature of the trouble, Sholmes?"

"It seems that some disaster has occurred, while he was away on a holiday, in connection with a portrait he has painted of Lord Popcorn, and another picture called 'Sunset on the Apennines.' He tells me that his lordship was painted with his favourite collie dog, Rover, at his feet, and that he is calling this very afternoon to see the finished picture. He was so very agitated that it is not easy to deduce what has really happened: but he is very anxious for me to go round at once, before Lord Popcorn arrives. So come, my dear Jotson: we must not lose a moment."

"But, my dear Sholmes—"

"This is no time for butting, Jotson," said Herlock Sholmes, severely.

"But," I persisted. "I have several patients to see this afternoon— I really must call upon my patients, Sholmes—"

"Not at all," answered Sholmes. "Let them live, my dear fellow. Come!"

And without waiting for a reply, my amazing friend hurried me out into Shaker Street and into a taxi.

We found Mr. Scrooluce pacing his studio in a state of wild agitation when we were shown in. Two large canvases stood leaning against the wall: and from moment to moment, the painter paused, and stared at one or the other of them, and shook his head despairingly. What was the matter was not clear: but it was evident that something was very much the matter.

"Which?" the painter was exclaiming. "His lordship will be here in a quarter of an hour—he must see the picture. But—which—which—which?"

The painter was obviously in a state of utter perplexity: from what cause I could not fathom. Indeed I doubt whether Herlock Sholmes himself was much wiser than I for the moment. Both of us, however, were deeply moved by the agitation and distress from the artist.

As our names were announced, Mr. Scrooluce, turned from the pictures, and rushed across to meet us, in his excitement catching my amazing friend by the arm.

"Mr. Sholmes! Can you help me?" he panted.

"Quite!" said Herlock Sholmes, calmly. "If you will give me a few details—you may speak quite freely before my friend Dr. Jotson—"

"But this is no ordinary case," said Mr. Scrooluce, hoarsely. "I am aware of your great reputation, Mr. Sholmes—I know how successfully you investigated the case of the missing marksman at Bisley—how you traced Lord Stoney de Broke's watch when it mysteriously disappeared after a visit to his uncle—how you, and you alone, tracked down the Lost Chord. But this case, I fear, must be beyond even your powers. Help me if you can—before Lord Popcorn arrives."

He led us towards the two pictures leaning on the wall. He pointed to them with a trembling finger.

We looked at them. What either was intended to represent, if indeed anything, was a secret known only to the painter. They were, I gathered, painted in his later, or blacking-brush style: but beyond that I could guess nothing.

"I will tell you the dreadful disaster that has occurred. Mr. Sholmes," went on Mr. Scrooluce, huskily. "I painted these two pictures before going on a week-end trip. One of them is the portrait of Lord Popcorn with his dog at his feet. The other is 'Sunset on the Apennines.' Before leaving, I gave strict instructions that nothing in the studio was to be meddled with. Nevertheless, an unthinking housemaid tidied up during my absence. On my return to-day, I found that the pictures have been moved, and, worse than that, that the labels attached to them had disappeared. Lord Popcorn is calling this afternoon for his portrait, Mr. Sholmes, to take it away with him in his car. He will be here is a matter of minutes now. His portrait is here—it is one of these two pictures. But which is it, Mr. Sholmes?"

Mr. Scrooluce paused, and wiped the perspiration from his brow.

Herlock Sholmes nodded, slowly. We now had an inkling of the cause of the painter's perplexity and distress.

"Which?" said Mr. Scrooluce, despairingly. "Which is which? One of these two pictures is the portrait of his lordship—the other is 'Sunset on the Apennines.' But which Mr. Sholmes, is which? Is that a problem beyond even your powers, Mr. Sholmes?"

Gazing at the two pictures, I could well understand the painter's perplexity. There was absolutely nothing in either to give a clue. Either might have been the portrait of Lord Popcorn, or a sunset scene in the Italian mountains: or, indeed, anything else. There was not the ghost of a clue.

"His lordship may be here any moment," muttered Mr. Scrooluce. "Every moment I expect to hear his car. He must take away his picture, Mr. Sholmes. But which is his portrait? Which? Can you help me?"

"I can!" said Herlock Sholmes.

"Bless you for those words," said Mr. Scrooluce, brokenly.

"Lord Popcorn was painted with his dog Rover?" asked Herlock Sholmes.

"He was! He and his dog are inseparable.

"Then Rover will be with him when he calls this afternoon?"

"Undoubtedly."

"Then all is simple," drawled Herlock Sholmes. "You may rely on the sagacity of the faithful hound, Mr. Scrooluce, to pick out his master's portrait."

"Do you think so?"

"I am sure of it, Hark! I hear a cry!" said Sholmes. "Go down and meet his lordship, please, and make sure that his dog accompanies him to the studio. I answer for the rest.

"If you are right—!" gasped Mr. Scrooluce.

"There is no 'if' about it," said Herlock Sholmes, coldly. "My friend Jotson could tell you that. Please go down—"

"You assure me?"

"I do!"

"I will trust you!" breathed Mr. Scrooluce, and he hurried out of the studio. Alone with Sholmes, I gazed at him. To my surprise, he drew from his pocket the unfinished fish-sandwich which was part of his interrupted lunch.

"Sholmes!" I exclaimed, "this is no time for finishing your lunch—"

"I am not thinking of finishing my lunch, Jotson."

"Then what—"

I broke off, in astonishment, as Herlock Sholmes stepped up to the nearest of the two canvases, and proceeded to rub the fish-sandwich on it. I gazed at him almost open-mouthed. Well as I knew my amazing friend's remarkable methods, I could understand nothing of this.

He stepped back, and replaced the remains of the fish-sandwich in his pocket. There was an inscrutable smile on his face.

"My dear Sholmes—!" I gasped. "What—?"

"Wait and see, my dear Jotson," he replied.

I had not long to wait. The door opened, and Mr. Scrooluce, ushered Lord Popcorn into the studio. A collie dog was prancing round their legs.

But in the next moment, the dog ceased to prance, made a rush at the canvas on which Sholmes had rubbed the fish-sandwich, and began to lick it with evey sign of pleasure.

Mr. Scrooluce stared, evidently amazed by this prompt verification of the assurance Herlock Sholmes had given him. Lord Popcorn smiled genially.

"Rover knows his master!" he remarked. "What?"

"Oh! Yes! He—he—he does!" stammered Mr. Scrooluce. "Undoubtedly! Good dog—good dog!"

"But—!" I remarked later, when we were back in our rooms at Shaker Street.

"But what, Jotson?" drawled Herlock Sholmes. "My client is satisfied. His client is satisfied. So what?"

"But Lord Popcorn's portrait, which his lordship took away in his car, may after all be the 'Sunset on the Apennines,' Sholmes."

"Quite possibly, Jotson. But as no one could ever know, that is quite irrelevant. You may add to your memoirs, as one more of my astounding successes—The Case of the Perplexed Painter."

HERLOCK SHOLMES—THE END

The name of Herlock Sholmes opened all doors.

"The missing Venus!" said Sholmes quietly.

THE ADVENTURES OF HERLOCK SHOLMES

CHECKLIST

No.	Title	Publication	Date
1.	**The Adventure of the Diamond Pins**	Greyfriars Herald	20/11/1915
2.	**The Case of the Biscuit Tin**	Greyfriars Herald	27/11/1915
3.	**The Bound of the Haskervilles**	Greyfriars Herald	4/12/1915
4.	**The Freckled Hand**	Greyfriars Herald	11/12/1915
5.	**The Sign of Fourty Four**	Greyfriars Herald	18/12/1915
6.	**The Death of Sholmes**	Greyfriars Herald	25/12/1915
7.	**The Return of Herlock Sholmes**	Greyfriars Herald	1/1/1916
8.	**The Missing Mother-in-Law**	Greyfriars Herald	8/1/1916
9.	**The Adventure of the Brixton Builder**	Greyfriars Herald	15/1/1916
10.	**The Case of the American Millionaire**	Greyfriars Herald	22/1/1916
11.	**The Foreign Spy**	Greyfriars Herald	29/1/1916
12.	**The Case of the Pipe-Clay Department**	Greyfriars Herald	5/2/1916
13.	**The Case of the Pawned Pickle Jar**	Greyfriars Herald	12/2/1916
14.	**The Munition Mystery**	Greyfriars Herald	19/2/1916
15.	**The Captured Submarines**	Greyfriars Herald	26/2/1916
16.	**The Sham Huns**	Greyfriars Herald	4/3/1916
17.	**The Kaiser's Code**	Greyfriars Herald	11/3/1916
18.	**The Yellow Phiz**	Greyfriars Herald	18/ 3/1916

19. The Case of His Lordship's Engagement	The Magnet	3/2/1917
20. The Missing Minister	The Magnet	17/2/1917
21. The Clue of the Chanting Cheese	The Magnet	24/2/1917
22. The Missing Moke	The Magnet	3/3/1917
23. The Vanished Aliens	The Magnet	10/3/1917
24. The Red Tape Mystery	The Gem	14/4/1917
25. The Case of the Escaped Hun	The Gem	5/5/1917
26. The Case of the Currant Bun	The Gem	12/5/1917
27. The Case of the Russian Revolution	The Gem	26/5/1917
28. The Last of the Potatoes	The Gem	2/6/1917
29. On the Scent	The Gem	16/6/1917
30. The Case of the Teuton's Trousers	The Gem	30/6/1917
31. The Missing Margarine	The Gem	21/7/1917
32. The Mystery of the Dustbin	The Magnet	25/8/1917
33. The Case of the American Clock	The Magnet	15/9/1917
34. The Case of the Hidden Hun	The Magnet	13/10/1917
35. The Secretary's Double	The Magnet	20/10/1917
36. The Lottery Ticket	The Magnet	3/11/1917
37. Herlock Sholmes at Monte Carlo	The Magnet	26/1/1918
38. The Case of the Financier	The Magnet	2/2/1918
39. A Murder Mystery	The Gem	9/3/1918
40. The Case of the Missing Wife	The Magnet	31/8/1918
41. The Case of the Missing Manuscript	The Magnet	30/11/1918
42. The Case of the Airman's Medal	The Gem	19/4/1919
43. The Missing Cricketer	Greyfriars Herald	12/6/1920
44. The Bacon Mystery	Greyfriars Herald	19/6/1920
45. The Chopstein Venus	Greyfriars Herald	26/6/1920
46. The Case of the Missing Heir	Greyfriars Herald	3/7/1920
47. The Mystery of the Studio	Greyfriars Herald	10/7/1920
48. The Case of the Musician	Greyfriars Herald	17/7/1920
49. The Mystery of the Taxi-Cab	Greyfriars Herald	24/7/1920
50. The Case of the Stolen Car	Greyfriars Herald	31/7/1920
51. The Case of the Ball Dress	Greyfriars Herald	7/8/1920
52. The Disappearance of Lord Adolphus	Greyfriars Herald	14/8/1920
53. The Mystery of the Garden Suburb	Greyfriars Herald	21/8/1920
54. The Case of the Sinn Feiners	Greyfriars Herald	28/8/1920
55. The Case of the Mysterious Soprano	Greyfriars Herald	4/9/1920
56. The Mysterious Bottle	Greyfriars Herald	11/9/1920
57. The Case of the Missing Patient	Greyfriars Herald	18/9/1920
58. The Purloined Pork	Greyfriars Herald	25/9/1920
59. The Case of the Bolshevik!	Greyfriars Herald	2/10/1920
60. The Case of the Orator	Greyfriars Herald	9/10/1920
61. The Trunk Mystery	Greyfriars Herald	16/10/1920
62. The Disappearance of Dr. Jotson	Greyfriars Herald	23/10/1920
63. The Case of the Boat Club	Greyfriars Herald	30/10/1920

64. The Case of the Gunpowder Plot	Greyfriars Herald	6/11/1920
65. The Case of the Lost Chord	Greyfriars Herald	13/11/1920
66. The Case of the Charlady	Greyfriars Herald	20/11/1920
67. The Case of the Corn-Plaster	Greyfriars Herald	27/11/1920
68. The Case of Podgers M.P.	Greyfriars Herald	4/12/1920
69. The Case of the Cubist	Greyfriars Herald	11/12/1920
70. The Case of the Dentist	Greyfriars Herald	18/12/1920
71. The Mystery of the Mince-Pie	Greyfriars Herald	25/12/1920
72. Pinkeye's New Year Resolution	Greyfriars Herald	1/1/1921
73. The Case of the Pink Rat	Greyfriars Herald	22/1/1921
74. The Case of the Lame Snail	Greyfriars Herald	19/2/1921
75. The Case of the Potato Jacket	Penny Popular	26/3/1921
76. The Sarah Jane Mystery	The Magnet	9/4/1921
77. The Mystery of the Vacant House	Penny Popular	23/4/1921
78. The Case of the Lost Sapphire	The Magnet	30/4/1921
79. The Case of the Haunted Coal Shed	The Magnet	7/5/1921
80. The Case of Creeping Krooboy!	The Magnet	28/5/1921
81. The Case of the Lost Nugget	The Magnet	9/7/1921
82. That Ghostly Xmas Knight	The Magnet	17/12/1921
83. The Lost Persian	The Magnet	14/1/1922
84. The Schwottem Ray	Penny Popular	26/7/1924
85. The Mystery of the Green Crab	Penny Popular	9/8/1924
86. The Golden Cow	Penny Popular	23/8/1924
87. The White Rabbit	Penny Popular	6/9/1924
88. The Unguarded Goal	Penny Popular	30/9/1924
89. The Mystery of Moldy Manor	Penny Popular	4/10/1924
90. The Silver Wishbone	Penny Popular	1/11/1924
91. The Secret in the Pudding Bag	Penny Popular	27/12/1924
92. The Great Waxworks Mystery	Penny Popular	3/1/1925
93. The Nabob's Elephant	Penny Popular	31/1/1925
94. The Missing Millionaire	Tom Merry's Own Annual	1950
95. The Case of the Perplexed Painter	Tom Merry's Own Annual	1952